A Love F

Kelly J. Goshorn

Janet,

    May you always
see yourself as your
heavenly Father does.

        1 Sam. 16:7b

        Blessings,

        Kelly

A Love Restored
COPYRIGHT 2017 by Kelly J. Goshorn

Contact Information: titleadmin@pelicanbookgroup.com

Scripture quotations, unless otherwise indicated are taken from the King James translation, public domain.

Cover Art by *Nicola Martinez*

Prism is a division of Pelican Ventures, LLC
www.pelicanbookgroup.com PO Box 1738 *Aztec, NM * 87410

The Triangle Prism logo is a trademark of Pelican Ventures, LLC

Publishing History
Prism Edition, 2018
Paperback Edition ISBN 978-1-5223-9760-1
Electronic Edition ISBN 978-1-5223-9759-5
Published in the United States of America

Dedication

To the two most important men in my life: My Lord and Savior, Jesus Christ, who wrote this story on my life, and to my husband, Mike, who lived it with me.

And for every woman who has questioned her self-worth because of unkind words or the reflection she sees in the mirror. Know that you are treasured by a loving God who sees your immeasurable value.

Acknowledgements

Sharing my courtship in written word has been a rewarding and oftentimes challenging endeavor. There were so many times I wanted to close the laptop and quit. I'm so thankful for all those who have inspired and encouraged me to keep pursuing the dream God had put in my heart.

First and foremost, my amazing God who surprised me with His answer to my prayer for a new passion in my life—writing a book! He has used this journey to grow my faith not only in myself, but more importantly, in Him.

My precious family, a/k/a my biggest cheerleaders, my husband, Mike, who first suggested I share our story; my children, Madeline, Michael, and Noah; my sister, Cindy Criste Scott, and my precious mama, Martha Criste. Mama, I'm so glad you had a chance to read *A Love Restored* before you went home to be with Jesus! A special shout out to my youngest son, Noah, whose dream to be a published author inspired my own. Keep writing, Noah, and trust God to handle the rest!

Chrissy Carr, Mike Goshorn, Alissa Hall, Cindy Kling, Tracey Levy, Becky Redman, Duane Scott, Cindy Criste Scott, Steph Sloan, and Lynn Whittington for accepting the challenge of reading and critiquing *A Love Restored* when I thought it was ready for public consumption! I'm so grateful for every suggestion and insight.

Colleen Hoernke for reading and re-reading *A Love Restored* so many times I'm positive you know the story as well as I do. Where would I be without your amazing proofreading abilities and descriptive insights? There are no words to express my gratitude except, I love you, Bestie!

For the amazing critique partners I found through American Christian Fiction Writers: Angela Couch, Jessica Konek Johnson, and Sarah Monzon, as well as the ladies of Scribes 204; Crystal Barnes, Linda Cushman, Tammy Kirby, and Jodie Wolfe. Thank you for making my story shine. I am forever grateful!

The talented and hard-working staff at Pelican Book Group including my incredibly patient editor and sweet friend, Paula Mowery. Thank you for believing in me and in *A Love Restored*, and most importantly, for following your "God nudges." Many thanks to Nicola Martinez for the beautiful cover design and to all those who have worked behind the scenes to bring *A Love Restored* to publication.

And I will restore to you the years that the locust hath eaten.
~ Joel 2:25a

1

Loudoun County, Virginia
August 1873

Land sakes it was hot.

Ruth Ann Sutton peeled the black stockings from her legs and stuffed them inside her boots. If only she could do the same with her insufferable corset. She wiped her brow. Perspiration moistened her hairline, tightening the loose strands on her neck into corkscrews. Buddy's tongue hung from the corner of his mouth as he meandered to the stream for a drink. She stooped beside him, running her fingers through his plush, red fur.

"You must be hot today, too, boy." He raised his head. Ears alert, mischief danced in his eyes, reminding her of the pup he'd once been. "You stay right there. You'll splash around and get me all wet."

Rarely did a week go by from March to November when she didn't visit this spot. She'd loved it from the first time Papa brought her fishing in the little nook sheltered among the dogwoods. If she remained

1

absolutely still, she could hear Papa laughing as he cast his fishing line into the creek.

The peaceful melody of the stream as it coursed around the bend beckoned her. What would Mama say? She glanced over her shoulder. Why not? No one was around. Gathering her skirts, she eased into the creek, mindful to avoid the mossy rocks that rested in the shade of the poplars. Cool water assailed her shins as she waded to the middle. Despite the gooseflesh forming on her skin, the knee-deep water offered respite from the sultry temperature and her sour mood.

Her thoughts drifted to the conversation she'd had with her mother. She'd promised to write James about her new teaching position at the Freedmen's School more than a month ago. How would she convince her beau to let her continue? No one else wanted to teach these children. They needed her, and in a way, she needed them. Wouldn't she be a better wife and mother if allowed to pursue her passion before surrendering it at the altar?

Tilting sideways, she skimmed her fingers against the current, spooking the dragonflies hovering above the water's surface. She didn't want to marry James. Truth-be-told, she didn't want to marry anyone—yet. No one hired a married woman to teach. At twenty years of age, she had plenty of time for marriage and children.

Or did she?

Suitors weren't exactly lining up at her door. While she had no trouble getting along with the opposite sex, as her bevy of male acquaintances attested, none pursued an attraction to her. If she delayed, she might lose her bloom, as mama suggested, and have more than her buxom figure prohibiting her from matrimony. Even if she could coax James into postponing an engagement, he would never allow her to teach Negroes.

What could she say to persuade him?

Did she even want to?

Tipping her head back, she released her cares to the only one who had her best interest at heart. "Oh Heavenly Father, guide my footsteps. May your perfect will be done in my life."

Sighing, she waded toward the creek bank. Mud squished between her toes. She dreaded the return home so soon. She scanned the meadow before glancing to her canine friend.

"Maybe just a bit longer. Huh, boy?"

She withdrew a bulging handkerchief from her skirt pocket and deposited it atop a large rock overhanging the creek. With a hearty thrust, she hoisted herself up beside her prize. Anticipating the treasure within, she untwisted the purple stained cloth. Hard to believe she'd found a whole cluster of black raspberries the birds had overlooked. She popped one in her mouth, savoring its mildly tart flavor. Leaning back on her palms, she dangled her legs over the edge, relishing her extended reprieve as her feet sashayed in the cool water beneath her. Singing might lift her spirits.

Besides, she really didn't need to fret about James. God would direct her path. He'd never disappointed her yet.

~*~

Benjamin Coulter cringed as the shrill tune hung

in the air. That woman sure knew how to ruin a Sunday afternoon. Sounded like something was dying and needed to be put out of its misery.

He shook his head. All he wanted to do was rest a while longer. His decision to go around his headstrong superior and talk to Mr. Farrell directly about his boss's inaccurate measurements had made for a nerve wracking week. That decision could have cost him his job. Thankfully, his discovery had been received well, saving the struggling railroad both time and money.

Benjamin leaned against the sycamore tree and tossed his line into the creek. A slight hint of remorse nicked his conscience. He now sat poised to guide the construction of the Washington & Ohio Railroad through the town of Catoctin Creek and over the Blue Ridge Mountains to Winchester, but he hadn't intended to get his boss fired. If only the man hadn't refused to admit he'd made a mistake.

Yep, it was all coming together. Just the way he'd hoped it would when he agreed to leave Texas and take this apprenticeship in Virginia. All he had to do was pass that examination next spring and…

He shuddered. The woman's screeching escalated to a bone-grating pitch. She'd frighten the fish away for sure. Like most folks, Sunday was his day off, and he didn't intend to spend it listening to her sing off-key.

Wedging his pole in the mud of the creek bank, he set off to investigate. Her ear-piercing slaughter of *The Merry, Merry Month of May* led the way. He spied his first glimpse of the lyrical assassin through the thin limbs of a dogwood tree. Perched on a large, flat rock at the edge of the creek, she swirled her bare feet in the water. Behind the rock sat a pair of woman's boots—fancy ones. Too bad she hadn't spent some of her shoe allowance on singing lessons.

Her voice cracked. *"The skies were bright, our hearts were light, in the merry, merry month of May…"*

Benjamin winced. That was the fourth time in a row she'd sung that part. *For the love of Pete, didn't Miss Fancy Boots even know the words?* He needed to put a stop to this so he could continue fishing—and napping. He stepped forward then stopped. The woman reached up and removed a pin from her hair, then another. Mounds of long chestnut brown ringlets spilled over her shoulders into the middle of her back.

Curls. He groaned. Why'd she have to have curls?

"The skies were bright. Our eyes were light…"

Never mind. Curls or not, the woman's voice could haunt the dead. Twigs snapped under his foot.

A stubby-legged dog spun in his direction, barking relentlessly. The woman pulled her feet from the creek and hopped off the rock. "Who's there?"

He held his breath.

She hummed her tune again, cautiously this time as her eyes searched the woods. She stepped around the dog and picked up a thick stick.

He chuckled. Did she think she could fend him off with that?

"It was probably just a rabbit, huh, boy?" She stroked the little fur ball behind his ears. Still clutching the improvised deterrent, she retreated to her perch. The dog wasn't fooled. He stood, ears pricked and eyes fixed in Benjamin's direction.

Benjamin shook his head as she sang the same line of the song—again. He hadn't meant to alarm her. He could fish another day.

The fragrant woodbine tickled his senses. He pinched his nose. No use. "Ah-choo."

The dog charged.

"I know someone's in the brush." She tightened her grip on the stick. "I heard you sneeze. Come out."

The feisty dog chased Benjamin into the clearing. His graying muzzle and deep bark contradicted the little scrapper's size and enthusiasm.

Miss Fancy Boots stood on the rock, holding the stick high above her right shoulder.

Benjamin held up his hands as he moved toward her. "I intended to leave before your mutt ferreted me out. My apologies. I didn't mean to frighten you."

Raising her chin, she edged backward. "I'm not scared."

The tailless critter nipped at Benjamin's heels then zigzagged around him. "Call off your...dog, Miss. If you can call that runt of a critter a dog."

Fear shifted to indignation as her dark eyes narrowed. "He's a corgi—a herding dog, from the finest breeding stock England has to offer."

"What's he herd? Rabbits?"

Resembling a batter for the Cincinnati Red Stockings, she readjusted the position of the stick. "What do you want?"

"I want you to stop your caterwauling so I can enjoy my Sunday afternoon."

She lowered her makeshift weapon and rested her hands on her hips. "My caterwauling? First, you insult my dog, now my singing. I suppose you could do better?"

"Decidedly better." His attention shifted to the stocky animal nipping at the leg of his dungarees. "Your dog, Miss."

"Buddy, come." The dog ambled to the base of the rock where she stood. She angled her head, brows furrowing. "You don't sound like you're from around here? Are you from up north?"

"Born and raised in Pennsylvania."

"Do you work for the railroad?"

"More or less. Is that a problem?"

She stiffened. "Not if you keep your distance."

"C'mon down from there before you slip." Benjamin moved toward the rock but halted when she raised the stick again.

"Don't come any closer."

Maybe he should leave since she still had concerns about him. He scratched his scraggly beard. His raggedy appearance no doubt added to her apprehension. He diverted his attention to her dainty shoes. She had no reason to worry. While her curls were definitely attractive, he had no designs on a woman like her. Marcy had cured him of an eye for women with a taste for the finer things in life.

Still, he couldn't just leave and risk her falling in the creek.

Stepping forward again, Benjamin held his hands high where she could see them. "I'm not going to hurt you."

The woman crept backward. "Keep your distance."

"I'd be careful if I were you, Miss. You're awfully close to the edge."

"I'll be fine." She inched back. "You just stay put."

The lady was feisty and tenacious—qualities he might like if she weren't threatening to pummel him. Too bad she couldn't carry a tune with a handle on it. "Let me help you down before you slip." He reached up to take her hand. "Then I'll be on my way."

"I told you to keep your distance."

The stick swished through the air. Benjamin ducked, the limb narrowly missing his head.

Splash.

He straightened and peered over the side of the rock. She sat bent-legged in shallow water—skirts knee-high, water dripping from her nose. The waterlogged woman glanced at him through damp lashes. What a sight. Benjamin clamped his lips together in a futile effort to contain his mirth. He knew enough about females to know Miss Fancy Boots would be fuming mad. Even more so if he laughed at her predicament. Despite his best effort, a hearty guffaw escaped him.

Until her glare silenced him.

Benjamin waded into the creek. "May I help you?"

"No, thank you." She searched the creek bed for the stick. "I can manage."

The dog sat at the edge of the water, the nub where his tail should be wagging playfully.

"I think he wants to join you."

As if Benjamin's observation had been a personalized invitation, the critter jumped in, splashing his mistress.

"Buddy, no!" She shielded her face in vain.

Bringing his fist to his mouth, he feigned a cough to stifle his laughter. Poor woman. This just wasn't her day.

She struggled to her feet and swiped wet tresses from her eyes. Without a glance in his direction, she lifted her soggy skirts and edged around him toward the creek bank.

"Watch your—"

Arms flailing, she wobbled as her foot slipped on a mossy rock.

Benjamin lunged forward and grabbed her waist, steadying the drenched woman. Mere inches apart, his gaze lowered to her rosy lips. He hadn't noticed those before. "Allow me to assist you?"

She sighed. "I guess I have no choice. I lost my stick when I fell."

With one arm wrapped around her waist, he grasped her elbow with his free hand and led her from the water.

Once on dry ground, she twisted the fabric of her skirt. Water pooled in the dirt beneath her. "Look what you've done!"

"What I've done?"

"Yes, I'm a mess." Mud-caked toes peeked out from underneath the hem of her dress.

A beautiful mess. Dark, wet curls plastered themselves against her creamy skin. Yellow flecks in her eyes sparkled like gold in the sunlight. She may be rounder than the other women who'd sparked his interest, but she was by far the prettiest.

"You probably could use a little putting back together." So could he. Benjamin rubbed his hand over wiry whiskers. Why hadn't he trimmed his beard?

Now that she was out of the creek, wet fabric cleaved to her ample curves. He shouldn't be staring. Averting his gaze, he cleared his throat. "Wait here, Miss. I'll be right back."

He returned with his fishing pole, three speckled trout and a wool blanket. He leaned the rod against a nearby tree. "The dog won't eat my fish, will he?"

"I don't think so."

Benjamin eyed the dog then handed the string of fish to her anyway. "Hold these, please." Unfolding the blanket, he draped it around her shoulders. "Name's

Benjamin Coulter, Miss."

"Thank you, Mr. Coulter." She grasped the blanket with her free hand. A smug grin crossed her lips as she lifted the string of trout. "Looks like my caterwauling didn't scare away all the fish."

Benjamin pushed his hat back from his forehead. "Begging your pardon, Miss, but I caught these before your serenade began."

"Here." She extended the fish in his direction. "I should be getting home." She grabbed her boots and stockings. "Come on, boy. Let's go."

"I'm heading back to town myself. May I escort you?"

"No, thank you." She pointed to her sodden clothes. "You've done more than enough already. Besides, I don't know you."

He should just let her go. Those fancy boots spelled trouble in his book, yet something about her captivated him. Benjamin grabbed his pole and followed her. "But I did come to your rescue. Surely, that must count in my favor."

She glanced over her shoulder. "True. But, if it weren't for you, I'd never have fallen in the creek in the first place. So that is a mark against you."

A mark against him? He wasn't some errant school boy. "Wait, please."

When she reached the edge of the clearing, she paused and removed the blanket from her shoulders. "Please, don't follow me. I can't be seen, like this, in the company of a stranger."

He tore his gaze away from the wet fabric determined to cling to her curvaceous figure. What was she thinking? She shouldn't be seen like that by anyone, including him. "All right, but you'd better keep the blanket. You'll be...indecent without it."

A dash of pink graced her cheeks. "Thank you."

Resisting the urge to admire her curves, he focused his attention on the storm clouds drifting toward town. Not nearly as interesting, but much safer. "Are you covered?"

"Yes."

He corroborated her statement from the corner of his eye before allowing himself to look her direction again. Even wet, she was fetching.

"But how will I return the blanket to you?"

"Just keep it."

"You won't need it?"

"Not unless fate requires me to rescue another obstinate woman from the creek."

A spark flashed in her eyes. "Fortunately for you, I'm the most stubborn woman in town."

"No doubt."

"Good day, Mr. Coulter."

Her pace quickened as she followed the dusty road toward town. Just his luck. He would've enjoyed walking Miss Fancy Boots home. Benjamin stopped in his tracks. Miss Fancy Boots? He smacked his palm against his forehead.

Doggone it.

Why hadn't he asked her name?

2

Ruth Ann tiptoed across the veranda. Clutching the green wool blanket, she peered past yellow toile curtains into the kitchen.

Where was Myra?

The scent of rain lingered in the air. Dark clouds hovered in the distance. Relieved she'd arrived home before the impending downpour, she hurried toward the door. A loose board creaked beneath her muddy feet. She cringed. A low throaty bark crept from Buddy's mouth. Bringing her finger to her lips, she glared at the snarling little scoundrel. "Shh, that's just me, boy."

His barking intensified.

"Traitor."

She stiffened at the faint click of the latch. Oh well, she shouldn't be skulking around the porch in the middle of the day anyway. She was a grown woman for goodness' sake—soaking wet or not.

The door handle slipped from her grasp.

"Lordy child, what happened to you? You's a mess."

Ruth Ann sucked in a breath, as her fist flew to her chest.

Myra's coffee-colored hands grasped Ruth Ann's. "Its fine, Missy. It just me."

"Oh, thank heaven." She glanced past the older woman. "Is Mama home?"

"Mmmhmm, and she on a tear about somethin'

Mrs. Hirst told her followin' services this mornin'."

Ruth Ann could well imagine. Why hadn't she told Mama about Mr. Janney's offer to extend her teaching contract before now? Hearing the news from Mrs. Hirst would only inflame the situation. "Can you help me clean up before Mama sees me like this?"

Myra shook her head. "Mercy, child, I not sure we has that much time. Let's get you out that wet dress and put it to soak." She tugged the blanket from Ruth Ann's shoulders. Pinching it between her index finger and thumb, she inspected the covering. "Where'd you find this ol' scrap of a blanket?"

"A man at the creek loaned it to me. He said I'd be indecent without it."

Myra's mouth fell agape. "Some man you don't know seen you like this?"

Ruth Ann nodded. "He sort of caused my fall in the first place then he waded in to assist me."

"I bet he's one of them railroad men?" She shook her finger at Ruth Ann. "You heard your Mama. They not to be trusted."

"I remember and his disheveled appearance had me fearful at first, but there was something about his eyes."

"His eyes?"

Ruth Ann nodded and grasped her confidant's arm. "They were a delicious shade of amber." She sighed. "Like honey drizzling on a warm biscuit."

Myra quirked a brow. "What 'bout Mr. Thornton?"

"You know I've never fancied him."

"Makes no never mind. You practically engaged to the man."

Ruth Ann rolled her eyes. "Don't remind me."

Myra opened the larder and retrieved the metal wash tub. Yellowing teeth split her grin. "And what your mama gonna say 'bout this railroad man with the fine eyes?"

"Nothing. It's our secret."

~*~

Ruth Ann forced a breath, steeling her nerves before sliding open the mahogany pocket doors. Mama sat in her wing back chair in the corner of the parlor, her fingers strumming its velvet upholstered arm.

"Myra said you wanted to speak—"

Mama sprung from her chair. "Is it true, Ruth? You agreed to another term at the Freedmen's School?"

She kissed her mother's cheek. "I take it the gossip mill of the Women's Benevolent Aid Society is working fine?"

"Don't get sassy with me, Ruth. I spoke with Genevieve Hirst this morning. Imagine my embarrassment when I learned this news from her. She is none too pleased either."

"I had planned to tell you earlier, but it slipped my mind. Mr. Janney offered the contract Friday afternoon."

"I thought we agreed this would only be temporary."

Thunder rumbled, shaking the thinly-paned glass.

Ruth Ann hurried to the parlor window and lowered the sash as the first droplets of rain splattered against the glass. She glanced at the darkening sky. A storm brewed—inside and out.

Taking a deep breath, she faced her mother. "Mr. Janney said my performance is exemplary and asked me to remain for the winter term while they continue their search for a qualified Negro teacher to replace me. I accepted. I don't see the problem."

Mama returned to her seat then adjusted her skirts to cover the thick sole of her left shoe. "You don't see the problem?"

Ruth Ann shook her head.

"Since you accepted the temporary position, Governor Walker has appointed James' father to fill the vacant state Senate seat. He's been courting you for nearly a year. You must realize by now that you are under perpetual scrutiny."

How could she not be aware of the scrutiny she was under? Constantly being told how to dress, what to say, and when to speak. Though he'd made his intentions clear, much to her relief, James hadn't proposed. She intended to retain her new teaching position as long as possible.

"Perhaps James can use my position at the Freedmen's School to his advantage."

Her mother's eyes narrowed.

"Aren't politicians expected to help those less fortunate and improve the lot of the poor?"

"Of course they aim to be seen as benevolent but not by teaching illiterate Negroes."

Ruth Ann crouched beside her mother's chair, resting her hand on the plush velvet arm. "Maybe it won't be quite as big of a problem as you think. James behaves rather... indifferent toward me."

The grandfather clock in the corner chimed four times. Ruth Ann's attention shifted to the pendulum as it swung inside its ornately carved walnut cabinet. "Mama, you should consider the possibility that my future may not include James Thornton."

"Nonsense."

Ruth Ann's gaze flitted from the grandfather clock to the delicate rose-papered walls of the parlor, anywhere but her mother's face. She didn't want to see the disappointment in her eyes—again.

"Look at me, Ruth." Mama placed her fingers underneath Ruth Ann's chin, guiding her head until their eyes met. "He could have any girl in Virginia, and whatever his reasons, he has chosen you."

James was kind and rich, to be sure, but he didn't love her. She had no illusions about that. He wanted the Sutton name and the connections that came with it, but she longed for a man to love and accept her, as she was. Did such a man exist? One who would share her love of literature and history? One who didn't mind fuller curves on a woman? "James rarely posts letters from Richmond, and when he does, little is of a personal nature. He's quite...dull."

Mama placed her hands on Ruth Ann's shoulders. "It doesn't matter if you find him dull, Ruth." The soft glint in her mother's eyes vanished along with her smile. "The point is he has not eliminated you as a prospect in spite of your obvious flaws."

"My obvious flaws?" Ruth Ann jerked to her feet, the timbre of her voice gaining intensity.

"Well-bred young ladies do not raise their voices."

Unbelievable. Pivoting on her heel, she stormed through the dining room, shoving the swinging door open to the kitchen.

"Where do you think you're going? We are not finished." Mama shuffled through the dining room in pursuit. "And well-bred young ladies do not stomp."

Ruth Ann held her hand a few inches above the stove. The surface had cooled considerably since the noon meal. She grabbed a stick from the kindling box, opened the cast iron door, and stoked the embers into a steady fire. Satisfied, she tossed the make-shift poker inside, closing the door with more vigor than she ought. Tea would calm her nerves.

She whirled to face her mother, fists lodged on her hips. "And what obvious flaws should I be so thankful James Thornton is willing to overlook?"

"There are those weaknesses that can be managed until after marriage, such as your stubborn, opinionated nature or your obsession with politics. However, the fact James continues to seek your company in spite of your robust figure speaks volumes."

Wind gusted through the open window, frantically blowing the curtains hanging in its path. Mama flinched as thunder rattled the china in the corner cupboard.

Ruth Ann reached over the dry sink and closed the window. Facing her mother once more, she leaned against the wooden cabinet, arms folded, studying her. How could she understand? With brilliant blue eyes and delicate features, Hannah Sutton was stunning. Her complexion rivaled the creamy white magnolia flowers that bloomed in April. She had been the belle of her hometown in Caroline County until the summer of her eighteenth year. The summer disease struck, rendering her left leg nearly useless.

"You must make a better effort to control your unruly curls, and tightening your corset strings will make your waist look thinner." Mama made a slight tsking sound before continuing. "It is a shame you are not slender and petite like Sarah and myself. Oh, and what I would not give for you to have just an ounce of your sister's acquiescent nature. However, your pretty face and lovely smile are no doubt assets. At least we have that to work with."

Ruth Ann tugged her lip between her teeth. She wouldn't cry.

Mama drew near and took hold of Ruth Ann's folded arms. "Because I love you, I will tell you what you refuse to admit to yourself. Gentlemen do not court and marry women who are plump and opinionated. They desire a woman who is a reflection of themselves and the image they wish to convey to their contemporaries."

Ruth Ann pursed her lips as her mother's words reverberated in her mind. The hurtful phrases seeped into her wounded heart, festering into a marinade of insecurity and self-doubt. Why was it so hard to believe a man might love someone like her? No matter the exact phrasing, it all boiled down to the same thing in her mind—she was undesirable and unlovable.

Forcing down the swell of emotion, she retrieved the whistling teakettle from the stove, and poured hot water into the porcelain teapot. A whoosh of air and the thud of the swinging door against the icebox announced her niece's arrival.

Chloe flung her small arms around Ruth Ann's skirts. "Aunt Roofie, you're home!"

"Chloe."

The child lifted her head before addressing her grandmother. "Yes, Mimi."

"You are not a baby any longer. You must act like a little lady and call your Aunt Ruth by her proper name."

"Yes, ma'am."

Ruth Ann stroked Chloe's soft, dark curls as a

gentle smile graced her niece's face. She was in no hurry to hear the end of the child's precious endearment for her. Chloe stretched her hands and Ruth Ann hoisted her niece onto her hip. "You promised we would use your pastels to color my paper dolls. Remember?"

"I remember." She drew Chloe snug against her and squeezed. A slight sigh passed her lips. She did want children of her own someday—but with James? If her mother was right, he might be her only choice.

Ruth Ann peeled Chloe from her side and set her on the floor. "My pastels are in the middle drawer of my desk. You go get them, and your paper dolls, while Mimi and I finish our conversation." She patted her niece gently on the bottom to send the child on her way.

"Perhaps James will not be as angry with you over this business with the Freedmen's School as we fear. Since he gave you his permission for the initial teaching assignment, it is only logical to assume he would approve an extension."

Ruth Ann grimaced. "As a matter of fact, Mama, I've never discussed my position at the Freedmen's School with James."

Mama's lips straightened into a thin line and a vein pulsated in her neck.

"It was only a brief assignment, and we have no firm understanding between us."

Mama hobbled toward the table. "Well, it is a good thing I have not lost my focus. This could jeopardize everything." She stopped mid-stride and faced her daughter. "You will write James today, explain what you have done, and tell him you will abide by his decision as to whether or not to continue teaching at the Freedmen's School."

"But—"

"You will thank me for this, Ruth, when you are Mrs. James Robert Thornton."

Ruth Ann nodded weakly, her chest tightening. Is that what she wanted? To be Mrs. James Robert Thornton?

And why did Mama insist on calling her Ruth? No one else called her that.

No one, except James.

3

Ruth Ann added the sum in her head. "Nice work, Sadie."

The girl smiled wide-eyed, exposing a dimple in her dark cheek.

"I think you understand how to add double digits." She opened her desk drawer and retrieved a peppermint stick from a small paper sack.

Sadie's eyes flitted from the candy to her teacher's face.

"Go on. Take it. Make sure to tell your mother you got all the sums right on the first try."

"Yes'm. I will. Soon as I gets home." Sadie stuck the red and white candy between her lips then gathered her things and left without looking back.

Ruth Ann surveyed the child's slate again, warmth spreading throughout her body. Two years at the Catoctin Creek Graded School hadn't compared to the satisfaction she experienced teaching these children who were so eager to learn. Humming, she recorded the child's mark in the grade book.

Her gaze rose at the heavy clop of a man's boots on the wooden floor. She glanced at her watch pin — three o'clock. Why wasn't her brother-in-law at the livery?

"I've come to bring you home."

On a beautiful day like this, she normally walked home. Her pulse quickened as she shot to her feet. "Is everything all right?"

Joseph rubbed the back of his neck while his eyes scanned the lesson on the chalkboard. "James is at the house."

"James? What's he doing here?" She twisted sideways, blocking her face from his view while she erased the blackboard. "I didn't expect to see him for a few weeks."

"Yes, and he didn't expect to hear you were teaching at a Negro school in a wire from Tilly Hirst sent to his sister either."

She blew out a breath and returned the eraser to the chalk tray before facing him again.

"You promised your mother you would write him." Joseph skimmed the brim of his hat through his fingers.

She had tried but found it difficult to put her enthusiasm for her new position into words, especially to someone with so little passion of his own. "I preferred to discuss it with him when he came home for his sister's wedding."

"He's not pleased."

"I guess not if it brought him all the way from Richmond."

"He's not alone either."

Ruth Ann pressed her eyes closed and forced herself to swallow the lump in her throat. "Mr. Thornton?"

Joseph picked up her satchel. "Mrs. Thornton, too. Let's get this over with."

Her stomach clenched at the mere thought of meeting with James and his parents. While both families were more liberal toward the Negroes than most of their acquaintance, the Thorntons swift rise in Virginia politics meant compromises were necessary.

"Let's not make matters worse by dawdling."

"Coming."

Joseph waited beside the Thornton's conveyance. As always, James insisted they use it whenever he called on her. The Rockaway was a beautiful carriage, with its glass doors and windows and two gas lamps to illuminate its path. The plush red interior and trim on the wheels made a striking contrast against its black exterior. She slipped her hand in Joseph's and stepped inside. He sat beside her, closed the door, then rapped once, signaling the Thornton's driver they were ready.

Muggy, oppressive air filled the carriage—August in Virginia. She retrieved the fan from her satchel. With swift flicks of her wrist, she created a cool breeze that lifted the loose, damp tendrils from her neck. The more she thought about the conversation awaiting her, the faster her fan flapped. Was there no relief from this suffocating heat?

Joseph gently lowered her hand. "If you wave that fan any faster, you'll sprain your wrist."

She gazed out the window at the purplish hue of the Blue Ridge. A humid haze had settled on the mountains, obscuring their beauty. Their rounded summits appeared blurry and indistinct—like her future with James.

She closed her eyes and leaned against the seat cushion, her fan waving nonstop. The heat and humidity were worse than last week when she had wandered to the creek. Images of speckled trout came to mind—and the broad shoulders of the man that had held up that string of fish. A sudden warmth rose to her cheeks as she recalled his thick, wavy locks. Dark, too—black as coal. But, he had whiskers. Scruffy ones at that. Nope, she couldn't abide a man with whiskers.

Why did she care, anyway? The man clearly had no scruples. He'd insulted both her singing and her dog.

Ruth Ann straightened in her seat, unable to wipe the smile from her face. But she could put it to good use before Joseph started asking questions. She extended her arm out the window and waved to Adam and Nancy Whitmore. Mr. Whitmore lifted his hand, but a stern glance from his wife appeared to make him think better of the idea.

"What in the world has gotten into the Whitmores?"

Joseph shifted to face her. "Many folks don't like the idea of a white woman teaching Negro students."

"Then why did they support the placement of a Freedmen's School in Catoctin Creek?"

"They assumed a Negro teacher would be the instructor."

She shook her head. "This is ridiculous. They are children, like the Whitmore's own, who need to learn to read and write."

"I agree, but I warned you how some folks would react to a white woman teaching Negroes."

"I remember." Standing up for what she believed in could have serious consequences. She'd already lost Tilly Hirst's friendship. "So much bloodshed, so much destruction, and the Negroes are little better off than they were before the war."

"Perhaps, but if I were you, I'd stick to reading and arithmetic. I happened to see the list of things written on the blackboard. What was the point of your lesson?"

Ruth Ann grasped the seat as the carriage veered left onto Colonial Highway. "We were discussing the values whites and negroes share." Her chin lifted with the conviction in her voice. "Things like honesty, fairness, faith, and freedom. It's time people started to think about what we have in common rather than what we don't."

"Ruth Ann, it's not good to fill their minds with ideas of equality. Many folks who were opposed to slavery don't consider Negroes their equals. Others have anger and hostility over the war and emancipation. They may explode at the slightest provocation." Joseph patted her hand. "Be patient. Change will come in its own time."

She leaned her head against the window frame. "I suppose."

The carriage slowed as the driver steered the team onto the path beside the Sutton's home. Buddy barked, announcing their arrival.

Without waiting for Joseph to assist her, Ruth Ann opened the door, hopped out, and stooped to pet Buddy behind his ears. The dog whimpered and jumped on Ruth Ann's knees, knocking her backwards. He placed his paws on her chest and licked her face with reckless abandon. "Okay boy, enough." She giggled. "Enough."

With a soft grunt, she pushed to her feet. What a sight she must be. She brushed the dirt from her skirt then felt her hair for any loose coils. Believing her appearance to be satisfactory, she approached the house. James leaned against a pillar on the veranda.

He'd witnessed the entire spectacle.

She smiled, hoping to lighten the tension that hung in the air like the dense humidity.

He didn't return her smile. Instead, he pulled his pocket watch from his vest and checked the time.

She chided herself. No doubt another error in ladylike behavior. Why couldn't she be more reserved? "Hello, James."

Handkerchief in hand, he wiped her face where the dog had licked her. He leaned over and gave Ruth Ann a quick buss to her clean cheek before opening the door. "You have made things very difficult for me." He refolded the cotton cloth then wiped his lips and returned it to his pocket.

"I planned to discuss my position at the Freedmen's School with you when you came home for Edith's wedding in a few weeks. I wanted to talk with you in person."

James nodded toward the door. "Everyone is inside."

Not one face looked happy to see her when she entered the parlor. No greetings. No smiles. Her stomach churned.

They had circled the wagons.

Mr. Thornton withdrew the cigar from his lips. "Sit down, Ruth. It is time we had a rather frank discussion." He motioned for her to sit on the settee, and she obliged him.

Mr. Thornton withdrew a cigar from his vest pocket and offered it to Joseph who declined. "Are you sure, Joseph? It's an Upmann, imported from Havana, Cuba. I won't smoke anything else."

Joseph held up his hand. "No, thank you, William. Despite their popularity, I prefer my pipe."

James, however, accepted. When had he started smoking cigars? She enjoyed the smell of Joseph's pipe, but cigars? She cringed.

The men clipped the ends of their tobacco sticks with a cutting tool Mr. Thornton removed from his suit pocket before swiping a matchstick against the mantel. Both father and son took several long draws on their cigars as they rolled the tip near the flame. James removed his and inspected the lit end. Satisfied, he stuffed it in the corner of his mouth and joined her on the settee.

Mr. Thornton cleared his throat. "No doubt Joseph has informed you why we are here."

She nodded. "Yes, but—"

Mr. Thornton held up his hand. "I will do the talking, young lady."

A sudden tightness gripped her throat. She resisted the temptation to cross her arms in protest. Instead, she placed her hands demurely in her lap. Perhaps she could throw him off guard by feigning attentiveness to his concerns. She bit the inside of her cheek while Mr. Thornton rattled off a list of reasons why she shouldn't teach Negro children.

When he paused to take a puff from his expensive Upmann, Ruth Ann grew bold. She wouldn't give up her position without a fight. "Certainly, Mr. and Mrs. Thornton, you who were so instrumental in the anti-slavery movement, must see the need to educate our freed slaves so they can contribute to society. What good is emancipation if they are now in chains to their own ignorance?"

Mama stiffened and raised her finger to her lips.

This might be her only chance to make her case. She ignored her mother's silent plea and forged ahead. "It's my Christian duty to meet the needs of the less fortunate."

Mr. Thornton's cigar waggled from between clenched teeth. "That may be, Ruth, but the politics of it are a mess. This part of Virginia has more support for the freed blacks than Richmond, but even here in Loudoun County, it is a very touchy subject." He inhaled deeply from his cigar then rocked back on his heels. A trail of smoke escaped his lips. "The point is, I must placate both sides on the issue to maintain my coalition of political supporters. If my future daughter-in-law is teaching Negroes, the scale will tip in a direction many of my financial donors will not like."

"But—"

"Ruth, this matter is no longer up for discussion. You will give the Freedmen's Bureau your notice and resign immediately, or James will terminate the courtship."

Mrs. Thornton sat in a wing back chair near her husband. She was mama's dearest friend. The only one who had stood by her mother when infantile paralysis ravaged her leg. The jut of her chin demonstrated that she could not agree more with her husband's proclamation. Mrs. Thornton's eyes met Ruth Ann's briefly then drifted slowly down her form, taking close inspection of her posture and attire before shifting to the window.

What was she going to do? She'd expected to stop teaching once she married. Since James hadn't made any declarations, she'd assumed she had more time before needing to face that reality. She sighed, earning her a look of disapproval from her mother.

Joseph clasped Mr. Thornton's shoulder. "Look, William, perhaps we can come to a new arrangement where James and Ruth Ann are concerned. Both our families have held moderate views toward the races. We are not unaccustomed to unkind remarks on this topic, are we?"

"No, definitely not."

"Your coalition of supporters must also include those who favored emancipation or you wouldn't have enjoyed such political success."

Mr. Thornton nodded.

"Besides, James hasn't proposed to Ruth Ann yet. Perhaps she could finish the term and give the oversight committee the opportunity to find a suitable Negro teacher for the school."

Ruth Ann searched her beau's face. Would he approve the plan? Did she want him to?

James stood and took a long puff from his cigar. He motioned for his father to join him by the window. They spoke in hushed tones. Then Mr. Thornton nodded and clapped his son's back heartily. James extended his hand to Ruth Ann, his grin broadened. "May I please have a word alone with you, darling?"

4

He intended to propose.

Ruth Ann trembled as she slipped her arm inside the crook of James' elbow. She rested her free hand against her stomach in a vain attempt to settle the queasiness. James guided her to the veranda at the rear of the house. Palms sweaty, her anxiety rose with each silent step. What was she going to do? She plastered what she hoped was a convincing smile on her face before her eyes darted away, following the antics of a hummingbird hovering above the butterfly bush. Buddy followed, unwilling to let Ruth Ann out of his sight. She slowed her pace to accommodate her four-legged friend.

"Must he follow us everywhere?"

Ruth Ann ignored his comment. At that moment, she preferred Buddy's company to his, and the conversation they were about to have. She lifted an unspoken plea for Heavenly wisdom then tried again to make amends for the mess she'd made. "I did intend to discuss my new position with you when you came home for Edith's wedding."

James patted her hand. "The entire situation has escalated beyond my control, Ruth." He motioned for her to take a seat on the bench and then leaned against a pillar, one hand in his pocket and the other holding his cigar. "The Vandenbergs have learned of your teaching position as well and are not pleased. Not only has Jonathan threatened to end his engagement to my sister, but his parents will pull their financial support from father's campaign as well."

She brought her hand to her mouth and covered a soft gasp. So, this is how the rich and powerful got their way. She had no idea her actions could affect so many outside of herself.

"The Vandenbergs have numerous wealthy and influential friends throughout the South. They will not only scrutinize me but my wife. These will be very powerful and influential connections, Ruth— connections that could take me to the United States Senate or beyond."

Beyond? Her head was spinning. The only thing she could imagine beyond the United States Senate would be the White House itself.

Taking her hands in his, James pulled her up from the bench. "I have thought about you considerably while in Richmond, and I have decided we should marry. You are a keen judge of character that will no doubt help me navigate the muddy waters of politics. And your frankness, while troublesome at times, will keep me humble."

She stared at him, unsure what to say, her pulse pounding in her ears.

"You are a smart woman, Ruth, well-educated, charitable. While your father may not have been from as prestigious a family as my own, his name is well-respected in the capital." He removed a gold timepiece from his pocket, manipulating it in the palm of his hand. "You will be an ideal wife for my future ambitions."

His eyes brightened as he spoke of their future together. "Imagine all we can accomplish. We will wine and dine with the most prominent businessmen and politicians in the South. We will negotiate deals in the boardroom and in the parlor. Our prodigy will lay the foundation of a business and political dynasty that will influence the halls of power from Atlanta to Richmond and possibly, Ruth, to Washington itself."

For a brief moment, his enthusiasm spilled over. What would life be like as Mrs. James Robert Thornton, entertaining influential businessmen, powerful politicians, and their wives? The image he painted enticed her.

His fingers glided over the smooth face of the timepiece as he spoke. "There are, of course, a few youthful indiscretions we will need to explain as "works of charity," and other subjects, such as women's suffrage, must be avoided. However, mother has convinced me that your potential benefit to my future ambitions far outweighs any detriment…"

Ruth Ann folded her arms tightly to her chest. *Youthful indiscretions? The only hesitation he has had? Certain subjects we need to avoid?* James rocked on his heels and puffed his cigar, smug and confident like his father had been in the parlor. Head spinning, she forced herself to concentrate.

"Yes, it does seem to be coming together nicely." He strolled to the edge of the veranda, dropping ashes from his Upmann on Myra's pristine floor. "We should marry next spring—you can fix the date. That should give you plenty of time to organize your trousseau and plan a grand ceremony. You will need to run every detail by mother as many of the Vandenbergs will be in attendance."

Her stomach roiled. His discussion of marriage lacked any of the romantic gestures she had always hoped her future husband would bestow. Her life seemed to be arranging itself before she had accepted his proposal. Did he even have any romantic feelings for her? *There was only one way to find out.* She swallowed hard, her tongue thick. "James, d-do you love me?"

He chuckled. "That is a rather impertinent question, Ruth, but you have always been forthright." James stepped closer, taking her hands in his again. "My affection for you, darling, is implied by the mere fact I want to marry you."

Ruth Ann shook her head. "You have acknowledged I have many of the characteristics you desire in a wife, but you haven't expressed any romantic sentiment toward me, nor have you proposed. You haven't even kissed me." Why had she blurted that out? Heat rushed up her neck and exploded across her cheeks.

"Well, darling, we can remedy that situation right now." He took one last puff of his Upmann, dropped it to the floor of the veranda, and then extinguished it with the toe of his shoe.

Now that the moment had arrived, she wasn't sure she wanted James to kiss her. But if they were to marry, she supposed kissing him would be inevitable.

James put his arms around her and drew her close. He was small for a man—barely a half-inch taller than her. His narrow shoulders and thin arms made her feel gargantuan. She tried to focus on his hazel eyes. His one feature she found attractive.

His fingers trailed along her cheek. "I know some may find your robust figure unattractive, but it's of little consequence to me." James sat on the bench then tugged Ruth Ann into his lap nuzzling her neck below her ear with his nose.

Ruth Ann stiffened.

"It's all right. No one can see us from the parlor." He wrapped a loose curl around his finger. "You smell wonderful. Is that lavender?"

Ruth Ann swallowed hard and managed to nod.

He cradled her cheeks in the palms of his hands. Their lips met briefly then parted.

She didn't know what to expect. She had never kissed a man before, but she didn't think much of it. Surely, it should have stirred something inside her, but there was no tingling sensation, no rapid heartbeat, and no shortness of breath. And no desire to kiss him again either.

His lips grazed her jaw.

"We mustn't, James."

A roguish grin spread across his thin lips. "Now that we are engaged, we are allowed to be a little more—*friendly*."

"Un-uh," she replied wedging her hands between them. "You still haven't answered me." She searched his eyes. "Do you love me?"

Silence.

He didn't love her. This wasn't surprising, but somehow, she had allowed herself to believe that he wouldn't propose unless he did. She pushed herself off his lap and slipped to the edge of the veranda.

James followed and placed his hands on her shoulders, nudging her to face him. "Look at me, Ruth."

Yearning to see love in the eyes of the man who sought her hand, she hesitated.

"Can you not sense my desire for you?" His soft breath tickled her ear. "Kiss me, Ruth."

She folded her arms across her chest. "Physical

desire and love are two very different things, James."

"Perhaps, but in time, I believe a deep affection for one another will blossom between us. My parents married not for love but for the excellent connections between their two families and the continued security their marriage would provide. Over time, they have developed a strong bond—a strong partnership."

A shiver traveled down her spine. Was a loveless marriage, a mere partnership, to be her fate? She stepped back from his embrace. "What are you proposing, James, a marriage or a business contract?"

He smirked. "Is there a difference, darling?"

She didn't find him the least bit amusing. "What did you mean earlier when you mentioned my youthful indiscretions?"

"Ruth, must we talk about this now? Sit on my lap again. Perhaps give me another kiss?"

"Please, James, this is very important to me."

"All right." James pinched the bridge of his nose and squeezed his eyes closed. "Sometimes you have a tendency to share your opinion when not asked." He paused and dabbed the back of his neck with a folded handkerchief. "There are certain situations when a woman needs to be seen and not heard."

She tapped her toe on the floor of the veranda and waited for him to continue.

"Topics, like women's suffrage, are not acceptable in polite society. You know this. Your dalliance at the Negro school must end as well." He patted the perspiration from his upper lip and returned the cloth to his pocket. He glanced down at her bouncing foot. "Don't be cross with me, Ruth." He wrapped her in his arms.

"James, if I agree to marry you—"

He shrank away from the embrace he had initiated moments before. "If you agree to marry me?"

"Yes, if I agree to marry you, I will give Mr. Janney notice of my intent not to return to my position in November, but I will need to finish the current school term. The children and their parents depend on me—I gave my word."

"That is unacceptable." The tenor of his voice rose as he massaged his brow. "You must resign so we can announce our engagement. It will make the society column of every major newspaper in the South, and I will not have it reported that my bride-to-be works for hire teaching illiterate Negroes." His voice softened. "I'm sorry, darling, but that is not negotiable."

She stepped closer, curious if the power of the attraction he held for her would persuade him. "What about volunteer work with organizations dedicated to improving the lives of Negroes?" She tilted her head, smiling as she fingered the buttons on his vest. "Isn't charity work expected from the wives of politicians?"

He lifted her hand from his chest and kissed it. "I'm sorry, darling, but volunteering to assist Negroes would not be an approved charity. Everywhere you go as my wife, from the opera to the market to a soirée, even to church, will be an opportunity to advance our status socially, financially, and politically. Besides, you will be plenty busy raising our family, managing our household, and making social appearances with me."

She stared at the hazy August sky. The muggy air pressed close against her, confining her. Her eyes darted to James. How had she gotten herself into such a mess? Her stomach churned. This wouldn't do. If she married James, he would turn her inside out until she no longer recognized herself. However, if what her mother said was true, she may never have another offer of marriage. *Oh Lord, what am I to do?*

James took her hands in his again. "Can you not see this is the opportunity of a lifetime?"

Ruth Ann bit her lip. "No. Not anymore. If we marry, Ruth Ann Sutton would be replaced by Ruth Thornton as she is packaged and presented by you and both our mothers."

"That is terribly unfair."

Not caring for his sharp tone, she shifted away from him. "Is it?"

He lowered his voice, but it sounded strained to her ear. "You are overreacting, darling."

"Overreacting?" She spun to face him, hands on her hips. "Tell me. If our families were not so intimately connected if our union wasn't the wish of both our mothers, would you seek my hand?"

Offering no response, James resumed massaging his brow as he paced.

She looked away from him. "That's what I thought." Her voice cracked.

He drew near to her then lifted her chin with his finger. "That's not important. Trust me. Mother is usually right about these things."

She jerked away. "James, I cannot marry you." The words had barely escaped her lips before the heaviness in her chest abated.

His jaw slackened. "You cannot be serious. You are not thinking clearly."

Ruth Ann raised her chin. "I am."

James tugged on his vest then patted the pocket that housed his watch. "Very well." He tipped his head in her direction, yanked open the screen door, and returned to the house through the kitchen.

She flinched when the wooden frame slammed into place. He'd rebound quickly enough. She hadn't injured his heart, only his pride.

Her fingers clutched the locket that adorned her neck, sliding it back and forth on its gold chain. She forced a breath.

What would Mama say?

5

Ruth Ann pulled open her reticule and searched for the list of items Myra had asked her to purchase. Had she left it at home? Mama had been so cross with her since Ruth Ann refused James that she hurried out the door this morning without breakfast. Missing Myra's cinnamon rolls was a hardship indeed, but one worth enduring if it meant avoiding another one of Mama's lectures on her impending spinsterhood. She found the list tucked inside a small copy of the Psalms and promptly handed it to the shopkeeper's wife.

Adelaide Turner scanned the paper before heading off in the direction of the dry goods. "Malachi got a new shipment of books," she called over her shoulder.

New books. Ruth Ann darted to the bookshelf near the window on the opposite side of the store. Teaching at the Freedmen's School was the only thing that rivaled her zeal for literature. Her sister, Sarah, preferred poetry, but Ruth Ann didn't have the patience nor the inclination for poetic gibberish. Whether riding with the calvary across the Great Plains or rescuing a princess locked in a medieval castle, she preferred to lose herself in the make-believe world authors created for her in the pages of their books.

She paused at the corner display. A man in faded dungarees and shaggy black hair thumbed through the books—her books. From the back, he appeared desperate for some soap and a haircut. Some clean clothes wouldn't hurt either. She slipped into the center aisle and observed him through the glass chimney of a kerosene lamp. He retrieved one book then another, skimming the first few pages before returning it to the shelf. If only he'd hurry up then she could have a moment to examine the new arrivals herself.

"I've got your order ready."

Ruth Ann jerked suddenly, catching the handle of a large cast iron skillet in the pocket of her skirt. The heavy pan knocked a Dutch oven from the shelf. Several pieces of cookware stacked inside the skillet careened to the floor, barely missing Adelaide's foot.

"I'm sorry, Adelaide. You startled me."

"No harm done. I'm fine."

"Everything all right over there?" Mr. Turner called from the storeroom.

Adelaide responded to her husband's concerns. "Yes, we're fine. Just knocked over some merchandise."

Ruth Ann stooped to pick up the frying pans. A pair of dirty work boots appeared next to the pile of cookware strewn across Adelaide's floor.

"Here, let me help you with those."

That voice. The disheveled person perusing her books was the man from the creek?

He squatted and reached for the cast iron skillet in her hand.

Now mere inches apart, her gaze locked on his amber eyes. Her tongue grew thick and lazy all of a sudden. "I-I-I..."

Adelaide returned the Dutch oven to its resting place on the wooden shelf. "When you're ready, Ruth Ann, your items are in a crate up front." She disappeared around the corner, leaving Ruth Ann to deal with the shaggy Mr. Coulter on her own.

A grin split his bearded face. "You were trying to tell me something before, but it came out a bit jumbled. Care to try again?"

She tugged the heavy cookware from his grasp. "I can manage quite nicely on my own."

Ruth Ann stacked the cast iron pieces according to size. Grunting, she lifted her heavy load. She listed slightly toward Mr. Coulter before righting herself and depositing her burden on the shelf next to the Dutch oven.

Chuckling, he shook his head.

She planted her hands firmly on her hips. "And exactly what are you laughing at?"

"You and your mulish ways. I offered to help you, but you'd rather grunt and groan and do it yourself." He stroked his overgrown beard, eyes twinkling. "If I remember correctly, refusing my help is what got you in a tight spot the last time we met."

Chin lifted high, she pivoted on her heel and strode to the back of the store. Mr. Coulter's laughter reverberated in her ears. She wouldn't let him get the best of her again.

"Hello, Ruth Ann, how are you?"

Malachi Turner's warm greeting brightened her mood as she approached the counter.

He wiped his hands on his crisp, white apron. "Come, tell me how things are going at the school."

"Very well, thank you. My students are making slow but steady progress."

"Splendid." His tone softened. "I imagine many folks don't understand what you're doing, but you are changing our community for the better."

"Thank you."

"Do the children need anything for the classroom?"

"No, sir, but thank you. We've had books and some maps provided and the Society of Friends has supplied the students with slates and slate pencils."

"Glad to hear it, but Adelaide and I have something set aside for you nonetheless." Mr. Turner motioned for Ruth Ann to follow him. He opened a cabinet door and pulled out a large, red book. "The missus and I want you to have this. Consider it a donation to your school."

Ruth Ann reached for the leather-bound volume. It was heavy. She couldn't believe her eyes—*An American Dictionary of the English Language.* "Oh, Mr. Turner, how wonderful. Thank you so much. I will put this to good use."

Mr. Coulter approached the counter, two books in hand.

Tugging her bottom lip between her teeth, Ruth Ann's gaze roamed to his selections. She hadn't reviewed the new arrivals yet.

He glanced at her, brow arched.

She redirected her gaze to the shopkeeper's face. "I almost forgot. Sarah asked me to purchase some Pears soap while I'm here."

Mr. Turner nodded. "All right, but first take a look at this." He directed Ruth Ann toward a soft bound book lying open on the counter. "Have you heard about the new mail-order catalog?"

She shook her head.

"A man named Montgomery Ward has put out a registry of general merchandise. Customers can select items to purchase from the catalog and pay for them here in the store. For now, the merchandise will be shipped to Leesburg. However, once the train comes to Catoctin Creek, goods will be delivered right here to my store for you to pick up."

"I can order merchandise from a book and have it delivered to your store?"

"That's right. Very clever idea this Mr. Ward had. He calls it mail-order shopping. Very exciting, isn't it?"

She had never heard of such a thing. "May I take a look?"

He nodded.

Pages and pages of ready-made clothing, farm equipment, and jewelry unfolded before her eyes.

"I'll get the soap for you in a moment after I wait on this gentleman." He stepped toward Mr. Coulter. "May I help you, sir?"

Ruth Ann's attention shifted again to the books Mr. Coulter had placed on the counter. She craned her neck for a better view. What was he purchasing?

"Yes, I'd like to buy these books." He nodded in her direction. "If they meet with the lady's approval."

He looked to be stifling a grin when their eyes met. Heat raced across her cheeks as she attempted a weak smile. Mr. Turner's gaze flitted between her and Mr. Coulter. She feigned attention to the catalog. "It's no matter to me what you read, Mr. Coulter."

"I don't believe we've met. Malachi Turner. My wife, Adelaide, and I own this store. My brother, Samuel, owns the Hampton Hotel across the street. Are you employed by the railroad?"

"Benjamin Coulter. No. I work for Dutton and Farrell Land Mapping Agency, but yes, I'm working to get the Washington & Ohio here to Catoctin Creek and then over the Blue Ridge."

"Land Mapping Agency—that's mighty

impressive. What do you do for them?"

Impressive. It would be impressive if he would visit the barber. She flipped another page in the catalog as she eavesdropped on their conversation.

"I'm a surveyor."

A chainman, a rodman, even a spikeman for the railroad would better fit his scruffy appearance. Why did he have to be a surveyor? She hated to admit it, but that was impressive.

"Well done, young man. You have a bright future ahead of you." Mr. Turner tore off a piece of brown paper. "That will be two dollars."

Mr. Coulter held up his hand. "No need to wrap them, Malachi. I'll take them as is." He reached in his pocket to retrieve a few coins for the shop keep.

"Thank you, sir." Mr. Turner pointed to the catalog she perused. "Care to take a look?"

Mr. Coulter stepped toward Ruth Ann and glanced at the catalog over her shoulder. He towered above her. He was taller than James, taller than Joseph and most likely taller than her father, and he had been six feet tall.

"The catalog is small now, but the Montgomery Ward Company has plans to expand it to include furniture, baby carriages, stoves, sewing machines, ready-made draperies, and the list will only keep growing. Anything you can think of will one day be for sale through the catalog."

Muscled forearms revealed themselves underneath the rolled sleeves of Mr. Coulter's work shirt. He pointed to one of the Winchester rifles listed on the page. "A Winchester Yellow Boy." His finger dragged across the page. "Eighteen dollars."

She placed her hand against her stomach. Why

was she suddenly jittery? "Does the catalog include books, Mr. Turner?"

"Oh, yes." He turned to the section with Bibles, dictionaries, and classic literature. I'm sure the list of titles will expand. In the back of the catalog there's an index listing all the categories of merchandise available and their page numbers. This truly is the way of the future."

Ruth Ann continued to peruse the catalog, stopping on occasion to comment on a particular item for sale. She flipped the page to find drawings of women's bloomers and stockings. She scrambled to turn the page, cheeks flaming. Her jaw dropped. Sketches of women modeling corsets stared back at her. She abruptly closed the catalog, not daring to glance at either man.

Mr. Turner cleared his throat. "Um, I'll just... go get the Pears soap for you, Ruth Ann."

Mr. Coulter wasn't as discreet. His head jerked backward, his shoulders shook, and a deep, hearty laugh escaped him.

The warmth in her cheeks had become a raging inferno. She smiled sheepishly. Why did she always seem to be stretching the bounds of propriety?

~*~

Benjamin's hand pressed over the aching muscles of his abdomen. He hadn't laughed that hard in a long time. Miss Fancy Boots spun on her heel and headed for the door. The ringing of the bell told him she'd found it.

Clink.

A young boy nudged Benjamin. "Excuse me,

mister. Dropped my penny. It rolled by your foot."

Benjamin moved to the side, allowing the boy to reclaim his coin.

Malachi returned a moment later with Ruth Ann's soap and laid it with the other items in her order. His eyes darted around the store.

"She left," Benjamin volunteered.

"She left? But all her... never mind." He shrugged. "I'll just deliver them to the Sutton's home this afternoon. It would've been difficult for Ruth Ann to carry it all anyway."

Benjamin glanced toward the door. "Say, Malachi, if you tell me where Miss Fancy...uh, I mean, Miss Sutton lives, I'd be happy to deliver those for you."

Malachi strummed his fingers on the counter. His glance flitted between the crate and Benjamin.

"I'd appreciate the opportunity to make it up to her. I think I embarrassed her when I laughed at her quandary."

"All right. That would be helpful, Benjamin. I promised the missus I'd get that storeroom organized today, and you know what the Bible says about living with an unhappy wife."

Benjamin raised a brow.

"You single, Benjamin?"

He nodded.

A knowing grin crossed the shop keep's face. "Proverbs 21:19. 'It is better to dwell in the wilderness than with a contentious and angry woman.' Knowing that, my friend, is the key to a long and happy marriage. You'll find the Sutton's house on Colonial Highway right at the edge of town. Big stone place on the left. Lots of ivy growing on it. Can't miss it."

Benjamin glanced at the red-haired boy now

eyeing the glass canisters of candy. "I'll take a penny's worth of lemon drops, too."

Malachi scooped the hard candies into a paper sack and handed it to Benjamin.

Benjamin laid two pennies on the counter then tilted his head in the direction of the little moppet. "How about a penny's worth for him, too?"

The boy twisted swiftly in Benjamin's direction and flashed him a gapped-tooth smile. "You mean it, mister?"

Benjamin nodded. He looked forward to having toothless little ones underfoot someday.

"Gee, thanks!"

Benjamin stuffed the candy in his shirt pocket and placed his books underneath the large dictionary. He grabbed the crate and headed for the door. Things were looking up. He had learned Miss Fancy Boots' name—Ruth Ann Sutton—and now he knew just where to find Catoctin Creek's spunky schoolmarm. Yep, it was shaping up to be a rather good day.

Benjamin leaned against the door, jingling the bell when he exited the store. He squinted. The late afternoon sun hung just above the tree line to the west. Someone tugged at his shirtsleeve.

"Excuse me. I believe those are mine." Miss Sutton hadn't gone far at all.

"Malachi gave me directions to your house. I was going to deliver these for you."

She reached for the crate. "That won't be necessary, but thank you."

Benjamin held firm to the container. "Nope, I insist, Miss Sutton. It wasn't very gentlemanly of me to laugh at your predicament a few moments ago. It's just—" He pressed his lips together. Despite his best efforts, a grin edged his face. "It's just... well, you seem to have a knack for finding yourself in tight spots."

"You have no idea." She tugged on the crate. "My things, please, Mr. Coulter."

She peered up at him with those dark eyes of hers. A man could get lost in those eyes. He cleared his throat. "Please let me make it up to you. I promise to be on my best behavior."

Miss Sutton angled her head and pursed her lips. Apparently, this was a big decision, and she didn't want to get it wrong. Probably the schoolteacher in her. She finally nodded and relinquished her hold on the crate. "Thank you."

They looked up as the bell on the door rang again.

The boy held up a brown paper sack, his freckled cheeks bulging like a squirrel in autumn. "Fanks agin, mitter."

Benjamin chuckled. "That reminds me." He set the crate on the porch and retrieved his own brown sack from his shirt pocket. He held out the bag. "Care for a lemon drop?"

She peeked into the bag then at him. Grinning, she reached inside for a piece. "Thank you."

Benjamin dropped a sour candy into his own mouth. He grabbed her purchases and followed her down the steps to the dirt road that ran in front of Turner's store, searching his mind for something to say. Images of her runty dog came to mind. "So tell me about that herding dog of yours."

She glared at him out of the corner of her eye.

If looks could kill, he'd be lying in a pine box.

"Despite popular belief, they aren't commonly used to herd rabbits." She lifted her hand to block the afternoon sun. "They were bred to herd cattle by nipping at their heels."

Benjamin couldn't picture a dog that size bossing anything around. To him, a dog should be able to protect him if need be and help him hunt perhaps, but... "He's barely a foot and a half tall. You sure they can handle cattle?"

"Most assuredly. Their short legs make them very agile. My brother-in-law's family uses them to herd the horses on their farm near Middleburg."

She flashed him a dimple-laden smile that made him tingly inside. Where had that little beauty been hiding the other day?

"Coulter, that you?"

They stopped as an older, bowlegged man approached, carrying a bulging, burlap sack over his shoulder. Great. Not the impression he wanted to make on the lady. "Ollie Harper, this is Miss Ruth Ann Sutton."

Ollie removed his hat and tipped his head in Miss Sutton's direction. He had less hair on top of his head than on his chin, and when he smiled, he disclosed more than one missing tooth. "Nice to meet ya." He swished tobacco around his mouth then spat. Ollie nudged Benjamin with his elbow and waggled his bushy brows. "Didn't take you long to find a pretty petticoat, even in this little town."

Benjamin glanced from Miss Sutton to Ollie. "Where you headed?"

Ollie tipped his head in the direction he'd come. "Me and the fellas is headin' to the general store."

Benjamin's eyes darted to the other men from his crew, all straining to catch a glimpse of Ruth Ann.

Ollie swung the sack off his shoulder. It landed with a thud in the dirt road, creating a small dust cloud. "I'll be needin' another jug. Found me a bushel o' corn, real cheap." He opened the sack so they could peer in.

Miss Sutton coughed and waved her hand in front of her face. She leaned forward. "I'm afraid I don't see what the jug is for. You'll need jars to can all that corn."

Ollie removed his hat and struck it against his leg. He guffawed and nudged Benjamin in the ribs a second time. "Your petticoat thinks we're cannin' corn in camp."

Heat burned in Benjamin's cheeks, and it wasn't from the afternoon sun. "Maybe you best be on your way, Ollie."

Ollie plopped his hat on his head and hoisted the sack to his shoulder. He waggled his brows. "She ain't nothing like Marcy, is she?"

"Mr. Harper?" Miss Sutton's eyes narrowed. "If you don't plan to can all that corn, what are you going to do with it?"

A grin spread across his unshaven face. He winked. "Makin' firewater, miss."

Miss Sutton tilted her head, all the while tapping her index finger against her cheek. Maybe if he hurried Ollie along, he could wriggle out of this uncomfortable situation before the teacher put two and two together.

"Moonshine, Miss."

She gasped.

Benjamin's shoulders slumped. Too late. Now he'd have some explaining to do. "You'd better get going, Ollie. I need to escort Miss Sutton home before her family worries about her. I'll see you back at camp."

He couldn't believe his eyes. Miss Sutton stepped toward Ollie and laid her hand on his filthy sleeve. "Mr. Harper, promise me you won't do that. Doc Rawlings told me about homemade spirits. He calls it rotgut and says its poison."

"Aw, Miss, you don't need to worry none. I'm so old and ornery nothing's gonna hurt me. But thank ya for yer carin'." He strode off in the direction of Turner's. "No siree, Coulter, she's nothin' like Marcy," he called over his shoulder. "Nothin' at all."

"Mr. Coulter?"

Oh boy, here it comes. She hadn't wasted a second. Benjamin steeled himself for what might be an ugly scene. What was he thinking, anyway? Women like Miss Sutton didn't associate with men like Ollie Harper. Men who drank and played poker—men like him. They wanted church-going types. Men like he used to be—before the war. Before Marcy.

Surprisingly, her tone softened. "Promise me, neither of you will drink that rotgut."

Those dark eyes stared at him, waiting for an answer, but he wouldn't make a promise he might not be able to keep.

They started walking again but slower now.

She spoke first, ending the awkward moments of silence. "Why do men like to drink firewater?"

"For some of us, like Ollie and me, it helps us forget."

"Does it work?"

Her questions were as probing as those eyes of hers. Who was he kidding? Nothing really helped. But for a few glorious hours every night he forgot about the death he had witnessed on the battlefield, the lives he took defending the Union. Women hadn't helped either. Marcy was just one more thing he didn't want to remember. "Only for a little while."

She stopped walking and searched his face. When she spoke, her voice was nearly a whisper. "I'm sorry."

Her gaze lingered on him as if she could see right through him. He looked away, hoping to discourage too close of an inspection. She wouldn't like what she found. And somehow, that mattered to him. He pushed down the lump in his throat and resumed their pace.

"How long have you known Mr. Harper?"

"Ollie and I go way back. He saved my life during the siege of Petersburg and even though he's a bit rough around the edges, a debt like that is hard to repay. He's got no family. At least none that will have anything to do with him. So he followed me west to find work with the railroad, and we've stuck together ever since."

She veered off the dirt road onto a stone path.

Benjamin's eyes drifted upward, like the ivy that clung to the impressive dwelling. *Woo-wee, I'm in way over my head.* His parents' modest farmhouse could easily fit inside her home three times. This little lady came from money. Although he had a bright future ahead of him as a surveyor, he'd never be able to afford a home like this one. Nor was he likely to spend his hard-earned money on such things.

They passed the stairs to the front door and followed the stone path behind the house. The dog barked at the sound of their approach. The feisty little critter scurried toward them and jumped against her legs.

"Hello, Buddy. I've missed you."

The dog trailed them down the remainder of the path to the back porch where two women, one Negro, one white, sat on the back porch snapping green beans into a large wooden bowl.

"You can set the crate on the veranda. Thank you."

The white woman stood and dumped her apron full of unsnapped beans into a basket on the floor. Her eyes drifted from Benjamin's plaid work shirt, to his faded dungarees, to his scuffed work boots, then back up again.

"Mama, this is Mr. Benjamin Coulter. We met the other day. He was in Turner's this afternoon and offered to carry that heavy crate home for me."

Benjamin removed his hat and bowed slightly in Mrs. Sutton's direction. "Ma'am."

Mrs. Sutton wiped her hands on her apron. She acknowledged him with a slight lift of her chin, but her scowl was tighter than the bun securing her dark hair at the nape of her neck.

"Mr. Coulter," Miss Sutton said, pointing with a nod toward the Negro woman. "This is a dear friend of our family, Myra. She works for us."

Myra stood and moved to the edge of the porch, shaking out her apron. "Can I gets you something cool to drink?"

Mrs. Sutton limped toward him favoring her right leg, her mouth curved downward. Was she unhappy with his presence, or was she in pain—or both? "That will not be necessary, Myra." She paused a moment as an involuntary shudder coursed through her. "I'm sure Mr. Coulter has things to do."

She may be in pain, but she definitely wanted him gone—far away from her little darling.

"Mr. Coulter has just done me a kindness, Mama, and I think it's only proper to repay him with a glass of lemonade."

"Very well, Ruth. Myra, you can remain on the

porch. Ruth and I will get the lemonade." Mrs. Sutton held the screen door open for her daughter.

"You'll wait for me? I-I mean the lemonade?" A smidgen of pink graced her cheeks. Miss Sutton wanted him to stay.

Benjamin glanced at her mother. She was a petite, but formidable, woman. He guessed she stood at least four inches shorter than her daughter, but they both seemed to possess the same determined spirit. "I have time for one glass. Thank you. Then I should be heading back to camp."

Miss Sutton headed for the door where her mother stood vigil then looked back over her shoulder and smiled before disappearing inside.

Benjamin stroked his beard. What was he doing? He knew better. When a man played with fire, eventually he got burned.

~*~

Ruth Ann poured three glasses of lemonade and placed them on a hand-painted tray. "Will you be joining us for lemonade on the veranda, Mama?"

Mama's fingers strummed on the wooden butcher block. "No, I am not joining you. This is not a social call, Ruth." Mama clutched her arm. "What do you know of this Mr. Coulter?"

"He is a surveyor with a land mapping agency, and he's assigned to the Washington & Ohio Railroad."

"A railroad man? What does he want with you?"

"Nothing, I suppose. He offered to carry my heavy crate, and I let him. He's kind and witty." Her gaze dropped to her forearm. "Please let go of my arm now. Mr. Coulter is waiting."

Mama tightened her grip. "You find him kind and witty? You prefer that scraggly, ill-mannered railroad man to the wealth and refined gentility of James Thornton?"

She preferred just about anything to James. "Mr. Coulter may be a bit unkempt, but he's not ill-mannered." Of course, he'd laughed at her predicament in Turner's. At least he had apologized. And earlier he had helped with the fallen skillets— before he had called her obstinate. But those eyes...

"You can do much better than a tracklayer who resides in a railroad camp, Ruth."

"Please keep your voice down, Mama. He'll hear you. Besides, Mr. Coulter is not a tracklayer. He is a surveyor. And just because a man is polite and offers to carry a heavy load for a woman doesn't mean he has taken a liking to her." She glanced at her arm. "Please let go. You're hurting me."

"Mind what I say. Be polite, but don't give him a reason to come back."

~*~

Benjamin ran his fingers through Buddy's thick coat. He was one lucky dog to have that pretty schoolteacher for his mistress.

Mrs. Sutton's voice drifted through the open window. "You can do much better than a tracklayer who resides in a railroad camp, Ruth."

He stood and donned his hat. "If you'd just let Miss Sutton know I had to leave, I'd appreciate it."

Myra sauntered to the edge of the veranda and leaned against a white pillar. She wiped her brow with the edge of her apron. "You gonna leave when she gettin' you lemonade?"

Mrs. Sutton didn't approve. She clearly saw him as a predatory fox, and she didn't intend to leave her baby chic unprotected. "It's just better this way, ma'am."

"Mmm-hmmm. You right. You best be on your way." She shooed him away with her hands. "Any man come callin' 'round here gonna need more spunk than that."

The woman had lost her mind. He'd merely assisted Miss Sutton with her crate. Benjamin massaged the back of his neck. He leaned forward and peered through the screen door. "You have the situation all wrong. We are acquaintances. I helped her carry a heavy load. That's all. No more. No less."

Myra shook her head. "I ain't never seen her eyes sparkle like that. She lit up like a firefly in July." The woman scanned him from head to toe. "You best clean yourself up if you come callin' on Miss Ruth Ann. You in pitiful need of a haircut. And you tell the barber to trim that beard while he at it. Never mind that. You just tell him to shave it clean off." She glanced toward the screen door then back at him, eyes twinkling. "Miss Ruth Ann don't cotton to men with beards, especially scraggly ones."

Benjamin scratched the course hair on his cheek. He'd been meaning to get to the barber.

The hinges creaked on the screen door. Myra meandered back to the bench and picked up the wooden bowl of beans. She raised a brow. "Mind what I tell you."

Miss Sutton returned with the tray of lemonade and offered them both a glass before setting the tray on the bench beside Myra. She picked up her own drink and drew a long sip. Her lips puckered from the tart beverage.

What he wouldn't give to be that glass—pressing against her lips.

Whoa. From where had that thought come? He was only helping an acquaintance. A stubborn acquaintance at that, but one with the most beautiful dimple-laden smile he'd ever seen.

If he needed a dose of reality, her mother offered it. She stood guard at the screen door as if his mere presence may sully her daughter's reputation. He gulped his lemonade then wiped his mouth with the back of his sleeve.

"Thank you for the drink." He placed his empty glass on the tray. "Nice meeting you." He tipped his head first toward Mrs. Sutton then toward Myra.

Mrs. Sutton returned to the house, probably satisfied the danger had passed.

Hat in hand, he extended his arm toward the crate. "I just need to get my books. They're under the dictionary."

"Oh, certainly." Miss Sutton set the large red book to the side and retrieved the novels. Her hand gently caressed the top cover.

"Is something the matter?"

"Not at all." Her eyes remained fixed on the book as if it were a rare and precious gem. "*A Journey to the Center of the Earth*. One of my favorite stories."

Benjamin's mouth fell agape. Miss Fancy Boots read Jules Verne?

She placed the top book underneath and spoke with a reverence he'd only heard in church. "*Around the World in Eighty Days*—his latest novel."

He stepped forward. "Y-you read Jules Verne?"

"Oh, yes." She finally lifted her eyes to him. "May I?"

Benjamin nodded.

She sat on the edge of the veranda reading the first chapter aloud.

He looked to Myra. She lifted a brow and motioned for him to sit beside Miss Sutton. He removed his hat and did as directed. Head bowed with book in hand, she was lost in the story.

Benjamin was lost in her—her creamy complexion, the wispy curls that had freed themselves from her bun and floated on the breeze, and her lavender scent. Oh, how he wanted to reach up and twist one of those curls around his finger.

He slid away and leaned against the nearest pillar, his long legs stretched out before him. Delighting in the sound of her voice as the story unfolded before her, Benjamin couldn't help but smile. She was enchanting.

Ollie had never been more right. She was nothing like Marcy.

A cold, wet nose nudged his hand. Benjamin scratched Buddy's chin. The dog rolled over, paws flapping, exposing his white belly. Benjamin chuckled, and he stroked the snowy fur. He lifted his head when he realized she had stopped.

Miss Sutton closed the cover. "I-I don't know what came over me."

They flinched when the screen door banged against the side of the house. Mrs. Sutton stood rigid beside them. "I didn't realize you were still here, Mr. Coulter."

Myra gathered the basket and wooden bowl. She stepped around Mrs. Sutton and hurried inside.

"We've kept Mr. Coulter long enough, Ruth."

Miss Sutton stood and offered him the book. "Here you go, Mr. Coulter."

Benjamin shook his head. "You keep it. I'll read the other one first."

She held the novel tight against her. "Thank you."

Mrs. Sutton held the door open for her daughter. "Go inside now and help Myra set the table."

Benjamin fiddled with the brim of his hat. He preferred to speak to Miss Sutton privately, but her mother didn't plan to leave them alone again. "I-I'm wondering if you would like to go fishing with me, Miss Sutton. We could talk about the books once we've both finished."

Her eyes brightened. "I—"

"Thank you for your kind offer, but that is out of the question. Ruth barely knows you and a trip to the woods...to fish? Surely you must see that is inappropriate for a young woman of Ruth's upbringing."

Miss Sutton's eyes widened. "Mama, it's just a fishing trip to the creek. Perhaps Sarah, Joseph, and the children could accompany us."

Could it be? Did she really want to spend time with him, too? He didn't know the folks she referred to, but if it meant he could see her again, he'd bring Ollie. "I would be happy to have them join us."

Her mother's jaw tightened. She tilted her head in the direction of the house. "Ruth."

Miss Sutton's gaze flitted between her mother and him while she weighed her options. Benjamin recognized the fire in her eyes as her chin lifted.

"Mama, you are being rude to our guest." She faced him, eyes bright. "I accept your invitation to go fishing sometime. Thank you."

Atta girl. There was that pluck he admired.

"You will go inside now, Ruth."

Miss Sutton looked at him, a shy smile spread across her lovely face, but her eyes looked—doubtful? "Good-bye, Mr. Coulter. Thank you again for the loan of your book." She patted her leg twice. Buddy yawned and stretched then followed after her.

"My pleasure."

Mrs. Sutton held her hands in front of her, fingers intertwined. "Thank you again for assisting Ruth with that heavy load. However, your services will not be required here in the future. Good day."

Benjamin lifted his hat. "Ma'am."

She left him alone on the veranda. He had been dismissed.

Benjamin plopped his hat on his head, picked up his book, and made his way along the stone path toward the road. Curtains swayed at the window. Was that Miss Sutton?

The lace coverings closed again and with it, any hopes of spending time with the spirited beauty. Her mother would most likely see to that.

6

Benjamin threw open the tent flap and slumped on the cot. It was dark and musty inside. He glanced around at his meager possessions. What did he have to offer a fine lady like Ruth Ann Sutton? She probably didn't want for much of anything when it came to material things—except singing lessons. He chuckled. He could buy her singing lessons. Her caterwauling would be a small price to pay if it meant spending time with the lady.

He raked his fingers through his hair. Her mother didn't approve of him. Even his position as a surveyor hadn't impressed her. A surveyor earned a good pay and with the west opening up, he would have his pick of opportunities. Though, if he were being completely honest, he wasn't a surveyor—yet. Only an apprentice. A tiny detail he'd neglected to mention.

Benjamin dropped to his knees and reached under his cot to the far back corner. He curled his fingers around the cool glass and pulled it from its hiding place. He'd intended to throw it out. Returning to his seat on the cot, Benjamin leaned forward resting his elbows on his knees. He stared at the amber liquid. Mrs. Sutton's disdainful glare flashed before him. Where was the respect his advancement from crew chief to surveyor should afford him?

He rolled the smooth glass from one palm to the other as thoughts of Marcy and his life in Texas surged through his memory. Pride swelled anew as Mr.

Farrell's words came to mind.

Never in the twelve-year history of the Dutton & Farrell Land Mapping Agency has anyone risen through the ranks as quickly as you have Benjamin. Seems we haven't found a job yet you can't do better than the man there before you. I see nothing but success in your future.

Filled with excitement about his good fortune, he'd gone to share his news with Marcy—and to propose.

Only she wasn't alone. She was in the arms of another man. Grant Jackson.

His thumb glided over the torn whiskey label. Why couldn't he just forget? The vein in Benjamin's neck pulsated, a steady throbbing sensation that mimicked his rampant pulse. He might've beaten the man within an inch of his life if it hadn't been for Marcy's pleadings. Like a fool, he'd professed his undying love in a futile attempt to persuade her to stay. It wasn't enough. She'd already decided to leave him. All that mattered to Marcy was the money.

Benjamin twisted the cork free. Lifting the bottle to his lips, he downed a long pull of whiskey then wiped his mouth on his sleeve. Maybe he wasn't Grant Jackson. Maybe he wasn't a civil engineer—but he was on his way. Marcy may have left him for a man with deeper pockets, but he'd make sure that never happened to him again. After he passed that examination next spring, he'd acquire a position others would respect, envy even.

The tent flap whipped open and Ollie ducked inside. He glanced at the whiskey in Benjamin's hand. "What's eatin' you? You look worse than a pig on butcherin' day."

"Nothin.'"

"Uh-oh, you got lady troubles?" Ollie chortled. "That pretty petticoat send you away?" Ollie slapped Benjamin on the back. "Well, never you mind. We men have to try, don't we? I got somethin' to take your mind off your ailin' heart. I'm headin' over to the livery for some poker. You want to join me?"

Benjamin stared at the bottle in his hand. He'd been trying to drink and gamble less since leaving Texas. Coming to Virginia was his chance to start over—clean slate. He'd even visited the local church a few times. But who was he fooling? He wasn't good enough for God anymore, and he sure wasn't good enough for Miss Fancy Boots—at least her mother didn't think so, and she was the gatekeeper. He let out a breath. Anything seemed better than sitting alone in his tent, dwelling on the afternoon's events. "Sure, I'll come along."

~*~

Perspiration made the cards stick to Benjamin's fingers. Smoke hung in the dank air, weaving its scent with the stench from unattended horse stalls and human sweat. He eyed the man across from him. Could his opponent's hand really be as good as he was indicating or was the man bluffing?

Artie smirked. "Looks like it's me and you, Coulter." The chainman lifted the jug, took a swig, and passed it to Benjamin.

As Benjamin brought the corn liquor to his lips, a sad pair of dark brown eyes flickered before him. *Promise me neither of you will drink that rotgut.* He sighed before surrendering the jug to the man beside him.

"Coulter. I raised you two dollars. You foldin' or

bettin'?"

Benjamin glanced at his cards, then the pot of money on the table, and finally at Artie who was taking yet another swig of rotgut. The gamble he'd taken earlier, asking Miss Fancy Boots to go fishing, had been a draw, at best. He didn't plan to lose again—at least not today.

"I'm in." Benjamin placed his two dollars in the pile. He leaned forward as he dropped additional money on the table. "And I'll raise you five dollars, Artie."

Mack reached for the jug. "Whooo-wheeee. This is gettin' good."

"Hold up, there, Coulter." Ollie swished a wad of tobacco to the other side of his mouth. "Ya sure yer thinkin' things through. Just 'cause that gal's mother gave ya the boot don't mean ya should risk an entire week's wages."

Benjamin glared at his friend. The man never knew when to keep his mouth shut. Refocusing his attention back to the game, he nodded toward Artie. "I raised you five dollars. You in or not?"

Artie ran his hand over his whiskers and stared at Benjamin. The sheen of perspiration glistened above his lip. He finally dropped five dollars in the pot and puffed his cigar. "I call. Three of a kind." He laid his three sixes on the makeshift table.

Benjamin stared at Artie's cards. Thoughts of Marcy's stinging rejection mingled with Mrs. Sutton's disapproving looks.

One of the tracklayers, Jim Tatem, slapped Artie on the back then handed him the jug. "Looks like you took him, Artie"

With a hasty shake of his head Benjamin divulged

his hand, snapping the cards as he laid them on the barrel. "Flush, boys, in diamonds. I believe that pot is mine." He swept the money into his hat.

"Well, I'll be." Ollie lifted the crock of moonshine. "Here's to ya, Coulter."

The bell rang at the livery door.

Mack stood. "Be right back." The foreman lowered his voice. "That's probably Peterson returning his carriage, but you fellas keep it down. Can't have word of our little game gettin' back to Mr. Palmer."

The men grunted.

Tatem shook his head. "I sure thought you had that one, Artie."

Ollie hoisted the jug to his mouth. "With that pile of winnings, Coulter, you can buy a fancy suit to go callin' on that pretty schoolteacher. Then her mama might take a shine to you."

Tatem chortled. "The gal you were talking to outside of Turner's earlier—she's a schoolteacher?"

Artie waggled his eyebrows. "The one with...the curves." His hands swerved generously through the air mocking her buxom shape.

"Don't go gettin' ornery now, Artie," one of the other men whooped. "How much whiskey have you had anyway?"

"Not nearly enough." He swaggered over to Benjamin and poked a finger in his chest. "God didn't make women with ample figures like that for marryin' boy. You oughta know that."

Benjamin's fists grasped Artie's shirt. "Shut your mouth. She's a fine lady."

Tatem snickered. "Fine for beddin' down."

The men guffawed.

Benjamin released Artie with a shove, removed his

winnings from his hat and stuffed them into his pocket. "See you back at camp, Ollie." He stepped around Artie and headed for the door.

Emboldened by the liquor, Artie blocked his path. "Well, you let me know if you're gonna pass on her. Because I can tell you right now, those plump little fillies are some of the sweetest ladies I've ever known."

That was it. Benjamin's jaw stiffened as scorching heat coursed through his veins. He'd tried to leave, but Artie just wouldn't let it go. Miss Sutton deserved better than to have this drunken sot maligning her.

He spun and lunged at Artie sending them both crashing into the crates. Cards and money flew through the air. Benjamin's fist connected repeatedly with Artie's face before the man was able to roll Benjamin over and get in a few punches of his own. The men whooped and hollered, encouraging the brawl.

"What the Sam Hill is goin' on in here?" Mack yelled. "Separate those men!"

Tatem wrenched Artie from atop Benjamin. "C'mon. Mack says you're done fightin'."

Ollie offered his hand then yanked Benjamin from the ground.

Benjamin's chest heaved. The rusty taste of his busted lip lingered on his tongue.

Mack stepped between Benjamin and Artie, one hand planted firmly in the chest of each man. "Mr. Palmer will fire my hide if he finds out what we're doin' in his livery."

Artie hawked a blob of bloody spit at Benjamin's feet.

That was all the incentive Benjamin needed. He broke loose from Ollie's hold. Mack ducked as

Benjamin took another swing at Artie.

Mack shoved himself in front of Benjamin, mere inches separating their noses. "That's enough!"

Gulping air, Artie leaned forward, resting his hands against his knees. "Not my fault...this fool...don't know women with figures like hers are good for one thing only."

Mack glared at Artie. "Sometimes you don't know when to shut your mouth."

Benjamin's gaze drifted past Mack, finally resting on the older man behind him. Could this day get any worse? He hadn't noticed the onlooker until now. Benjamin avoided Neil Peterson's piercing eyes—the kind that bore into a person's soul. Peterson was an elder from the church he'd been visiting. Benjamin could already hear the tongue-lashing he'd get following tomorrow's services. He picked up his hat and dusted it off against his pant leg. Pushing past Artie and the others, Benjamin hastily exited the livery without another glance in Peterson's direction.

~*~

Benjamin trudged down the muddy road, water splashing from puddles he couldn't avoid in the dark. The sounds of late summer filled the warm September night. Crickets and bullfrogs swapped mating calls, creating a peaceful harmony that usually soothed his soul when troubled. Not tonight. He was furious with himself—drinking and gambling. When would he ever learn?

"Benjamin, wait up!"

Hearing the older man call out his name, Benjamin stopped. *Great. On top of everything else, now I'm going to get a sermon from Neil Peterson.*

"You all right, son? Do you need to see the doc about that lip?"

Benjamin dabbed his hand against his bloody mouth. "Nah, I'm fine."

Neil set a hand on Benjamin's shoulder. "Where are you heading?"

"Back to camp."

"Why don't you come along with me, instead? My wife, Trudy, made a delicious peach pie this afternoon. I'm on my way home to have a piece."

Benjamin searched the older man's eyes for the judgment and condemnation that he deserved, but all he found was heartfelt concern. "I'm a bit of a mess, sir. I should probably go clean up."

Neil patted him on the back. "We're all a mess, son. That's why we need a Savior." He pointed in the direction from which they'd come. "It's a short walk from here."

Benjamin hesitated. He didn't relish the idea of going back to his tent—alone. And, there was something about Neil that drew Benjamin. What was it exactly—his quiet confidence, his unswerving faith? If he spent time with this man, would it rub off on him? He didn't know, but he aimed to find out. "Sure, pie sounds great."

"Good."

A few minutes later, the two men sat on the back porch of the Petersons' three-story boardinghouse. Neil gently pumped his rocking chair. "So why don't you tell me what's troubling you. Why were you fighting with Arthur Johnson?"

Benjamin ran his fingers down the length of his course beard. "He said some disrespectful things."

"About you?"

"Mostly about a woman I met recently."

"Punches flew over a woman you barely know? Very honorable. You must care about her."

He avoided Neil's gaze, preferring instead to fiddle with his hat perched on his knee. There wasn't anything honorable about him or his behavior tonight. "I do care for her, but it doesn't matter. I'm not..."

Neil rested his hands on the arms of the rocking chair. "Not good enough for her?"

Benjamin lifted his head. "H-how did you know?"

"I was a young man, too, once—full of myself and my pride. I was determined to make the world bow in recognition of me instead of bowing to the One who made me." Neil paused while his wife served them peach pie and coffee.

"Thank you, ma'am." Benjamin set his mug on the porch railing, then broke off the point of his pie with his fork and stuffed it in his mouth. He washed it down with a sip of coffee while he waited for the door to close behind Mrs. Peterson. "It's too late, Neil. I veered away from God a long time ago. Even if He were to forgive me, a lady like Miss Sutton would have a hard time overlooking my past."

Neil raised his bushy brows. "Ruth Ann Sutton is the woman you were referring to?"

Benjamin nodded.

"She's a fine young woman—the kind that looks past the outside and into the heart."

"That's exactly what concerns me. There's nothing good there for her to find."

Neil's eyes remained fixed on him. "There's nothing God can't forgive Benjamin."

He swallowed another bite of his pie. "Those are

pretty words, and I believed them once. But God doesn't have much use for me—not anymore. You saw me tonight—drinking and gambling. And that's nowhere near the worst of it."

Neil lowered his coffee cup. "You know, Benjamin, even when we are walking with the Lord, we still stumble. That's all you did tonight. You stumbled a bit."

"I've been stumbling for years."

"Tell me what's troubling you, son. Sounds like it's time to get it off your chest."

Benjamin listened to the rain's sorrowful melody. He wanted to believe Neil—to believe it wasn't too late for him. Why not? What did he have to lose? Benjamin scraped a hand along his beard. Eyes trained on his coffee mug, he forced the words from his mouth. "Growing up, my family didn't have much. My pa owned a successful orchard but drank away most of the profits. I couldn't wait to leave home and strike out on my own. I worked hard in school, especially in arithmetic. Pa, however, expected me to take over the farm and forbade me from taking advanced courses. I finally told him I didn't want to work the farm but preferred to go to college instead. He drew me close, putting his arm around my shoulder. His whiskey-laden breath filled the air between us, as sour as the words he spoke. 'Son, let me set ya straight. No Coulter has ever amounted to anything in this world, and neither will you. You'll take yer place on this land, and scrape out yer living beside yer Pa as I did mine.'"

There it was. The truth Benjamin had been running from for nearly nine years. The truth he'd become determined to dispel. Staring at the rain running off the edge of the porch roof, Benjamin bit back the bitterness threatening to overtake him. "A few days later, the Confederates burned Chambersburg to the ground. Determined to prove my father wrong, I ran off and enlisted in the Union army. I was only fifteen, but anything was better than a future trapped on that farm. I was a good soldier, too. A lot of Rebs died at the point of my bayonet, and I have the medals to prove it." He shook his head. "But no matter how much I drink, I still see their eyes pleading for mercy. After the war I followed the railroad west. I worked my way up from a tracklayer and spikeman to the position of chainman and rodman on a surveying crew. I met a woman, too. One I wanted to share my future with, but she left me for a man who made more money than I did."

Benjamin scoffed. "Appears Marcy's refusal fulfilled Pa's prophecy, wouldn't you say?" He folded his arms across his chest and pumped his rocker. "I tried to forget it all and move on, but I can't. Truth is, no amount of liquor or cheap women will ever be enough to make me forget my father's grim predictions, the lives I took on the battlefield, or Marcy's stinging rejection."

Neil leaned back in his rocking chair. A lamp in the window behind him partially illuminated his face. Calm and expressionless, his eyes held no censure. Knowledge that both comforted and unnerved Benjamin.

The older man finally broke the silence. "And you think that's unforgiveable? You're not the first man to take a life in the line of duty or share a bed with a woman he wasn't married to. I'm not excusing your behavior, mind you. The Bible is clear that knowing a woman other than your wife is sin. However, the Good

Book is also full of men who made far more grievous errors than you."

Benjamin shook his head.

Neil leaned forward in his rocker. "You don't believe me? One such man lusted after another man's wife, committed adultery with her, and then sent her husband to the front lines in battle so he would die."

Benjamin's eyes narrowed.

"King David."

He nodded as the Sunday school story flooded his memory.

The runners of Neil's chair groaned as they steadily rocked back and forth. "Despite his sin, God refers to him as 'a man after Mine own heart.'"

Benjamin massaged his jaw, still smarting from one of Artie's licks. "That doesn't make any sense. How could God say that after all David had done?"

"Because God looks upon the heart. And when he looked upon David's, He not only saw the wrong David had done, but a man of strong faith—a man who was quick to repent. The Psalms are full of David's pleas for forgiveness and his joy that God had absolved him."

Benjamin wanted to believe Neil's words could be true—that God could forgive him. But the weight of his own sin pulled him into darkness, like a drowning man sinking into the depths of the sea. His desperation pounded in his own ears. He needed to reach out and grab hold of something, anything, or he would be lost—for good this time. He slumped forward in his chair, resting his elbows on his knees. "Neil, I-I..." The lump in his throat prevented any intelligible words from forming.

"It's all right, son." Neil leaned forward and

placed his hand on Benjamin's shoulder. "God doesn't expect perfection, but He desires a contrite heart that will keep coming to Him for forgiveness and guidance."

Maybe Neil was right and it wasn't too late. Maybe God would forgive him. Benjamin couldn't speak as the emotion swelled within him. He managed a nod of his head then blinked back the moisture pooling in his eyes.

"Good." Neil patted his shoulder. "A man should never be ashamed of tears of repentance, Benjamin—they are cleansing to the soul. Let's pray."

The two men bowed their heads as Neil prayed aloud. "Heavenly Father, thank You for the gift of Your grace and Your mercy. Thank You for sending Your Son to seek and save the lost. Guide Benjamin on his journey to reconcile his past and repent of his sin. May Your word guide his path and lead him in the way everlasting. Amen."

Benjamin's faint voice caught in his throat. "Thank you."

Neil nodded. "Any time. Have you ever considered leaving the railroad camp? I realize the arrangement is financially beneficial, but I'm not sure it's advantageous spiritually. We have room here in the boardinghouse if you're interested."

"That's probably a good idea."

"Good. It's late now. How about you stay tonight and fetch your things in the morning?"

"All right." Benjamin touched his busted lip and winced. "I think I'll stay out here a minute or two longer."

"Fine. Take room four. Second floor, third door on the right. Just make sure you lock up when you come inside."

Benjamin nodded. The rain had subsided while he'd been talking with Neil. Now the world smelled fresh and clean—like Benjamin desired his heart to be. He leaned against the porch railing, eyes drifting heavenward.

Father, forgive me for staying away from You. Forgive me for blaming You for the mess my life has become instead of taking responsibility for the sinful choices I've made. Someday I pray You will see in me a man after Your own heart.

7

Ruth Ann tugged at the collar of her plain brown linsey-woolsey. How she hated the scratchy thing, but it was appropriate for the task. Rather than arranging her hair in its normal bun, she braided her tresses and allowed the thick plait to fall over her shoulders. She folded a square of beige calico into a triangle, laid it on top of her head then tied the ends underneath her braid. She checked the time on her watch pin—quarter past seven. Forty-five minutes before meeting with her students and their families to do some much-needed work at the schoolhouse.

The smell of bacon frying wafted up the stairs, calling Ruth Ann to breakfast. She grabbed her shawl and headed downstairs.

"Good morning, Myra."

"Mornin', Missy." Myra scanned the length of her then arched her brow. "Does your Mama know you goin' out in public in them old rags?"

Ruth Ann shrugged her shoulders. "It's best for what needs to be done."

"You better hopes no one from the Women's Benevolent Aid Society sees you. That'd ruffle your mama's feathers somethin' terrible."

She leaned toward Myra, grinning. "A truer word has never been said."

"I been meanin' to tell you I is proud of you for teachin' at the Freedmen's School. Not many white folks would be doin' that. I knows your mama has mixed feelings about it, but I also knows your papa would be mighty proud."

A tear threatened to spill from the corner of Ruth Ann's eyes as she hugged Myra. She was more than a woman who worked in their home. She was part of their family. Myra and her husband, Amos, had been wedding gifts to Ruth Ann's parents. Papa had given them their emancipation papers shortly afterward. An act never completely forgiven by her mother's side of the family. They had been working for her family ever since, earning a fair wage for their efforts. "Thank you, Myra. That means a lot to me."

Myra patted Ruth Ann's back before whispering in her ear. "I loves you, child."

She kissed Myra's cheek. "I love you, too."

Bacon grease popped and sizzled in the frying pan, beckoning Myra back to her preparations. She cracked an egg on the side of the skillet. "Breakfast is nearly done cookin'." Spatula in hand, she motioned toward the back door. "Mr. Palmer and Amos is out back puttin' everything you needs in the wagon. Let 'em know to hurry and wash up. I ain't servin' a cold meal."

Ruth Ann snitched a piece of bacon, narrowly escaping Myra's swat, and scurried out the back door. "Joseph. Amos. It's time for breakfast!"

Joseph waved. A smile graced his clean-shaven face. Unbidden images of Benjamin Coulter crept to mind. She tried to envision the handsome face lying beneath those overgrown whiskers. A strong jaw, maybe a cleft in his chin—something that would match the breadth of his shoulders and the height of his stance. Pleased, a slight grin inched her lips upward.

Joseph kissed her cheek. "Morning, Ruth Ann. You

don't look like a schoolmarm today."

Amos nodded, a toothy grin offset his dark features. "Not today she don't."

She pointed at the washbasin and rags on the bench. "Myra says if you two don't wash up, you'll get no breakfast."

Amos snickered. "She's a tough ol' bird."

"I'll tell her you said that," Ruth Ann teased.

She reached for the handle on the door. "Mmm." The heavenly aroma of cinnamon glided through the mesh screen. She licked her lips in anticipation of the doughy delight awaiting her inside. She couldn't imagine this day getting any better.

~*~

Benjamin whistled a happy tune as he strolled toward the schoolhouse. He cut through the field, eager to visit with the pretty schoolteacher. Mingled among the overgrown grasses were tall, flat-topped white flowers with tiny yellow-buttoned centers and feathery leaves. Plucking several from the ground, Benjamin fashioned a bouquet.

He hadn't seen hide nor hair of Miss Sutton for the last few weeks, but her plucky personality, dark eyes, and endless curls were never far from his thoughts. Her mother may not approve of him, but the glint in Miss Sutton's eyes when she said she'd enjoy a trip to the creek had given him hope. Neil believed her to be a forgiving woman, if he made an earnest attempt to improve himself. The more he'd thought about it, the more he agreed with Myra. He'd need to show more tenacity if he planned to earn her mother's blessing and win the lady's heart.

Pausing at the bottom of the stairs, Benjamin removed his hat and heaved a deep breath, before slowly releasing it. No woman had ever gotten under his skin like this one had. He smoothed his dark hair into place, then ran his fingers down the length of his shirt. His attire would have to do. Why hadn't he visited the barber yet?

Taking the steps by twos, he entered the one-room school, flowers in hand. The teacher hummed as she wrote arithmetic problems on the blackboard. Funny, he didn't remember her figure being so ... straight. It reminded him of the track he laid across the Texas prairie. Where were the curves he remembered? *Never mind*. Best not to linger on those thoughts.

He grinned as her humming grew more animated. "No caterwauling today, Miss Sutton?"

The teacher faced him.

Heat flashed up Benjamin's neck. Small beady eyes peered at him through wire spectacles perched atop a pointy nose. Not only were the curves missing — so was Miss Sutton.

"Umm. Uh." Benjamin swallowed the lump in his throat that had nearly choked him dead. "Excuse me, ma'am. I expected someone else." He tipped his head and fled the way he'd come.

Once outside, he sat on the second step, his arms folded around bent knees. This had to be the right place. How many schools could a small town like Catoctin Creek boast? He should go back inside and speak with the woman. Maybe Miss Sutton was ill and she was taking her place. Benjamin's head lifted at the thumping of small feet trudging up the wooden steps. He sighed. It'd have to wait 'til later.

Depositing his hat back on his head, he strode to

Turner's. He wanted to check on the special order he'd placed from that new-fangled catalog.

The rich aroma of coffee mingled with the scent of pipe tobacco greeted Benjamin when he entered the mercantile. He navigated his way to the front counter, ducking an assortment of lanterns that were recently displayed from a rope hanging across the ceiling.

Malachi greeted him before his eyes drifted to the flowers in Benjamin's hand.

Benjamin shrugged. "I seem to have misplaced Miss Sutton."

The shopkeeper's eyes narrowed.

"I stopped by the schoolhouse this morning, but the teacher wasn't the one I had hoped to find."

A knowing grin spread across Malachi's face. "You'll find Miss Sutton at the Freedmen's School. It's on Hillsboro Road across from the smithy."

"The Freedmen's School?" Miss Fancy Boots taught Negro children? Maybe things were different here in Virginia, but in Texas, no white woman would ever be found near a Negro school, much less teaching in one. "Is that safe?"

"Some folks protested, but most of the community supports the school. There've been more rumblings since Miss Sutton became the teacher. The Freedmen's Bureau promised a Negro instructor for the school but hasn't been able to find a qualified candidate."

Benjamin made a mental note to ask her about safety precautions while she taught at The Freedmen's School.

Malachi studied Benjamin for a moment before he glanced at the flowers again. "Say, Benjamin. If you're planning to deliver those to Miss Sutton this morning, I have a wagonload of supplies I need delivered there.

She's organized a work day to spruce up the place, and I assured her they would arrive no later than half past eight."

He'd deliver supplies to the Oregon Territory if it meant spending time with Miss Sutton. "I'd be happy to help you out."

Malachi motioned for Benjamin to follow him through a maze of barrels containing apples, pumpkins, and potatoes. "The wagon is out back." The shopkeeper paused to shove an assortment of rakes and hoes into the corner so they could pass. "I understand Miss Sutton can use all the help she can get. So, if you have a mind to stay, I won't need the wagon for afternoon deliveries until two o'clock."

Benjamin extended his hand to the shopkeeper. "Thanks."

As he climbed into the wagon, Benjamin grinned at his sudden change in fortune. He'd be lying if he said he hadn't been disappointed earlier when his plans to visit with the spirited young woman had been derailed. But now, he'd not only have the opportunity to deliver the wildflowers, he'd get to spend the entire day with Miss Sutton—without her mother's interference.

~*~

A fly dipped and soared around Ruth Ann's face. She had taken several good swats at it, but the pesky insect seemed determined to exasperate her. Mid-September and the weather was still warm, but the towering pine trees marking the edge of the property would cast shadows across the schoolyard by noon, providing a nice haven from the afternoon sun.

She poured water into a large kettle hanging from an iron tripod. A strong fire burned beneath it, assuring the liquid would be boiling in no time at all. "As soon as this water is hot, I'll help Sadie and Eula May scrub the floors. They're inside sweeping now."

Joseph nodded. "But I don't want you carrying buckets of hot water. You get Amos or myself when you're ready."

"I can man—" Joseph's arched brow stopped her mid-sentence. Hands up, she succumbed to his wishes. "All right, I promise."

"Good. Anthony and his father are chopping and stacking firewood." He motioned toward the Hillsboro Road. "I hear the wagon coming now. I'll tell Malachi where to put the supplies." Joseph pointed toward the blaze. "Keep stoking the fire."

Ruth Ann nodded then stooped to add another piece of wood to the fire. She grabbed an iron poker and pushed the logs around, allowing more oxygen to feed the flames as she mentally prioritized the jobs she hoped to accomplish today.

"Ruth Ann, this man says he knows you."

She glanced up at the honey-colored eyes of Mr. Coulter. A smile spread unbidden across her face before she quickly reined it in. Not entirely sure what kind of man he was, she didn't want him to know how delighted she was to see him—not yet anyway.

He removed his hat. "Hello, Miss Sutton."

His eyes sparkled. Could he be happy to see her too? She wiped her hands on her apron. "Joseph, this is Benjamin Coulter. I met him in town a few weeks ago. Benjamin, this is my brother-in-law, Joseph Palmer."

Benjamin rubbed his whiskers. "Any relation to Palmer's Livery?"

"One and the same. Have we perhaps done business before?"

Perspiration beaded on Benjamin's brow. "No, sir." He extended his hand to Joseph and the two men shook. "I-I'm just familiar with the establishment."

Joseph glanced at the flowers in Benjamin's hand, and then to Ruth Ann. "So, how did you end up delivering supplies for Malachi this morning?"

Benjamin held out his offering of wilting wildflowers. "I wanted to deliver these to Miss Sutton." He cleared his throat. "They looked much better an hour ago."

Ruth Ann smiled. Their fingers grazed each other as she reached for his offering. "I think they look lovely now."

Benjamin skimmed the brim of his hat through his fingers. "I hope you don't mind that I agreed to bring the supplies out for him."

She didn't mind one bit. Her gaze locked on Benjamin. "Not at all. That was very thoughtful of you."

Joseph cleared his throat. "Benjamin, why don't you and I unload the wagon?"

Benjamin nodded, but his eyes never wandered from hers, nor did his feet move from where they'd planted themselves.

Joseph tugged on his sleeve. "The wagon is this way."

"Right."

Ruth Ann bit back a grin as Joseph dragged him toward Mr. Turner's wagon. She sniffed the bedraggled wildflowers and peeked in Mr. Coulter's direction. My, he cut a fine figure of a man—tall and broad shouldered, with a keen wit...but that beard.

She ventured inside and rummaged through the supply closet until she found the glass bottle she'd seen earlier. It could serve as a vase for Mr. Coulter's flowers. She returned to the water bucket behind the school clutching the container in one hand and cradling her bouquet in the other. "You'll be looking fine again in no time," she mused, pouring a ladle full of the cool liquid inside the jar.

Unable to shake the feeling someone was watching her, she glanced over her shoulder. No one in sight. She shrugged and continued arranging the wilting posies as best she could. "That ought to spruce them up." Pleased with her results, she ascended the back stairs. "Won't they be a lovely greeting come Monday morning?"

"Miss Sutton?"

She turned to find Jolene and Missy approaching. Eyes wide, they pointed toward the ridge. "Them white men been there awhile now. What you think they want?"

Ruth Ann put a hand to her brow. "I'm sure I don't know. Perhaps they're curious." She faced the frightened girls, hoping to reassure them. "Most folks around here aren't accustomed to seeing whites and Negroes working together like we're doing today."

Jolene nudged her older sister. "Go on. Tell her."

Missy lowered her chin and fiddled with a string on her sleeve. "W-we sorry to disappoint you, but we leavin'. We don't want trouble."

Ruth Ann gently lifted Missy's chin. "That's fine. I have plenty of help."

Missy and Jolene nodded before embarking toward the wooded path behind the school.

Slipping her hand into her apron pocket, Ruth

Ann retrieved the note she'd found nailed to the schoolhouse this morning. A shudder ran down her spine as she scanned the message a second time. Taking a deep breath, she marched toward the kettle and tossed the menacing letter into the fire.

Why did some folks hate others because of the color of their skin? Her eyes wandered heavenward.

Lord, heal the angry soul that wrote these vile threats and all those who think like them. May Your children learn to love one another, as You love us.

She glanced back to the fire. The white paper curled and turned to ash.

~*~

Benjamin lifted a fifty-pound sack of limestone from the wagon and handed it to Joseph. Joseph passed it to Amos who stacked it against the rear of the schoolhouse. He stood and wiped his brow against his shirtsleeve. Miss Sutton tossed something into the fire. She'd left her fancy boots home today, but even in her work dress, her smile made his pulse race.

"Ahem." Joseph stood next to the wagon, arms empty, awaiting the next bag of limestone.

"Oh. Sorry. Here you go." Benjamin shoved the heavy sack toward Joseph without shifting the focus of his attention.

Joseph followed Benjamin's line of sight to Ruth Ann's position near the kettle. He took the limestone, but kept his brow arched, letting Benjamin know he'd seen his wandering gaze.

Benjamin refocused on the task at hand, grunting as he passed Joseph the remaining limestone sacks. "What's next?"

We'll need to mix the limestone, salt, and water in those wash tubs. Then we can distribute the whitewash to the workers in smaller buckets."

Benjamin nodded absently, but his attention once again centered on Miss Sutton.

Joseph nudged him. "Benjamin."

"Huh?" Benjamin dragged his gaze toward Joseph. He'd missed something.

Amos snickered.

Joseph tipped his head in Miss Sutton's direction. "Why don't you see if she needs help carrying the hot water inside? Then you can carry cold water back here to mix with the limestone.

"All right." He placed a hand on the side of the wagon and hopped down. With his long strides, he was by her side without delay. "Miss Sutton?"

She jumped.

"My apologies. I didn't mean to startle you. The whitewash supplies and paint have been unloaded like you asked."

She swatted at a troublesome fly buzzing around her face. "Thank you."

He grinned. Black soot lined her cheek and the tip of her nose.

"Is everything all right, Mr. Coulter?"

"Oh, sure, everything's fine. It's just"—Benjamin paused, unsure if he should continue "If you don't mind me saying so. You have black streaks on your face."

"Oh my heavens." She wiped her cheek against her shoulder.

Just when Benjamin thought she couldn't get any prettier, a hint of pink dusted her cheeks. "I thought I'd stay and help out today if that's all right with you."

Ruth Ann picked up a wooden bucket and tipped the edge into the hot water. "That would be wonderful and greatly appreciated, since most of the laborers are women and children."

Benjamin reached for the pail. "May I?"

She handed him another bucket and stepped away from the fire. "Will you help Joseph mix the whitewash?"

"Yes." He lifted both containers with ease. "As soon as you tell me where you want these."

"Follow me." She walked ahead of him and opened the rear door of the schoolhouse. "I appreciate your help with those. I would've had to make two trips."

Once inside, she introduced him to Sadie and Eula Mae who had been sweeping the floors.

"Set them over there, please, Mr. Coulter." She pointed to the platform that housed her desk then unbuttoned her cuffs.

Buckets in hand, Benjamin stared as she rolled up her sleeves.

She shrugged. "The floor won't scrub itself, Mr. Coulter."

"No, Miss Sutton, I suppose it won't." He set the buckets down, tipped his hat and headed toward the back door. Was Miss Fancy Boots really going to scrub the floors? Curiosity got the best of him as he peeked over his shoulder. He wouldn't have believed it if he hadn't seen it with his own eyes. There she was, on her hands and knees, working beside her Negro students.

She looked up from her task and smiled.

Benjamin shook his head as he reached for the doorknob. She lived in a lavish ivy-covered house, had Negro help to serve her, yet she toiled beside Sadie and

Eula Mae. She was a mystery—one Benjamin looked forward to solving.

~*~

Ruth Ann kneaded the small of her back with her fist. After removing the handkerchief from her sleeve, she wiped the perspiration from her neck. She moved near the window and allowed the cool breeze to refresh her. Peering through the glass, she spied Isaac and Josiah whitewashing the outhouse and chuckled. Her Negro students would have the nicest privy in the entire county.

The rhythmic plodding of horse hooves on packed earth drew her attention to the opposite window. Benjamin steered Mr. Turner's wagon into the side schoolyard. Where had he gone? She unrolled her cuffs as she moved toward the door. Oh no, not her linsey-woolsey. She closed her eyes. Benjamin had seen her in this old rag? Her hand flew to her head—the kerchief. Her first instinct was to rip it from her hair, but then she thought better of the idea. Not only did she have more work to do, but he'd already seen her in the ugly headscarf anyway. She sighed. "Oh well."

He climbed from the wagon seat, his shirt taut against his muscled chest and biceps. Something fluttered inside. She doubted James Thornton had muscles like that.

Benjamin thundered up the steps and ducked his head around the door. "Good. You're here. Come with me, please. I want to show you something." He reached for her hand and pulled her toward the stairs.

She'd never again have to wonder what lightning felt like. A fiery tingle rippled down her arms and legs then shot out the tips of her fingers and toes, tempting her to see if the heat had burned a hole in the sole of her work boots. He dragged her all the way to the wagon before releasing his hold. She stared at her hand, secretly wishing it remained snug inside his.

Benjamin removed his hat, using it to point toward the wagon. "They're for you. For the school, I mean. I hope you like them."

Ruth Ann stepped toward the wagon. "Mums? Saplings?"

He nodded. "While you were organizing the supply closet, I went to the feed and seed. I hope you're not disappointed that I didn't let you select them yourself. Ma always told me ladies liked to do their own choosing."

Ruth Ann's heart skipped a beat. "Ladies also like surprises."

A shy smile crossed his face. She couldn't help but see a glimpse of the boy he'd once been. She resisted the urge to kiss his cheek. He'd think her wanton for sure.

"It'll take a while for the saplings to mature, but in time, your students will have some shade for recess. Anthony and his father are going to take care of planting the saplings for you. You'll need to show them where you want the holes dug."

"Thank you, Mr. Coulter. The children and I appreciate your kindness and generosity."

"My pleasure." Benjamin stooped to pick up an acorn from the ground. He rolled it back and forth between his fingers. "I'll need to be leaving soon."

"Oh?"

"I told Malachi I'd return his wagon by two o'clock so he'd have it for his afternoon deliveries."

Ruth Ann nodded.

"I need to speak with Joseph before I leave. Do you know where he might be?"

"Yes, he was working on the windows the last I saw him." They walked to the far side of the school where Joseph knelt, sanding the wood trim.

"I'm not sure if you are aware of it, Joseph, but we've had some folks watching us this afternoon." Benjamin tilted his head in the direction of the men at the top of the rise. "I'm not saying they mean any trouble, but I wanted to make you aware of it."

Ruth Ann stretched her neck to see where Benjamin pointed. She trembled. It looked like the same men she'd seen earlier with Missy and Jolene. They were still there—still watching them. Her thoughts drifted back to the message nailed to the schoolhouse. A cold, prickly sensation crawled up the back of her neck.

Dust billowed underneath Joseph's boots as he trudged toward the road. "Looks like Silas Hench and Levi Hamilton."

Ruth Ann gasped. "Nate and Elias' father? Why would Mr. Hamilton be watching the school?"

Joseph waved.

The men didn't acknowledge him. Instead, they guided their horses toward town.

Joseph turned to Benjamin. "I don't know much about Silas, but the Hamiltons have been around these parts for a long time. Ruth Ann went to school with his younger son, Nate. Levi, and his eldest son, Elias, have been opposed to the school—same with Hench. So far, it's been nothing but verbal sparring. Thanks for pointing it out. We'll keep an eye on them."

"Good." Benjamin's attention shifted back to her.

"Accompany me back to the wagon?"

She nodded. Silence stretched between them as they walked. She sneaked a glance at him. His eyes focused ahead, somewhere off in the distance.

Benjamin paused. His golden eyes met hers and she noted a fierce determination she hadn't seen before. "I hear there's a barn dance next week following the county fair."

Never at a loss for words, she suddenly couldn't utter a sound. She barely managed a nod.

"If you're planning to attend, I'd like it if you'd save me a few dances."

His words came out in a free-flowing tumble that had taken her by surprise. Her tongue twisted in a knot. "Uh...um...I-I—" She only needed to configure one simple three-letter word, but the traitorous appendage refused to form any comprehensible sounds.

He stared at the ground, kicking at a clod of dirt.

"Yes!" she blurted. She softened her voice to a more lady-like pitch. "Yes, I'd be delighted to save you some dances—the first, if you'd like."

He lifted his chin, a gleam of white peeked through his whiskers.

She averted his gaze. Why had she suggested the first dance? He'll think her desperate for certain.

Benjamin offered his arm. "I'll hold you to your word, Miss Sutton."

Knees wobbling, she peered up at him, no longer able to contain the broad smile that spilled across her lips. She slid her hand in the crook of his elbow, grateful for the support.

Mama had been wrong. It was possible for someone other than James Thornton to take an interest in her.

Her friends had gathered at the rear of the wagon admiring the plants Benjamin had purchased.

Charlotte Peterson's fingers gently traced the bright yellow blossoms. "These flowers are lovely, Ruth Ann."

"Benjamin bought them for the school." Ruth Ann grabbed two of the mums. "Where should we plant them?"

Charlotte and her Aunt Trudy each carried a plant toward the schoolhouse.

Mrs. Peterson pointed to a sunny patch of grass near the steps. "That looks like a nice spot."

Benjamin removed the last sapling from the wagon then approached the ladies. "I'll be leaving now, Miss Sutton, but I look forward to that first dance."

Heat raced up the back of her neck and burst onto her cheeks at his pronouncement.

He touched the brim of his hat, climbed into the wagon, and guided the team onto Hillsboro Road.

Without making eye contact with her friends, Ruth Ann attempted a hasty retreat. "I'll go find Amos and see if he has a shovel so we can plant these flowers."

Trudy Peterson looped her arm around Ruth Ann's waist, preventing her escape. "Charlotte didn't tell me Benjamin Coulter was sparkin' you, Ruth Ann."

Ruth Ann's eyes flitted between Charlotte and her aunt. "I-I don't know if I'd call it sparkin', Mrs. Peterson, but we're getting better acquainted."

Trudy pulled Ruth Ann snug against her side. "Yes, we can see that. But just remember, Ruth Ann, it only takes a little wind to turn a spark into a raging fire."

She gulped. Benjamin Coulter was everything she could ever wish for in a man—handsome, thoughtful, and a hard worker. But she shouldn't have encouraged him by asking for the first dance. What was the point? Even if he could look past her fuller figure, he would expect her to quit teaching as well. She'd just freed herself from one overbearing man. She didn't need another.

Raging fire or not.

8

Ruth Ann studied herself in the full-length mirror—not one of those passing glances to see if her hair was askew. Blowing an exasperated breath from the corner of her mouth, a loose strand floated up then gently down again. Observing her profile, her hands glided across the slight bulge in her stomach that she dreaded containing with her whalebone corset. Why couldn't she be thin and petite like Sarah and Mama? Like a woman was supposed to be. She sighed. Would she be able to keep Benjamin's attention once inside the large barn with every other unattached woman in town present?

Sarah came behind her and placed her hands on Ruth Ann's shoulders. "Why the long face? You've already secured a gentleman for the first dance of the evening. I doubt many young ladies can make that claim."

Ruth Ann lowered her chin. What would Sarah think if she knew her sister had been brazen enough to offer the first dance to Mr. Coulter? He had asked for a few dances tonight, but still—to offer the first? What had she been thinking?

"Perhaps, but..." Ruth Ann glared at her less than perfect image staring back at her. "I wonder if any man will ever find me attractive."

Sarah gently turned Ruth Ann's shoulders until their eyes met. "You mustn't think so little of yourself. There are many young men who would be honored to step out with you."

"Mama doesn't agree." She plopped herself on the rose chintz cushion lining the window seat and fingered the lace on her chemise. "Not only did she consider James a highly desirable match, she believes he may be my only offer of marriage." She glanced at her older sister. With eyes the color of sapphires and hair dark as midnight, Sarah was the spitting image of their mother. "You'll never understand...you'd already married Joseph by your twentieth year."

Ruth Ann stood and paced across the floral rug at the foot of her bed. "I'm not as petite or gentle-spirited as you. My voice is too loud, and I'm too expressive with my thoughts and opinions. My curls are unmanageable. My shoulders and hips are too broad. My bosom is too large and my—"

Sarah held up her hand. "It's tempting but unwise to compare ourselves to others. We have a tendency to glamorize their best qualities and emphasize our worst." She took a seat on the bed and tugged on Ruth Ann's arm until she sat beside her. "You have a lengthy list of features you don't like in yourself, but have you considered a list of your best qualities?"

Ruth Ann shook her head.

"No?" Sarah's voice softened, matching the concern in her expression. "Because you haven't considered it, or because you can't think of any?"

Ruth Ann buried her face in her hands, tears threatening to spill from her eyes. "Because all I see are... my shortcomings."

Sarah pulled her close. Resting her cheek on Ruth Ann's head, she caressed her sister's hair. "You have no idea how much I admire you. You are so full of life and eager to experience new things. You express your thoughts, and you stand up for the things and people that matter to you, like teaching at the Freedmen's School. And you're wrong about your curls—they're lovely. I much prefer them to my straight hair. However, my favorite feature is your smile—it's friendly and inviting." Sarah raised her head and lifted Ruth Ann's chin until their eyes met. "Listen to me. You are much taller than Mama and myself, but your shoulders and hips are not too broad. They are in proportion as they should be." Sarah released her chin and leaned forward whispering in her ear. "Men like curves, and they never believe a bosom too big."

Ruth Ann chuckled as she wiped a stray tear. "Well then, I should have plenty of gentlemen vying for a dance tonight."

Knuckles rapped against the door, and Mama breezed in without an invitation, her thick shoe clopping against the polished floors. "Are you almost—why, you're not even dressed yet. Nor is your hair pinned."

Ruth Ann sniffled and dabbed her nose with her handkerchief. "We were...uh..."

Sarah interceded. "We were just talking a bit."

Mama arched her brow. "Talking can wait until after you're dressed. Hurry up, now, Ruth. You'll make us all late." She reached for the doorknob. "Sarah, make sure you pull her corset strings snug."

Ruth Ann rolled her eyes.

Sarah patted her sister's hand. "It may not always seem like it, but Mama really does have your best interest at heart."

Ruth Ann shrugged. She didn't doubt Mama loved her. She just never felt accepted for who she was. She was a project. Something Mama needed to fix so that

Ruth Ann wouldn't reflect poorly on the family.

Sarah moved to the vanity and motioned with her hand for Ruth Ann to take a seat. "Did Mama ever tell you about her first serious beau, Matthias Campbell?"

"A serious beau—besides Papa?"

Sarah lifted Ruth Ann's thick tresses and began inserting pins. "When Mama was our age, all the young men swarmed around her like bees to honey."

Ruth Ann didn't need reminding. Her mother remained one of the most beautiful women of their acquaintance, and her youngest daughter clearly didn't measure up.

"He was from one of South Carolina's wealthiest families. Matthias and his father planned to travel to India to investigate different types of rice that might turn a larger profit for their plantation. Totally smitten, he convinced Grandpa Garrett to allow Mama to accompany him on the journey. His sister, Louisa, came along as Mama's companion and chaperone. After touring Bombay, Mama and Louisa were stricken with an upset stomach, muscle aches, and a high fever that lasted for days. Louisa made a full recovery, but for Mama, things ended very differently. The pain in her muscles returned and she had trouble walking. By the time they returned to Virginia, Mama could barely move her right leg and her left had been rendered useless. Grandpa Garrett immediately took her to New York City. The doctors there diagnosed her with a very rare paralytic virus. Matthias ended their courtship and left without saying good-bye."

"Poor Mama." Her heart pinched at the heartache and rejection her mother must have endured.

Sarah leaned low over Ruth Ann's shoulders, catching her sister's gaze in the mirror. "She learned that only physical perfection would keep a man's attention. Eventually Papa came along and married her despite her crippled leg, but—"

"But she always keeps herself impeccably dressed and groomed because she doesn't believe she will be loved otherwise." Ruth Ann stared at her sister's image in the vanity glass. "So that's why she's so hard on my appearance."

Sarah nodded. "Though she can be harsh at times, Mama does mean well. But remember, while a pretty package may attract attention, you'd be sorely disappointed if you opened the box and there was nothing inside."

Ruth Ann smiled, thankful for her sister's encouraging words.

Sarah patted her shoulder. "We can't procrastinate any longer. It's time to get this over with."

Ruth Ann sighed and moved to the end of the bed. She gripped the footboard then glanced over her shoulder. "Not too tight, all right, Sarah?"

~*~

Benjamin hurried his pace. He'd been promised the first dance, and he didn't intend to miss it. Although the crickets and bullfrogs serenaded him as he walked, he preferred the melodies of the banjos and fiddles for dancing tonight. He glanced toward the late September sky. Stars abounded. The perfect night to woo a woman, and if things worked out as he hoped, Benjamin intended to do just that.

He paused before entering the barn and smoothed his hands over his hair, making sure the pomade held his newly shorn locks in place. Satisfied, he took a deep breath and reached for the latch. The noisy chatter of the crowd inside Dillon's barn filled him with anticipation. His palms were sweaty, and his pulse thundered in his ears. *C'mon Coulter, you've taken a turn with lots of pretty girls in the dance halls of central Texas.* But that was just it—Miss Sutton was no dance hall girl.

Benjamin moved along the wall, nodding at passersby, until he spotted her with several people on the far side of the barn. His heart skipped. She'd loosely pinned her hair—allowing those twisted tresses to dangle. Several loose strands framed her face. She looked so pretty in the soft light from the candles and lanterns lighting the dance floor that, for a moment, he was content just to watch her.

Another fella stepped forward and scribbled on her dance card. Benjamin's throat tightened. He'd better get over there before that claim jumper took all her dances.

Their gazes caught.

Benjamin waved, but she didn't acknowledge him. He glanced down at his attire—tan vest, tan and brown plaid shirt, black necktie, dark brown trousers and boots. Nothing appeared out of place. Why had she looked away?

~*~

Ruth Ann slipped the dance card from her wrist. "Thank you, Nate. Any dance but the first, I promised that one already."

Nate raised a brow as he signed his name. "Anyone I know?"

He and his older brother, Elias, had been her

friends since childhood. Nate was the brother she never had. At least not until Sarah had married Joseph. "Maybe." She grinned. "You'll just have to wait and see."

Elias joined the group with drinks for the ladies. She thanked him then scanned the barn hoping to spy Mr. Coulter. At well over six feet, he shouldn't be hard to find. While the banjos and fiddles tuned their instruments, she craned her neck in all directions. Nowhere in sight. What if he'd changed his mind and didn't come? Or worse, what if he came but changed his mind about taking a turn with her? Her stomach churned, and she forced herself to swallow the spiced cider.

Frannie tugged on her dress sleeve. "I think that man is trying to get your attention."

Ruth Ann tilted her head to see past Elias. A stranger waved from across the barn. Her eyes narrowed. "That's odd. I've never seen him before."

Charlotte followed Ruth Ann's gaze until it rested on the man under scrutiny. She chuckled. "Well, Mr. Coulter will be sorely disappointed to hear that. He told me you promised him the first dance."

Ruth Ann snapped her head in the stranger's direction. Her jaw dropped so far it nearly came unhinged. Benjamin Coulter? His long hair...his scraggly beard...gone? Shaky hands threatened to wash the cider over the side of her full cup.

Frannie reached for her drink. "I'll take that."

Her eyes darted to Frannie as she nodded, unable to form an intelligible word. Her gaze returned to him, now only a few feet away. Her pulse charged through her veins as she gulped down a breath. He was the handsomest man in the room, and he was coming to claim a dance with her.

~*~

"Hello, Miss Sutton," Benjamin greeted.

She smiled, one dimple gracing her left cheek.

"Mr. Coulter."

Charlotte cleared her throat. "Perhaps you could introduce him to your friends."

"Oh, yes. Mr. Coulter is a surveyor with a land-mapping agency. You know Charlotte from the boardinghouse and this is my dear friend, Maggie Wythe and her beau, Edward Simms." She pulled the blonde woman closer. "This is Edward's younger sister, Frannie." She pointed to the gentlemen beside her and continued with the introductions. This is Nate Hamilton and his brother Elias. Their family owns a dairy farm north of town."

He shook hands with the men but eyed the younger Hamilton especially close. Nate had been the one signing Miss Sutton's dance card. He still had a baby face. Probably couldn't grow a beard if he tried. Relieved, Benjamin rubbed his naked jaw, still getting used to his clean-shaven face. He had a good four inches on the young buck, too, but still, it would be wise to keep Miss Sutton away from him as much as possible.

The music started in earnest, and Edward swept Maggie onto the dance floor, followed by Elias and Charlotte.

Benjamin reached for her hand. "I believe this dance is—"

Miss Simms jerked on Miss Sutton's sleeve and pointed behind Nate.

As Miss Sutton's eyes widened, Benjamin glanced over his shoulder hoping to discover what had alarmed her. A man, appearing way overdressed for the simple country barn dance, headed in their direction. Benjamin didn't know who he was, or how Ruth Ann and the others knew him, but it was clear they did.

Miss Simms' hand covered her mouth as she whispered in Miss Sutton's ear.

Miss Sutton shook her head. "Surely, he won't ask me, not after..."

Benjamin couldn't make out the rest of her words. He looked helplessly toward Nate, hoping he could shed some light on why the appearance of this gentleman seemed to be causing such a stir among the ladies.

Nate rolled his eyes. "Great. I was hoping Thornton would remain in Richmond."

Before Benjamin could ask who this peacock Thornton was, he had swooped in, eyeing Miss Sutton.

"Hello, Nate. Ladies." He tipped his head in the general direction of the women then held out his hand to Benjamin. "James Thornton."

"Benjamin Coulter." Benjamin squeezed the stranger's hand more firmly than necessary. He wasn't sure why, but he took a measure of delight in the man's wince before he released his grip.

"Hello, Ruth. You look lovely, as always."

Ruth? Who did this dandy think he was, referring to Miss Sutton by her Christian name?

Thornton reached for her wrist and examined her dance card. "Excellent. You're free." He signed his name in the empty space. "Shall we dance?"

Her eyes landed on Benjamin's, overflowing with

confusion and disappointment.

He stepped forward. "See here, Thornton. Miss Sutton and I have an understanding. She's promised the first dance to me."

Thornton slipped the card from her wrist and waggled in front of him. "That's not what this says. If you want to claim a dance, you sign the lady's card." He tucked the card in Benjamin's vest pocket and pulled Miss Sutton toward the dance floor.

Benjamin's jaw tightened. He ran his fingers along the inside of his collar which suddenly attempted to strangle him. "Would someone please tell me who James Thornton is?"

"He's Ruth Ann's former beau." Miss Simms leaned forward. "But you have nothing to worry about. He proposed to Ruth Ann a few months ago, and she refused him."

Benjamin's gaze remained fixed to the dance floor. "It doesn't look that way to me."

Nate shook his head. "Well, what do you know about that? The entire town assumed it was James who had ended their courtship." Nate chuckled. "Ruth Ann declined a Thornton? She's always had her own mind about her."

The fiddlers rested their bows against the strings of their instruments as the banjos picked the last notes of the song. Thornton escorted Miss Sutton to the punch table.

Nate rubbed his hands together. "I'm up next. Ruth Ann promised the second dance to me."

Benjamin put his hand against Nate's arm. "Hold up." He yanked her dance card from his pocket and scanned the list of names already written. "Sorry." He tore the card in two and handed it to Nate. "Not tonight." Benjamin pivoted on the heel of his boot, determination pounding in his veins. He would step out of the way if she had a beau, but he wasn't going to sit idle while some dandy she'd rejected took another shot.

~*~

Ruth Ann glanced over her shoulder. Mr. Coulter ripped something between his fingers. Was that her dance card? Was he as mad about James claiming her first dance as she was? *Please don't leave.*

"Ruth? I asked if you'd like a cup of cider."

"Hmmm. Oh, no, thank you."

"Fine. Let's sit over there." He directed her to a couple of empty hay bales in the corner. James took her hand in his. "I made a special trip home for this dance. It's been a few weeks since our discussion of marriage."

She tried to wriggle her hand loose from his grip. Who could see them?

James tightened his hold. "I am confident by now you realize the sensibility of my proposal and regret your previous decision. Therefore, I have decided to allow you to reconsider."

She closed her eyes and pressed her lips firmly together, willing herself to stay calm. The audacity of this man not only to assume she would have changed her mind, but that he would address such a private matter in a public setting. What was she to say? What words could she use to make him understand that she wouldn't marry him?

"James, I'm flattered that you would renew your intentions toward me, but I ..."

"Excuse me, Miss Sutton." Mr. Coulter extended his hand. "Would you join me in a fast-moving two-step?"

Unsure how to respond, Ruth Ann's gaze flitted between the two men. Her etiquette book had never addressed this predicament.

James stood, hands on hips, preventing the black jacket of his tailored suit to close over his red jacquard vest. "See here, Coulter. Ruth and I were having an important conversation."

"Well, I'm sure it can wait. How important can it be if it's had in the middle of Dillon's barn?"

Beyond his shoulder, she caught a glimpse of her mother, eyes fixed on the trio. Mama shook her head and nodded toward James. She must have known he was coming to the dance. She'd probably been encouraging him to renew his affections.

Ruth Ann's gaze drifted to Mr. Coulter's open palm. He probably wasn't aware of it, but he was offering her more than a dance. He was offering her a choice. A choice she wanted to make. "Thank you, Mr. Coulter. I'd like that very much." She placed her hand in his, dispelling any hesitation. "James, it was nice seeing you again. Thank you for the dance."

After the little scene with James, more than a few pairs of eyes were on them. As they stepped onto the crowded dance floor, Benjamin slipped his arm around her waist and twirled her toward him. Before long the two were gliding, spinning, and circling the dance floor as if they were riding a carousel. She would remember this dance the rest of her life.

Three dances later, Benjamin had finally relinquished his hold on her. Guiding her by the elbow, he led her to the table laden with refreshments.

He dropped a coin in the open cigar box and grabbed two cups of cider. "Would you like to step outside? There's a nice breeze tonight."

Crowded with people, the barn was stifling, yet she hesitated, unsure if she should leave the dance unchaperoned. Across the dance floor, she spied James moving toward them. "Y-yes. That would be nice." After taking the cup he offered, she waited while he opened the door. She stepped through and a star-studded canopy greeted her.

Ruth Ann sighed. "Have you ever seen anything so beautiful?"

"Yes."

The soft whisper of his voice drew her eyes toward him. He was studying her. She glanced away, glad for the darkness that hid the warmth creeping across her cheeks.

Mr. Coulter narrowed the distance between them.

Heart pounding, she gulped her cider.

He took the cup from her hand and set it on a nearby tree stump along with his own.

Ruth Ann swallowed hard and tried to calm her quivering insides. The light of the half-moon shone on his face. His eyes softened as he tucked a loose curl behind her ear. His feathery touch made her pulse skitter. When her lips parted, Benjamin leaned forward. His lips slowly descended towards hers.

He's going to kiss me!

She wasn't ready to be kissed-yet. Just as his mouth neared her own, she jerked her head to the side and his lips found her jaw instead. Mortified, she hid her face in her hands. "I'm sorry," she whispered, peeking between splayed fingers.

He shook his head, mirth dancing in his eyes. "No

apologies necessary."

She lowered her hands, confident her face glowed red like the setting sun. Her heart thundered in her chest. Why had she recoiled? She already regretted that decision.

"I guess it's no secret how I feel about you. The only question left is, do you feel the same about me?"

Resisting the urge to shout yes and throw herself into his arms, she managed to nod in response to his question. She glanced away, her tone softening. "I like you Mr. Coulter, but I enjoy my position at the Freedmen's School, and I don't have any intention of quitting in the near future."

"I realize where your heart lies, Miss Sutton."

Her head snapped in his direction. "Then you have no objections?"

Shaking his head, he inched closer. "As a schoolmarm, are you allowed to keep company with men?"

"It wasn't allowed according to the terms of my contract with the Graded School. However, Mr. Janney was desperate to find a teacher and since I was already courting James, the only social restrictions pertain to drinking alcohol and scandalous behavior."

A cocky grin spread across his face. "Then if it's not too scandalous, I'd like to call on you regular."

She wanted to pinch herself. This couldn't be happening—not to her.

~*~

Benjamin swiped damp palms against his vest. Tiny rivulets of moisture formed above his lip while she contemplated her answer. Why had he tried to kiss her so soon? He knew better than that. She wasn't one of the cheap women he'd known in Texas. She was a lady, and ladies liked to take things slow.

He couldn't read anything in her eyes. No hint of what her answer might be. What if she said no? She sure was pretty standing in the starlight, ringlets bobbing with the slightest tilt of her head. Artie's words shoved their way into his thoughts. *God didn't make women with ample figures like that for marryin' boy. You oughta know that.* She may be a little more generously proportioned than some women, but he liked her curves. And there were worse qualities—like a woman who only wanted a man who earned lots of money. Marcy had taught him that lesson.

She pursed her full red lips before she spoke. "What exactly do you mean, 'call on me regular'?"

He didn't doubt for a minute that Miss Sutton understood what he was asking, but she was going to make him say it. She would definitely keep him on his toes. Then again, he liked spirit in a woman. "I'm saying I'd like to ask permission to court you proper, Miss Sutton. That is, if you're friendly to the idea."

Her eyes grew bright, and she flashed him one of those two-dimple smiles he'd come to adore. "I can't think of anything I'd enjoy more."

Benjamin released a breath. "Wonderful. I'd like to stop by tomorrow and speak to your father."

She looked away, thumbing the gold locket that adorned her neck. "My father passed when I was thirteen."

He reached for her hand. It fit perfectly, as if designed to complement his own. "I'm sorry."

She threaded her fingers between his and squeezed. "In many ways, you remind me of him. Papa was a hard worker, intelligent, and most of all—he had a keen wit." She grasped the necklace. "This was the last present he gave me."

"It's lovely."

Moisture glistened in her lashes. "Thank you." She laid it gently against her shirtwaist and smiled. "If you're wanting to come calling, then you'll need to speak to Joseph."

Great. Just when things were going so well. Joseph Palmer—owner of the livery where he'd been drinking, gambling, and fighting with Artie and the others.

"Is there a problem, Mr. Coulter? You met Joseph at the Freedmen's School. The two of you appeared to get along fine."

Benjamin scraped his hand along his jaw. There was no getting around it. He'd have to tell her of his behavior when he'd like nothing more than to forget his stupidity. But if he wanted to honor God and have a shot with Miss Sutton, honesty was the only way. If she rejected him, better to find out now before he grew any fonder of the lady. He motioned toward the stump with his hand then picked up their cups. "Have a seat."

He peered into her empty cup. "Still thirsty?"

She nodded.

He poured some of his cider into her cup before he spoke. "You should know that a while back I was involved in a scuffle at the livery. I'd been drinking a little and gambling, and one of the men pushed me too far. I have a short temper when I drink. A brief fight broke out, and the foreman asked us to leave." He folded his arms across his chest. "So it's possible Joseph will say no."

She lowered the cup from her lips, a slight frown etching her features. "Do you drink and gamble frequently, Mr. Coulter?"

"Until recently...yes. When I came to Virginia, I was in a bad way. It had been a long time since I had stepped inside a church. My actions surely demonstrated that. I'd taken to drinking to dull the pain of the war. Gambling soon followed."

Miss Sutton tilted her head and idly ran her finger over the rim of her cup, maintaining her silence. The faint echo of fiddles and laughter from inside Dillon's barn filled the night. Only her sigh broke the quiet between them. Her disappointment hung heavy in the air like the mournful croaking of the bullfrogs from the nearby pond.

He ran his fingers through his hair. So that was it. His past would be too much for a lady like Miss Sutton to overlook.

She studied him, and even under the cover of darkness, Benjamin knew she was taking his measure. "That was then, Mr. Coulter. That doesn't sound anything like the man I've made acquaintance with over the last few weeks. What about now?"

Maybe there was still hope. "I've been attending church regularly. More importantly, I've sought God's forgiveness, and I haven't had a drop of whiskey or gambled since the incident in the livery." He took a deep breath. "Will you still have me?"

Benjamin waited impatiently as she deliberated, the seconds ticking by slower than molasses running up hill in winter. He could say nothing more to persuade her. He'd laid himself bare before her, and if she was the kind of woman he believed her to be, she wouldn't hold his past against him.

She stood and smoothed her skirts. "Mr. Coulter, if our merciful heavenly Father has forgiven you, who am I to hold judgment against you?"

Benjamin closed his eyes briefly, savoring his victory. When his eyes lighted on her again, she had increased the distance between them.

"May I speak frankly, so there is a proper understanding between us?"

He nodded.

Miss Sutton lifted her chin and squared her shoulders before continuing. "You are welcome to ask permission to call on me, but you must know I intend to continue my employment at the Freedmen's School, and I won't abide by any drunkenness or gambling."

She was refreshingly candid, especially for a female. "Understood."

"Good. Have you made amends with Joseph prior to now?"

"No, but I'll be as honest with him as I've been with you this evening." Benjamin massaged his neck. "Do you think Joseph will hold the scuffle in the livery against me?"

"No. Joseph is a godly and reasonable man. Besides, he has a sweet spot for me." She paused and bit her bottom lip. "It's Mama you need to worry about."

9

Ruth Ann placed the last coffee cup on the tray of refreshments she would serve in the parlor. "Please give Mr. Coulter a chance."

Mama set her mouth in a firm line. "I'll try, but he is no James Thornton."

"You're right." She leaned over and kissed her mother on the cheek. "And I like him all the more for it."

Mama reached for her daughter's arm. "Sit down, Ruth."

"But he'll be here—"

"Never mind that. It does not hurt to keep a young man waiting."

"Yes, ma'am."

"I know you refused James because you felt he didn't love you, but you must be leery of this romantic tendency of yours. Tingly sensations and rapid heartbeats cloud a young woman's good judgment. A man may offer you the moon and the stars, but rarely can he provide it."

Ruth Ann squeezed her mother's hand. "I know you had your heart broken when you were young— Sarah told me. But not all men would've made the same choice Matthias Campbell did if they'd been in his shoes. Papa wouldn't have hurt you that way."

Mama withdrew her hand. She sat straighter in her chair. "Your father married me for my dowry—a sensible decision. The affection between us grew over time. Just as I believe it would between you and James if given the chance."

"That's not going to happen. And you're wrong about Papa. He relayed many times how smitten he was with you from the moment he met you. I think you told yourself otherwise to protect your heart."

Mama removed a monogrammed handkerchief from her sleeve. "Mark my words, child. This romantic foolishness will only lead to heartache." Tears pooled in her eyes. "I could not endure watching you suffer as I did."

Ruth Ann slipped her arm around her mother's shoulders. "I know you love me and want what's best for me."

Her mother nodded and placed her hand on Ruth Ann's.

She kissed the top of Mama's head. "I believe that might be Benjamin Coulter."

Joseph pushed through the swinging door. Buddy, fast on his heels, barking repeatedly. "I believe your guest has arrived. He's ten minutes early." Joseph waggled his eyebrows. "Someone is eager to see you."

~*~

Benjamin straightened his tie and removed his hat, tucking it under his arm. He ran his fingers along his hairline making sure his derby hadn't mussed it. Shifting from one foot to the other, he rapped his knuckles against the frosted glass of the front door. He glanced around—ivy-covered pillars, wicker furniture and more potted plants than the feed and seed.

He eyed his new charcoal gray sack suit. He'd been so proud of it when he'd first tried it on. Malachi assured him the haberdasher's label was the finest in Montgomery Ward's catalog. He gulped. *What have I gotten myself into?* Footsteps approached the door, and Benjamin took a deep breath. *Your will be done, Lord.*

Joseph answered and offered his hand. "Hello, Benjamin. It's nice to see you again."

The two men shook hands. "Nice to see you again, too, sir."

Joseph nodded toward the parlor behind him. "Come inside."

Benjamin cleared his throat. "If you don't mind, I'd like to have a private word with you."

Grinning, Joseph slapped him on the back. "No need, Ruth Ann has already informed us you've come to ask permission to call on her."

"It's not about that, sir. At least not directly." Although he'd eaten a sizeable midday meal, an empty pit formed in Benjamin's stomach.

Joseph stepped onto the porch, closing the door behind him.

Oh Lord, give me Your strength and wisdom. Help Joseph understand that I've changed. Benjamin squared his shoulders, locking his gaze on Joseph. If Benjamin was going to come clean regarding his past, then he'd look him in the eye while he did it. "I owe you an apology, Mr. Palmer. I was involved in a scuffle at your establishment back in August. A group of us were playing poker and drinking, and some punches flew."

Joseph leaned back on his heels and stuffed his hands in his pockets. He scrutinized Benjamin. Deep creases formed between his brows. "I'm not sure I want a man who is inclined toward drinking and gambling calling on Ruth Ann."

Perspiration beaded on Benjamin's forehead. He

could only hope Joseph had sowed a few wild oats of his own when he was younger. "I understand, sir. She deserves only the finest type of man seeking her affection. I'm pleased to tell you that I'm attending church regularly now, and I won't be drinking or gambling anymore. You have my word."

"Ruth Ann knows all this and has encouraged you to come call?"

He nodded.

The seconds ticked off like hours as Benjamin waited for him to respond. Would Joseph send him home before he even had a chance to see her?

Joseph studied him a moment before his pronouncement. "Do I have your word? No more gambling or drinking—not even once?"

"Yes, sir, you have my word. Not even once."

Joseph patted his shoulder. "That's good to hear. Ruth Ann is a special young woman. I don't want to see her hurt."

The tension drained from his taut muscles. "Thank you, sir."

Joseph motioned for Benjamin to follow him. "She's in the parlor. The rest of the family and I will join you in a few minutes."

Benjamin entered the parlor and froze. Miss Sutton stood near the fire, Buddy curled at her feet. She shifted toward him, a shy smile spreading across her face. Benjamin stared, his mouth agape. He blinked twice. Was she real? A russet dress trimmed in black lace complimented her dark hair and ivory skin. Layers of fabric gathered behind her, accentuating the curve of her hips. Combs loosely secured her hair on either side, allowing cascades of curls to fall over her shoulders. Her father's gold locket adorned her neck.

He'd always thought her pretty, but tonight—

~*~

Ruth Ann bowed her head. The confines of her whalebone corset made breathing difficult. Her mother had insisted Sarah pull it tighter than she usually did, and Mr. Coulter appeared to notice immediately. She smiled and looked away briefly, embarrassed by his perusal of her figure.

"You look...stunning."

She reached for the wing back chair to steady herself as heat soared through her body. Suddenly, the room was way too warm. "Forgive my manners, Mr. Coulter." She motioned toward the settee. "Please have a seat."

Benjamin sat on one end then patted the space beside him.

She smiled and obliged him.

They sat side-by-side, the ticking of the grandfather clock providing the only sound. Her knee bounced as her gaze traveled around the room briefly meeting his before finally settling on the antics of a squirrel outside the parlor window.

She bit her bottom lip. Why couldn't she think of anything to say? Conversation usually flowed with ease between them. She searched her memory for her mother's instructions on entertaining. *When all else fails, speak of the weather.* "Unseasonably cool weather we're having, isn't it?"

"Hmm? Oh, yes. It's very chilly for late September."

He'd answered her but offered little else to keep the conversation going between them. She fidgeted with the black buttons on her sleeve. This was dreadful. If she didn't find something clever and witty to say, he'd find her terribly dull. Even if she could think of something, it wouldn't matter, her tongue felt thick, and she doubted any of her words would be discernible. Why did her tongue get tied-up in knots every time he was near?

The awkward silence stretched out between them like the vastness of the prairie she'd read about in one of her books. Of course, why hadn't she thought of it sooner? She jerked to her feet.

His eyes grew wide. "Are you all right, Miss Sutton?"

"Hmm, oh yes. Would you like to see the new cards Mama purchased for the stereoscope?" Ruth Ann retrieved them from the walnut secretary in the corner without waiting for his reply. "We have pictures of the Great Plains and the Rocky Mountains." She placed a picture card in the slot then motioned for Benjamin to follow her to the window. "This is my favorite."

Mr. Coulter leaned closer to the glass. After a brief inspection of the image, he pulled away from the pane and stared at her. "It's a bison."

"You don't like bison?"

"It's just not what I expected a woman to favor. Fields of wildflowers or prairie dogs perhaps."

She arched a brow. "I'm not like most women, Mr. Coulter."

~*~

She certainly wasn't like any woman he'd ever met. He managed to shake his head and smile. Her lavender scent inhibited his ability to think clearly. He needed to shake off this troublesome stupor before he made a fool of himself. She unnerved him and that was new territory for Benjamin.

The swinging door in the dining room pushed open. Joseph returned with Mrs. Sutton and the rest of their family. Benjamin stood and tilted his head in Mrs. Sutton's direction. "Ma'am."

Her eyes narrowed. "You've done something to your appearance." She waved her hand in a circular motion. "Very much improved, young man."

He let out the breath he'd been holding as his hand inadvertently rubbed his smooth jaw.

He followed Joseph to the parlor where introductions were made to Joseph's wife, Sarah, and his daughters, Chloe and Lily. The youngest of which curled against her mother half-asleep.

Chloe's dark ringlets and deep brown eyes reminded him of Miss Sutton. She must have been an adorable child as well. "You're a beautiful young lady, Chloe," he said.

She giggled and waved her pudgy hand, encouraging her father to come closer. She covered her mouth as she pressed close to Joseph's ear. "Is he Aunt Roofie's beau?"

Benjamin grinned. Chloe's whisper was tantamount to a bugler playing Reveille. He held out his hand to the youngster. When she put her little hand in his, he bent down and kissed it. "Between you and me, I'm only Aunt Roofie's beau because you are too young for me." He glanced at Miss Sutton, a touch of crimson graced her cheeks.

Chloe covered her mouth and giggled again.

"All right, Chloe, it's time for bed." Mrs. Palmer looked at him. "I promised them they could stay up to meet you, but Lily just couldn't keep her eyes open. She'll be disappointed in the morning." She steered Chloe toward the stairs. "I'll bring coffee and dessert when I'm done."

Mrs. Sutton nodded then took a seat in the wing back chair across from the settee.

Benjamin swallowed the lump in his throat. Now that the introductions were over, the inquisition would begin.

Benjamin eased onto the settee, relieved when Miss Sutton sat beside him again.

"Ruth has informed us that you work for the railroad, Mr. Coulter."

"Actually, ma'am, I'm employed as a surveyor by the Dutton & Farrell Land Mapping Agency. They won the contract to build the Washington & Ohio from Alexandria to Winchester."

"A surveyor?" Mrs. Sutton lifted a brow indicating that she doubted what she was hearing. "Then you have a college education, Mr. Coulter?"

"No, ma'am. I did go to school until I was fifteen though."

Joseph struck a match against the mantel, lit his pipe, and puffed on the stem. "How did you manage to become a surveyor without attending college?"

Benjamin slid the brim of his derby between his fingers. He glanced at Miss Sutton. He'd told her that he was a surveyor already, and of course, that's what she'd told her family. Oh well, if this was going to work, he needed to be honest about who he was. He licked his lips. "I'm in an apprenticeship program."

Surprise registered on Miss Sutton's face, but to her credit, she didn't challenge him in front of her family.

Mrs. Sutton's brows furrowed. "An apprentice?"

"I was hired by the Central Texas Railroad as a tracklayer and spike man. Dutton & Farrell then hired me to work on one of their surveying crews as a chainman. They eventually promoted me to crew chief. Nearly two years ago they offered me an apprenticeship. I'll take the surveyor's exam in March. Assuming I score well, I'll be a surveyor in my own right and poised to build the rails from Catoctin Creek, over the Blue Ridge and on to Winchester."

"I see." Mrs. Sutton sounded genuinely impressed. "That is quite an accomplishment."

Benjamin let his gaze roam to Miss Sutton, pleased that her mother had given him a compliment. "Thank you, ma'am."

"Your family is in Texas?" Joseph asked.

"No, sir. My parents live in Pennsylvania. I joined the Union Army in '64 and served in Tennessee. When the war ended, I went west looking for work with the railroad."

Mrs. Sutton tilted her head. "What's your father's occupation, Mr. Coulter? I believe one's parents offer great insight into a person's...potential."

Here we go. What potential did his father have? He had barely scraped enough together to keep food on their table and shoes on their feet when Benjamin was a boy. He'd prefer someone or something else to be the center of the discussion for a while. *Buck up, Coulter. This is why you came—so her family could get to know you, to win them over.*

He licked his lips. "My father owns an orchard near Chambersburg. My younger brother will inherit it."

Mrs. Sutton lifted her chin. "Younger brother?"

"I would have inherited it if I had chosen to, but I've never wanted to be a farmer. My younger brother, Matthew, loves the land, so it's best all around."

Relief washed over Benjamin when Mrs. Palmer entered the parlor with a tray of refreshments, providing a welcome distraction from Mrs. Sutton's scrutiny.

For the first time that evening, Benjamin noticed the fine furnishings of the Sutton's parlor—marble-top tables, floral arrangements, store-bought rugs, and the rich maroon drapes that framed the parlor windows. A slight hint of cinnamon emanated from the mixture of dried flowers, leaves, and pinecones occupying a glass dish on the table. The room reeked of elegance. Nothing in his own parents' home could compare.

"You have a lovely home, Mrs. Sutton."

She lifted her chin and smiled. "Thank you, Mr. Coulter."

Miss Sutton handed him a slice of warm apple cake. "Did you make this?"

She nodded and sat beside him.

He breathed deeply, the scent of warm apples mixed with lavender filling his senses. "Mmm, you smell delicious."

She arched her brow. "Pardon?"

"Uh..." Benjamin sized up the marble coffee table, wondering if he'd fit beneath it. "I mean the cake—it smells delicious."

She chuckled. "Thank you."

Mrs. Sutton set her plate on the side table and resumed her questioning. "I imagine a surveyor for the railroad does not stay in one place very long?"

Benjamin tore his attention away from Miss Sutton and refocused it on her mother. "It depends. Working on a job for the railroad requires me to follow the progression of the job." He pierced the cake with his fork. "The W&OR is having financial difficulties and is making slow progress. They haven't advanced more than eight miles in two years." His gaze briefly shifted to Miss Sutton. "However, it has allowed me to stay in Catoctin Creek longer than I'd expected."

Joseph shook his head. "Well, I'm glad it's benefiting someone. The investors are bleeding money, and the railroad wants to raise more bond funds. The farmers and merchants were told this thing would be done two years ago."

"I know, sir. The rate at which the Virginia Creeper is progressing has me concerned for my own job. They've already cut back my hours, and if I didn't need them desperately to gain certification, I'd be forced to look elsewhere for work."

Benjamin caught Mrs. Sutton's gaze. She frowned before looking away. *What a fool.* He shouldn't have indicated his job may be in jeopardy.

"Is surveying usually so unpredictable, Mr. Coulter?" She looked at her daughter as if to make a point.

Benjamin shook his head then sipped his coffee. "No, ma'am, but like any profession, it's susceptible to the whims of the economy. The way I understand it, when the Baltimore & Ohio beat us to Harper's Ferry, several large investors backed out. It looks like the W&OR will be sold."

An awkward silence filled the room.

Miss Sutton leaned forward, her brows furrowed. "Mr. Coulter, the railroad will make it here to Catoctin Creek, won't it?"

"Without a doubt, the line will make it beyond

Catoctin Creek to Round Hill, but if new funds aren't raised, I may never get my chance to take it over the Blue Ridge."

Her expression softened. "I'm sorry to hear that. I'm sure that would be an excellent opportunity for you."

"Then what will you do for employment, Mr. Coulter? I will not have an idle young man calling on Ruth."

Benjamin ignored the icy tone in Mrs. Sutton's voice. "There are many good prospects for surveyors, ma'am. Towns all across the south are rebuilding, railroads are expanding in every direction, and the west is opening up as well. My employer gave me a list of contracts they have with the government. I'm considering heading west to Colorado, Wyoming, or maybe even Alaska."

Mrs. Sutton lowered the coffee cup from her lips. "Alaska? Why on earth would you want to go to a cold, barren wilderness? There would be no culture—no educated people with whom to spend your time." She certainly spoke her mind, much like her daughter.

"I want to see the western territories before they become overrun like the eastern states. The chance to make something out of nothing—to help tame that wild land. The west is a great equalizer, and opportunities like that don't come around very often."

Mrs. Sutton's eyes narrowed. "How so?"

Benjamin rubbed his jaw, carefully weighing his words. He didn't want to give this woman any reason to prevent him from calling on her daughter. "It provides a man with the chance to meet one of his most fundamental needs—to be judged on his abilities rather than his bank account."

She straightened in her chair. "Is that what you think I'm doing?"

He glanced at Miss Sutton. Her eyes widened. *Oh, boy.* If he found his collar tight before, it strangled him now. "No, ma'am. Not you specifically. It's just the way things are back here."

Mrs. Sutton lifted her chin. "Young man—"

Joseph placed his hand on Mrs. Sutton's shoulder, quieting her. "It sounds like a wonderful plan. I have a mind to head west and start my own horse ranch someday."

Mrs. Palmer stared wide-eyed at her husband.

Benjamin stifled a grin. He surmised that was the first she'd heard of his westerly ambitions.

As the grandfather clock chimed, Benjamin took one last swig of his coffee and gathered his hat. He'd prefer to stay and visit with Miss Sutton longer, but he'd determined ahead of time this first visit would be brief. He wanted to make a good impression on her family and leave early without overstaying his welcome.

"Thank you, Mrs. Sutton, for allowing me to visit in your home tonight. It was a pleasure."

"I hope we'll be seeing more of you, Benjamin." Joseph's gaze landed on his mother-in-law. She gave the slightest nod of her head in affirmation. "You are welcome to call on Ruth Ann again."

"Thank you, sir."

"If you ever need work, Benjamin, come by the livery. If I don't need help, I usually have a good idea of who's hiring."

"Thank you, Mr. Palmer. I'll do that."

"If I'm to be seeing you socially…" Joseph paused and glanced at Ruth Ann's smiling face, "and it appears I will be, then you'd better be calling me Joseph."

Benjamin smiled and took Joseph's hand. "Thank you, Joseph."

~*~

"I'll see you out, Mr. Coulter." Ruth Ann removed her shawl from the hall tree.

Benjamin opened the door and stepped onto the porch. He reached for her hand and brought her beside him before closing the egress behind them. At his touch, that familiar lightning bolt shot through her.

He raised her hand to his lips. "Now that I'll be paying calls on you, I'd prefer you call me by my Christian name."

A shy smile spread across her face. "All right, Benjamin. If you'll call me, Ruth Ann."

He pressed another kiss against the back of her hand.

Glancing to the window where her mother hovered just beyond the lace curtains, she lowered her voice to a whisper. "I'm sorry about Mama."

"It's all right. She's just being protective of her daughter. I respect that." Benjamin stepped backward, guaranteeing he was out of Mrs. Sutton's line of sight, then drew her close to him. He brushed her cheek with his fingertips. "You are striking in that dress, Ruth Ann."

He leaned forward and kissed her cheek then took his leave.

She slid her hand to the spot where his lips had been then closed her eyes and willed her knees not to buckle out from under her. What power did he have over her? She hadn't wanted James to touch her, but she longed for Benjamin's caress. This couldn't be real—she must be dreaming.

Reaching for the doorknob, she glanced back to where they'd stood moments earlier. Hopefully, she wouldn't wake up for a very long time.

10

The cool October wind shuffled colorful autumn leaves around Ruth Ann's feet. A squirrel, cheeks laden with treasure, hustled across her path before making his way up a nearby maple tree. He deposited his bounty in a nest before crawling back out and scurrying along the branches. Chuckling at his antics, she drew her shawl close and resumed her pace. As she walked, she reviewed the list of items she needed to purchase at the mercantile. Benjamin offered to teach her to make sugar cookies this afternoon. He guaranteed they would melt in her mouth.

Benjamin. She sighed. The last month had been a whirlwind of romance. Nothing fancy like the cotillions James had insisted they attend. Instead, he'd eaten dinner with her family several times a week, they'd read Jules Verne together on the porch swing, and he'd even made good on that fishing trip he'd proposed so long ago. She'd out-fished him, too. Unsure how his male pride would take that, she'd thrown a few back when he wasn't looking. Even Mama seemed to be enjoying his company, although she wouldn't admit it.

Ruth Ann hadn't told him yet, but Benjamin Coulter had already captured her heart.

As she neared Turner's store, she discovered two men studying her. One pointed in her direction as she approached. Lowering her gaze, she climbed the stairs. The taller, dark-haired man stepped in front of her, blocking her path.

"Excuse me, please, sir."

The taller man spoke, his gravelly voice setting her nerves on edge. "We don't move for darkie lovers."

Ruth Ann froze. She'd experienced some censure from people she knew because of her position at the Freedmen's School, but these men were strangers. Alarmed by his coarse manners, she bit her lip and kept her tongue in check. This was not the time or place to challenge these men. Avoiding his scrutiny, she attempted to sidestep the shorter red-haired man who thus far had remained silent.

He repositioned himself, preventing her from entering the store. "Where do you think you're goin', little lady?"

Ruth Ann locked eyes with him, determined not to show fear in their presence.

"Well, now, I guess when your mama forgot to teach you to stay away from darkies, she forgot to tell you it's rude not to speak when you're spoken to."

Alcohol reeked on the shorter man's breath. She took a step back, her frustration barely contained beneath an attempted show of indifference. The dark-haired man screwed up his lips and spat tobacco juice at her feet. The brown liquid landed atop her right boot, splattering the hem of her dress.

"Aw, now ain't that somethin'? I missed the spittoon, darlin'." He swished the wad of tobacco from one side of his mouth to the other. "I got an idea, teacher. Why don't you get one of those coloreds you love to clean your boot for you so they learn their place?"

She tightened her jaw.

The redhaired man guffawed. "That's a good one,

Silas." The taller man gave him a stern look that immediately silenced his companion. He stepped closer to Ruth Ann and grabbed her wrist. "Some folks around here don't like the idea of you teaching them darkies to read and write. Might make 'em get all uppity."

Ruth Ann's heart pounded in her chest. Silas Hench? The man Joseph saw watching the school with Mr. Hamilton? She struggled to free herself, but Silas tightened his hold and yanked her toward him. Her face now inches from the brown liquid oozing between his tobacco-stained teeth. Her stomach churned.

"Me and my friend here would take it as a personal favor if you was to stop teaching 'em darkies."

"Only the ignorant fear the education of others."

"You watch yer mouth, missy, and mind what I say. I'd hate to see anything happen to that purty face of yours."

A bell jingled and voices resonated from the open doorway.

The dark-haired man released her with a little shove.

"Good-bye, Morgan," Mr. Turner called. "Give my best to Clara." He paused, eyes darting between the men and her. "Everything all right here, Ruth Ann?"

She nodded, massaging her wrist.

"If you folks don't need anything from the store today, why don't you go on your way so my paying customers can get inside?"

The two men obliged his request, but not before tipping their hats in Ruth Ann's direction. "Sorry again about your shoe, Miss."

Mr. Turner's gaze shifted to Ruth Ann's feet.

"What happened to your shoe?"

Ruth Ann took a deep breath, relieved the two men had gone. "Oh nothing, really. The taller man missed the spittoon." She raised her skirt a bit so he could see. "It will clean up easy enough."

He wrinkled his brow then took Ruth Ann by the elbow. "You're shaking."

She didn't offer any explanation. If word of this got back to Joseph, he might make her resign her position.

"Come inside and sit down. Adelaide has the kettle simmering in the storeroom. A cup of tea will warm you up and calm your nerves."

"Thank you. Tea would be appreciated."

He guided her to the alcove at the back of the store and pulled out a chair for her at the checker table. "I still remember you and your father playing here during winter. Charles Sutton was a fine man. I'll be right back with your tea." Mr. Turner disappeared behind the curtain dividing the store from the backroom.

Ruth Ann's hands shook as she removed her shawl. She brushed a lone tear from her cheek. What might have happened if Mr. Turner hadn't come when he had? She didn't want to think about that right now. Instead, she stared at the checkerboard painted on the surface of the round table. She hadn't played in years. Running her hand over the smooth edge, she closed her eyes and breathed deep, certain the smell of her father's pipe tobacco still hung in the air.

"Wait, Ruthie. Think before you move," he'd say.

"But I can take your king, Papa!"

"Yes, but before you make a move, even one which might take my king, you should look at every option." Her father paused and looked at her. "Every choice you make will have different results—some better than others."

Ruth Ann then examined the entire board with renewed vigor. She'd study each of her red pieces, reviewing every move it could make. Then she'd find it. Picking up the red checker two squares over from her original move, she'd jump two of her father's single blacks and the coveted king.

"That's my girl! Remember, Ruthie, a wise person contemplates all their choices before making a decision." He'd reach up and put his hand on her cheek. "Some choices, once made, can never be undone."

"So true, Papa," she whispered as her thoughts drifted back to the confrontation outside moments earlier. What counsel would he offer her regarding her position at the Freedmen's School?

"Here you go, dear." Adelaide Turner set the teacup on the checkerboard table, worry etched on her face.

"Thank you." Ruth Ann held the steaming liquid close, allowing its warmth to calm her anxious nerves.

"Malachi is going to fetch Joseph from the livery to escort you home so those ruffians don't bother you again."

She sat up a bit straighter and lowered her cup. What would Joseph do? He would feel obliged to tell Mama, and Mama would want her to resign. Maybe she could hint to Mr. Turner that Joseph might have gone to the livery in Hamilton or the horse farm in Middleburg today? No. Lying was never a good solution to any problem. "I hate to be a bother. Besides I have a few things I need to purchase."

Adelaide patted her hand. "It's no trouble, I assure you. Tell me what you need. I'll fill your order while you drink your tea."

Mr. Turner untied his apron and laid it across the counter. "I'll be back in a few minutes."

She forced a nod, hoping he wouldn't make the situation out to be more than it was.

~*~

The bell jingled above the door as Benjamin entered the mercantile.

"Benjamin, nice to see you today."

"You as well, sir. Myra said Ruth Ann came to the store a while ago, but she hasn't returned home." Benjamin's eyes swept the inside looking for Ruth Ann. "Is she here?"

Malachi nodded toward the alcove where Ruth Ann sat cradling a teacup. "There was an incident with two men on the porch. I'm not sure what they said exactly, but she looked fairly shaken. Adelaide noticed a red mark around her wrist, so we figured one of the fellas must have grabbed her."

Benjamin's hands clenched at his sides at the thought of someone manhandling Ruth Ann.

Malachi's gaze drifted to Benjamin's tightly balled fists. "She's all right, Benjamin. A little shook up, but fine otherwise. I was on my way to fetch Joseph to make sure she made it home safely."

"No need, Malachi. I'll see her home." He walked to the alcove and laid a possessive hand on Ruth Ann's shoulder. "Myra was getting worried."

She gave his hand a little squeeze in return, letting hers linger on his for a moment before returning it to her lap. "I was visiting with Adelaide, but I'm hoping you're still planning to teach me your secret sugar cookie recipe today."

"Nothing's changed." He squatted down beside her. "But Malachi told me some men were bothering you on the porch. Are you all right?"

"I'm fine. They were expressing the opinion many have about me teaching Negroes."

Benjamin reached for Ruth Ann's hand and examined her wrist. "How did you get this red mark?" He waited, but she didn't answer. "Did one of them touch you?"

She looked away.

That was all he needed to know. Benjamin stood again, keeping one hand on her shoulder. "Did you recognize the men, Malachi?"

"Yes, I've seen them both around here before. The fella with the red hair might be from the railroad camp, but I don't know his name. He always pays in cash, so I've never run a tab for him. But the taller one was Silas Hench."

Ruth Ann trembled beneath his fingertips.

Silas Hench—he recognized that name. And soon, Silas would know Benjamin's.

~*~

Benjamin was thankful for the distraction making cookies provided. Occasionally, his thoughts wandered back to the men who had harassed Ruth Ann earlier. He couldn't stop dwelling on the fact that some ruffians had touched his woman. Benjamin shook his head. When had she become his woman? They'd only been courting a month. He was supposed to be moving slowly, letting the Lord direct his path. The sudden realization that he considered Ruth Ann his both warmed his heart and filled him with trepidation.

Smiling, Ruth Ann set the bowl on the counter. "All done."

Benjamin peered at the dough resting inside. "Nope, not yet. There are two secrets to this recipe. One is the powdered sugar and the other is blending the dough until there is not a lump of butter left in it."

She kneaded her upper arm. "I'm getting tired. Wouldn't you like a turn?"

He didn't know what was cuter—her flour-covered cheeks, or her pouty lip. But he didn't intend to let her off the hook too easily. "Why don't you tell me about your students' progress or the latest novel you're reading? It will help take your mind off your work."

"You're probably right." She slid the bowl away from him, shielding his view with her body. "Myra told me that slaves would sing songs as they worked together in the fields or the barns. It helped to make the drudgery of their work more bearable."

"Drudgery?" Benjamin chuckled. "I'd hardly call making a batch of cookies drudgery."

She leaned slightly to the right. "To each his own, I suppose."

What was she up to? He came up behind her. Peeking over her shoulder, he caught Ruth Ann red-handed with a blob of cookie dough on her index finger. "Eh, eh, eh," He shook his finger. "No snitching either."

She attempted an innocent smile. "I thought it would be a shame to continue beating the batter so diligently if it didn't taste good."

Benjamin raised his brow, skeptical of her story. She was good, almost convincing. "You may have a point." He wrapped his fingers around her hand then raised it closer to his face, examining the dough this way and that. "But since you've never had these cookies before, you wouldn't be a good judge as to whether the dough tastes right."

Her protests rang out a moment too late as Benjamin deftly brought her hand toward his mouth and licked the dough clean from her finger. She gasped, rousing her faithful dog from his slumber by the stove. Buddy barked, calling attention to some perceived injustice against Ruth Ann. Benjamin placed his finger across his lips to shush the old dog. Determined to protect the honor of his mistress, Buddy persisted relentlessly.

Benjamin's eyes drifted back to Ruth Ann. She stood with her back against the counter, mouth agape. His gaze dropped briefly to the quick rise and fall of her chest. He scooped a blob of dough onto his finger and raised an eyebrow. She licked her lips. They stood eyes locked on one another.

Myra pushed open the swinging door from the dining room. "How's that dough comin'?"

Ruth Ann spun in Myra's direction, causing the bowl to wobble precariously close to the counter's edge.

Benjamin reached toward the counter, grabbing the dish before it toppled to the floor.

"Huh? Oh, it's coming along fine."

He licked his finger clean. "And delicious, too."

Myra stooped and scratched underneath Buddy's chin. "Good dog." Her eyes met Benjamin's. "He a fine watch dog, Mr. Benjamin."

Benjamin raised his shoulders and lifted his hands suggesting he was completely innocent, but Myra stared him down. "All right. I'll be on my best behavior. You win."

"Mmm hmm, I always do. The sooner you get that in your thick skull, the better it gonna go for you 'round here."

Sensing the excitement had concluded, Buddy returned to his blanket by the stove, this time keeping his eyes on Benjamin instead of sleeping.

Benjamin sighed. "Care for a taste?"

Myra grinned. "Don't mind if I do." She pinched the dough then smacked her lips. "Mmm, that's so soft, it like floatin' away to heaven on a cloud." She gave the contents of the bowl a closer inspection then furrowed her brows. "But I still see lumps of butter in that dough, Missy."

Ruth Ann rolled her eyes and stirred the dough again.

Benjamin chuckled. "I've been trying to tell her that, Myra, but she thinks it's fine the way it is."

A burst of air rushed from of the corner of Ruth Ann's mouth in a failed effort to blow a strand of wayward hair from her cheek.

"Let me show you how it's done." Benjamin reached for the bowl.

"That's quite all right, Mr. Coulter." She bit back a grin. "I can manage."

He tugged on the dish. "C'mon give me the dough, Miss Sutton."

Ruth Ann shook her head. "Un-uh. You go get the sugar ready so when I finish beating this dough until its silky smooth, we can get these cookies baking."

Benjamin grinned. She was a stubborn woman.

Keeping up with her would be a challenge—one he was happy to take on. Grabbing the canister from the counter, he scooped sugar into a glass bowl to sprinkle on the cookies before they went into the oven.

Myra gave Benjamin a stern look. "I gonna be in the next room polishin' the silver."

Benjamin glanced at Buddy still awake, eyes trained on him. "All right. Buddy has everything under control in here."

She paused at the door. "I'm sure he do."

~*~

Tongue pressed against her upper lip, Ruth Ann continued working the ingredients with a heavy wooden spoon. "I've never met a man who enjoyed baking. How did you learn?"

"My grandmother, mostly. She loved to bake, and I enjoyed spending time with her."

"Were you close to your grandmother?"

"Yes. She passed while I was in Texas."

Ruth Ann set the bowl on the counter in front of Benjamin and reached for his arm. "I'm sorry."

"Thank you. I suspect she's up in heaven, watching us now, pleased to see that I'm sharing her recipe with you."

Ruth Ann closed her eyes. She imagined Benjamin rolling dough balls alongside his white-haired grandmother. She liked the images it conjured in her mind—images of home and family and warm cookies baking. There was something good and decent about a man like that.

"I dare you to find any more lumps."

Benjamin pushed the wooden spoon through the

dough. "Well done. You're ready to graduate to pie-making."

"Y-you know how to make pies?"

"Yep—blueberry, peach, rhubarb, mincemeat, raisin, pumpkin, but apple is my specialty."

She arched a brow.

"Honest. I even won second place at a county fair when I was fourteen."

She shook her head and grimaced. Her baking skills suffered grossly in comparison.

"Come on over here, Ruth Ann, and I'll show you what we do next." He pinched a blob of dough, rolled it between his palms, and placed it on the pan.

Ruth Ann did the same.

"Next, take the glass and dip it into the dough, then into the sugar, then flatten the balls, like this." Benjamin proceeded to squash the round mixture with the sugar-laced glass.

They worked quickly and soon had two trays ready for the oven.

"How long do the cookies bake?"

His eyes narrowed. "You don't bake much, do you?"

She shook her head.

"It varies depending on how hot the fire is." He opened the door and checked the blaze inside. "Hmm, maybe nine or ten minutes. You have to keep a close eye on them so the edges don't burn."

She noted the time on her watch pin. While the first batch baked, they continued making dough balls.

"Ruth Ann." Benjamin waited for her to look at him. "We need to let Joseph know about the incident at Turner's this morning."

She frowned and shifted from him, wiping her

hands on a kitchen towel.

Benjamin placed a hand on Ruth Ann's shoulder, angling her toward him again. "It's important that you're safe."

She nodded then heaved a sigh. She thought he'd forgotten about the men in front of the mercantile. Benjamin hadn't said much about her teaching position one way or the other. Would he oppose her now? Her teeth tugged on her bottom lip. And what would she do if he did?

11

Ruth Ann moved from desk to desk observing the marks her adult students wrote on their slates, each one forming the letters that spelled their name. She leaned near Bea's ear and whispered, "The 'e' is backward."

The older woman wiped the letter away with a tattered piece of white cloth and tried again.

Ruth Ann patted Bea's shoulder. "Well done."

Her eyes drifted toward the back of the classroom where a handsome surveyor's apprentice studied for his upcoming certification exam. She'd been worried he'd oppose her efforts at the Freedmen's School after Silas Hench had accosted her outside Turner's store. Instead, he'd offered to escort her to and from her evening classes. Heat flashed across her cheeks when Benjamin caught her staring, pride beaming from his eyes. His presence made it difficult to concentrate on her lessons.

Forcing her attention back to the task-at-hand, she peered over Isaac's shoulder. "Nice work."

She surveyed the burgeoning class. In only three weeks, the number of adult students had quadrupled. There were already three adult students for every book and slate she had. Class members filled the benches Benjamin had made. If any more students showed up, she wouldn't know where to seat them.

Ruth Ann referenced her watch pin. "That's all for tonight." She pulled her shawl tighter around her shoulders and shivered. "Remember, Thursday is Thanksgiving, and there will be no class." She pointed to the bench where Benjamin sat in the back of the room. "There are jars of peaches, green beans, beets, and preserves in the crate next to Mr. Coulter. Enough for every family to take one. Please add them to your family's supper on Thursday. It's my way of saying how thankful I am for each of you and your eagerness to learn."

Thank yous hummed across the classroom as students filed toward the front of the room stacking slates, chalk, and primers on her desk.

A hand rose in the back of the room. "Miss Sutton, when we gonna learn cypherin'?"

Conversation ceased. All eyes shifted to her. "I don't know, Francis. With so many of you and only one of me, we are progressing slower than I had expected. We'll need to be at a point where most of you can work independently so that half the class can receive instruction in arithmetic while the other half can practice their reading." Ruth Ann tapped a slate pencil against the edge of her jaw line. "Hmmm, I'd say it won't be until mid to late spring."

Eyes dropped and smiles faded. Others shook their heads. Grateful for any opportunity to learn, none gave voice to their unhappiness.

"Thank you, Miss. We appreciate what you doin' for us." Francis tipped his head in her direction. Many others echoed his gratitude as they funneled out of the schoolhouse.

Ruth Ann collected the McGuffey readers and placed them on the shelf in the supply closet.

Benjamin followed with the slates and slate pencils. "Don't be discouraged, Ruth Ann. You're doing a wonderful job."

She pressed her palm against her temple and sighed. "I sense their frustration with their slow progress. It's important that they learn arithmetic soon. Too often, they're taken advantage of when selling their crops or buying items in some of the local stores. Many Negroes travel a long distance to buy from Mr. Turner because of his reputation for fairness and honesty." Her hand trailed the shelf where the books sat stacked in neat rows. "I don't want to let them down."

"You won't, but be patient." Benjamin held her by the arms. "They're learning. I hear improvement already."

She nodded and removed the key to the supply closet from her pocket. "We'd better get going. It's already half past eight."

Benjamin opened the door to the potbelly stove then closed the valve. He picked up a poker and pushed the logs away from one another, spreading the ashes in a thin layer. "What if you taught reading on Tuesday evenings and arithmetic on Thursdays?" He closed the door and leaned the poker against the wall, then brushed his hands against his pants. "If they're all doing math, you wouldn't need to worry about whether or not they could work independently."

"I've considered that, but I don't like the idea of waiting a week to reinforce their reading concepts." She slipped into the cape Benjamin held for her. "I'm positive their progress would slow nigh unto a standstill, and some are already frustrated with their sluggish improvement." She paused and put her lessons and books in her satchel. "I know they're disappointed, but I'm confident it's better to stay with this course."

~*~

Benjamin removed the haversack from Ruth Ann's hand. "I'll carry that."

"Thank you." She locked the door with the larger of the two keys on the ring.

When she faced him, the moonlight lit her features. Disappointment and doubt still lingered in her eyes. Even sad, she was the prettiest woman he'd ever escorted. "No thanks necessary. It's really very selfish of me."

Ruth Ann cocked her head.

He extended his arm. "Now your arm is free to take mine."

A gentle smile graced her lips as she slipped her hand into the crook of his elbow. He brought his arm snug against himself, enjoying her closeness as they walked.

"Perhaps I should offer arithmetic on Saturdays," she said.

"You're already teaching the young ones Monday through Friday and the adults two evenings each week. You'll wear yourself out."

"But—"

"I think what you need is patience."

A heavy breath pushed from her lungs. "You're right."

Seeing Ruth Ann lost in contemplation, worrying that she would let her students down, tugged on his heart. But why? This wasn't his problem, nor was it a problem that she couldn't resolve with a bit of patience. But it did matter. He wanted her world to be perfect, as silly as that sounded—to be her protector and her problem solver. There had to be a way. He just needed to think.

As they approached the path beside her home, Benjamin broke the silence. "What if I taught arithmetic to half the class while you taught reading, and we switch after the first hour?"

She paused. Eyes narrowing, she faced him.

He swiped his palm over his face. He didn't know anything about teaching arithmetic. She would think him ridiculous now.

Ruth Ann took a step backward, her arm slipping from his hold. "I can't believe you would—"

"I know, foolish idea, huh? What do I know about teaching arithmetic? However, I do know numbers. They are my strength, and you'd be—"

"No, Benjamin, it isn't a foolish idea. It's a brilliant one."

He hooked his thumb through his belt loops and straightened his shoulders.

"But what about your certification exam? You need to study."

Desperate to find a solution for her problem, he hadn't given any thought to the exam. He'd figure something out. "You let me worry about that. I'll manage."

Her smile broadened, revealing the twin beauties in her cheeks.

"I just can't believe you'd go to all this trouble to help my students."

Her students? Is that what she thought? Maybe he was going about this wooing thing all wrong. He narrowed the distance between them. "Not for your students, Ruthie. For you."

A gentle sigh slipped from her lips. "My father called me Ruthie when I was a girl."

Benjamin cringed. Why had he called her that? She was a grown woman, not a child. He resisted the urge to crawl under the hydrangea bush nestled against the porch. "I didn't mean to imply...I mean I don't see you as...ugh." His eyes drifted away from hers, too embarrassed by his slight. "Sorry, it just slipped out."

Delicate fingertips grazed his chin, directing his eyes toward her again. "I like it, Ben." Her voice faded to a whisper. "It's...special, like you."

Ben. He never liked the shortened version of his name and always insisted on people calling him Benjamin. It emanated respect. He liked the sound on her breathy lips, however, hinting at something only they shared.

Benjamin's palm slid across her skin until it cupped her jaw. She rested her hand atop his as he cradled her cheek, all the while trembling at his touch. His gaze wandered to her mouth. Her lips called out to him, begging for a kiss. Desire surged through his veins. He was drawn to her, the way moths succumbed to flames. One kiss and he'd be doomed, forever at her mercy for another. Benjamin lowered his chin. Soon his mouth would find her moist, soft...fingertips?

Feathery light words floated in the evening air. "Not yet, Ben."

He groaned. She'd done it to him again. "All right." He rested his forehead on hers. "I'll wait a while longer, Ruthie."

She gave him a gentle kiss on the cheek, lingering a moment before climbing the porch stairs.

"Ruthie, wait."

"We mustn't. You agreed, and I can't stay out here

any longer without risking Mama's ire." She tipped her head toward the window where her mother watched through the lace parlor curtains.

Benjamin took the stairs two at a time. "You'll need this." He handed her the satchel he'd been carrying.

"Oh, right." She bit her lip. "Thank you."

"But don't think I wouldn't mind getting a chance to hold you a bit longer." He tucked the same wayward curl behind her ear. "If that's what you had in mind."

Eyes wide, she gasped, opened the door, and stepped inside. "Good night, Ben."

He chuckled as he made his way down the stairs. The click of the latch returned his attention to the porch.

Her head poked through a space no wider than her shoulders. "Oh, I almost forgot. Sarah asked me to remind you that dinner will be served at noon on Thursday, and you're not to be late. She's looking forward to tasting your award-winning apple pie."

"I'll be here." He grinned. "I look forward to eating the delicious meal you ladies plan on making without Myra's help."

"We can cook you know, Benjamin Coulter." She disappeared behind the beveled glass door.

Benjamin whistled as he made his way home to the Petersons' boardinghouse. He may not have gotten that kiss yet—but he would, eventually. He was growing more confident that Ruthie, and her kiss, were worth waiting for.

~*~

Ruth Ann poured the steaming tea through the sifter into each of three porcelain teacups on the kitchen table then offered one to Mama and Sarah. "Ben has—"

Mama's brow lifted. "Ben? I thought he preferred Benjamin."

"Yes, well I—" Ruth Ann's cheeks flushed but she was determined not to let mama goad her. "I mean, Benjamin has offered to teach arithmetic during my evening classes."

Sarah lowered the cup from her upturned lips. "Really? It seems like someone can't spend enough time with you, little sister."

"He's just being kind." She spooned sugar into her tea and stirred. "With so many students, we are progressing very slowly. His offer means we can begin arithmetic much sooner than I had originally planned."

Sarah grinned. "Yes, I'm sure that's why he's doing it."

Mama set three slices of apple cake on the table then positioned herself between her daughters. "I am growing fond of Benjamin. He is a very smart young man with a bright future in spite of his upbringing."

Ruth Ann smiled and reached for a plate.

Mama slid the dessert away from Ruth Ann. "That one is for Sarah. I cut this one especially for you."

Ruth Ann stared at the piece of cake in front of her. Her slice was twice the size of the one Mama had cut for Sarah. Why did Mama do this? Why did she tell her she was too plump to find a beau then offer her such large portions? It took considerably more will power to refrain from eating the dessert once it was on her plate. "I shouldn't eat all of this, Mama."

Mama's hands fluttered in front of her face.

"Nonsense. You love dessert, and apple cake is your favorite."

"It is my favorite, but I'm trying to eat less sweets." She moved to the counter and cut the wedge in half, returning a portion to the serving dish.

Mama's lips thinned, and she folded her arms across her chest. "Sarah had suggested lemon cake, but I had Myra make this especially for you. You have been working very hard lately."

"Thank you, Mama." She placed her hand on her mother's arm. "I do appreciate it, and I am having some. I just don't want such a big piece, that's all." She took a small bite and swallowed.

"Please do not trouble yourself on my account." Mama stood, removed Ruth Ann's plate, and scraped the remainder into the garbage.

"Mama—"

"I am going to bed. Good night." The swinging door whooshed closed as Mama's uneven cadence faded into the parlor.

Ruth Ann glanced from the swinging door to her sister. "Is her leg troubling her tonight? I've been remiss at applying the liniment to her hip."

Sarah shook her head as she swallowed.

"Then what has Mama so upset?"

Sarah lowered the fork from her lips. "I'm sure you know she was watching at the window when Benjamin brought you home."

She nodded.

"Mama saw Benjamin try to kiss you."

Ruth Ann bit her lip and grinned sheepishly. "But she must have seen that I didn't let him. Is that why she's angry with me? Does she think I'm too free with him?"

Sarah dabbed her mouth with a cloth napkin before lying it on the table. "No, she thinks she's losing you to him."

Ruth Ann sat up straighter in her chair. "What?"

"She's worried you'll marry Benjamin, and he'll take you away from home, following the rails west, never to be seen again."

"Oh." Ruth Ann sipped her tea. "We haven't discussed marriage."

"You love him, don't you?"

She chuckled under her breath at Sarah's frank remark. And folks thought she was direct. "I think so."

"Then why haven't you let him kiss you?"

She shuddered at the unbidden image of James holding her close, pressing his lips against her own. It had nearly sickened her. "I think something might be wrong with me, Sarah."

"What do you mean?"

"When James kissed me, it was like squeezing a soggy dishrag against my mouth. I didn't like it one bit." She lowered her gaze and stared at her hands. "I couldn't bear it if kissing Ben felt the same."

Sarah grinned. "I don't think you'll have to worry about that."

Ruth Ann lifted her head. "Why?"

Sarah squeezed her sister's hand. "Because kissing someone you love sets your insides on fire." Sarah covered her mouth to suppress a yawn. "Do you mind cleaning up so I can go to bed?"

"I don't mind, but it's awfully early."

"I've been so tired lately." She hugged Ruth Ann. "Trust your heart. You'll know when it's the right time."

She nodded. "Good night."

Ruth Ann poured water from the stove's reservoir into the sink. She cut a sliver of soap from the bar and watched it sink in the hot water. Sarah seemed confident there was a difference between kissing someone you loved and someone you didn't, but Ruth Ann wasn't so sure.

She sighed and returned her mother's uneaten dessert to the serving dish then covered it with the glass lid. Her own portion sat atop vegetable peelings and soggy coffee grounds in the compost pile. Did mama really think Ben might marry her and take her west? Did she see something between them that Ruth Ann hadn't seen herself? It was all so confusing.

Ben had wanted to kiss her earlier, and she'd nearly let him—until fear took over. Something more than apprehension over another lackluster kiss festered inside her. Twirling the dishrag through the soapy water, painful memories flooded her mind—snickers from the children in the schoolyard and cotillions with empty dance cards. Her grandfather commenting that he couldn't get his arms around her when she was a girl or mother telling her not to eat sweets if she wanted to be thin like Sarah.

What was she so afraid of? Ben hadn't seemed bothered by her fuller figure so far, but what if her figure became an issue?

What if it didn't?

What would it be like to melt into his arms and let him 'set her insides on fire'? She'd like to know, but that would mean he'd need to hold her—tight.

She forced out a breath. Would she ever be brave enough to find out?

~*~

Deep laughter came from the darkness. Benjamin squinted. Two, maybe three, men wobbled in his direction.

"Get up, Ollie. Yer so dag blasted drunk, you can't stand up straight."

Artie Johnson. Benjamin shook his head. He'd been remiss in looking out for Ollie since he left the encampment. He hustled across the green in the direction of the boisterous men.

"Ollie, you okay?" He offered a hand to the older man, still splayed on the ground.

"Hall-ooo Ben-fa-men."

"I'm right here, Ollie. No need to yell."

Ollie took Benjamin's hand and allowed the younger man to maneuver him upright. He swayed on his feet. "Where's yer purty gal tonight?"

He put his hands on Ollie's shoulders. "Whoa. Steady there, Ollie. I already took Miss Sutton home."

"Thaf's too bad." Ollie belched, filling the air between them with the pungent odor of rotgut and tobacco. "She's reeeeeal nice."

Artie snickered. "You still moonin' over that plump schoolteacher? It's a good thing her face is purty, cause everything south of her chin ain't." He guffawed and smacked his hat against his leg.

Benjamin's jaw clenched. *Just ignore him. He's drunk.*

Artie slapped Benjamin's back. "Ya know, Coulter, the more I think on it, the more I realize her shape ain't all bad." Artie's hands sliced the night sky in the curvaceous form of a woman's figure with ample breasts. "After all, when they's round, they's round *all* over."

Benjamin leaned Ollie against an obliging oak tree then grabbed the foul-mouthed, cantankerous spikeman by the shirt, nearly lifting Artie from the ground. "I would've thought you'd have learned by now not to talk about her that way."

Benjamin released the crumpled fabric of Artie's shirt from his grip, giving the man a backward shove. "Open your mouth again and I'll bust your jaw so you can't speak against her for a long time."

"Aw, you need a drink. You're no fun anymore." He grabbed his hat off the ground and dusted it against his trousers. "See ya later, Ollie. Coulter."

"Let's get you home, Ollie." Benjamin positioned his friend's arm across the back of his shoulders. "Lean on me."

The two made their way toward the tent encampment, Ollie occasionally stumbling on a tree root. "Don't pay no mind to Artie. Fool wouldn't know a good woman if she—"

"You don't look so good, Ollie."

Cheeks bulging and shoulders heaving, Ollie gagged and doubled over, emptying the contents of his stomach onto the hard Virginia clay. It splattered atop Benjamin's right boot.

"Sorry, about that."

Benjamin removed the handkerchief from his pocket and offered it to his friend. "Nothing a bit of water can't fix."

Ollie wiped his mouth then handed it back to Benjamin.

"That's okay. You keep it." He lifted the tent flap and guided Ollie to the cot. "Why are you drinkin' so much?"

He shrugged. "Lonely, I guess."

Benjamin reached down and tugged on his friend's boot. He needed to spend more time with Ollie, encourage him to give up the drink. How was he going to do that? He spent nearly all his free time with Ruth Ann and, somehow, he couldn't imagine the two of them together in her mother's fancy parlor.

Ollie's thick sausage-like fingers squeezed Benjamin's shoulder. "You don't need to worry about me, buddy." He belched. "Excufe me. You got yer filly, and soon you'll be a surveyor."

Benjamin yanked on Ollie's boot again, wrenching it free from the man's chunky calf.

"I know some fellas make fun of yer gal's buxom figure, but I remember her kindness that day we met. I reckon she'd be mighty disappointed to see me right now."

"She'd be worried about you, same as me." He pulled off Ollie's other boot and shoved them both underneath his bunk.

"Well, don't—" Ollie's hand clamped across his mouth.

Benjamin scrambled for the chamber pot and thrust it under Ollie's chin as the remainder of his stomach gushed from his lips like steam bursting from a racing locomotive's chimney.

Ollie blew out a putrid breath. "Much better."

Benjamin's stomach heaved at the rancid smell permeating the tiny tent. Holding his breath, he slipped the pot outside.

"Don't you listen to Artie neither? Just 'cause he likes 'em slender and petite, doesn't mean we all do." He nudged Benjamin's shoulder.

"Ollie—"

"I'm serious." Ollie listed sideways, and Benjamin

righted him. "There's lots to be said for a buxom woman." A liquor-induced grin spread across his face, and he waggled his brows. "They're real soft."

Benjamin shook his head and leaned Ollie back against the thin straw ticking.

"And you don't have to worry about 'em runnin' off on ya neither like my Hattie did." Ollie yawned and his eyes drifted closed. "Cuz...nobody else...wants 'em." His words trailed off until soft, grunting breaths replaced them.

Benjamin pulled the wool blanket over his sleeping friend and headed out into the night. Raucous laughter spilled from the gaming hall on the outskirts of the encampment. He quickened his pace toward the Petersons' boardinghouse, flopping on the porch steps when he'd reached their sanctuary. What was he running from anyway? He wasn't a kid anymore. He didn't have to let the unkind remarks of others bother him as they had when he was a boy.

"Let me...rest...a moment...Benjamin." Liza Coulter had grabbed her skirt and leaned her outstretched arm against the post.

Benjamin and his little brother and sister had stopped beside her.

Rivulets had dripped down Ma's temples and the hair at the nape of her neck had been soaked from the short walk to town. She'd pulled a tattered fan from the basket she carried and waved it near her face.

Snickers had drawn Benjamin's attention to a group of boys on the far side of the building. One pointed at his mother and laughed.

"Okay, son, give yer ma a hand."

Benjamin had taken her sweaty hand in his and grimaced. He tugged with all his might and managed to pull her up the stairs.

"You stay here and mind Alice and George. Keep 'em close, ya hear?"

Benjamin's eyes drifted down to his worn boots. He'd nodded.

Ma leaned into his ear. "Don't pay those Kent brothers no mind. Ya hold yer head up high, son. Yer a Coulter."

"Yes'm."

Ma had released his hand and kissed his head. "I won't be long." Lifting her basket shoulder high, she'd angled sideways and disappeared through the narrow doors of the Fayetteville Mercantile.

Benjamin had wiped the sweat from his mother's hand against his trousers and glanced at Alice and George. He'd offered to go to town for his Ma—alone. But she'd insisted they all needed to get off the farm for a while and a walk would do them good. Alice had stood barefoot. Her skirt, close to knee-length, had already been let down as far as it would go and she had been in desperate need of new shoes before winter. George's trousers hung several inches above the top of his boots. Benjamin had been no better off. Skin had peeked through the hole ma had mended in his britches last week. Course, if Pa didn't drink away all they made, they'd have money for shoes as well as material for new clothes.

What a spectacle they'd made.

"Hey, Coulter."

Benjamin had glared at Bobby Kent. The Kents owned one of the largest dairy farms in the county. Although Bobby was only one year his senior, the boy had been more than a few inches taller and broader than Benjamin.

"Your folks own a milking cow?"

He'd nodded.

"I think she's loose in the mercantile."

Bobby's younger brother doubled over laughing. "Maybe if she didn't eat so much you, your brother, and your sister could get some decent clothes."

Benjamin's fists balled at his sides. He'd grown tired of the taunts from the Kents about his mother's size. He had tired of never having enough to eat or proper clothes to wear despite a thriving orchard. Most of all, he had tired of the laughter and disrespect. He couldn't wait 'til he was grown—he'd never be the butt of others jokes again.

The nearby trill of a screech owl shook Benjamin from his remembrances. Thoughts of Artie mocking Ruth Ann's figure streamed through his mind, his drunken laughter echoed in his head. Benjamin rested his elbows on his knees, tapping the brim of his hat against his left palm. Why did it matter to him what Artie Johnson thought? He liked Ruth Ann's fuller curves and all that came with them. She was smart, kind, and very pretty. He'd be a fool to let her go.

Ollie hadn't meant to slight him, but his words had stung, too. *Cuz nobody else wants 'em.* Is that how other men perceived Ruth Ann? As the consolation prize? He'd been feeling pretty good about his draw in the game of love, but if other men thought she was just the honorable-mention ribbon, the kind of girl any man could get and never had to worry about another man wanting, he wasn't so sure.

12

Benjamin slipped the strap of his guitar over his shoulder and plucked a few chords, checking that his instrument was in tune. "I learned this one in Texas. I'll play through once and then I want everyone to join me in the chorus."

"There's a yellow rose of Texas that I am going to see— Benjamin winked at Ruth Ann while he sang. Her cheeks blossomed with color like spring flowers.

—And if I ever find her, we never more will part."

He played the tune through a few more times, encouraged by Chloe's vigorous clapping.

"That's all for me. I don't play as much as I used to and my fingers have lost their calluses. Any chance you have a fiddle, Joseph?"

Joseph shook his head.

Ruth Ann's eyes widened. "You play the fiddle too?"

"My father taught me the fiddle when I was a boy. I haven't gotten around to purchasing one yet." Benjamin's palm glided across the smooth spruce wood of his guitar. "I won this in a po—" His eyes darted to Mrs. Sutton as he cleared his throat. "—a card game in Tennessee during the war." He expected censure, but instead, a hint of a smile twinkled in her eyes. He grinned. "Double or nothing in the next hand earned me some lessons as well."

"Well, it appears you have put your talent for card playing to good use then, young man." Mama stood and smoothed the wrinkles from her skirt. "It is time to see if your talents at pie making are as good as we have been led to believe."

Sarah adjusted a sleeping Lily on her shoulder. "Thank you for entertaining us. That was the most fun I've had in quite a while, but it's time for two young ladies to go to bed."

Chloe protested, but Joseph swooped her up in his arms. "Time for bed, Missy."

"Please come back," she called over her father's shoulder. "You're the best beau Aunt Roofie's ever had."

Ruth Ann kissed her niece on the forehead as she whisked by. "Let's not make Mr. Coulter's head swell, or it won't fit through the door when he takes his leave."

Benjamin patted the space beside him on the piano bench.

"I should help Mama with dessert, Ben."

"C'mon. One minute won't hurt." Benjamin slipped the guitar strap over his head and leaned the instrument against the wall. "Dinner was delicious, Ruthie. I must admit I doubted whether or not you ladies could pull off such a fine meal without Myra's help."

Her posture stiffened "Well, it goes to show you that we are perfectly capable in the kitchen."

"Whoa now." His hands flew up in a defensive posture against her clipped words. "I didn't mean to ruffle your feathers. I just assumed because Myra cooks for your family, you wouldn't need to learn such tasks."

"Myra helps our family four days a week and Amos tends to the horses, garden, and handiwork, but

Papa insisted we know how to run a house. 'Help is a privilege,' Papa said, 'and you need to know how to do without.'" She crossed her arms snugly across her chest. "So, you see Benjamin Coulter, I do know how to cook, clean, sew, and plant a garden."

He dragged a palm across the back of his neck. They'd pulled off one meal, but day after day?

Her eyes narrowed. "I can cook, Ben. I can make eggs, pancakes, cinnamon rolls, and chicken soup. And my biscuits, while not as fluffy as Myra's, are definitely edible."

The tap-tap-tap of Ruth Ann's foot against the polished hardwood floors drew Benjamin's gaze downward.

"If I was spoiled, Benjamin, I wouldn't teach at the Freedmen's School."

He brushed a loose hair from her face. "I don't believe you're spoiled, sweetheart, but look around your parlor. You haven't wanted for much of life's necessities."

Ruth Ann pressed her lips together as tightly as her arms were folded against her.

He hadn't intended to hurt her feelings or injure her pride. Buddy curled up at his feet, and he stroked the dog's reddish-brown fur. At least the old dog wasn't mad at him. If they married, her life would be vastly different from the one she enjoyed now. *How am I going to make her understand?*

"Ruthie, there's a difference between making a nice meal a few times a year and being responsible for all of the family's meals each day. Plus, all of the household chores Myra does and some that Amos does as well. Like tending the garden regularly."

She didn't look at him. Instead, she kept her eyes

focused on her hands resting in her lap.

"I grew up very differently, Ruthie. I didn't have any of the advantages that you've had." He paused and waited for her to look at him.

"None of that matters, Ben."

He covered her hands with one of his own. "What I'm trying to say is that everyone pulled their own weight in my family—no hired help. While I might be able to afford hired help on a surveyor's salary, I'm not inclined to spend my money on such things—not if my wife is perfectly able."

~*~

A faint creak enticed Ruth Ann to lean past the Grandfather clock and peer into the dining room. Her mother's blue gown was visible below the swinging door to the kitchen. She shook her head. "I think Mama can hear us."

Benjamin shrugged. "When I go west, I won't be settling down in a town or even homesteading. I'll be on the move three quarters of the year surveying and mapping the western territories. I'll be living out of a tent and wagon. Are you ready for that?"

Ruth Ann studied her hands enclosed in Benjamin's. Was she ready for that? Many of her domestic skills suffered in comparison to other young women her age, even to Benjamin's apparently. She couldn't make an award-winning pie. Did he see her as some fragile, silly girl who'd fuss and cry when things got hard? That's not who she was. She was the kind of woman who rolled up her shirtsleeves and worked hard.

A fierce determination rose within her. Lifting her

chin, she looked directly into his golden brown eyes. "I'm often told that my strong will is a negative quality in a woman, but hear me when I tell you, Benjamin Coulter, the other side of that coin is perseverance." She wriggled one hand loose and clutched it against her bosom. "I have within me what it takes to work hard and sacrifice, if necessary, for what I want."

He lifted her hand and kissed it gently. "You're an amazing woman, Ruthie, and I have no doubt you will accomplish whatever you set your mind to, but you need to consider what I'm telling you. It won't be easy."

"Ruth," Mama called from the kitchen. "I need help with dessert."

"Coming, Mama." Pausing at the swinging door, she glanced over her shoulder, giving Benjamin what she hoped was a confident smile. "I can do it, Ben."

The aroma of cinnamon and cooked apples greeted her when she entered the kitchen. Her mouth watered as she glided her tongue across her lips.

"Ruth, I wish to speak with you about Benjamin." Mama placed the cream and sugar on the tray beside the coffee cups.

Ruth Ann tugged her bottom lip between her teeth and waited. What was wrong now?

"I overheard part of your conversation with him. He raised a good question. Are you sure you are willing and able to live in circumstances immensely different from how you were raised?"

Not this again. Why did everyone doubt her? Did everyone think she was a pampered princess? "I think so, Mama. Suttons don't shy away from a challenge."

Mama placed her hands on her daughter's shoulders. "Promise me you will think about this matter seriously."

"I will. I promise."

"You know, Ruth, the more time I spend with Benjamin, the more he endears himself to me. While he doesn't have the money and societal graces of the Thorntons, it is not hard to see he cares deeply for you. There is something about his easy manner that reminds me of your father."

She hugged her mother. "Your good opinion of Benjamin means a great deal to me."

Mama stroked Ruth Ann's hair before breaking their embrace. "Are we ready?"

She glanced over the serving trays. "We need napkins. You go ahead, and I'll be right there." She grabbed the cloth napkins and tucked them under her arm. The whoosh of the swinging door brought a mischievous thought to mind. *I wonder if Mr. Coulter has ever had pointless pie.*

~*~

Benjamin reached for the plate Ruth Ann offered him. Where was the point of his pie? Glancing toward the piece she had set aside for herself, he discovered hers missing too. *How odd.*

The smell of warm apple pie roused Buddy from his nap by the hearth. Being honor bound to clean up any crumbs that might land on his mistress' rug, the old dog lumbered toward the table.

Dessert in hand, Benjamin joined Joseph near the fire. After taking a sip of coffee, he placed his cup on the mantel. He stared at Joseph's serving. The point was intact on his piece. He scratched his cheek. *What was Ruth Ann up to?*

Joseph leaned toward Benjamin. "I see you were properly initiated into the family ritual this evening."

Benjamin pulled his head back slightly and furrowed his brow.

Joseph pointed to his plate. "Ruth Ann took the point of your pie."

"I can't make any sense of it."

"Charles Sutton was quite the prankster. One of his favorites, besides snitching the icing the girls would save for last, was to steal the point of their pie. It quickly became a game amongst them to see who could steal the other's point first."

"Ah. So why didn't she take everyone's point?"

"Ruth Ann wanted to single you out. I'd wager she took her own as well, so you couldn't."

Benjamin chuckled, imagining her giggling as she stole the tips of their pie.

Joseph laid his hand on Benjamin's shoulder. "But you know, Benjamin, in nearly a year of courting she never stole Thornton's point."

A warm contentedness covered him like a blanket on a cold winter's night. It was silly, but he liked the fact she'd included him in the family tradition and not Thornton.

Mrs. Sutton wiped her mouth then laid the napkin across her lap. "Benjamin, I would appreciate a copy of your receipt. I am unsure how we will get Myra to switch without offending her, but this is the best apple pie I have ever eaten."

"Thank you, ma'am, but that won't be necessary. I intend to be around for a long time to make them myself."

Ruth Ann returned his gaze with a tender smile then continued her conversation with Sarah.

"Think I'll go get a drink of water then I'd better head home."

Benjamin removed a glass from the cupboard beside the sink. He pumped the handle two times, filling the glass halfway. After he drank, he noticed the second pie sitting on the butcher block and chuckled again at the thought of Ruth Ann taking the point of his pie. He shook his head. She must be awfully proud of herself for pulling one over on him.

He rejoined the family in the parlor, gathered his guitar, and thanked them for the delicious meal. After removing his hat and coat from the hall tree, he placed his hand on Ruth Ann's shawl. Without words, he invited her to accompany him outside. She nodded and joined Benjamin in the foyer. After placing the wrap around her shoulders, he grabbed his instrument and escorted her to the porch.

His eyes flitted to the window. It was Joseph's turn on guard duty. Undeterred, he caressed her cheek. "I had a nice time today. Your family is wonderful, and I get the impression that your mother is warming up to me."

"I believe you're right."

Benjamin pulled her close, his chin resting on top of her head. "Only one thing was missing and it would have been the perfect day."

Ruth Ann stepped back, a scowl crossing her face. "Not yet, Ben. You promised, remember?"

Benjamin puckered his brow. "My dear, Ruthie, whatever are you talking about?"

"You know perfectly well what I'm referring to." She playfully poked her finger in his chest. "While you might be tempted to kiss me, we agreed last night to wait a while longer."

He had her now. Garnering as much innocence as he could muster, he fought to keep an impish grin under control. "Kiss you?" He shook his head. "Ruthie, I was talking about the point of my pie."

She blushed then gave him another little swat. "You'll never get another point of pie if I have anything to say about it."

"We'll see about that."

~*~

Oh, that man. She was fit to be tied. Twice in two days she'd misunderstood his meaning and thought he wanted to kiss her when he hadn't.

The foyer and parlor were empty when she entered the house. Curious. Hadn't Joseph been at the window only moments before?

No sooner had the latch clicked behind her than Mama's voice rang out from the other end of the hallway. "Ruth, come to the kitchen please."

Mama's clipped words hung in the air. Now what? The day seemed to have gone so well. She hung her shawl on the hall tree. "Coming."

Sarah leaned against the cook stove. Shoulders shaking, her hand attempted to hide her amusement.

Ruth Ann's gaze shifted to Joseph who merely shrugged and tipped his head toward her mother.

"What is the meaning of this, Ruth?" Her mother held Benjamin's other pie in her hands, a perfect circle cut from its middle.

Strange. Ruth Ann shrugged her shoulders. "I didn't do it, Mama, and I don't know who—"

"Yes, you do," Sarah interrupted.

Ruth Ann cocked her head. How should she know

who cut the center of the pie? Why did they think she—a hearty laugh escaped her mouth.

Benjamin Coulter had bested her again.

13

Ruth Ann pulled her shawl tighter around her shoulders. The day had been sunny with mild temperatures for early December when they set out. The sun, now shrouded behind darkening clouds, refused to yield its warmth. Shade from the trees by the creek added to the chill.

"The first night we will need to assess the adults' knowledge of arithmetic." She tapped her index finger against her cheek. "My guess is they do basic arithmetic every day without realizing it—measuring food or using their foot to mark off distance." She glanced over her shoulder. The old dog trudged along behind them, eager for a rest. "Perhaps we should point out as many of those things as possible so they will have confidence in their abilities."

Benjamin motioned toward a spot for them to sit. He spread the blanket he carried over a large rock, the tip of which jutted out over the edge of the creek. Buddy curled up at its base.

Her hand landed on her hip, and she cocked her head to the side.

Unable to hide his own amusement, Benjamin chortled. "What?"

"I hope you don't plan on pushing me in the creek today."

"I wondered if you'd recognized this spot. And for the record, I didn't push you. You backed up and fell, too mulish to let me help you down."

"Too mulish?"

Chuckling, he climbed up on the rock then stretched out his hand to Ruth Ann.

She looped the satchel across her shoulders before taking his arm and claimed a seat beside him.

"Perhaps you were too mulish. If you recall, I insisted you leave more than once."

Benjamin grinned. "Maybe. But I was doomed from the moment you unpinned those curly locks—caterwauling or not."

Her jaw dropped.

Laughing, he pulled her near. "As long as you stay close to me, you should have no trouble avoiding the water today."

Strong arms engulfed her. Pulse skittering, she strained to form a coherent thought. "I...I don't know what I'm going to do with you, Benjamin Coulter."

He waggled his brows. "I have a few ideas."

"You better keep your mind on the lessons you'll be teaching this week." She pulled the arithmetic book from her satchel and poked the primary volume in his stomach. "I plan to work on numbers in their reading lesson as well. So you'll teach them to recognize numbers in numeral form, and I'll do the same in written form."

"That makes sense. If we both are working on the same concepts, the students will learn them quickly. Perhaps I could bring some nails or apples and begin with pattern recognition, and basic addition and subtraction."

"That's a wonderful idea." Benjamin was thinking like a teacher and would have his students learning arithmetic in no time. Ruth Ann dug around in her satchel. "Here, Benjamin." She offered him another book. "You should take this since you'll be responsible for teaching arithmetic. You won't need the advanced volume for a while, but you can take it too if you like."

Benjamin perused the primary book. "How will I know when they are ready to progress to the next topic?"

"I'll help you with assessments."

Benjamin let out a breath. "Good. I was worried about that part."

The gurgling streamed flowed over the rocks below them. "This is my favorite place. I used to come fishing here with Papa when I was little and..." She hesitated. "It's where I first saw you."

Benjamin squeezed her shoulders. "I like it here, too. It holds special memories for me as well."

"Really?" She tilted her head to see his face, hoping he would tell her again how he was smitten with her from their first meeting.

"Yep," Benjamin said, eyes twinkling. "Some of the best fishing I've ever done was right over there in that fishing hole."

"Oh, you." She gave him a playful swat, accidentally knocking the arithmetic books from his hand.

"Sorry, I didn't mean to—"

"I'll get them." Benjamin slid off the rock and grabbed the manuals. A white slip of paper floated to the ground. "What's this, Ruthie? Are you sneaking me love letters?"

She gulped a breath, eyes blinking rapidly. "Certainly not." She held out her hand for the paper. "May I have that, please?"

Benjamin opened his mouth and feigned disappointment. "What? You aren't trying to woo me as Darcy did Jane?"

"Darcy didn't woo Jane. He wooed Elizabeth. You'd know that if you had read *Pride and Prejudice* like I suggested." She reached for the note.

"That's not likely to happen, Miss Sutton. Now, if the content of this message is not for me," he teased, holding the missive above his head, "perhaps it's a letter to you from a former beau. Thornton perhaps?"

Her eyes tracked the paper. "Please, Ben." Voice wavering, she locked her gaze on him. "Pleeease give me the paper."

~*~

Benjamin turned his shoulder slightly. "No, Ruthie dear, I'm just going to have to—"

We, the citizens of the Loudoun valley, do not favor the education of darkies, young or old, and find it disgraceful for a white woman to keep company with coloreds for any reason. You must end your instruction immediately or violence will be used to make you comply with this request.

Benjamin stared at the slip of paper in his hands. He shifted to face her, his gaze waffling between Ruth Ann and the note. "How long ago did you receive this?"

She bit her bottom lip and shrugged.

He squared his shoulders. "Ruth Ann?"

She flinched.

Benjamin climbed onto the rock and squatted down in front of her. Taking her by the arms, he tried to force her to look at him, but she wouldn't. Still holding the menacing note under his thumb, he cradled Ruth Ann's face between his hands. His voice firm, but even. "Answer me, Ruthie."

"I-I'm not sure. A week now…or maybe, two."

Benjamin's thumb glided across her skin briefly before releasing her. Hadn't he proven his support for her position at the Freedmen's School despite mounting threats? Still she'd kept this secret from him. He rubbed his jaw and commanded himself to stay calm. She would be the death of him. "And you mentioned nothing about this? Not even to Joseph?"

Tugging on her bottom lip again, she shook her head then pulled her knees tight against her chest and wrapped her arms around them.

Benjamin softened his tone and sat beside her. "You kept this quiet because you were fearful Joseph wouldn't allow you to continue teaching there?"

He'd barely finished before her excuses tumbled from her lips. "I seriously doubt they'd do anything to harm a woman, Benjamin. They're just hoping to scare me away."

Benjamin read the short note again and shuddered. "Maybe, or maybe not, but have you given any thought to the danger you're placing your students in by continuing to teach them?"

She lifted her head. "What do you mean? Why would they be in any danger? The note is directed to me."

"I know you've read the papers. You must've seen the news reports about the attacks on Freedmen's Schools across the South and the teachers who taught in them. Many schools have been burned to the ground, some with the students and teacher inside."

Her shoulders straightened as if preparing for battle. Did she see him as the enemy?

"Yes, but in every one of those accounts the teachers were Negroes or white men from the North."

Rolling on to one knee, he grabbed Ruth Ann by the shoulders. "Silas Hench put his hands on you at Turner's. What might have happened if Malachi hadn't come when he did?" He shook her gently, hoping to rattle some sense into that beautiful head of hers. "What makes you think someone like that will respect a code of honor when it comes to the treatment of women? Especially women whom he believes are a 'disgrace to society.'"

Her lips flattened to a thin line, mimicking the tightness of her jaw. She pushed his hands from her shoulders. "Okay, Ben, you've made your point, but neither of us can say for sure that Silas Hench had anything to do with this letter."

How could she be so headstrong? Couldn't she understand the danger she was in? Why hadn't she confided in him? The reality of that last thought swept over him, nicking his pride. For some reason, she didn't trust him to keep her safe. Heavy with frustration, Benjamin's arms and legs moved like lead weights as he shifted away from her to a sitting position.

She forced a breath then scooted beside him. "I'm sorry for being snippy. I know you're only trying to protect me, but teaching at the Freedmen's School is —"

"Very important to you. I understand." He covered her hand, his thumb caressing her smooth skin. "But do you understand that you are very important to me?"

Chin tucked low, she nodded.

"I think I've demonstrated that I'm supportive of your position at the Freedmen's School."

She lifted her gaze. "Yes, but—"

"Then why didn't you come to me when you

received this?" He waved the note for emphasis. "Why didn't you trust me to find a way to make it safe for you?"

She shrugged her shoulders. "Because I knew you'd want to protect me."

"Of course I do but—"

Ruth Ann held up her free hand. "I wouldn't expect anything less from either you or Joseph, but to me, some things are worth the risk." Her gaze attached to his. "Teaching at the Freedmen's School is worth the risk. If people like Silas Hench get their way by threatening women, nothing will ever change."

"I agree with you."

She narrowed her eyes as if doubting the veracity of his words. "You do?"

"Yes, I do, but it's also time to get help before someone gets hurt. We need to talk to Joseph."

Ruth Ann sighed. "I'm not sure a conversation with Joseph will go as well as you think."

"You let me handle Joseph. It's time we organize a meeting of those folks, white and Negro, in favor of the Freedmen's School and its mission. We need to let them know of the threat so they can protect themselves and their children. We need to find volunteers to patrol the school anytime it's in use, and we probably should contact the Freedmen's Bureau and the sheriff in Leesburg and—"

Ruth Ann leaned forward and kissed his cheek. "Thank you, Ben. I should've known I could depend on you. I won't keep secrets from you again."

Benjamin huddled close. When had she become so important to him that her dreams, her safety, superseded his own?

Thunder rumbled nearby and the darkening skies

prophesied more than rain coming their way. Benjamin could feel it in the air.

A reckoning was coming.

~*~

Ruth Ann shoved the ivory lace curtain away from the parlor window. Where were they? Sighing, she released the window covering. "They should be home by now."

Mama looked up from the embroidery in her lap. "Sit down for heaven's sake. All this fretting will not bring either Joseph or Benjamin home sooner."

"I suppose." She flopped onto the settee where she could keep watch out the window for them. "I don't understand what's taking so long. They've been gone nearly two hours."

Sarah put her book aside. "I'll make tea."

The swinging doors hadn't stopped swaying before Ruth Ann renewed her pacing. Buddy lifted his head, his old ears perked. A low throaty bark erupted from his mouth moments before the front door creaked open.

Ruth Ann spun around in the direction of the foyer where Joseph and Benjamin brushed snow from their outer garments. Winter had finally decided to show its true colors.

She hurried to Benjamin's side, stepping back as he yanked a muddy boot free in the wooden jack. "How did the meeting go?"

His eyes twinkled. "Is that the only greeting your beau gets on a cold winter's night?"

She nodded toward the parlor.

Mama cleared her throat.

"Evenin', Mrs. Sutton."

"Good evening, Benjamin." She deposited her embroidery on the side table then stood straightening her skirts. "I'll help Sarah with the tea and coffee. Please join us in the kitchen."

Ruth Ann waited for the soft shuffling of Mama's shoes to fade then obliged Benjamin with a kiss to his cheek.

Joseph scanned the room before meeting Ruth Ann's gaze. A question loomed in his eyes.

"Sarah is in the kitchen making tea to calm my nerves." Ruth Ann's gaze flitted between Joseph and Benjamin. She was anxious for any information. "How did the meeting go? How many people attended? Did they vote to keep the school open?"

Benjamin rubbed his hands together. "Let's join Sarah in the kitchen, Ruthie. We'll tell you everything while we have a drink to warm us up." His gaze wandered to the parlor hearth. He patted the outside of his thigh. "C'mon, Buddy."

Buddy rose from his resting place by the fire. The old dog stretched before ambling after them toward the kitchen, his hind feet slipping on the polished wood floors.

Ruth Ann smiled. James had always treated Buddy as an unwelcome nuisance. Benjamin, on the other hand, seemed fond of her dog. Her pulse quickened. How could such a simple gesture endear him to her? A warmth spread throughout her body as his calloused hand enveloped hers.

He brought her hand to his lips and placed a gentle kiss there. "Everything will be fine, Ruthie. Trust me."

She did trust him, and with something way more

important than her teaching position—her heart.

Sarah and Mama made quick work of serving the tea and coffee. Too nervous to pour her own drink, Ruth Ann took a seat at the table beside Benjamin.

Joseph removed his pipe and tobacco bag from his shirt pocket. "It was a good meeting, Ruth Ann."

She pressed a hand against her stomach. "It was?"

"Sheriff Johnson came from Leesburg and brought Captain John Reynolds with him."

Mama's teacup halted midway to her mouth. "Captain?"

"Yes, he's a captain in the Army, decorated for valor at Gettysburg. Lost his left arm in the fray. Now he works with the War Department to transition the Freedmen's Schools to self-governance or with oversight from the American Missionary Society. He'll board at the Petersons' while he's in town."

Benjamin added a spoonful of sugar to his coffee and stirred. "We had about twenty men there tonight—Negroes and whites. Most of them volunteered for the safety patrols the captain is establishing."

She squirmed in her seat like one of the children in her class waiting for the bell to announce recess. "So the school will remain open?"

Joseph cocked his head to the side, arms folded tight against his chest. "Yes. In the long run. Assuming you are willing to continue."

Her head flinched back slightly. Of course she was willing. "What do you mean, 'in the long run?'"

His eyebrows squeezed together. "The school will be closed until after Christmas."

Ruth Ann stood abruptly, jarring the table. Teacups clanked against their saucers sloshing hot liquid over the sides. "Not until after Christmas! My students will regress!"

Mama reached out to right her daughter's teacup. "Goodness gracious, Ruth. Sit down and let them finish."

Benjamin patted her hand. "Captain Reynolds needs to train his replacement, and he doesn't want the school to operate until the safety patrols are established."

Shoulders slumped, she returned to her seat.

"The captain believes this is best, Ruthie, and it's only two weeks before the school closes for the Christmas break anyway."

Elbows on the table, Ruth Ann hunched forward and sipped her tea. At least she wasn't being forced to resign. The captain was only looking out for her safety, and the safety of her students, and that was a blessing in itself.

Mama cleared her throat. "Perhaps by the new year, a suitable Negro teacher will be found."

Ruth Ann pressed her eyes closed. Not that again. Weren't all these precautions arranged to keep the school open with her as the teacher?

"I understand how much this means to you, Ruth, but the situation is growing increasingly dangerous," her mother added.

Benjamin and Joseph exchanged glances.

Joseph leaned back on the hind legs of his chair. "We're all concerned about Ruth Ann's safety. More than a dozen men volunteered to take shifts guarding the Freedmen's School whenever it's open, and Tom Hardy offered the use of his smithy as a base for overnight operations. This is a temporary solution until the authorities can find the culprits responsible for the threats against Ruth Ann and the school."

Mama clutched the cameo fastened to the collar of her shirtwaist, her eyes darting between the two men. "What aren't you telling us?"

Joseph returned his chair legs to the floor. "Silas Hench had the nerve to show up at the meeting—and he wasn't alone. Levi and Elias Hamilton came also. Levi seemed friendly with him."

Ruth Ann quaked at the mention of Silas' name. She stroked her wrist as if he'd only relinquished his vice-like hold on her moments before. Voice wavering, she whispered, "I can't believe Elias or his father would be mixed up with these threats."

Mama's voice cracked. "I'm no longer confident Ruth Ann is safe. I think we should reconsider."

Ruth Ann widened her eyes, but before she could protest, Benjamin addressed her mother.

"You have every right to be alarmed, ma'am, but rest assured the captain is taking this very seriously. He is personally overseeing the investigation and the assignment of volunteers. Joseph and I are convinced these provisions will keep everyone safe."

Mama knit her brows together, concern etched in the frown lines at the edge of her lips. "You'll continue to personally escort her to and from evening classes?"

Benjamin nodded.

"And you'll stay with her the entire time?"

"Yes, ma'am. You have my word. I'll do everything in my power to keep your daughter safe."

Mama's eyes glistened. "I know you will." She reached for Joseph's hand. "I know you both will."

14

Benjamin peeked between the pocket doors. The tree they had cut yesterday afternoon stood proudly in the corner of the parlor, displacing Mrs. Sutton's wingback chair for the remainder of the Christmas holidays. Fire blazing in the hearth, the scent of pine, cinnamon, and clove lingered in the air. Christmas Eve. Ruth Ann pointed to a spot on the tree for Chloe to hang an ornament. Holly graced the mantel, swags of pine wrapped in ribbon adorned the windowsill, and velvet bows dotted the tree. Everywhere he looked something gold or silver sparkled. The scene reminded him of a Currier & Ives lithograph he'd seen in the newspapers—not reminiscent of the childhood holidays he'd known. It was perfect.

She was perfect.

"The first day of Christmas, my true love sent to me…"

He cringed. Almost perfect.

Maybe he should've bought her a bucket for Christmas so she could carry a tune in it. Grinning, he slid the doors into their nesting space. "What fine decorating you ladies have done since last we met."

Ruth Ann spun to face him, eyes wide. "Goodness gracious, Ben, you startled me."

He kissed Ruth Ann's cheek.

Chloe giggled.

Benjamin picked up the little moppet, one shoe dropping to the floor as he lifted her high above his head. "And what are you giggling about?"

She responded with more infectious laughter.

He lowered the child into his arms and pecked her ringlet-covered head. He glanced to Ruth Ann. "How's my best girl doing this morning?"

She smiled. "I—"

A tiny voice interrupted. "I'm good."

Ruth Ann tickled her niece. "Benjamin was speaking to me."

Benjamin retrieved a card from the inside pocket of his winter coat. "Charlotte has sent me with an invitation for a Twelfth Night Party. She is hoping you will help decorate. And from what I can tell, she's chosen the right person."

The child's little hands realigned his face with hers, excitement dancing in her eyes. "What's a Twef Night Party?"

"I'm not sure, little miss, but there will be singing and games and treats of all kinds."

Ruth Ann tied a burgundy bow to one of the ornaments then held it high, inspecting her work. "Twelfth Night is the eve of the Epiphany and marks the end of the Christmas holidays. Every year Charlotte hosts a party with all the traditional foods and games her grandmother taught her."

Anticipation filled Chloe's eyes. "May I come, too?"

"I wish I could take you, but your Aunt Ruthie gets terribly jealous." He winked at Ruth Ann.

"Aunt Roofie and I are decorating the tree. We're going to string the popcorn and cranberries this morning too. Do you want to help us?"

Benjamin boosted Chloe high enough to hang an ornament from one of the taller branches then set her feet back on the rug. "Popcorn and cranberries? Homemade ornaments? I expected fancy store-bought ornaments to go along with all this holiday frippery."

Ruth Ann's lips pinched closed, refraining her speech.

"What?"

"My father's family has a tradition of only using homemade decorations on the tree. Our family has been making cinnamon-clove ornaments since Sarah was a little girl. It's a tradition I hope to continue when I have children."

Benjamin shook his head. He seemed to have a talent for ruffling her feathers lately. "I only meant that your home is so lovely and filled with fine things. I assumed you would want only the best on your tree as well."

She raised her chin. "That's not what you meant." She handed an ornament to Chloe then pointed to a spot on the tree the child could reach. "You still consider me spoiled."

Spoiled? Not exactly. Pampered maybe, but he had no intention of debating the fine nuances of those terms with a teacher. Still he couldn't help but worry that she romanticized what it would be like to live far from the refined offerings of the east in a tent and wagon. What if she came to resent him when she discovered she'd made a terrible mistake?

She waved her hand in a circular motion. "I don't care about any of this. I want more from life than pretty dresses and fine things."

He put his arms around her waist and rested his cheek against her temple, an obstinate curl tickling his neck. "I don't believe you're spoiled. Honest I don't. I just don't think you realize how difficult life in the west will be."

Ruth Ann straightened abruptly and wriggled free of his embrace. "Would you like to take a sleigh ride with me? I want to show you something."

He nodded. "Where are we going?"

"You'll see."

Twenty minutes later, they were bundled and heading north out of town. Ruth Ann gave Benjamin directions but wouldn't answer any of his questions about their destination. In fact, she didn't say much during their outing. If it weren't for the fact her arm intertwined his, he would have thought she was still cross with him.

"Okay, we'll see it from the crest of the hill."

He reined in the horses. Catoctin Creek snaked its way through the valley below them. Red barns distinguished themselves as majestic structures against uncluttered fields laden with snow. Although beautiful, it didn't stand out as unusual. Certainly, nothing to inspire the mystery she had placed on their destination.

Ruth Ann pointed to the right. "Please guide the sleigh to that farmhouse."

Dilapidated didn't begin to describe the rickety log home she had directed him to. Obviously vacant for some time, broken windows and a partially collapsed roof demonstrated years of neglect. More light than chinking was visible between the logs, and the garden, that probably once had been the delight of the woman who lived here, had been reduced to a bed of weeds poking out between layers of ice and snow.

Ruth Ann exited the sled. "Let's go inside."

"It doesn't look safe, Ruthie."

"You need to watch your step, but its fine. I've

been here before."

Benjamin remained seated, watching Ruth Ann traverse the slight incline. Confusion and disbelief adhered him to the bench.

Nearing the front steps, she called to him. "Are you coming, or am I going on this adventure by myself?"

He rubbed his jaw. She was a stubborn woman, but that wasn't news to Benjamin. He pushed the brake into place before hopping down and hanging the reins over a nearby tree limb.

"Where are we?"

She still didn't answer but motioned for him to follow.

"Ruthie, wait."

She disappeared inside, leaving him no choice but to trail after her.

Debris littered the inside of the cabin. Cobwebs and dust covered every surface. Snow lay six inches deep in the center of the single room beneath a three-foot hole in the roof. What on earth would attract her to this ramshackle?

Straddling a rafter that had fallen from the ceiling, she warned him to be careful. "The wood is rotten over there." She pointed to the unobstructed snow-covered path that stood between them. "Climb over the joist."

He complied. "What's so important we're going to all this trouble?"

She stood near the hearth, her hand caressing the oak mantel. Magnificently crafted, scrolls and rosettes adorned the wooden perch.

Benjamin wiped cobwebs from the edge. Engraved inside a circle were the letters HSJ, the S appearing twice as large as the other two letters. The craftsman's initials. Below the monogram, etched in smaller letters, was Pr. 28:6.

Her voice reverent, she pointed to the letters. "HSJ—Harold Joseph Sutton—my grandfather." She continued stroking the mantel, tenderly embracing the link to her ancestors. "I know you worry that our backgrounds are exceedingly different and that I won't be able to survive in the west. I wanted to bring you here to show you that we are not as different as you assume."

"I didn't mean—"

"Generations of Suttons have lived and died on this land since they emigrated from Ireland in 1762. My father was born and raised on this dairy farm. Papa worried mother's love of fine things would spoil us. As I told you, he insisted Sarah and I learn how to manage a home, and he brought us here on several occasions so we would never forget our modest heritage."

Benjamin took her hand in his. "Sorry, Ruthie. I shouldn't make assumptions, but I see your fine home, your study filled with books, and your nice clothes, and I wonder what in the world you're doing with a man like me?"

Ruth Ann tilted her head until he looked her in the eyes. "You're a fine, hard-working, intelligent man, Ben."

"Ruthie, there's something I've wanted to ask you." Benjamin took a deep breath, unsure if he wanted a truthful answer or not. "Why did you refuse James Thornton? He could have supported you very comfortably—given you everything you could ever want."

She held his gaze. "You're right. James could probably give me everything I could ever desire."

What a fool. Why had he brought up that dandy anyway?

"But, he couldn't give me everything I need."

Benjamin narrowed his eyes.

"What good are nice things if the people you share them with don't love you?" Ruth Ann pointed to the inscription underneath her grandfather's initials. "Have you ever read Proverbs 28:6?"

"Most likely, but I can't quite say I know it by memory."

"It says, 'Better is the poor that walketh in his uprightness, than he that is perverse in his ways, though he be rich.'" She took his hand. "Your story is so much like his—my father's, I mean. His father struggled to provide for his family. My grandfather couldn't read, but my father attended the university and became a lawyer and then a judge. Like you, my father grew up on a farm and chose to leave it. Not because it wasn't good enough, but because he wanted something different." They stood in silence for a moment. She squeezed his hand. "You are a kind and godly man. You have nothing to be ashamed of."

Bullseye. How'd she do that? He was embarrassed by his own modest beginnings. Benjamin closed his eyes as he recalled his illiterate parents, their constant struggle to provide for their family, and the taunts from other children about his mother's appearance and their threadbare clothes. He was ashamed of his upbringing and had assumed Ruth Ann would be as well.

~*~

How would she make him understand?

Swallowing the lump in her throat, Ruth Ann stepped closer to Benjamin. Her skirts brushed against him. "I know you worry that I'm not strong enough for life in the west, but I think it would be a grand adventure—with the right person." Shaky fingers glided across his cheek. "I will learn anything I need in order to take care of those I love."

"You'd really give up your fine home to live out of a tent and wagon with me most of the year?"

Unspoken devotion in his honey-colored eyes transfixed her. She managed a nod.

Benjamin's gloved fingers trailed the length of her arms before he pulled her close against him. Warm breath lingered against her cheek as smooth lips shadowed her jaw, inching toward her mouth. The heady scent of bay rum and spice disoriented her. An unfamiliar heat rose within, weakening her limbs. She could no longer resist him. He was going to kiss her, and this time, she longed for it.

Soft musings tickled her ear. The pounding of her heart between her temples made his words indiscernible. A quiet murmur escaped her lips. What had he said?

Benjamin broke their embrace and stepped back.

Her half-lidded eyes had trouble focusing. Where had those feather-light kisses gone?

He cleared his throat. "We should head back. We have popcorn and cranberries to string."

Dizzy from his abrupt change of course, she grabbed his arm to steady herself. "But I thought you were going to—"

A roguish grin crossed his handsome face as he regained surrendered ground between them. "To what?"

"N-Never mind." Embarrassed by her own brazenness, she forced her gaze away from him.

Pulling her close with one arm, his teeth yanked the glove free from the opposite hand. "Are you finally wanting that kiss, Ruthie?"

She bit her bottom lip, refusing to look his direction.

A tender palm slid across her face until it rested at the nape of her neck, strong and confident. His husky voice matched the cat-that-had-eaten-the-cream-look in his eyes. "I thought you'd never ask."

Before she could protest his cheeky remark, his mouth nestled her own. Her eyelids fluttered closed as she succumbed to his gentle kisses. Like delicate butterfly wings against her skin, each one explored her face...her earlobe...her neck. Her knees shimmied like jelly at his touch. A breath hitched in her throat. Without prodding, her arms slid around his neck.

When Benjamin's lips returned to capture hers, she matched his passion with her own. For a frenzied moment, she couldn't kiss him deep enough to squelch the blaze that burned inside her. Just as quickly as the spark had ignited, Ben's mouth softened against hers then faded away.

Her pulse raced frantically. James' kiss had been nothing like this.

"Ruthie," he whispered, lips brushing against her temple. "That was worth waiting for."

~*~

"Whoa there, little miss. You're putting way too much popcorn in your mouth. We're supposed to be stringing it for the tree, remember?"

"I can't help it, Uncle Benjamin. It's so good."

The Suttons' parlor fell silent.

Benjamin quirked a brow. *Uncle?*

Like a marionette waiting for the puppeteer's direction, Sarah's hands froze, suspended in air above the pine bough where she'd hung the first strand of popcorn and cranberry garland. Eyes wide, Joseph's pipe dangled from the corner of his mouth. Mrs. Sutton's needle hovered above the fabric, waiting permission to sew the next stitch. And Ruth Ann had her eyelids pressed closed so firmly, Benjamin thought if she didn't soon release them, they just might stick. The crunch of popcorn between Chloe's teeth provided the only evidence of conscious life in the room. What a scene. He shook his head and chuckled.

Ruth Ann stiffened and cast a sideways glance in his direction. "Benjamin, I never—"

"That's all right, Ruthie." He grinned as he tousled Chloe's ringlets. "I like the sound of that."

Air seemed to rush from every set of lungs in the room as the chatter of the Sutton women resumed.

He studied Ruth Ann as Lily lay sleeping against her chest. This was what he wanted—a home and children, and with this woman. He loved her. It was clear to him now. Why hadn't he told her? Because there was no going back from telling a woman you love her, that's why.

What had she told him earlier? *I will learn anything I need in order to take care of those I love.* He thunked his head. *Those I love.* She'd hinted at her feelings for him and he'd missed it. He was slower than the Virginia Creeper heading up Leesburg Mountain.

Ruth Ann shifted Lily from her shoulder to her lap, the child's head rested in the bend of her arm.

"Her thumb had slipped from her lips. I think she'll sleep all night now."

Joseph bent and gathered his slumbering daughter in his arms.

Benjamin glanced at Ruth Ann. Her gaze darted away. A lovely shade of pink adorned her cheeks.

She stood and smoothed her skirts. "I'll get dessert."

Sarah reached for her daughter's hand. "Chloe, give Mimi and Aunt Ruth Ann kisses good night."

"What about Uncle Benjamin?

"Him, too."

Benjamin nudged Chloe from his lap then pecked her on the cheek. "'Night."

Mrs. Sutton positioned her wooden embroidery hoop in her lap. "Benjamin, would you mind helping Ruth Ann? I hate to ask that of you, but I just don't seem to have the energy tonight."

"My pleasure, ma'am."

Benjamin peeked over the top of the swinging doors. The smell of roasted duck still lingered in the kitchen. Ruth Ann sat with her back to him, her dark tresses dangling past her shoulders. A hot prickle crept across his shoulders, picking up intensity as it swept down his arms and legs. What would it be like to lose his fingers in her mass of wavy locks?

~*~

Ruth Ann lurched forward at the whoosh of the door, hairpins lodged between her teeth. "Bem, I widm't hear you." She hastily wrapped curls against the nape of her neck.

He steadied her frenzied hands then removed the

pins from her lips. "Let me see."

She reached for one of the clips he held. "I-I shouldn't."

He stretched his arm above his head then leaned forward and whispered, "Not 'til you let me see."

His husky voice made her pulse skitter. She managed a faint shake of her head. "Mama's in the next—" A gentle finger silenced her. She needed to flee from the kitchen—from his smoldering gaze, but her lead feet wouldn't budge.

Benjamin's hand grazed hers as his lips brushed her cheek. "Please, Ruthie."

Her double-crossing hand fell to her side. Uncontrollable curls flowed in every direction.

Benjamin's eyes grew wider than Catoctin Creek when the winter snow melted.

"Why are you looking at me like that?" she asked.

He gently touched the twisted, wavy mass of dark locks that tumbled well past her shoulders. "Your hair is so curly. It's—"

"Unruly."

Benjamin shook his head. "Breathtaking. I've never seen anything like it. It's slightly quirky and untamable. It suits you."

Struggling not to squirm, she avoided his longing gaze.

Benjamin took a seat and tugged her to follow.

Her heart thundered. She couldn't. If she sat on his lap, he'd have to put his arms around her round middle, feel her less than tiny form on his legs.

"Come sit with me. I have something I want to tell you."

He pulled her hand again. The pounding inside her chest echoed in her head, making it difficult to think. She needed to find a way to stall him.

Strong hands encompassed her waist. She cringed as they lowered her to his lap.

He wrapped a curl around his finger. "You've never looked lovelier than you do right now."

She should spring from his lap before he changed his mind, but she couldn't move. His amber eyes held such love, such promise. What remained of her resistance vanished. He had broken through all the defenses she'd constructed around her heart and in this moment, she allowed herself to believe he found her attractive, that he desired her—fuller curves and all.

His thumb caressed her cheek. "I love you, Ruthie."

~*~

Benjamin studied her, determined to lock this image of her away in his memory.

"I love you, too, Ben Coulter. With all my heart."

Moisture glistened in her eyes as she cradled his cheek in her palm, her thumb gliding over his skin. Trembling fingers traced the line of his jaw then the cleft of his chin. Why would she cry? He thought telling her how he felt would make her happy. He'd never understand women.

She kissed his forehead. "We should grab the coffee and dessert and return to the parlor."

He held her firmly. "Just a bit longer."

"Ben, Mama will—"

He quieted her protests with his lips. She made a vain attempt to push him away before relenting to the will of his mouth. Gentle kisses charted a slow, deliberate path along her cheek. He nibbled her ear then nudged the high collar of her shirtwaist down. A soft murmur escaped her, before she angled her head granting him unfettered access. He paused briefly and grinned then continued his tender assault on her neck, savoring every morsel of her soft skin.

Benjamin's gaze drifted upward as another gentle sigh passed between her parted lips. Her eyes remained closed, a delicate smile adorning her face.

She was beautiful, and she was his.

His hands froze in place. She wasn't his yet.

Her eyes flickered open.

Benjamin deposited one last, chaste kiss on her sweet lips then gently nudged her from his lap.

He stood and combed his fingers through her glorious curls. "How about I take my best girl out to supper next Saturday night at the Hampton Hotel?"

She grinned. "Really?"

He nodded. "And wear that beautiful dress you wore when I first called on you."

She stretched to place a kiss on his cheek. "Are we celebrating anything special?"

He pulled her into a light embrace. "I hope so."

15

The candles clipped to the tree in Charlotte's parlor flickered near the source of Benjamin's amusement. He chuckled as Ruth Ann vigorously sang off-key.

"Four colley birds, three French hens, two turtledoves…"

He remembered her rendition of "The Merry, Merry Month of May," curls flowing then a splash. What a sight she'd been—and still was. Despite what Artie Johnson said about her figure, she was by far the prettiest woman in the room.

Nate Hamilton brought Ruth Ann a cup of mulled cider. "Well done." His eyes flitted around the circle, before landing on Benjamin. "Who's next?"

Lost in his reminiscences, he'd forgotten about the game. Hands up, begging for mercy, he declined. "I know next to nothing about parlor games."

Nate slapped his shoulder. "Perhaps, but you're a smart fellow, and you've seen us go around once." He leaned into Benjamin's ear. "Besides, the ladies like this game. In the even rounds, when they make a mistake, you can demand a sweet—either candy or a kiss, your choice. It's likely Ruth Ann will err for your benefit."

He agreed and followed Nate to the front of the parlor. "We have our next leader. Benjamin will pick up the tempo. Remember ladies, the stakes are high. If you make a mistake, Benjamin can have his choice of sweet."

The fair-haired woman in the corner flashed him a smile, brazenly holding his gaze. Benjamin looked away but felt her stare follow him. Ruth Ann had introduced them earlier. Rose Martin was her name. She had come with Elias but seemed to be saving her smiles for Benjamin.

He ran his finger along the inside of his shirt collar. "After I lead in, we'll begin with—" Had the woman batted her eyes at him? Benjamin shook his head then glanced at Ruth Ann. Had he imagined it? He cleared his throat and started again. "After I lead in, we'll begin with Charlotte and go around the circle in Maggie's direction."

"On the first day of Christmas, my true love sent to me…"

Several rounds later, Rose stood to sing. "Seven swans a swimming, six ducks a laying, five golden—"

Benjamin held up his hand. "Hold up there, Miss Martin. It's six geese a laying."

"Oh my, you're right." Her lashes fluttered like a flag waving in the breeze. She covered her mouth with one hand. "I don't know how I could have made that mistake."

Ruth Ann shifted in her seat, lips pursed.

Elias's voice strained through clenched teeth. "Keep your mind on the song, Rose. It's the same line you've already sung twice, dear." He reached into his jacket and retrieved a peppermint stick and handed it to Benjamin. "This should take care of her debt, Coulter."

"Much obliged." Benjamin broke the peppermint stick in half and popped one piece in his mouth.

Charlotte moved to the center of the room. "Let's take a break from Memories and Forfeits. Perhaps we can coax Maggie into playing carols while we enjoy the refreshments."

He stood and motioned toward the dining room. "Would you like a mince pie and cider, Ruth Ann?"

She nodded and extended her cup toward him. "Only cider, please. Thank you."

He patted her shoulder. "Stay here and enjoy your friends, I'll be back in a moment."

Ben placed two mince pies on the plate for himself. Spying some date cookies, he put a couple on the plate. Perhaps a different sweet could tempt her. He reached for the ladle resting against the side of the punch bowl. Dainty heels clicked on the wooden floor behind him.

"Would you be kind enough to pour me a cup of wassail, Mr. Coulter?"

Miss Martin's southern accent drizzled from her lips, slow and sweet, like molasses slathered on cornbread. Funny, he hadn't noticed that in the parlor.

Benjamin set his plate on the table. He'd be polite and pour her a drink, but that was it. He'd caught her both staring and smiling in his direction earlier. Perhaps he should be flattered, but he didn't want to give this young woman the wrong impression or embarrass Ruth Ann in front of her friends. "All right."

She smiled. "Thank you. Ruth Ann is a lucky woman to have a beau as attentive to her as you are."

Elias's voice rose over the group. "You can't be serious."

Benjamin craned his neck. "Who was he speaking to?"

Sighing, she glanced over her shoulder. "He appears interested in everyone else here tonight, except me."

If that was true, Elias was a fool. With blonde hair,

blue eyes, and skin the color of fresh cream, she was reminiscent of the porcelain doll in Turner's window. Any number of men, would line up to spend an evening with a woman like her. "Nonsense. He quickly paid your debt with a peppermint stick, remember?"

"Yes, but it should've been my choice..."

Elias's thundering voice pulled Benjamin's attention to the parlor for a second time. "You can't really believe that nonsense, Ruth Ann. Why must you constantly swim upstream?"

His six-foot frame towered over her. She stood toe to toe with him, chin lifted high in a show of will that Benjamin recognized all too well.

"Excuse me, Miss Martin." He shoved the drink in her hand, its contents perilously close to erupting over the cup's edge.

"They need a good education, Elias. Teaching Negroes the trades will encourage their independence from white land owners who want to force them into tenant labor."

Elias thrust his index finger in her direction. "I don't understand you anymore. You keep talking like that, and you'll have no friends left in this town."

Nate grasped his brother's arm. "Calm down, Elias. Charlotte and the ladies went to a lot of trouble to make this a nice evening for all of us, and you're being a pig-headed fool."

Elias wrenched his arm free, his jaw clenched as tight as his fists. "Stay out of this, little brother."

Benjamin approached the verbal sparring match as Ruth Ann's hands bolted to her hips. Slipping his arm in front of her, he gently nudged her backward, placing himself between the two. "What's the problem here?"

"The problem is women like her who don't know their place. You'd be best to keep your woman under control."

Her strained voice called over his shoulder. "Under con—"

With a slight shake of his head, Ruth Ann stopped short. "I don't need to control Ruth Ann. She's a bright young woman, entitled to her own opinions."

"No respectable white woman teaches darkies to read. It isn't proper, and you know it, Coulter."

"All this talk of being proper—since when is it proper for a gentleman to raise his voice to a lady?"

Ruth Ann entwined her fingers with Benjamin's, and he responded with a gentle squeeze of her hand.

"Get our things, Rose. We're leaving." Elias focused his stony, green gaze on Ruth Ann. "You may want to rethink your position. Some people in this town don't like what you're doing. And if you persist, it might cost you more than just Thornton's hand."

~*~

Ruth Ann's free hand flew to her mouth in a failed attempt to stifle a gasp. Elias had been her friend since childhood. How could he speak to her so?

Benjamin stepped forward, his nose mere inches from Elias. The two men locked eyes. Even though Benjamin had three inches on him, Elias didn't seem deterred. Her pulse skipped erratically through her veins making it difficult to breathe. Were they going to come to blows?

"I don't cotton to people threatening Ruth Ann."

Rose handed Elias his hat. He plopped it on his head and shoved his arms in his coat sleeves. "Then take it as a friendly suggestion."

"All right. Here's a friendly suggestion for you, Hamilton. Stay away from Ruth Ann, or you'll answer to me."

Elias exited the parlor. "Let's go, Rose."

Ruth Ann's fist pressed against her chest. What had just happened? How had an evening of singing and games transformed into a shouting match? Her eyes traveled the silent circle of friends. Tears threatened to spring down her cheeks. Charlotte had gone to such effort to make the evening enjoyable for all of them.

The crackling of embers shifted her attention to the hearth. Nate and Edward conversed in hushed tones. Were they upset with her, too?

She let out a breath. "Charlotte, I-I don't know what to say. I-I'm so sorry for ruining—"

"You did no such thing, Ruth Ann."

Nate laid the poker against the hearth. "My brother has always had a short fuse. Lately, it's shorter than ever."

Warmth drew her focus downward. Safe and secure, her hand rested in Benjamin's strength and confidence. What would she do without him? He'd proven himself her advocate and protector time and time again. Did he know he held her heart in the palm of his hand as well?

Edward slipped his arm around Maggie's waist. "Go on, Nate. You be the one to tell her."

Eyes wide, she chewed on her bottom lip. Was she destined to alienate all her friends?

"Edward and I want to join the safety patrols to protect the Freedmen's school."

She studied him for any sign of hesitation. "Nate,

you don't need to prove anything to me."

"I know, but I do need to prove something to myself. There comes a time in a man's life when he needs to stand up for what he believes in no matter the cost."

Knowing how Nate's family felt about her position at the Freedmen's School, she knew exactly what it might cost Nate—what it might cost all of them.

~*~

Ruth Ann climbed the stairs to the schoolhouse, stomping excess snow off her boots before entering the building. As she grabbed the latch to insert the key, the door creaked open. She pushed it again, this time with her foot, and peered inside.

"Captain Reynolds?" Perhaps he had come early to light the stove.

The room was empty.

Brrrr. She rubbed her gloved hands together before cupping her mouth and nose to warm them as she made her way to the stove in the center of the classroom. Frigid air blew the tendrils at the base of her neck, drawing her attention to a broken window. What on earth? A shiver ran down her spine as she examined the broken windowpane and the rock that lay beneath it. Where was Captain Reynolds?

Stepping around the glass, she made her way to the stove then started a fire. She retrieved the broom and dustpan from the closet and swept the floor. Footsteps pounded in the entryway. She swallowed a lump in her throat. *Please, Lord, let that be the captain.* She glanced around. Nothing but a broom to protect herself. Ruth Ann took a deep breath, closed her eyes, and raised the makeshift weapon high above her shoulder, all the while asking God to give her courage.

A familiar voice hung in the brisk air. "This brings back memories of our first meeting. You're not planning to pummel me with that are you?"

She lowered the stick, pressed her hand to her stomach, and slumped against the wall. "Certainly not."

"I'm sorry. I shouldn't tease." Benjamin held his arms wide. "Come here. You all right? You look a bit frightened."

She flung herself into his open arms. "I am now. Seeing this broken glass and with Captain Reynolds nowhere in sight, when I heard your boots on the steps I—"

"Shhh. It's all right, Ruthie. I'm here now."

He tightened his embrace, thawing not only her cold bones but her fear as well. "Captain Reynolds came by earlier to light the stove and found the broken window. He noticed some tracks in the snow he wanted to trail. He came back to the Petersons' and asked me to stay with you and the children until he returns."

"Thank you," she whispered.

Benjamin kissed her forehead and released her from his hold. "It's colder than a dead man's nose in here." Tiny white clouds trailed his words as he spoke. "Neil is going to the hardware store to have a piece of glass cut for the window. With any luck, we'll have it fixed today."

She swept the broken glass into a pile. "Mr. Martin isn't likely to sell him glass if he knows it's for the Freedmen's School."

Benjamin lifted a skeptical brow. "I doubt a

businessman would refuse a sale." He held the dustpan for her then dumped its contents into the bin by her desk.

"Believe that if you will, Ben, but neither Mr. Martin nor Rose has spoken a civil word to me since I started teaching here. She barely acknowledged me at Charlotte's party. Rose's older brother, Patrick, fought and died for the Confederacy at Antietam. She told Maggie that the renewal of my contract here was the last straw."

Benjamin lifted the rock from its resting place.

"Look, Ben. There's black paint on the side of it."

Their eyes met briefly before returning to the foreboding message. *February 1.*

She breathed deeply in a vain attempt to quell her anxious heart. *February first is only three weeks away.*

The door opened. Chatter and laughter filled the classroom.

Benjamin shoved the crude deterrent into Ruth Ann's satchel. "No need to worry the children with the message. The broken window is enough to explain." He gave her a quick peck on the cheek. "It's a normal school day." He tilted his head toward the rear of the classroom. "I'll be right over there."

She nodded.

"Please be seated boys and girls. Leave your coats on. A prankster decided to break one of our windows, so it's a bit chilly in here today."

The students gawked at the tall white man, adding kindling to the stove. "Class, this is Mr. Coulter. He helps me teach arithmetic to many of your parents and older siblings in the evenings. He is…uh…observing this morning."

Ruth Ann called the class to order, took

attendance, and then had the children recite the Lord's Prayer. Finding a sense of normalcy in the daily schedule, her pulse no longer raced out of control. The routine brought a measure of comfort, but not as much as the presence of the man in the back of the room. When her gaze lingered, the snickers of the older children brought Ruth Ann from her thoughts.

"We will begin our recitations now. Primary students, you may rise and walk to the recitation bench, please." The students filed from their row of desks to the bench perpendicular to her own in the front of the room.

Ruth Ann stooped and drew a chalk line on the floor about one foot in front of the bench where the children stood. "There. That shall do nicely." She brushed the white dust from her hands as she continued. "Remember, this assignment is not only about memorization but also elocution. Pronouncing words clearly and correctly is the mark of an educated person."

The children responded in unison, "Yes, Miss Sutton."

"Flossy, please recite the first stanza. Toe the mark when you are ready. Remember, Flossy, loud and clear."

The young girl stood, her booted foot aligned to the chalk streak on the floor. Chin down, her dark eyes concentrated on her hands, busily picking a string from her pocket.

"Flossy?"

The girl's head remained low, but her eyes met her teacher's.

"You can do this. I know you can."

"Yes'm." She lifted her head.

Ruth Ann straightened in her seat, squaring her shoulders.

Flossy mimicked her teacher and straightened her posture. "Doing right—"

Neil Peterson cleared his throat. "Sorry to interrupt, Miss Sutton, I need to speak with Benjamin for a moment."

~*~

Benjamin's boots crunched against the icy remnants clinging to the schoolhouse steps.

Captain Reynolds sat astride his bay mare in front of the building. "The tracks led to a farm a few miles north of town—the Hamilton family farm."

Doubt etched Neil's expression. "The Hamiltons?"

Benjamin thought it admirable that Neil tended to give everyone the benefit of the doubt, but now was not the time. Not with February first only weeks away. "You are probably correct where Nate Hamilton is concerned, but his older brother, Elias, can be a bit of a hot head. I've witnessed his anger firsthand."

Neil rubbed a gloved hand along the back of his neck. "I'll be the first one to acknowledge that Levi has strong opinions about Negroes that he's imposed upon his family. He was in favor of secession. That's public knowledge. But Nate, Elias, and Levi attended the community support meeting to organize safety patrols for the school."

Captain Reynolds reached inside his coat and pulled a piece of paper from his pocket. He scanned it quickly. "That may be, but so far none of the Hamiltons have volunteered for patrols."

"Nate told Ruth Ann and myself that he planned

to volunteer. Edward Simms as well." Benjamin shook his head. This was ripening into a real mess. How would he tell Ruth Ann that her friend and his father may be involved?

The captain patted his mount. "We'll need to talk with the Hamiltons."

"And the Martins," Benjamin added.

Neil's eyes narrowed. "What do the Martins have to do with anything?"

"Isn't Elias paying calls on Rose Martin?"

Neil nodded.

"Ruth Ann didn't think Mr. Martin would sell you the glass for repairs if he knew it was for the Freedmen's School." Benjamin took a quick glance around. "Where is it, Neil?"

"Martin said he was too busy to cut glass today."

Benjamin cocked his head, brows raised.

Neil rubbed the back of his neck. "So, you believe the Martins could be involved in this as well?"

"I think what Benjamin is saying is that since the tracks led to the Hamiltons, they need to be questioned. It only makes sense that their friends, who share similar views, should also be questioned." Captain Reynolds shifted on his horse as the mare foraged through the snow with her nose for anything green she could find. "I'd like one of you to go with me. I can do the questioning, but a witness is good, and there's safety in numbers."

Benjamin put his hand on Neil's shoulder. "I'll go. I'm not as friendly with the Hamiltons as you are."

"I appreciate that, Benjamin. Thank you."

"Can you repair the window and stay with Ruth Ann and her students while we're gone?"

Neil nodded.

"Good. When I go to the livery, I'll ask Joseph if he has some wood you can use to board up that window. I'll be back shortly." He paused. "Oh, I nearly forgot. The rock used to break the window had a message painted on it—February first."

Neil furrowed his brow. "What is that supposed to mean?"

Captain Reynolds straightened in his saddle. "It means we'd better root out this brood of vipers—the sooner, the better."

16

Ruth Ann shifted nervously. Her arrival in the railroad camp with Maggie and Charlotte had garnered more attention than desired. Several men, reeking of whisky and sweat, stood nearby, ogling them from head to toe. She should have known a rainy day such as this would keep the men in camp. Her gaze drifted over the sea of canvas tents stretched across the soggy meadow. How would she find Benjamin? She glanced at the ragtag bunch assembled nearby. Letting them know they were lost was not an option.

The door jingled behind them. A tall clean-shaven man emerged from the company store and telegraph office. He touched the brim of his hat. "Ladies."

He was there best hope. Who was she kidding? He was their best hope. "Good afternoon. Might you direct us to Benjamin Coulter's office?"

"My pleasure. Name's Sam Denning."

They dismounted the wagon, lifted their skirts from the mud caked road, and followed Mr. Denning to a large tent bearing the sign Surveyor and Engineer's Office.

"Boss, some ladies here to see you."

Benjamin stood behind a small wooden table, books and papers strewn about in haphazard fashion covered its surface. "Ruthie—" his attention flitted to Maggie and Charlotte. "What are you ladies doing here unescorted?"

Tugging her bottom lip between her teeth, Ruth Ann handed him a tin filled with cookies. "I brought you these."

He cocked his head, eyebrows raised.

"I know I could have given them to you tonight, but I was curious about where you work so I convinced Maggie and Charlotte to stop. We can't stay long. We're headed to Charlotte's."

"You didn't have any trouble from the men when you arrived?"

"Mr. Denning ushered us to you safe and sound as you can see."

Sam cleared his throat. "A few of the men were taking in the scenery, but they kept their distance."

"Thank you, Sam."

Sam nodded. "I sent the telegraph to Williams. I'll let you know the minute I get an answer from him." Sam disappeared between the folds of the tent.

Ruth Ann walked to the rear of Benjamin's makeshift office, passing several desks and bookshelves. Various types of equipment lined its canvas sides. She paused and examined an instrument with a miniaturized telescope mounted on a tripod, several knobs and gears of various sizes fastened to its sides. "I think I've seen a picture of this in father's Encyclopedia Britannica. Is it a theodolite?"

"You own a cloth-bound edition of the Encyclopedia Britannica?"

"Yes. No. I'm not sure what difference it makes, but its leather bound. Papa was a judge and a scholar. His library is filled with books." She tilted her head. "Haven't I shown you his study?"

Benjamin shook his head.

"I'll show you first thing tonight." She ran her

fingers over the apparatus. "So, am I correct?"

"Yes, but we refer to it as a transit."

"What's a transit?" Maggie covered her mouth to hide a yawn.

"It measures the horizontal and vertical angles of the earth. We use it to determine the best route to lay the track for the railroad."

Ruth Ann bent forward, aligning her eye with the telescope. "Fascinating."

Charlotte snickered. "That is the last thing I would call fascinating."

"Ruthie, would you like to take the equipment out when the weather warms up and learn how it works?"

She jerked upright. "Yes, I would."

Maggie rolled her eyes. "I'd rather pluck feathers from a chicken."

~*~

Benjamin laughed at Maggie's saucy remark. "All right, we'll do it one day this spring." He kissed Ruth Ann's cheek. "I'll see you ladies safely to your buggy and then I have some things to finish up here before a two o'clock meeting."

Benjamin pushed open the flap to his tent and let the women exit before him. He spied a herd of ruffians gathered around their carriage.

"What's going on here?"

"Nothin'," said one. "Jest bein' social is all."

"Back up. Make room for the ladies." Benjamin glanced past the men, hoping for a glimpse of Sam. "None of you louts should be within fifty feet of their buggy. And I don't want to hear any indignities either."

"Yes, sir, Mr. Coulter. We'll be on our best behavior."

Benjamin perused the rag-tag assembly, doubting their sincerity. He assisted each of the girls into the buggy and thanked Ruth Ann again for the cookies. "I'll see you later tonight for supper at half past six." Benjamin untied the reins and handed them to Charlotte. He put his fingers to his hat and nodded as the ladies departed.

The buggy was barely out of sight before the men started whooping and hollering.

A skinny fellow, not more than seventeen or eighteen, kicked a rock into the muddy path. "How'd you git them there ladies to come visit ya?"

John Tatem, a man from Benjamin's crew, pushed to the front of the crowd. "Which one are ya sparkin'?"

A tall blonde fellow Benjamin didn't know nudged the man beside him with his elbow. "I bet he's sweet on the one drivin'. She's the prettiest."

Giddy with excitement, the skinny lad piped in. "They're all pretty, even the plumper one."

The blonde man snickered. "But did you see the eyes the plump one gave him? She's after you, Mr. Coulter. Better watch out!"

Tatem slapped Benjamin on the back. "Boss, here, can do much better than her."

The skinny youngster smiled shyly. "I don't think she's all that bad. She's purty 'nough."

Benjamin waved his hat toward the muddy road, his voice gravelly. "That's enough fellas. Move it along. Those ladies deserve better than the likes of you drooling over them."

He returned to his tented office, took off his hat, and threw it on the table before flopping in his chair.

Opening the ledger, he reviewed his calculations for what seemed like the hundredth time. Heavier now, the water pelted against the canvas exterior. It had been raining on and off for days getting him way off schedule. Would it ever let up?

"I think we hit the nail on the head. The boss must like 'em mighty round in the hips and bosom."

"Nothin' wrong with that. Jest a little more to love!"

"Yeah and with those broad hips, she'll drop his babies like they were peanuts."

Benjamin slammed the ledger shut before shoving it toward the rear of the table. Even the rain showers couldn't drown out their merriment at his expense. Why did their buffoonery bother him? He'd been asking God to bring a wonderful woman into his life. One he could share his future with. God had answered his prayer in Ruth Ann. So why couldn't he shake the nagging hesitation regarding her figure? An even better question was what was he going to do about it?

~.*.~

Ruth Ann moved to the full-length mirror and gave her appearance one last check. She slid her hands over the slight bulge in her stomach. Her mother's words came from nowhere to invade her thoughts. *Gentlemen do not court and marry a woman who is plump and opinionated. They desire a woman who is a reflection of themselves and the image they want to convey to their contemporaries.* Ruth Ann sighed. "I hope it's good enough, Benjamin Coulter, because this is the best I can do."

Sarah placed her hand on Ruth Ann's shoulders.

She leaned forward, joining her sister's image in the looking glass. "You're stunning. Let's go downstairs. Benjamin will be here any minute and won't he be surprised when he doesn't have to wait on you."

Ruth Ann swatted her sister. "He doesn't usually have to wait on me."

Sarah cocked her head and placed her hands on her hips.

Ruth Ann smiled at her sister's posturing. "Besides, Maggie says it's good to make a man wait on you occasionally. She says it lets you know he thinks you're worth waiting for."

Sarah laughed. "Leave it to Maggie."

As Ruth Ann entered the parlor, her mother looked up from her embroidery. "You are positively striking, Ruth." Moisture glistened in the corner of Mama's eye.

Unaccustomed to seeing even the hint of a tear from her mother, Ruth Ann furrowed her brows. "What's wrong, Mama?"

"You have become such a lovely young woman. Your father would be so proud." Mama pulled a handkerchief from her sleeve and dabbed her eyes. "I do not always say it, I suppose, but I want you to know that I am very proud of you."

"Thank you, Mama." She squeezed her mother's shoulders then placed a kiss on top of her head.

Joseph slipped his arm around Sarah. "Seeing you dressed for a special evening with your beau has made us a bit nostalgic."

Sarah smiled. "You are no longer the young girl who dug worms in Mama's cutting garden to fish with Papa."

Joseph laughed. "Or spied on your sister and me

while I was sparkin' her on the porch swing."

Ruth Ann chuckled.

Mama looked up from her stitching. "Or refused to practice singing lessons, preferring instead to curl up with a book." Mama sighed and laid the wooden embroidery hoop on her lap. "Well, you may still be that girl."

"Mama, you're teary again."

Mama sniffled. "Nonsense."

Ruth Ann stooped in front of the fire to pet her sleeping dog. What had gotten into everyone?

The clock in the foyer chimed—half past six. Benjamin should be here any minute. She stood and placed her hand to her stomach to calm her jittery nerves. Her eyes glanced to the hearth. Memories of Benjamin's passionate kiss in front of a dilapidated fireplace a few weeks earlier spread through her like flames devouring dry kindling. She fanned her face and stepped away from the blaze, heat scorching through her veins.

Joseph reached for his pipe, resting on the mantel. "You're flushed, Ruth Ann. Are you feeling all right?"

She nodded. "I just got a little too warm by the fire."

~*~

Benjamin was running late. He had been looking forward to this evening with Ruth Ann the entire week. At least he had been before Tatem and the others had commented about her appearance. *They're all pretty, even the plumper one.* The sound of the men guffawing echoed inside his head. *Jest a little more to love.*

He raked his fingers through his hair as he looked in the mirror above the washstand. Blast it all. Why did it bother him what those ruffians at the railroad camp thought anyway? He sighed, tilted his head to the right, and eased the straight razor downward against his neck. After running the blade through the last path of foamy cream, he rinsed the blade in the basin before laying it on the washstand.

He'd never met a woman better suited for him. Ruth Ann was pretty, smart, kind, humble, and she possessed just enough spunk to keep his prideful tendencies in line. Her quiet confidence and inner strength resulted from a deep abiding faith in God that made him a better man just by being with her.

"What the blue blazes is your problem, Coulter? It's not as if she's ready for the circus sideshow. She is everything you ever wanted except for one little, measly thing, and you can't see past it." Benjamin's shoulders sagged as he wiped the remaining shaving cream from his face and neck. He hated to admit it, but her figure was becoming a problem. Although, he hadn't fretted about it when she sat on his lap in the kitchen. Unbidden memories flooded his mind—her unbound curls, the taste of her lips, and the heady scent of lavender. She had roused his passion that night, and he had wanted her—fuller curves and all.

Benjamin pulled his freshly pressed white shirt off the hook behind the door, slipped it on, and proceeded to slide the tiny pearl faced buttons through their corresponding buttonholes. Leaning forward, palms against the washstand, he took a long look at himself in the mirror. It wasn't about loving her or even desiring her. It was about what he really wanted—a woman on his arm who represented the culmination of all he'd labored to achieve. A woman so attractive, every man around would take notice of him, and for the first time in his life, he would be respected. Didn't he deserve that? He'd worked his way to the top, no longer the son of a poor dirt farmer. He would soon be a surveyor—all his dreams within his grasp.

Lifting his collar, Benjamin wrapped the thin, black tie around his neck. With a jut to his chin, his nimble fingers made quick work of tying the silky fabric into a bow. He buttoned his charcoal gray vest then stuffed his arms into the sleeves of his matching sack suit jacket and took one last glimpse in the mirror. The cloth was the finest he'd ever owned. A splurge, he'd bought it when he first called on Ruth Ann.

Benjamin reached into his pocket and removed his grandmother's pearl ring. His mother had given it to him during his visit home last year. He had no idea his mother possessed such a treasure. She relayed how his grandfather had won it in a poker game during the Mexican War. Benjamin remembered his mother pressing the ring into the palm of his hand.

This is the only inheritance I have fer ya. I've been hidin' it from yer Pa so he wouldn't hawk it fer whiskey money. When ya find the woman God has fer ya, a woman who loves ya second only to the Good Lord himself, ya give her this.

The ring should've gone to his sister since she was the only granddaughter, but ever-practical Alice had chosen a small cash dowry instead.

Benjamin closed the treasure in a tight fist. He'd planned to propose during dinner. However, after the ribbing he took earlier that afternoon, he would switch tracks and put the proposal in the stabling yard for now. Ruth Ann was entitled to a husband fully committed to her. One with no lingering doubts. He sighed and returned the ring to its green velvet bag. He cinched the golden strings closed and returned it to the top drawer of his bureau.

Oh, Ruthie, forgive me. I'm not the man you deserve—not yet anyway.

Plopping his bowler on his head, he grabbed his wool coat and headed for the front door. Stepping into the moonless night, he pulled the collar up to protect his neck from the cold, January wind. He contemplated his decision again as he walked. Just a bit more time. That was all he needed. Wasn't it?

As he passed the front of the Hampton Hotel, he paused under the gas lamps and noted the time on his pocket watch—6:40. He needed to hurry or they would be late for their reservation. The thought did nothing to improve his sour mood. As he stuffed the watch back in his coat pocket, a familiar voice drifted his direction.

"Hello, Mr. Coulter."

"Hello, Miss Martin, Mr. and Mrs. Martin."

"It's nice to see you again." Smoldering cornflower eyes latched onto his own. "I don't believe I've had the pleasure of your company since the Twelfth Night party."

Despite the chill in the air, Benjamin warmed. "I think you're right." He recalled the gathering at the Petersons' boardinghouse and the numerous smiles she so willingly bestowed upon him.

The deep timbre of Mr. Martin's voice interrupted his thoughts. "If you're dining alone tonight, you're welcome to join us for supper."

"Oh, well I have other…" Benjamin paused and glanced at Rose. "Won't Elias be joining your family tonight?"

Rose blinked. "Elias? No."

"I was under the impression you were stepping out with him, Miss Martin."

A delicate smile spread across her full lips. "Elias calls on me occasionally, but there is no understanding between us."

Benjamin rubbed the back of his neck. He should leave. Ruth Ann was expecting him. But lovely Rose was right here. Right now. Even though she wore a heavy wool coat, her trim feminine shape remained evident. With golden hair and bright blue eyes, she had a face and figure any man would desire.

"I'm afraid I must..." Tatem's words replayed in his mind. *Boss can do much better than her.* He glanced at Rose. She was no consolation prize—she was the blue ribbon.

Benjamin pulled in a deep, fortifying breath then offered Rose his arm. "If that invitation is still open, sir, I'd be happy to join your family for supper."

She arched a brow. "What about Ruth Ann?"

"I'm afraid Miss Sutton and I are to remain only friends."

Rose fluttered her lashes then slipped her hand into the crook of his elbow.

Benjamin's muscles flinched. He stared at her slender arm entwined with his. What was he doing? He loved Ruth Ann, didn't he? He'd never be able to forgive himself, but this was his chance. Maybe his last chance, and Rose was exactly the type of woman he wanted on his arm.

He led Rose up the stairs and held the door open for her and Mrs. Martin.

If only the men back at camp could see his dinner companion tonight—that would silence their laughter.

~*~

Ruth Ann attempted an air of confidence as she climbed the stairs to her room, but on the inside, her emotions roiled. More than an hour had passed since Benjamin said he would arrive to escort her to dinner. All the excitement and anticipation for their special evening had disappeared faster than the dogwood blossoms after a spring thunderstorm, leaving her physically and emotionally exhausted.

She slumped against her bed pillows. Sarah's words echoed in her thoughts. *If you love him as you say you do, then you owe it to him to believe only the best about him, and wait to hear his explanation.*

"You're right, Sarah."

Perhaps reading would take her mind off her troubles. Flipping open *Pride and Prejudice*, her eyes landed on Mr. Darcy's scathing pronouncement. 'She is tolerable, but not handsome enough to tempt me.' Ruth Ann flung the book toward the foot of the bed.

She didn't want to read anyway.

Grabbing the afghan her grandmother Sutton had crocheted for her, she nestled herself in the window seat. Pulling her knees up to her chest, she rested her head against the window frame. The wind moaned outside, mimicking the mournful ache within. She sighed. *Benjamin, where are you?* Folding her arms against the top of her knees, she bowed her head and did the only thing she knew how to do—cry out to her Heavenly Father—the only one who could calm her anxious spirit.

O Lord, You know why Benjamin didn't come tonight, even if I don't. Please watch over him and keep him safe. If he is ill, heal him. If he is injured, bring someone along to help him. If he is having second thoughts about our courtship, then may Your perfect will be done in our lives. Amen.

Buddy's incessant barking roused Ruth Ann from her slumber in the window seat. She yawned then kneaded her sore neck muscles. What in the world was he barking at this time of night? She opened the bedroom door and crept into the hall. Male voices drifted up the stairway.

"Do you have any idea what time it is, Benjamin? She's gone to bed—the entire house has gone to bed."

Ruth Ann lifted her skirts and made her way down the stairs. Her left hand trembled as it slid along the walnut banister.

Joseph raised the kerosene lamp. "You don't look ill or injured."

"No, sir. I'm fine."

Joseph straightened his shoulders, his voice strained. "Then why might I ask—"

The creak of the step under Ruth Ann's slippered foot gave Joseph pause.

"I'm awake, Joseph. I'd like to speak with Ben if you'll allow it."

He nodded, his green eyes boring into Benjamin. "Only briefly and you must remain in the parlor. Please keep your voices soft so you don't wake the others."

"Thank you," she whispered.

Joseph kissed her cheek then lit the gas lamps in the parlor. He sent one last, steely glance in Benjamin's direction. "I'll be in the kitchen."

Her eyes took his measure—no tender smile, no twinkling eyes. Despondency threatened to overwhelm her before she wrestled her emotions into submission.

"Hello, Ben."

Benjamin fidgeted with the hat he held in his hands. "You wore the dress."

"As you requested."

She waved her hand toward the settee, silently inviting him to sit. Taking the seat opposite him in her mother's wing back chair, she noticed his gray suit, slicked hair and the scent of bay rum and spice. He appeared dressed and ready for their engagement. Why hadn't he come? Her mouth dry as cotton, she licked her lips and swallowed. "Y-You're all right?"

Benjamin nodded.

"I'm glad." She pressed her palm to her chest. "I feared you had taken ill or become injured."

"I'm fine."

Her gaze drifted to Benjamin's bouncing knee before wandering upward. Furrowed brows and lips pressed into a hard, thin line characterized his features, a look she was unaccustomed to seeing on his handsome face. She scanned her memory trying to recall the events of the afternoon. Had she said or done anything that would cause him to be upset with her?

"I apologize for not arriving to take you to dinner this evening."

Her shoulders slouched, eyes focused on the lace ruffle adorning her sleeve. "You didn't forget?"

"No, I didn't forget."

~*~

Benjamin ran his fingers through his hair. "There is no easy way to say this, Ruthie, so I'm going to be direct." He sucked in a breath and swallowed hard, the words sticking to the back of his throat. "I was on my way here when I happened upon Rose Martin. Her family invited me to join them for supper, and I accepted."

The color drained from Ruth Ann's face. "Y-You had dinner with Rose? Tonight? W-Why would you do that?"

What could he say to explain the situation to her when he still grappled himself to make sense of what he'd done? "I...I don't know. I didn't plan it, Ruthie. It just happened."

Ruth Ann pushed herself from the chair and walked toward the window, her back to him. "Do you no longer love me, Ben?"

She got right to the point, as usual. Of course he loved her, but was that enough? He certainly couldn't tell her about the comments the men had made about her figure. That would be too unkind. But wasn't she better off without him anyway? He could never give her all that she was used to and certainly not what she deserved.

"I'm uncertain."

Her spine stiffened. "And do you wish to call on Rose?"

He owed her an answer but his mouth, too cowardly to form the words, remained silent.

"I see." She shifted to face him, steadying herself against the piano. "And Rose is agreeable?"

He nodded.

"Then there is nothing more to say."

What was the matter with him? Why couldn't he shut out the rest of the world and just love her the way he wanted to—the way she deserved to be loved? What he did know was that he alone was responsible for the woeful sadness that had replaced her usual joyful countenance. What could he do or say to ease her suffering?

"I enjoy your company enormously, Ruthie, and I hope you will allow me to remain your friend so we can discuss books and current events. And I still want to demonstrate the transit and other surveying equipment for you this spring."

Her lips thinned, then without warning, the back of her hand pressed against her mouth, muffling her cries. She looked away from him, but he noticed the gentle quake of her shoulders.

Don't cry, Ruthie. Please, don't cry.

"Ruthie, did you hear me? I'm hoping we can remain good friends so we can enjoy each other's company on occasion."

She shook her head repeatedly. "While I appreciate the sentiment behind your offer, I don't deem that appropriate under the circumstances." Still avoiding his gaze, her voice faltered. "I will...always treasure...the time we spent together...and I wish you...only the best." She brushed past him into the foyer and opened the door. "Good night, Mr. Coulter."

Mr. Coulter. No longer Ben. His name sounded cold and distant on her lips. He followed her into the foyer and grasped her hand. "Please consider what I said—about remaining friends?"

~*~

Friends. She liked the sound of that. If only it were possible. Whatever his feelings for her, she still loved him. Her heart wouldn't mend if Ben remained in her life even as a friend. She extracted her hand from his grip. "You need to leave."

"I'm sorry that I've hurt you, Ruthie. I'll never forgive myself." He kissed her cheek. "Good-bye."

Ruth Ann shut the door behind him. Shoulders heaving, her breath hitched as tears tumbled down her face. She pinched her eyes closed and clamped a hand over her mouth to squelch the aching sobs that wrenched from her lungs.

The floorboard in the foyer groaned. She blinked, clearing the moisture from her eyes. Joseph stood in the hallway, arms outstretched. Without hesitation, she flung herself against him and allowed the safety of his embrace to comfort her.

17

Puffy eyes and a swollen nose greeted Ruth Ann in the vanity looking glass. Despite her best efforts, she'd cried frequently throughout the day, finally seeking refuge in her room. It still didn't make any sense. Ben had seemed happy to see her and as eager for their dinner engagement as she'd been. What had gone so horribly wrong? A chance meeting with Rose Martin? Was that all it took for Benjamin's professed love to stray? Well if it was, then she was better off without him.

If she really believed that, then she wouldn't be moping around her room. She stroked Buddy's fur. At least he hadn't abandoned her. Sighing, she wrapped herself in her grandmother's afghan, its soft warmth providing comfort and strength.

Sarah prodded the bedroom door open with her elbow, placed a tray on the vanity, and immediately poured her sister a cup of tea.

"Thank you, Sarah. You're a godsend."

"Don't thank me yet." A brown bottle rested in her hand. "I've also brought the remedy. Mama's orders."

Ruth Ann crinkled her nose. "Laudanum?" She hated the bitter medicine and always tried to avoid it when Mama suggested it for relief of her monthly discomforts.

Pointing to the ceramic honey jar, Sarah grinned. "No need to fuss. I came prepared. Besides, what will your students think if you come to school with dark circles and swollen eyes?"

Ruth Ann lifted the lid off the golden sweetener. Raising the dripper over her cup, she allowed a liberal amount of honey to glide from its grooved edges. She swished the spoon through the steaming liquid, then sipped cautiously and shuddered. "Bleck."

Sarah nudged a warm cinnamon roll in Ruth Ann's direction. "You haven't eaten since noon yesterday."

Ruth Ann glanced at the offering. "Mama's orders?"

"No, but like me, she's worried about you."

"I'm not hungry."

Sarah pushed a stray curl behind her sister's ear. "I'll leave it just the same."

"Excuse me, ladies." Joseph stepped inside, his arms laden with firewood. "Amos and Myra have gone home for the evening."

"Thank you."

He placed several logs in the woodbin beside the fireplace. "I'll stoke the fire then carry Buddy outside one final time."

If her heartache over Benjamin wasn't bad enough, Buddy's sudden ailing health and inability to climb the stairs certainly provided no consolation.

Joseph scooped the dog into his arms. "We'll be back shortly."

Sarah reached for the doorknob. "Make sure you drink it all."

Ruth Ann lifted the cup to her mouth. "I will." She forced a smile. "I need the rest."

Tea in hand, the ping of sleet and ice against the house drew Ruth Ann to the window. Relieved to be alone once more, she leaned against the glass and shivered. Maggie's news that Ben had escorted Rose Martin to church earlier that morning still plagued her. Maggie had told her it was all she could do to keep Edward from pulverizing Ben when he'd assisted Rose into a rented buggy and drove her home. Unwelcome images of Rose Martin on Ben's arm flashed before her. What would she do when she came across Ben in town? Or worse, Ben and Rose together? Of course, her heart would mend, in time. But not yet. It was too soon.

The Lord is nigh unto them that are of a broken heart. She'd been repeating the verse Charlotte had shared all day, finally committing it to memory. Sipping the bitter tea, she pondered what it meant to be 'nigh unto the Lord.' She pictured God sitting beside her as Sarah had earlier that morning—gently rocking her and stroking her hair. Tears spilled from a well she thought long dry. "Be nigh unto me, Lord, for my heart is broken."

~*~

Benjamin sat at the Petersons' kitchen table dunking oatmeal cookies in lukewarm coffee. Sleet plinking against his bedroom window usually encouraged him to burrow down under the covers and slumber. But tonight, it taunted him.

He'd spent the entire afternoon in Rose's company. Mrs. Martin had insisted he join them for Sunday supper. Thrilled at first to get a nod of encouragement from her parents, the day had dragged on. Rose was pretty to look at but not much good at conversation. At least not the kind that didn't involve gossip. She and her mother criticized the attire of nearly every young woman at the morning service. Not to leave the men unscathed, she proceeded to disparage Elias in front of him as well. Is that how she would speak of him when they were not together? Though he didn't think the two ladies were fond of each other, he couldn't recall Ruth Ann ever saying an unkind word about Rose—or anyone for that matter.

He'd tried to change the subject several times, but Rose had never heard of *Twenty-Thousand Leagues under the Sea*. What's more, she didn't like to read—anything. Not even dime novels. She'd inquired about his work as a surveyor but yawned and stared out the window, leaving him convinced of her indifference. Truth was, he couldn't imagine enjoying himself more than the time he'd shared with Ruth Ann, reading Jules Verne together, teaching her to bake cookies, or assisting her at the Freedmen's School.

Rose was nothing like Ruth Ann. She might be soft and sweet like a French pastry on the outside, but inside—she was as stale and unappealing as week-old bread.

He was a fool. What had he done? Why did it matter what anyone else thought of Ruth Ann? Especially men that meant nothing to him.

O, God. Please heal whatever is broken in me, hindering me from sharing my life with her.

"May I join you?"

Lost in thought, he hadn't heard Neil enter the kitchen. He rocked back in his chair, lifting its front legs from the wood floor. "Sure."

Neil poured himself a cup of coffee and joined Benjamin at the table. "Some decisions are hard to live with."

Benjamin's head jerked. "You know?"

"I saw you with Miss Martin at church. How long have you fancied her?"

"Not long. I mean, I don't really fancy her. She's pretty, but she's not Ruth Ann." Benjamin lowered his chair. "I've made a huge mistake."

"This can be worked out, Benjamin. It may take time, but Ruth Ann will forgive you."

"I wish it were that simple. I love Ruth Ann, but I can't be with her—at least not right now."

Neil furrowed his brows.

Benjamin leaned forward, elbows on the table, his head resting in his hands. "I don't know how to explain it, and frankly, I'm ashamed to admit what I'm struggling with."

Neil grabbed the pot from the stove and refilled Benjamin's cup. "Well, there is plenty of coffee. Why don't you get whatever is bothering you off your chest?"

He raked his fingers through his hair. "I love Ruth Ann—enough that I had planned to give her my grandmother's ring when I proposed to her. I've had it all this time, and although I'm confident she is the woman God has chosen for me, I'm still hesitant."

"Marriage is a huge commitment, son. You are taking on the responsibility for another person. Not only their physical needs, but their spiritual ones." Neil reached for another cookie. "It's not unusual to be cautious."

"That's not the problem." His fingers strummed the table. Would Neil understand or think him a louse? His opinion couldn't be any worse than what he already thought of himself. He took a deep breath and forged ahead. "Her appearance is not what I desire physically in a wife."

Neil placed his mug on the red-checkered table covering. "You believe God is directing you to marry Ruth Ann, but you won't because you're not physically attracted to her—as a husband is attracted to his wife?"

"Yes. No. I don't know." He paused, dragging his hand across his face. "On Christmas Eve, I surprised her in the kitchen when she was rearranging her hair. You should have seen her, Neil." Benjamin closed his eyes, savoring the memory of holding Ruth Ann on his lap. "Mounds and mounds of the most beautiful curls I've ever laid eyes on. I could barely breathe let alone speak. "And when we kissed...it stirred—"

Neil held up his hand. "Yes, I can well imagine. It doesn't sound to me like you find her unattractive."

"It's not her face, Neil. It's...her figure."

Neil jerked the mug from his mouth, coffee sloshing over its edge. "Is that what you told her?"

"No, I told her I wanted to pursue Rose Martin."

"Well, let's be thankful you had the good sense to say that instead. For a moment, I feared you may be touched in the head."

Benjamin blew out a breath. "Most of the time I don't think on her fuller figure one bit. Then someone will remark that she's plump, and it dredges up memories I'd rather forget. Scornful mockery about everything from my overweight mother to my patched-up clothes or my drunken father. I've worked hard, Neil. I promised myself I'd end up better off than the way I was raised and that includes the type of woman I marry."

Neil lowered his chin and looked at him over the top of his spectacles. "You promised yourself?"

Benjamin shifted sideways in his chair to avoid Neil's scrutiny. "Yes. It's shameful to voice, but I won't settle for a woman who others mock and nobody else wants."

"What makes you think nobody else wants Ruth Ann? It's my understanding she refused a previous suitor."

He scoffed. James Thornton. The dandy that could give Ruth Ann everything money could buy.

Neil took a cookie and nudged the plate toward Benjamin. "So you don't want the woman God has chosen for you if she doesn't turn the heads of other men and make them envious of what you have—like a fine suit or an impressive stallion?"

Benjamin closed his eyes and pinched the bridge of his nose. "It sounds so horrible the way you say it, but I'm afraid if I marry Ruth Ann, I'll be heading down that same path—a path of ridicule and rejection instead of respect."

"Respect?" Neil wiped crumbs from his shirt. "Sounds more like you want them to envy you."

"No, of course not."

Neil raised a brow.

Benjamin fidgeted in his seat. He heard truth in Neil's words, yet part of him didn't want to settle for less than he wanted. Trouble was, he wanted Ruth Ann—or at least part of him did.

"It's deep within a man to seek the good opinion of his peers, his neighbors, his wife, and his family. But envy will only lead to jealousy, bitterness, and regret. Respect is earned through a man's character, not his possessions." Neil paused, locking eyes with Benjamin over the rim of his wire spectacles. "Nor his wife's appearance."

The flickering lamp light drew Benjamin's eyes from the older man's penetrating gaze. Truth crushed against his chest, constraining his breath. In a moment of weakness, he'd tossed aside the woman he loved to pursue a fleeting image of perfection. Why? So others would look upon him and covet what he had?

"I'm concerned this promise you've made to yourself not to marry a woman whose figure is less than perfect has become a vow—a vow whose strength has replaced the truth of scripture in your heart and committed you to a course of action you now regret."

Heat tinged Benjamin's skin from the inside. How could he have gotten everything so twisted?

Neil scooted closer. "God wants you to value His opinion above that of man and to judge others by their character, not their appearance."

"But how—"

"With a lot of hard work on your part. You willing?"

Benjamin nodded.

"Good. Let's meet next Sunday, following the noon meal." Neil opened his Bible and jotted several scriptures down on a piece of paper.

Benjamin scanned the list. He'd study the verses Neil had suggested. Hopefully, in time, they would change his heart. But what good would they do his relationship with Ruth Ann? Why would she ever consider him again after the way he'd treated her?

~*~

"Evening, Ruthie."

Ruth Ann flinched at the sound of his voice. What was he doing here? She glanced at Benjamin, her finger frozen in place where it pointed on the page. Her stomach flipped at the sight of him.

"I-I wasn't expecting to see you tonight, Mr. Coulter." Why had she stammered? It sounded odd to call him Mr. Coulter again after the intimate connection they had shared. What else could she do? She couldn't very well continue as if nothing had changed between them.

Benjamin removed his hat and stroked the wide felt brim between his fingers. "It's Tuesday night. We teach tonight. I came to the house for you, but Joseph informed me you'd already left. I didn't want to interrupt your class, so I waited until you'd finished."

Captain Reynolds acknowledged Benjamin with a nod of his head then erased the blackboards.

Ruth Ann bit her lip and glanced over her shoulder at the captain. He wasn't blatantly trying to eavesdrop, but he probably couldn't help but overhear them either. Her eyes rested on Benjamin again. "After our conversation Saturday, I had no reason to expect you this evening."

"I promised I'd help you teach arithmetic, and I intend to keep my promise."

Captain Reynolds moved to the stove in the middle of the room and banked the coals for the night. The sound of the metal poker grating against the woodstove brought a momentary distraction for Ruth Ann. It should be Benjamin banking the coals and erasing the blackboards. Why was this happening?

Fingers trembling, she shoved the record book and lesson outlines into her satchel. "I've made other arrangements, Mr. Coulter, but I appreciate your willingness to help my students."

The captain wiped his hand against the dark blue pant leg of his army uniform. "I'm going to bring in some wood for you, Miss Sutton. Then we should be leaving."

"Thank you, Captain. I'll be ready."

"I'd still like to help, Ruthie."

A cold chill scurried the length of her arms and legs. She'd rather drink two heaping teaspoons of castor oil than hear him call her Ruthie. The very sound of the endearment recalled moonlight conversations and tender kisses on her front porch.

"Please refer to me as Miss Sutton. As I said, Mr. Coulter, I have made other arrangements for the lessons, but I will need the arithmetic books to plan for Thursday's class. Would you please bring them by before school tomorrow?"

"I can do that, but you aren't having classes next Thursday are you? It's the first of February."

Ruth Ann didn't answer him. Instead, she concentrated on packing her satchel, careful not to meet his gaze. She picked up her cape. He attempted to assist her, but she stepped backward out of his reach.

"Ruthie?"

She fastened the last button on her cape as cold vibrations spread down her spine. Fingers splayed wide, she pulled on one glove then the other.

His posture stiffened along with his tone. "Ruthie. Answer me. Are you holding classes on February first?"

The continued use of the sweet nickname grated on her nerves. She wasn't a child, and she didn't owe him any answers. Lifting her head, she glared at her former beau. "Please refer to me as Miss Sutton."

Benjamin winced.

"As for February first, the decision hasn't been made yet, but I'm in favor of holding classes, if you must know."

"You are in favor of it?" He raked his fingers through his hair. "You are the most obstinate, bull-headed woman I've ever known. It's way too dangerous, Miss Sutton." He grabbed her by the elbow. "I forbid it."

"You forbid it?" Her jaw tightened as she struggled to maintain a ladylike tone. "You have no right to tell me what to do, Mr. Coulter. You gave up that right when you decided to step out with Rose Martin. I am no longer your concern." She lowered her gaze to where he held her elbow and then lifted her eyes to meet his again. "Now, please unhand me."

Benjamin released her. Shifting away from her, he scraped his hand across the stubble shadowing his cheeks.

Captain Reynolds finished stacking the firewood along the back wall. He cleared his throat and motioned for Benjamin to follow him.

Benjamin extended his arm, pointing his hat in Ruth Ann's direction. "We're not finished with this conversation."

Ruth Ann rolled her eyes and flopped in her desk chair. He made her so fuming mad she was sure smoke must be coming out her ears. Why had he come anyway? If he wanted to pursue Rose Martin, why wasn't he doing just that?

~*~

Benjamin slapped his hat on his head and stomped down the steps of the schoolhouse, icy snow crunching beneath his boots. She had to be the most headstrong, hard-headed woman God had ever made. Surely, Captain Reynolds would not allow the school to be open on February first. He wouldn't be able to sleep a wink between now and then if he didn't get some reassurance.

He followed John on the partially shoveled path that led to the main road. "Ruth Ann seems to think she will be teaching next Thursday, John. She doesn't understand how dangerous it could be. Please tell me you aren't in agreement."

"No, I'm not in favor of it. However, Miss Sutton seems quite determined. As you know, she is a stubborn woman."

He smirked. "You don't know the half of it." If this kept up, he'd have a sour stomach for sure.

"There's been another note, Benjamin, and security patrols found fresh foot and hoofprints near the woodshed. We've identified the redhaired man. His name is Frank Bender, but he's not talking. We've arranged for extra patrols, especially for the evening classes." The captain placed his hand on Benjamin's shoulder. "She and her students will be well protected."

Benjamin's stomach churned. Did Malachi sell sodium bicarbonate by the pound? "What about February first, John?"

"Since she'll fight me, I'm going to make an announcement at the end of class next Tuesday evening. The students will hear it and stay home."

He didn't envy Captain Reynolds. Benjamin envisioned Ruth Ann's ivory complexion veering into a lovely shade of crimson and her soft brown eyes hardening to stone. "She's not gonna like it."

The captain nodded. "Well, I'm not here to be her friend. I'm here to keep her safe."

"I want in, John. When Ruth Ann is teaching in the

evenings, I want to be here. What about her home? Is anyone watching it?"

"Only Joseph. We don't have the manpower."

"I'll do it. Every night if necessary." Why not? He wouldn't be able to sleep anyway.

Captain Reynolds stroked his beard. "All right, Benjamin, we can use all the help we can get. I don't plan to inform Miss Sutton you're part of the team unless she asks me directly. I need her to do what I tell her and not give me any excuses."

The uneasiness in Benjamin's gut subsided. Ruth Ann had no idea how much she meant to him. It had only taken one afternoon with Rose to realize the mistake he'd made.

Benjamin extended his hand. "I guess you'll be seeing her safely home?"

He nodded. "She's safe with me."

"Thanks. I'll be here Thursday night."

"Report to the smithy shack for your watch. The man before you will alert you to any suspicious activity." Captain Reynolds headed for the stairs then paused. "Benjamin. Bring your gun."

18

Ruth Ann placed her satchel on the floor near the Petersons' door. "Hello, Captain Reynolds has brought me for a visit."

"Come on in," Mrs. Peterson called. Charlotte and I are in the kitchen."

Her stomach growled as the smell of warm bread wafted into the Petersons' spacious parlor, reminding her that she'd barely eaten in the last few days. At Myra's insistence, she'd taken a hard-boiled egg, cheese, and a few soda crackers with her to school, but she had no appetite. Instead, she'd given her fare to Sadie Houser who'd forgotten her lunch and accepted Ruth Ann's offering with a gracious smile.

Anticipating the taste of melted butter on warm bread, the delicious yeasty scent enticed Ruth Ann to quicken her pace. She deftly unbuttoned her cape, laid it on the back of Mrs. Peterson's rocking chair, and made her way to the kitchen. Relieved that Benjamin would be working until supper, she'd be able to enjoy her visit with Charlotte without fear of seeing him. The thought of another encounter like the one at school last evening made her growling stomach turn suddenly queasy.

Having never mastered the art of hiding her emotions, she plastered what she hoped was a convincing smile on her face. "Good day, Charlotte. Mrs. Peterson. It smells wonderful in here."

"I do love baking day." Trudy Peterson paused

and wiped her hands on her apron. Tiny lines creased her forehead. "Are you all right? You look a bit pale, dear."

"I'm fine." She worried her bottom lip. "You aren't expecting Benjamin any time soon are you?"

Mrs. Peterson pushed the handle on the kitchen pump twice then washed her hands at the sink. "It's hard to say. His hours vary, but we don't usually see him for about another hour or so." She yanked on the middle drawer of her red corner cabinet. "Remind me, Charlotte, to have your uncle...fix...this drawer." Finally freeing the drawer from its recess, she removed the large bread knife and set to work cutting thick slices from a loaf of brown bread cooling on the counter.

"You may have the first piece."

Ruth Ann tore off a piece of crust and popped it in her mouth. Closing her eyes, she savored the warm, fluffy treat. "Mmm, tastes like heaven itself, Mrs. Peterson. Thank you."

Charlotte placed a ball of dough into one of the many greased loaf pans on the counter. "Have you seen Benjamin since Saturday night?"

Ruth Ann peeked in the captain's direction. She appreciated his attentiveness to her, but she had no intention of discussing Benjamin with him seated at the table. She lifted a cautious brow when their eyes met.

Gathering his newspaper and pipe, Captain Reynolds stood. "If you'll excuse me, ladies, I'd prefer to read my newspaper by the fire if you don't mind."

"Just one minute, John." Mrs. Peterson handed him a piece slathered with apple butter. "Just the way you like it."

He smiled and nodded his appreciation.

Ruth Ann traced a knot in the bench beside her while she waited for Captain Reynolds to retire to the parlor. She leaned forward making certain he wouldn't overhear their conversation. Satisfied, she faced Charlotte and her mother. "Benjamin came by the school last evening. He thought he was going to teach arithmetic with me. I told him he was no longer needed." She squared her shoulders. "I'll do it myself before I let him help me."

Charlotte glanced at her mother.

Mrs. Peterson placed her hand on Ruth Ann's shoulder. "Kneading dough is a wonderful way to work through the trials and sufferings of life. Would you like to help us?"

"Thank you. I think I will." Ruth Ann stood and rolled up her sleeves before sprinkling flour on her section of the table. She grabbed a huge chunk of bread dough and got to work. Pressing her hands deep into the dough, she folded it over and over again. Leaning forward, she pressed her full body weight into the flour mixture. "Myra says her bread tastes best when she and Amos are having words."

Mrs. Peterson laughed. "I suppose that's true."

"When Benjamin discovered that we may still hold classes on February first, he looked me straight in the eye and said he forbade it."

Charlotte grabbed another chunk of dough and placed it on the table. "He still has feelings for you. I'm sure of it."

Ruth Ann pressed her eyes closed. Ben didn't want her. He wanted Rose. She brushed her temple with the back of her flour-covered hand. That woman attracted men like hummingbirds to larkspur.

"What's done is done. He made his choice, and I'm

allowed to make mine—without interference from him." Ruth Ann placed her dough into a greased loaf pan then peered out the Petersons' kitchen window. Rain splattered against the glass. How fitting. The weather seemed to match her dismal disposition.

Mrs. Peterson separated another chunk of dough and placed it on the table for Ruth Ann. "Maybe, with God's help, he'll work out what's gnawing at him on the inside and come back for you a much-improved man."

Ruth Ann returned to the table. "That's not likely. Not with Rose Martin on his arm." She pressed her weight into the new ball of dough, massaging it with her palm. Flipping it over, she squeezed the mixture firmly, watching it squish between her fingers. "I'm not holding out for that, Mrs. Peterson."

Charlotte covered the dough-filled loaf pans with a red and white checked kitchen cloth. "I know you're angry with him, but you can't allow your heart to grow bitter."

Ruth Ann glanced from Charlotte to her aunt before smacking the dough.

Charlotte took a deep breath. "The Bible tells us to pray for those who have wronged us, even if we don't feel like it. The discipline of obedience will change your heart from anger to forgiveness."

She folded the dough in half. "What if I don't want to forgive him, Charlotte? What has he done to deserve it?"

"Absolutely nothing."

She wiped her brow with her forearm. "Benjamin broke my heart, and I have to forgive him?"

Charlotte met Ruth Ann's gaze and nodded. "While Christ hung on the cross He asked His Father to forgive those who crucified Him."

Her shoulders slumped. Charlotte was right, but she didn't like it. She pounded her fist into the mixture several times. *Fine.* She'd ask God to help her forgive Benjamin, but hopefully, someone would talk to him about seeking forgiveness as well.

Mrs. Peterson gently grasped Ruth Ann's wrist. "All right, Ruth Ann, that dough you're…uhh…kneading is ready for the loaf pan."

Ruth Ann winced. "Sorry, Mrs. Peterson, I shouldn't have pummeled it."

"No problem. Why don't you wash up and make us some tea?"

Ruth Ann cleaned up, set the water to boil then went in search of the tea. Mrs. Peterson whispered as she stepped from the larder, tins in hand.

"You've got to ask her, Charlotte."

"Ask me what?"

Mrs. Peterson locked eyes with her niece and nodded encouragingly.

Charlotte patted the space next to her on the wooden bench. Ruth Ann placed the tea on the table and took a seat between Charlotte and her aunt.

"Aunt Trudy and I have been praying for you frequently the past few days and each time we pray, I have this nagging feeling something bad may happen to you."

Her eyes narrowed. "Something bad? I assure you, whether at home or at school, day or night, I am never alone. I'm always well protected."

"It has nothing to do with the Freedmen's School." Charlotte placed her hand on Ruth Ann's arm. "The danger is from your own hand."

Ruth Ann's head drew back slightly. Her lips

parted, eyes blinking rapidly. "From my own hand? Are you suggesting I might hurt myself—intentionally?"

Charlotte slid her hand across Ruth Ann's palm until their fingers knitted together. "While Aunt Trudy and I were praying yesterday, I felt this overwhelming sense of sadness and loss. Then I saw your face, and you were dead."

She sucked in a breath then quickly covered her mouth. "I would...never—"

Charlotte kept her eyes trained on Ruth Ann's as if she were searching them for any hint her friend harbored harmful thoughts.

Mrs. Peterson's flour-covered hand rested on Ruth Ann's shoulder. "All right then, we are going to pray for your protection."

The seriousness of Mrs. Peterson's voice unnerved Ruth Ann. She was a quiet woman with the heart of a warrior when it came to prayer, much like her niece. Ruth Ann looked to Charlotte and nodded. "I don't understand any of this, but since I have no desire to harm myself for any reason, then yes, let's pray against it."

Ruth Ann and Charlotte bowed their heads.

"Lord, we ask Your protection over Ruth Ann. May she know deep down in her heart that her value rests in being Your daughter, not in the fleeting opinion of man. Put Your angels around her and keep her safe. Ruth Ann is Your child, Lord, and Satan has no hold on her. Amen."

The tea kettle whistled as Charlotte and Ruth Ann said amen.

Charlotte rose quickly. "I'll get it."

The gentle pitter-pat of the rain against the kitchen

window soothed Ruth Ann. She removed a handkerchief from her sleeve and wiped her nose. The information Charlotte shared should've left her fearful and overwhelmed. Instead, peace prevailed, wrapping her snug like her grandmother's afghan had done so many times lately.

Mrs. Peterson put her arm around Ruth Ann, her eyes intense. "You are welcome here anytime, Ruth Ann, no matter the time of day or night."

She was as at home in the Petersons' kitchen as she was in her own. "Thank you."

Mrs. Peterson kissed Ruth Ann on the cheek. "How about a nice cup of tea?"

Men's voices drifted from the parlor—Benjamin.

"No, thank you, ma'am. I'd better be going now. Mama will be expecting me for supper soon." Ruth Ann hugged Charlotte and walked with Mrs. Peterson to the parlor.

Benjamin stopped mid-sentence when she entered the room. "Ruthie. I didn't know you were here."

Too busy concentrating on preventing her wobbly knees from buckling, she managed to nod in his direction. Why couldn't he remember to call her Miss Sutton? And why did he have to look so handsome? The rain had dampened his hair, and a few curls appeared at the base of his neck. She had never noticed that before.

Benjamin reached for her cape. "Can I walk you home?"

Walk me home? Not likely anytime soon. Hadn't he broken her heart only days ago to pursue another woman? "No, thank you, Mr. Coulter." She glanced at Captain Reynolds. "I have an escort."

Benjamin scowled in the captain's direction then

plucked her satchel from the floor and offered it to her. "I don't mind. The captain can stay here."

She shook her head then closed her eyes briefly. "It's better this way."

~*~

Benjamin's stomach roiled. What was taking so long? He hadn't been this nervous standing outside the Suttons' front door since he'd first called on Ruth Ann. Seeing her leave church earlier that morning with Captain Reynolds had unnerved him. Where was her family? Maybe he was growing paranoid or perhaps he didn't want to leave Captain Reynolds as Ruth Ann's sole protector. It was bad enough he escorted her on his arm everywhere she went, but now he'd volunteered to teach the adult classes with her. Fate was putting them together entirely too much for Benjamin's liking. He lifted the brass knocker a second time and swallowed hard. Would she listen to him? Could he persuade her to wait for him?

The door creaked open, and Captain Reynolds offered his hand. "Benjamin, nice to see you today."

Great. He's here now? Answering her door? "Hello, John." Benjamin firmly grasped the captain's hand. "I've come to see Ruth Ann."

"Follow me. Miss Sutton is in the parlor."

Benjamin scanned the spacious room. Captain Reynolds and Ruth Ann alone—fire blazing in the hearth, newspaper, book, and coffee mugs on the side tables. For the love of Pete, the man was even smoking his pipe. John had become a bigger threat than he'd realized.

He wiped sweaty palms against his pant legs as

his eyes locked on Ruth Ann. "May I speak with you, Ruthie?" His head tilted toward the dining room. "It will only take a few minutes."

Her fiery gaze shot flaming arrows in his direction. "I'm not sure that's a good idea, Mr. Coulter."

"Please, Ru—uh, Miss Sutton. There are some things I'd like to discuss with you."

Captain Reynolds gathered his pipe and newspaper. "I'll wait in the kitchen."

"Nonsense, Captain. Enjoy your paper by the fire."

The smile she had given John vanished when her attention shifted to Benjamin. "Mr. Coulter won't be staying long. He can speak to me in the kitchen while I ready the soup for our meal." She pivoted and walked briskly through the dining room.

Feeling like a pup, Benjamin followed on her heels.

Ruth Ann lifted the apron loop over her head then tied its strings behind her back. Grunting, she lifted the cast iron pot onto the work table. She eyed Benjamin. "What did you want to speak to me about?"

He glanced around the kitchen. "Where's your family? I noticed they weren't with you at services this morning."

"They've gone to Oak Hill to visit Joseph's family." She removed a large jar from the icebox and set it beside the pot.

"You didn't wish to join them?"

"No, I preferred to stay here."

Benjamin's fingers skimmed the brim of his hat. "With Captain Reynolds?"

"No, not with Captain Reynolds. I have lessons to plan and the outing to Middleburg will bring them home after supper. And I haven't been the best company of late." She gripped the jar lid with a damp rag and twisted with all her might. "Is this...what you wanted...to discuss...with...me?" Ruth Ann straightened, apparently frustrated that her efforts hadn't opened the container.

Benjamin reached for the soup. "Let me help you with that."

She slid the jar away. "I can manage."

He leaned forward and swiped the container from her hold. "Like you managed at the creek the day I met you? When are you going to learn not to refuse my assistance?" With little effort, he loosened the lid and pushed the jar in her direction.

Her gaze flitted to the soup before zeroing in on his face. "Why exactly are you here, Mr. Coulter? I thought you wanted to pursue Rose?"

"I'm concerned about the unprofessional manner Captain Reynolds has taken in protecting you."

Her eyes narrowed.

"Maggie says he has been 'very attentive.'"

"Maggie is a dear friend. She's just trying to get your dander up."

He scraped his jaw. "From the looks of the cozy scene inside your parlor, she's right. Since when is it required of him to read his newspaper and smoke his pipe in your home? Shouldn't he be out patrolling the grounds or questioning suspicious people?"

She blew out a breath and poured soup into the pot before placing it on the stove.

Benjamin paced the short distance between the ice box and the dry sink. "The captain escorts you about town on his arm as if he is courting you rather than protecting you."

"The captain offers his arm because that shows courtesy to me. In truth, it felt a little awkward at first."

"But not anymore?"

She shrugged.

He stopped abruptly and waggled his hat in her direction. "He's nearly twice your age. Have you forgotten me so quickly, Miss Sutton?"

She squared her shoulders. "I'm not the one who stepped out with Rose Martin."

He slapped his hat against his thigh. "Rose Martin. Rose Martin. Will I never hear the end of that name? There's nothing between Rose and me, but apparently the same cannot be said for you and the captain."

Fisted hands landed on her hips. "There is no understanding between Captain Reynolds and myself other than that he is here to protect the children and me from harm. He has been a perfect gentleman."

Ruth Ann returned to the stove and stirred the soup. She glanced over her shoulder. "Why weren't you sitting with Rose in church this morning?"

Benjamin sighed. "As I said, there is nothing between us. She's not what I want."

~*~

Ruth Ann's voice caught in her throat. "W-what do you want?"

In an instant he was behind her, his chest brushing against her back. "You."

The spoon slipped from Ruth Ann's grasp and clanked against the iron pot before slipping beneath the golden broth. Shivers rolled over her skin, racing behind his fingers as they traced the length of her arm. She should step away from his reach. Unable to fight the desire for his touch, she faced him instead.

His thumb caressed her cheek. "I've never stopped loving you, Ruthie."

Her insides quivered at the sight of his honey-colored eyes, his words nourishing her desiccated heart. She was willing to try and mend fences if he was.

"I've never stopped loving you either, Ben."

He took her hand in his before lifting it to his lips. "Please understand how it pains me to say this, but we can't be together just yet."

The quick tightening in her chest matched the brisk fluttering of her eyelids. What had he said? Her eyes darted from the coffee grinder to the handle of the ice box, before pairing with his. "I don't understand. If you love me as you say, why can't we be together?"

He reached for her hand again, but she stepped away from him.

"I can't say, not yet. I need you to trust me, Ruthie. I need you to wait for me."

"Wait for you?" Emotions reeling from his contradictory declarations, she leaned against the kitchen chair, needing its strength to remain on her feet. "Is this a game to you, Ben?"

He shook his head.

She rested her fingers on parted lips. "You stirred hope of reconciliation with your pronouncements of love. Then you ask me to wait for you without any explanation?" Frustration simmered below the surface as she balled her fists. She swerved abruptly to face him. "Tell me why. I'm entitled to know what's troubling you."

"You're right, but I can't say. Trust me. It's better left unspoken." He grasped her by the arms. "Wait for me to get my heart right with God—for me to be the husband you deserve."

Ruth Ann searched his eyes. Husband? "We've never spoken of marriage."

"I've wanted to marry you for a long time, but—"

She'd heard enough. Wiggling free of his hold, she jabbed her finger in his chest. "You don't love me, Benjamin. If you loved me, you'd want to be with me—now. Nothing would keep us apart." She pointed toward the swinging doors. "You need to leave."

"Blast it all, Ruthie." He raked his fingers through his hair. "All right, you want to know what's keeping us apart?"

"I have a right to know."

"You're not gonna like it."

She folded her arms tight to her chest, her foot tapping briskly beneath her skirts. "Maybe not, but I can't fix what I don't know is broken."

He shook his head. "Ruthie, you've done nothing wrong. The fault—the problem is entirely my own." He forced a breath and continued, "This is hard for me to say, so please bear with me." He motioned toward the table. "Let's sit."

Anxious to uncover the problem, she nodded and eased into the chair beside him.

Taking her hands in his, he stroked them with his thumbs. He took a deep breath, pausing as the air slowly escaped his lungs. "I love you, Ruthie. I love your inquisitive nature and the way you tap your pencil against your cheek when you're thinking. I love your stubborn streak and that you stand up for what you believe. I love that we can talk about anything or nothing and it's equally wonderful." His eyes lingered on her face. "I love your curly hair, your dark brown eyes, and the smell of your lavender dusting powder."

She squeezed his hand. "Just say it, Ben."

"My issue is with your form."

Her eyes narrowed. "My form?"

The words tumbled from his lips. "You are broad through the shoulders and hips, and your waist is thicker than I prefer." Pressing his eyes closed, he lowered his head. "I'm sorry, Ruthie."

Her breath hitched. This couldn't be happening. Not now. Not after all the time they'd spent together. An eerie groan wrenched from her lungs. She swayed to the left. Benjamin reached out a hand to steady her. He continued talking, but she couldn't make sense of his words. Eyes pinched closed, she shook her head. Pressing one hand against her stomach, she covered her mouth with the palm of the other. Suddenly her corset was two sizes too small.

"Did you hear me, Ruthie? I said I'm sorry. I've been praying for the Lord to heal whatever is broken in me that such a trivial thing would keep me from marrying the woman I love."

Ire quickly replaced all reason as the meaning of his words settled in her heart. She lunged at Benjamin, sending him and his chair careening to the floor. Leaning over him, her fists pummeled his chest as liberated tendrils bounced and swayed with a fury of their own.

Tears spilled down her cheeks. "I believed you when you professed your love for me."

Boots thundered in the dining room, rattling the china in the corner hutch.

Eyes wide as saucers, Benjamin grabbed her wrists, fending off her angry attack.

She struggled to free herself from his grip and

injure him like he'd wounded her, if only he'd let go. "I gave you my heart, and you threw it away."

"I didn't want to hurt you this way. I'm going to become the man you deserve—a man we both can respect, and then I'll be back for you."

Her body went limp in his grasp. Exhausted from the maelstrom of emotions Benjamin's confession evoked, she reclined on her heels. "Don't bother coming back, Benjamin. You don't know how to love."

The swinging doors whooshed open, banging against the icebox. "What the Sam Hill is goin' on in here?" Captain Reynolds grasped Ruth Ann's elbow and tugged her to her feet. "You all right?"

Despite her quivering shoulders, she nodded. "Mr. Coulter was just leaving."

19

Too ashamed to look at Captain Reynolds, Ruth Ann lifted her skirts and brushed past him. She scurried through the swinging doors and disappeared upstairs.

His voice trailed after her. "Are you all right, Miss Sutton?"

Ruth Ann flung open her bedroom door then slammed it quickly behind her. She tugged on the apron strings before yanking it over her head. Catching on her hair, it loosened another pin, freeing more curls from her bun. She flopped in the window seat and buried her face in her hands. *Benjamin loves me but doesn't want me, and James wants me, only if he can change me.* The only man who had ever truly loved her in the unconditional way she hungered for was no longer around to fill the deep void inside her. *Oh, Papa.*

Stomach churning, she dove for the washstand and wretched in the basin. She wiped her mouth on a cloth and looked at her red, swollen face in the mirror. Fighting the urge to wretch again, she crumpled to the floor and sobbed, her arms cradling her head. Her mother's words pressed in all around her. *No man will ever want to marry you...* Mama had repeated them frequently enough. Just fill in the blank with one of Ruth Ann's *obvious flaws*—her stubborn streak, her opinionated nature, or her robust figure. Sarah had tried to put a favorable twist on Mama's words, saying she meant that Ruth Ann was healthy and vigorous.

But deep down she knew her mother meant she was built strong and sturdy like a ship—the S.S. Ruth Ann.

She had gone to Doc Rawlings once, without Mama knowing about it. With gentle eyes and a hand to her shoulder, he'd told her she had a larger frame than most women. She could lose ten to fifteen pounds if she wanted to but no more. Doc had indicated that her broad hips would be a blessing when it came to childbearing. She'd turned five shades of red at his pronouncement. He'd assured her she was healthy but would never be petite like her mother and sister. She was big-boned—a workhorse, not a filly.

A knock on the door briefly interrupted her thoughts. "Miss Sutton, I brought your soup."

She pulled the handkerchief from her sleeve and wiped her eyes. Had Captain Reynolds overheard her conversation with Ben? Mortified, she brought her knees closer to her chest and covered her mouth, hoping he wouldn't hear her muffled cries.

He knocked louder this time. "Miss Sutton, are you all right? I'll leave the tray in the hallway. If you need anything, I'll be in the parlor."

His footsteps faded on the stairs, and she allowed pent up sobs to escape her lungs. Her shoulders quaked. Would any man ever love her unconditionally? She wanted a home and family of her own—a man to love her as Joseph loved Sarah. She placed her hands on her ears but nothing seemed to drown out the sound of her mother's words. *Young gentlemen do not court and marry women who are plump and opinionated. A gentleman wants to step out with a woman other men will envy.* No one would envy her. She was undesirable and unlovable.

Ruth Ann sat up and leaned against her bed. The

word *unlovable* resounded in her mind. It wasn't exactly the word her mother had used, but that is what she'd meant. The sum total of her entire being wrapped up in two words—plump and opinionated, neither of them good.

Although it was the middle of the day, darkness engulfed her, pressing against her chest like a lead weight. The slightest breath difficult. A chill bristled her. Her skin prickled. She glanced to the window. Closed. She rubbed her arms and rested on her heels. A cold, raspy voice hissed in her ears.

Unworthy of love…unworthy of love…

The toxic phrase echoed in her thoughts, taunting her.

What was the point of her life if everything else came down to that? She was unlovable. Ruth Ann moved to her knees and rummaged through her vanity drawer. Then she found it, way in the back. Shoving her hairbrush aside, she retrieved the bottle of laudanum Sarah had given her to alleviate her headache.

The container was more than three-quarters full.

She twisted the cap and brought the brown bottle to her lips. Thoughts of tasting the bitter liquid made her stomach heave.

Drink it. You will fall asleep and never wake up. It will be so easy.

Heart hammering in her chest, she stared at the bottle. Shaky fingers stroked the smooth brown glass. It would be easy.

No man will ever love an ugly, round, stubborn, opinionated woman such as yourself.

There it was. The truth she'd spent her entire life avoiding. She couldn't deny it any longer. Not after

Benjamin. Tired of never being good enough, she tilted the container and took a swig. Shuddering, she wiped her mouth on her sleeve.

Good. Now, do it again. Nobody loves you. Nobody will ever love you. You're undesirable and unworthy of love...unworthy of love... unworthy of love...

The reproachful words became an unholy refrain, speaking death to her weary soul. She eyed the bottle. Could she do it?

The voice grew more desperate. *Just drink it.*

Reclining on her heels, she clutched the bottle to her chest. Head tipped back, a mournful plea extricated itself. "Oh, God, why can't anyone love me the way I am?"

I love you.

She paused, the bottle halfway to her mouth.

I made you in My image, and I do not make mistakes. You are worthy of love.

But which voice to trust? As much as she wanted to believe she was worthy of love, there wasn't much proof of that. Ben's words assailed her. *You are broad through the shoulders and hips, and your waist is thicker than I prefer.* How could she have been so foolish? Only appearances mattered. On that score, she failed miserably.

You're undesirable and unworthy of love...unworthy of love...

Still grasping the laudanum, she swayed back and forth as thoughts of gulping the bitter liquid returned. "God where are you?"

I am here child. With you, always. I love you unconditionally, in a way no man ever could.

His voice draped her in love and affirmation, like her grandmother's afghan on a cold winter's night.

I sent My son to die for you so that you would have abundant life on earth and eternal life with Me after death. Do you remember?

"Yes. I remember." The preacher expounded many times on the unconditional love of God. He'd told the congregation that God had chosen us before we ever chose Him by sending His Son to die on the cross for us and that God loved us in spite of our sin. She gasped. He loved her, Ruth Ann Sutton, fully—even the stubborn, selfish, opinionated inner parts of her. Even with her less than attractive figure. Maintaining her white-knuckled grasp, she lowered the laudanum to her lap.

"If He loves me unconditionally and He made me in His image, then He must love me in spite of my form."

I do not regret making you. I do not look upon you as man does. I look upon your heart and what I see is beautiful. You are worthy. You are worthy of My love.

How could she have forgotten? How had Mama or Ben's opinion of her appearance become more important than the Lord's? She was one of His works, and He found her marvelous. What had she almost done? She returned the cap to the bottle and shoved it away. Covering her eyes, she wept.

She remained silent before God, relieved the cold, raspy voice had left her. All the tension drained from her muscles as her pulse flowed serenely through her veins. Light and carefree, she imagined herself as a cattail blowing in the breeze along the creek bank.

Exhausted, she crawled into bed, cradling her Bible. How had she become so deceived? She reflected on her mother's words—words she had chewed on repeatedly over the years. Although her mother could be harsh at times, she had never said that Ruth Ann was unlovable or undesirable—those phrases she'd chosen for herself. She'd twisted her mother's words into something completely different in her mind. Dwelling on the unholy phrases until they became her excuse for everything that didn't work out in her life the way she wanted. Phrases that had reshaped the image she saw in the mirror until her reflection no longer held value in her own eyes.

"Oh, God, please forgive my stubborn and rebellious heart. Please forgive me for denying the truth of scripture that says I am fearfully and wonderfully made, and that You find me marvelous!"

Her thoughts flashed to Benjamin and his declaration that her figure was unpleasing. Poor Ben. Bound by opinions and perceptions of the world, he was unable to see the heart of the woman who loved him desperately because the wrapping on the gift was not to his liking.

Ruth Ann swiped at one remaining tear before rolling over, her Bible snuggled close to her heart. She'd nearly made an irreversible decision tonight, but the voice of truth had spoken and silenced that of the Great Deceiver.

~*~

Benjamin sat in the Petersons' kitchen, his Bible open. It had been nearly a week since his careless words had devastated Ruth Ann. How could he have been so reckless?

Elbows spread wide across the table, his head rested in his upright arms. He'd read the verse Neil jotted down for him several times, but like many things in life, it seemed easier said than done. *Casting down imaginations, and every high thing that exalteth itself against the knowledge of God, and bringing into captivity every thought to the obedience of Christ.* If he knew how to take his thoughts captive, he wouldn't be in such a mess. Why had he let jealousy and desperation trick him into telling Ruth Ann he had an issue with her figure?

The more he thought about it, the more he realized he wasn't any better than Marcy. He'd been so angry when she'd rejected him for a man who made more money than he did. His character or temperament didn't matter to her. It all came down to something shallow and superficial. Wasn't that what he'd done to Ruth Ann? She loved him despite the differences in their social standings, but he'd reduced their relationship down to her appearance—something shallow and superficial.

"A-hem." Neil cleared his throat as he leaned against the entryway to the kitchen. "How's the study coming?"

Benjamin glanced at Neil before returning his gaze to the open Bible in front of him. "Not good."

"You look glum."

"Thanks."

"Mind if I join you?"

Benjamin pushed a chair away from the table with his foot. "Perhaps you can help me make sense of these verses I'm reading."

Neil moved to the stove and refreshed his coffee. He took a mug from the shelf and poured one for Benjamin before joining him at the table. Hooking his wire spectacles over his ears, Neil leaned forward and glanced at Benjamin's Bible. "Which verse are you having trouble with?"

Benjamin lowered the coffee mug from his mouth and sighed. "This one in 2 Corinthians. I don't understand what it means to take thoughts captive to Christ. I've tried not to dwell on the negative comments of others about Ruth Ann's figure. When I've had disparaging thoughts, I've chastised myself, but they keep coming back." He set his mug on the table and placed his head in his hands again, his fingers kneading his hair. "I miss her so much, Neil, it hurts. I start thinking about everything I love about her, about myself when I'm with her and then, out of nowhere, some unfavorable remark by one of the men lunges to the surface, and I feel defeated all over again." Benjamin's voice cracked as he fought to keep his emotions under control. "I'm not worthy of her, Neil, yet I don't know how I can live without her."

Neil reached forward and put his hand on Benjamin's arm. "Taking thoughts captive doesn't mean we never have that thought again. It means when controlling thoughts enter our mind, we denounce it and replace it with truth from Scripture...every time."

Benjamin shook his head in his hands. "I hear what you're saying, Neil, but it's like I've built this strong fortress around myself, and I can't break free."

Neil placed his mug on the table and scooted his chair closer to Benjamin. "You couldn't be more correct. The vow you've made to yourself about marrying a woman who other men would envy has formed that strong fortress you mentioned. But replacing those negative thoughts about her fuller curves and what other men will think of you for being with a woman who is less than perfect, with the truth from His word and prayer is how you break free." He arched a bushy brow for added emphasis. "Lots of prayer."

Drumming his fingers on the table, he eyed Neil cautiously. The path his friend suggested wouldn't be easy.

"First, you change the way you think and that, son, will change the way you feel. Do you still have that list of verses I gave you?"

He flipped his Bible to the front and pulled the sheet of paper from inside its leather cover.

Neil unfolded the paper and smoothed out the creases. Coffee stains dotted the list and the bottom right corner had ripped off. He dipped his chin and peered at Benjamin over the rim of his spectacles. "I'm glad to see you've been studying these verses. Now, which one of these do you feel most applies to your situation with Ruth Ann?"

Glancing at the list of verses, Benjamin pointed to Proverbs 31:30 before strumming his fingers idly on the table again. "Favour is deceitful, and beauty is vain: but a woman that feareth the Lord, she shall be praised."

Neil briefly covered Benjamin's restless hand. "Excellent choice. As soon as the disparaging thought comes to mind, denounce it. Then pray and recite this verse, repeatedly reminding yourself that this is how God sees Ruth Ann. Ask Him to give you His eyes where she is concerned." Neil peered over his spectacles. "What about pride and envy? Which verses speak to your heart about those issues?"

Benjamin pressed his lips into a thin line, choking back the emotion the verse brought forth in his heart. "The one from Proverbs fourteen, "A sound heart is the life of the flesh: but envy the rottenness of the bones." Benjamin's shoulders slumped as he shook his head. "That's me—rotten inside, full of pride and more desirous of man's blessing than that of the God I profess to love."

Neil's lips inched upward.

"What are you so happy about, Neil?" The sharp edge of frustration had returned to Benjamin's voice. "I'm miserable."

"Yes, you are, son." He slapped Benjamin on the shoulders, his slight grin stretching into a broad smile. "Praise God. The first step to healing is a contrite and broken spirit." He rocked back in his chair, front legs off the floor. "Once we are broken, then God can refashion us in His image. So just like we talked about a few moments ago, you need to pray specifically for God to purge this need you have to win the approval of men so your heart will be pure before Him."

Benjamin's fingers strummed against the white table covering. "You believe this will work?" Skepticism rang in his words.

Neil stared at Benjamin's fingers.

He followed Neil's gaze. "Sorry." He reached for his coffee mug to busy his idle hands.

"Absolutely. God has never failed me yet, and He won't fail you either. He wants to heal us so we can live lives of joy and blessing. He doesn't want to see us enslaved to Satan's lies."

"All right, I'll try this." Benjamin gritted his teeth and swallowed the emotion that fought to erupt from within. "Will you pray with me?"

"I'd be honored." Neil leaned forward, gently returning all four chair legs to the floor. He nodded and placed his hand on Benjamin's shoulder.

"Lord, I come before you with a broken and contrite heart. Forgive me of my sin and foolishness—my pride and arrogance. I only desire Your approval, God. Give me a sound heart, Father, and heal the rottenness in my bones. Amen."

He glanced at Neil. This man was more of a father to him than his own—at least in the spiritual sense. Where would he be without Neil? "Thanks."

"I love you like my own son." He slapped Benjamin on the back. "Now be vigilant. Temptations will come. Satan won't want you to experience the fullness of freedom in Christ and all the blessings God has in store for you."

"I will."

"Good." Neil retrieved the blue crock from the hutch. After removing the lid, he offered it to Benjamin. "Oatmeal raisin."

He removed two cookies and set them beside his mug. "Do you think Ruth Ann will forgive me?"

Neil searched Benjamin's eyes. "I think she will—in time."

Benjamin smiled, relief flooding his beleaguered heart as he dunked the baked treat in his coffee.

Neil stood, pushing his chair under the table. "But forgiveness doesn't necessarily mean your relationship will be restored, Benjamin."

The cookie slipped from Benjamin's fingers into his mug. Coffee sloshed over the rim onto Mrs. Peterson's crocheted tablecloth. "But why would God have us go through all of this if we aren't to marry?"

Neil's eyes softened. He leaned forward against the back of the chair. "I don't pretend to know the will of God, and I'm not saying you won't ever marry Ruth Ann, but God will have to heal her heart, too. She will need to walk in obedience and trust you again if you're to marry."

The momentary peace after praying with Neil disappeared as quickly as it had arrived. He couldn't imagine his life without Ruth Ann in it. "But I'm confident God told me Ruth Ann would be my wife."

"Then pray fervently for her as well, Benjamin, that she would be healed, too."

Benjamin's eyes narrowed. "Neil, is there something you're not telling me about Ruth Ann. You said she needed to be healed, too. What did you mean by that?"

Neil sat again, straddling his chair. He took a sip of coffee and paused. "I may be breaking a confidence in telling you this, Benjamin, but I think it's important for you to understand the spiritual battle that's going on here—a battle not only for your hearts and souls, but for Ruth Ann's life."

Benjamin sat up straight in his chair. "What are you talking about?"

"Charlotte and Trudy have prayed with Ruth Ann several times in the last week. After you told her about your issue with her figure, she came close to swallowing an entire bottle of laudanum."

"W-what?" Benjamin scrambled to comprehend Neil's words. "W-why would she do such a thing?"

"Just as you have spoken lies to yourself, others have done the same to Ruth Ann. Falsehoods she internalized and twisted in her mind. Untruths that distorted the reflection she saw in the mirror and prevented her from seeing herself as God does."

"What lies?"

Neil held up his hand. "I'm not sure I should say any more."

Images of Ruth Ann drinking laudanum plagued Benjamin's thoughts. He jumped to his feet, nearly knocking his chair backward. Slapping his hand on the table, more coffee spilled from his mug onto the already stained tablecloth. "Blast it all, Neil, you know I love her. Tell me what lies you're talking about."

"She'd been told her figure would keep her from attracting suitors."

Benjamin remained standing, his hands spread across the table. "What else?"

Neil angled his head, studying Benjamin over the rim of his glasses.

"Please, Neil."

He pressed his lips together firmly and shook his head. "She was told gentlemen only want to court and marry women that other men will envy."

"Oh no." Benjamin closed his eyes and flopped in his seat. "This can't be."

Neil lowered his chair to the floor. "In her mind, she twisted that to mean no man would ever love her, so when…"

"So when I told her that I had issues with her fuller curves, my words poured salt in a tender wound." Benjamin winced as he recalled Ruth Ann's eerie gasps and gut-wrenching sobs as his foolishly cruel words penetrated her heart. "What have I done, Neil? I nearly killed the woman I love."

Neil patted the younger man's hand. "She's fine. She barely drank enough to rest from her tears and the headache that followed them. Ruth Ann chose to live. She's doing much the same as you are these days— taking those destructive thoughts captive and praying for a new self-image in Christ."

"She'll hate me, Neil—forever." Benjamin hung his

head, unable to control his emotions again. "Why would God do this?"

Neil rubbed Benjamin's shoulder. "Regardless of how your relationship with Ruth Ann unfolds, each of you needed purging of these lies if you are ever to give and receive love unconditionally in marriage—to anyone. Hopefully, God in His infinite mercy will choose to mend your relationship. But if not, it will serve His greater purpose—each of you having a more abundant life in Christ."

"But that's not enough, Neil." Benjamin's faint voice seeped with desperation.

Neil stood and gathered the dishes. "It may have to be. But we'll add praying for contentedness to our list."

Benjamin tucked the list of verses inside his Bible's leather cover. No longer able to contain the brokenness inside, he called to his friend. "Neil..."

Neil tugged him into a tight hold. "It's going to be fine, son. Remember, God promises us that He will turn those things Satan intends for our detriment into blessings if we allow Him to have full reign over our hearts and minds.

Benjamin clung tight to Neil, and with one heavy sigh, released all his doubts and fears to His God.

Your will be done, Lord.

20

Benjamin chucked a few pieces of wood into the pot-bellied stove that heated the smithy shack. He peered through the window. A dark, moonless night awaited him. The wind howled, rattling the glass inside the sash. He slid the coffeepot forward so there would be a hot drink to warm him when he returned from his rounds then shrugged into his wool coat. Pulling his collar up against the back of his neck, he plunged into the cold—gun in one hand, lantern in the other.

Snowflakes driven by the relentless wind stung his cheeks as he inspected the perimeter of the schoolhouse. Faint voices drifted from inside. February first had passed without incident. Captain Reynolds had given permission for evening classes to resume, but Benjamin wasn't convinced the threat had diminished.

They were biding their time.

Progressing to the wood shack, he examined the frozen ground. Boot prints. He glanced at the school. Should he inform the captain? His eyes flitted back to the imprints in the snow. He'd investigate a little further before raising the alarm. Nate and Edward held positions in the brush beyond the tree line on the northern and western sides of the building. He'd check in with them on this round.

The tracks continued to the well. His boot kicked something hard. He lowered the lantern—a whiskey bottle.

An owl hooted.

He jerked upright, blood pounding in his veins. *Stay calm and focus.* Ruthie depended on him, even if she didn't know it.

Fighting against the wind, Benjamin followed the snowy trail to the privy. The prints stopped in front of the door. Were the impressions a sign of danger or merely one of the men from class who'd taken a swig of booze on his way to the outhouse? He bent on one knee and once again examined the ground. Raising the lantern, no boot prints returned in the direction of the school. He inched forward and found another set of fresh tracks joining those he'd been following. Benjamin scooped a small mound of packed snow in his palm and raised it to his nose. The crisp smell of snow mingled with whiskey and...kerosene.

Horses whinnied.

The wind whipped around the outbuildings and trees, but he was certain the sound hadn't come from the direction of the smithy. He flattened himself against the side of the privy and slowly cocked the hammer on his revolver. Breathlessly he waited, listening for sounds of horses or men moving in the brush. A dim light moved beyond the thick stand of pines—Nate.

Snowflakes clung to his lashes, obscuring his view. Easing around the corner of the outhouse, he peered into darkness, straining to see. He ran across the open yard toward the light and the cover of brush.

"Nate? It's Benjamin."

Between the gusting wind and the pounding in his chest, Benjamin couldn't hear any response. He continued moving along the perimeter calling for Nate.

Then he saw it again.

The dim light flickered a few hundred feet away, off to his left this time. Was it his imagination, or had he become confused in the darkness? An uneasiness settled in his gut. He glanced over his right shoulder. Nothing. Again, he called for Nate with no response. A cold prickle catapulted from the nape of his neck to the tips of his fingers. Something was awry.

Enough stalling. It was time to alert Captain Reynolds. But what if he was wrong? What if he'd merely become disoriented? He'd look a fool. His gaze darted to the schoolhouse. Ruthie was inside. His pride no longer mattered. If he'd learned anything these past few weeks, it was the necessity of taming that beast. Selfish pride made him turn away from the only woman he'd ever truly loved. He would not allow it to jeopardize her safety as well.

Committed to his choice of action, Benjamin barreled along the tree line until he was even with the rear of the schoolhouse. Leaving the cover of the tall timbers, he charged toward the building and the protection it would afford. Multiple lights glowed through the woods on the opposite side of the school, halting Benjamin mid-stride. The eerie wail of a wounded animal pierced the night air. Men on horseback charged from the trees, torches in hand. Their faces covered with white flour sacks, two holes cut for their eyes. A half dozen more joined the assault on foot.

"Captain!" Benjamin raised his revolver in the air and fired a single shot before a punishing blow to his back dropped him to his knees. A second strike across his shoulders knocked him forward onto his palms. Throbbing pain pulsated through every muscle between his neck and his waist. He groaned and lifted his chin, eyes honing in on the school. Had the captain heard his warning?

"Ooooof." A stiff boot connected with his gut, flipping him over, forcing the air from his lungs.

"Ruthie." Gasping for breath, Benjamin's voice fell flat, no match against the wind. Wincing, he grunted as he forced himself off the frozen schoolyard. He had to get inside. Had to protect her.

Once upright, he lunged at his attacker, sending them both crashing to the ground. Benjamin scrambled on top of his assailant and pinned him down. He raised his fist, ready to return some of the punishment the man had inflicted.

Gunfire rang in his ears.

Searing heat punctured his shoulder.

He listed sideways then descended into darkness.

~*~

A cold shiver coursed over Ruth Ann as the spine-chilling cry echoed on the wind.

Captain Reynolds ran to the window and shoved the curtain aside.

Ruth Ann hurried beside him. Men and horses moved in the night. Bright lights bounced in the darkness—torches. Even the strong wind couldn't mask the distinct crack of gunfire. Her knees wobbled like Myra's peach jelly, and she bit back the impulse to scream.

The captain grabbed his revolver from its holster and spun to face the others. "We're under attack!" With decisive urgency, he barked a series of commands.

"Francis, ring the bell! We need more men from town! Isaac, give him cover."

"Miss Sutton, stay with me!"

"Everybody out! Men first, take your stand! Women, head for the trees!"

Gunfire erupted.

Bea's eyes bulged from their sockets. "They's gonna kill us."

Women stampeded toward the rear exit, knocking over benches, sliding on slates and books that littered the floor.

The bell tolled, pleading in the darkness for men to join their defense.

Captain Reynolds grabbed Ruth Ann's arm. "Come on. Let's get you to safety."

Bullets pierced the window.

"Get down!"

Ruth Ann dropped to the floor, covering her head as broken glass sprayed overhead.

Using his elbow, the captain knocked out the remaining glass from the pane then fired his weapon. "Is everyone else out?"

She lifted her head just enough to glance around the classroom. "I think so."

Staying low, the captain hugged the wall as he made his way to the rear door. He motioned for Ruth Ann to join him. "Stay close behind me. When I tell you, run for the trees. I'll give you cover. Don't look back and don't stop until you make it to the creek. I'll follow if I can."

She nodded and drew close behind the captain. Gun raised, he opened the door and peered outside.

Crack!

The captain stumbled backward, knocking her off-balance. Blood oozed from a hole in his side as he slid to the floor.

"You're—"

He kicked the door closed with his foot. "Shove the chair under the knob! Now!"

She grabbed the chair and did as instructed.

He lifted his finger to his lips and shook his head.

"Come on out, Captain. We know you're in there."

The pounding in Ruth Ann's chest matched the heavy fists pummeling the door. How would they escape? She snapped her attention toward the front door. Why wasn't the bell ringing? Her eyes darted to the captain.

He grunted and leaned forward. "Get under your desk. Do you have the knife?"

She instinctively slid her hand to the garter strapped to her calf. "Yes."

"Good. I have to keep that bell ringing. Stay put until I, or someone you know, comes for you. Do you understand me?"

She nodded and watched as he crawled along the wall beneath the windows. "Be careful," she whispered.

He looked back and motioned for her to get underneath the desk.

Knees to her chest, Ruth Ann crammed herself into the tiny space. She retrieved the knife from its sheath and held it between her trembling hands. Closing her eyes, she rehearsed the captain's instructions.

Thrust the blade upward, swiftly, as hard as you can. You'll only get one chance.

One chance. *Lord protect us—*

Glass shattered.

~*~

Benjamin groaned and lifted his head, his body slumped against a wagon wheel. His breathing labored, he forced air in and out of his lungs. How had he gotten here? The stink of blood and gun powder permeated the air. Prickly heat radiated through his shoulder and down the length of his arm leaving his right hand numb. He opened and closed his fist several times before shaking his wrist. He'd be of no use in this dogfight if he couldn't hold a weapon.

Vigilantes whooped and hollered. "This is what happens to darkie lovers!"

He jerked as a rifle fired above his head.

Edward squatted beside him. "You're awake. How's your shoulder?"

"Feels like it's on fire. Where's Ruth Ann?"

"Not certain, most likely hiding in the woods. Captain Reynolds emptied the school after your warning shot. The women headed toward the creek. A couple hoods followed them. I'm hoping Nate can take them. He's still out there."

Gritting his teeth, Benjamin compelled himself upright and leaned against the sideboard. He tenderly examined his side and flinched. A couple broken ribs would certainly explain the nagging, pinching pain. Instinctively, his good hand remained at his side, as if it offered some measure of protection.

Edward eyed him. "You sure you can stand?"

"I'll be...fine." The words, more strained than he would've liked, didn't sound convincing to his own ears. He scanned the schoolyard littered with bodies. Dead or injured? How had this happened? They'd been patrolling for weeks and watching both the

Hamilton and Hench farms.

"Why isn't the bell ringing?"

Edward lined up his sights and fired then removed shells from his coat pocket and reloaded. "Ringer and his cover's been shot. Probably killed."

With unsteady fingers, Benjamin checked his gun and added three rounds to his Yellow Boy repeater.

"I'm trying to keep those men by the steps from entering the school. Someone's firing from inside. One of the hoods just fell."

Benjamin flipped the chamber closed and leaned the rifle against the wagon wheel. "Inside? That must be Captain Reynolds. You got an extra weapon?"

Edward reached inside his coat, retrieved a small revolver, and offered it to Benjamin. "It's loaded."

He gripped the handle, moaning as he shoved the weapon in his rear waistband. "Give me cover."

"Where are you going?"

"Through the back door."

Edward took another shot. "Are you crazy?"

"Yeah, about a certain stubborn brunette."

Edward crouched behind the wagon bed. "You could get yourself killed, and you don't even know if Ruth Ann's in there."

"There's a good chance the captain kept her close-by, and I have to know she's safe."

Armed riders from town galloped into the fray. "Reinforcements. This is my chance."

Grunting, Benjamin hopped over the wagon's tongue. Still clutching his ribs, he trudged toward the schoolhouse moving slower than anticipated. Each step laborious, as if shackled to a cannon ball. A bullet whizzed by his left ear. He ducked for the slight protection afforded by a large tree. Bracing himself against its thick trunk, he raised his rifle. When had it gotten so heavy? He aimed at the masked rider and fired a couple rounds. The man set his sights on Benjamin and returned the volley. Benjamin took a deep breath and aimed again, this time finding his mark. The vigilante fell from his horse, his foot tangled in the stirrup. His horse bucked then lurched forward, dragging his rider away from the maelstrom.

The schoolhouse now stood only a few feet away. Benjamin surged forward, praying Ruthie had escaped with the other women. Tripping over a tree root, his body hit the frozen ground with a thud, jarring the rifle from his grip. Propelled by his feet, he thrust himself forward, blindly searching for his weapon. Agonizing pain rippled through his bruised and broken ribs with each stretch of his arm. Maybe he should just let it go. He needed to get inside, and he still had Edward's revolver.

Clamping his eyes shut, he shoved himself off the ground. Hands resting on his knees, he gasped for breath, wincing as his lungs labored.

Breaking glass drew his attention to the schoolhouse.

Orange light flickered inside.

Where was Ruthie?

~*~

Ruth Ann unfolded her limbs and crawled from beneath the desk. She peered into the classroom. Books and papers strewn on the floor shriveled beneath a kerosene soaked torch. Stuffing the knife in her skirt pocket, she sprang to her feet. She grabbed the water bucket beneath the chalkboard and doused the fire.

A second flaming torch burst inside the schoolhouse. She shrieked as shards of glass pricked her cheeks. She inspected her face. Blood stained her fingertips.

Abandoned coats caught fire.

She glanced at the bucket. Empty.

Fire leapt from coats to books and back again like children playing hopscotch in the schoolyard. Her heart thundered in her throat, leaving her breathless and confused. Her gaze hastened to the barricaded door. Should she leave or stay as the captain directed? What fate awaited her out there? If she stayed, what could she use to put out the flames? She needed to make a decision and commit herself to it. Her gaze landed on her cape draped across her desk. She grabbed the woolen garment and beat the flames feeding on the remnants of her once orderly classroom.

Heat kissed her ankles...her skirt.

Dropping to the floor, she rolled over broken glass, smothering the flames.

Red binding caught her eye. Mr. Turner's generous donation lay beneath a water soaked torch. The dictionary's gold leaf pages, singed black. Her fingers traced its charred leather cover. Maybe she could salvage it.

Flames hugged wooden benches in the corner of the room. She covered her mouth and coughed. Heart racing, her attention darted between the two exits. Where was Captain Reynolds?

Ruth Ann waved her hand frantically in front of her face, attempting to clear the thin veil of smoke hanging in the air. She had to get out before the entire building was ablaze. Clutching the dictionary in her left arm, she aimed for the nearest exit.

Gasping, she teetered to a halt.

Three hooded men blocked her path.

She willed her trembling knees not to buckle.

The taller of three took charge. "Go tell 'em we found her. Tell Bender to bring the horses 'round back. And shove those burning benches toward the front doors. With any luck, that will slow any rescue party."

Hair bristled on the nape of her neck.

Silas Hench. She scurried backward, but the other masked intruder blocked her retreat.

Silas chuckled as he tapped his club-like weapon against his palm. "Ain't nowhere to go, teacher." He stepped forward, pinning her against a blackboard. "No need to be afraid. We're here to be social. You're gonna be our special guest at a shindig in your honor." He nodded at his cohort. "Toss the place with kerosene. On my word, burn it to the ground."

His partner raised the firkin and removed its lid. "My pleasure."

An icy shiver ran its course over her quaking limbs. There was something familiar about that voice, too. She stared at the disguised man. Angry, green eyes engaged her own. But who? She couldn't imagine anyone she knew, besides Silas, being involved in something like this.

His thumb grazed her cheek. "We'll have to tend this at the barn. Can't have our prize bloody and bruised."

She swatted his hand away. "Don't touch me."

Silas dropped his club then yanked the dictionary from her hand and flung it across the room. He grabbed her chin and pressed her firmly against the blackboard. Through jagged eyeholes, his gaze burned with rage. "We're gonna teach you what happens to disrespectful, darkie-lovin' white women 'round here." Hatred spewed from his lips.

She slid her hand inside her pocket and grasped the smooth handle of her concealed weapon.

You'll only get one chance.

Her grip tightened. This was it. Now or never.

Yanking the knife from her pocket, she thrust it upward into his ribs.

He gasped and staggered backward.

Side-stepping his wavering form, she bolted toward freedom.

Thick hands circled her waist, pulling her down. Her body crashed into a desk, then slammed to the floor.

The unknown assailant grabbed her wrists and yanked her to a sitting position.

Silas knelt close-by, blood seeping between the fingers pressed against his shirt. "We can do this the hard way or the easy way. Makes no never mind to me."

Chest heaving, defiance surged through her veins. "I won't do anything to make it easy for you."

"Hard way it is." He nodded at his accomplice.

With lightning speed, the man's calloused hand struck her cheek.

Her head wrenched sideways. Throbbing pain burst across her jawline as liberated tendrils fell across her face. If ever there was a time to keep her mouth shut, this was it, but she could no more contain her tongue than a raging river could alter its course. Her eyes narrowed as she lifted her chin. "You're nothing but cowards hiding behind those hoods like children behind their mothers' skirts!"

"You were right, kid. She has a mouth on her."

Kid? Who was hiding behind the other mask? How would he know…?

Silas' cohort grabbed her hair, forcing her head back.

She screamed and clawed at the man's hand. *Smack.* Another whack to her face sent sharp, stabbing pain through her cheekbone and exploding across her temple.

Silas sneered. "Keep talkin', and you'll get more of that."

Warm blood dribbled from her mouth, leaving the faint taste of iron on her lips.

The other man stood and chucked the small cask in the corner before peering out the window. "We've gotta get out of here. The place is crawling with men from town."

With both hands, she shoved Silas's chest, knocking him off balance. She scrambled backward, wincing as window shards pierced her palms.

Silas grabbed her ankles.

She kicked and flailed as he dragged her toward him. Outstretched fingers grabbed a thick wedge of glass. She thrust her hand toward Silas' face. The makeshift weapon tore through his flour sack mask. Finding her target, she jabbed its pointy edge into his flesh.

Silas reeled, hands covering his cheek. He cursed as crimson stains formed on his white hood. He shoved Ruth Ann to the floor. Straddling her, he pinned her arms above her head. "You're gonna pay for that, teacher."

"Ruthie?" Benjamin pounded on the rear door. "You in there?"

Silas covered her mouth then yelled to his partner.

"Get rid of whoever that is. Then help me restrain her so we can be on our way."

The hooded man nodded and pulled a knife from a sheath secured at his hip. He reached for the chair barricading the door. "I have a few scores to settle with Benjamin Coulter."

~*~

Benjamin stepped back from the rear door of the schoolhouse, clutching his side. Sounded like a struggle inside. And if he was right, Silas was in there.

Bracing for the impact, Benjamin breathed as deep as he dared then hurled himself, shoulder first, against the wooden barrier. It gave way, and he stumbled inside, biting back foul words as agony ignited his shoulder, arm, and ribs. His eyes drifted closed briefly as he swayed on his feet. He willed himself to stay conscious. Forcing his eyes open, he shook his head, hoping to do the same for his mental acuity.

The sudden whoosh of air drove the smoldering fire toward the trail of kerosene. Invigorated sparks sent new flames bouncing and skipping across the classroom.

For a fateful second Benjamin froze, paralyzed by the image of the masked vigilante astride Ruth Ann. Bile rose in this throat.

She jerked free of her assailant's hold against her mouth then bit his hand.

The man writhed and cursed.

Silas.

"Ben, beside you. He has a knife!"

A flash of white caught the corner of Benjamin's eye a moment too late. The hooded man pounced.

Benjamin dodged his blade. Grimacing, he compelled his injured arm behind him. Tingling fingers freed the pocket revolver from his waistband. He flung his arm around and fired without taking aim, grazing his attacker's shoulder. Undeterred, the man surged forward. Benjamin squeezed the trigger twice more, piercing the vigilante's leg and knee. This time the masked raider lurched forward, before slumping to the floor.

Muscles convulsed in Benjamin's side, shoulder, and head as he spun toward Silas and Ruth Ann. He coughed as smoke constricted his already overworked lungs. Eyes pressed firm, he wagged his head in a futile effort to ward off the encroaching blur. He couldn't black out now. Ruthie needed him. The stinging sensation returned to his arm. Numbness flowed to his hand, his fingers. He stared helpless as the revolver slipped from his grasp.

Silas leapt from the floor and lunged at Benjamin, ramming his head into Benjamin's gut.

He doubled over, gasping for breath as he careened backward still engulfed in Silas' bear-like hold of his chest and arms.

"Get out...Ruthie! Now!"

21

Ruth Ann darted toward the busted rear door.

Benjamin moaned.

She looked over her shoulder. Silas knelt next to Benjamin, repeatedly smashing his head against the raised platform that housed her desk. How could she leave when he was unable to defend himself? He had just saved her from a horrible fate. But what could she do? Silas was much bigger, stronger than she. If only she had—

Where was it? Smoke irritated her lungs and clouded her view. Embers floated from the ceiling where flames licked the crossbeams. Soon there would be no escaping.

Then she spied it, lying on the floor beneath the blackboard. She maneuvered swiftly around a burning bench, grabbed the club, and came up behind Silas.

You'll only get one chance.

Ruth Ann raised the weapon over her shoulder. Heart pounding in her chest, she swung the instrument. An eerie bone-snapping crack split the air when the cudgel collided with Silas' skull. Blood splattered on her clothes, her hands. His body swayed above Benjamin.

Footsteps thundered over the popping, hissing fire. Two, maybe three men were coming.

She struck Silas again.

A loud groan passed from his lips before he collapsed.

Chest heaving with fear, she raised the club overhead and prepared to swing again.

"Stop, Miss Ruth Ann. You gonna kill him."

Panting, her gaze landed on the origin of the familiar voice. Loose strands of hair mingled with blood from her busted lip clung to the side of her face.

Amos slowly lifted his hands and removed the weapon from her grasp. "We needs to get you outta here."

She nodded.

A ceiling beam crashed to the floor.

"Go on." He nudged her toward the rear door.

Her gaze jumped to Benjamin.

"I gets him." Amos stooped beside Benjamin. Grunting, he tugged his limp body forward and onto his shoulder.

Fire blocked their retreat. She glanced toward the front. Taller, four-foot flames consumed everything in that direction. Where were they to go?

"No choice, miss. We gots to run those flames 'fore they get big like them others. You gots to run then jump like when you was little playin' in the garden."

Her eyes widened. "You first."

Amos shook his head. "No, miss. I won't leave lessen you does."

Amos and Benjamin were depending on her. She took a deep breath and hiked her skirts then sprinted toward the door.

Beyond the open doorway a voice called from the darkness, interrupting her retreat. "Wait!"

She halted at Joseph's warning.

"Bucket brigade!"

Frigid water splashed against her. She gasped. Before she could wipe her eyes, another cold dousing soaked her skirt. She staggered backward. Three more buckets followed, spraying the hem of her skirt.

Joseph stomped the remaining flames with his boot then grabbed her by the elbow and whisked her to safety.

Amos followed, carrying Benjamin.

"Is anyone else inside?"

She nodded, shivering as the cold, night wind whipped against her sodden form. "Two…raiders…one unconscious. One is Silas, but I think he's dead."

He yelled to the volunteers. "Keep the water coming. We got two more inside."

Two men rushed passed her into the burning schoolhouse. She shook her head. Silas wouldn't have done the same for any of them.

"Are you all right? Let me look at you." Joseph struggled to keep her at arms length to inspect her injuries.

Ruth Ann wriggled free and grasped hold of him. "I'm fine. Nothing serious, cuts and bruises." For the first time since the raid started, she was safe. Fear released itself in a torrent of tears.

Wrapping his coat around her shoulders, Joseph pulled her close, patting her back. "Shhh, it's all over."

Benjamin moaned.

She knelt beside him on the ground and gently placed his head on her lap. A warm, sticky substance covered her hands. Her eyes widened then darted to Joseph.

Grabbing a lantern, he lowered himself beside her.

Tenderly Ruth Ann adjusted Benjamin's head so Joseph could get a better view.

"He'll need stitches. We need to cover that wound to keep the dirt out."

"My petticoats."

Amos cradled Benjamin's head while she tore the bottom of her underskirts then wrapped the eyelet fabric securely around his injury.

Joseph fingered a hole in Benjamin's jacket. "He's been shot."

Ruth Ann's throat constricted. "Shot? Is it bad?" She searched Joseph's eyes for any shred of hope.

"I don't know. Help me roll him over."

Benjamin moaned as they repositioned him.

Joseph inspected the back of Benjamin's shoulder. "Looks like there's an exit wound. I'm no doctor, but that's a good sign." They rolled him gently onto his back, his head once again resting on Ruth Ann's lap.

She let out a breath and swiped at the last of her tears. "Why was Benjamin on my security patrol? I...I told him to go away and never come back."

"He insisted. He told Captain Reynolds that if you were teaching, he wanted to help protect you. He's been guarding our house most nights by himself as well."

She shook her head in disbelief. "That doesn't make any sense. Why would he do that? Why would he risk his life for me after—?"

Joseph squeezed her hand. "He may not know it himself, but he still loves you."

Memories of their last conversation flooded her thoughts. He'd professed his love and had requested she wait for him. Maybe he did still love her—just not the way she was.

Two men hurried from the burning structure carrying hooded cargo. The raider writhed and struggled to break free of their grasp. "There's still one more man in there."

Joseph glanced toward the schoolhouse. "It's too dangerous."

Pop. Crack.

Ruth Ann sucked in a breath and clutched her chest.

The last of the windows exploded and large plumes of black smoke floated over the schoolyard. Creaking timbers gave way as the remaining section of roof collapsed.

Mr. Turner assisted the men in subduing the rescued vigilante.

Amos tied the man's hands behind his back. He winced as they jerked him to his feet and removed his hood.

Ruth Ann gasped, her eyes widening. "Elias!"

"You knows this man?"

She nodded. "I can't believe you'd do such a thing. That you would let Silas..." She shuddered at the thought of what Silas and the others might have done to her at their 'shindig' had Benjamin not been able to break down the door.

Angry green eyes glared at her. "You brought this on yourself, Ruth Ann. We tried to warn you to stop teaching here."

Joseph's eyes narrowed, fists clenched at his sides. "And you've brought jail—maybe even a hanging on yourself."

A hand flew to her mouth. "Hanging?"

Joseph nodded. "There are three dead men, one Negro and two raiders. Two Negro women were assaulted in the woods. Captain Reynolds has been shot. Nate was ambushed before the raid, tied to a tree, and beaten unconscious. We haven't counted the wounded yet and then there is all of this." Joseph's gaze swept over the burning school. "So, yes, perhaps a hanging is in order, but that's not up to me. We'll send for the sheriff in the morning."

~*~

"Good Morning, Doc. Mrs. Rawlings." Ruth Ann set the pot on a small table in Doc's waiting room. "How are our patients today?" She stuffed her gloves in the pocket of her cape before hanging it on the coatrack. "I brought more of Myra's chicken broth."

"That's lovely dear." Violet Rawlings greeted Ruth Ann with a quick buss to the cheek. "I'll put that on the stove immediately. I don't know how we would have managed this many injured without you—or Maggie and Myra for that matter." She took the pot from Ruth Ann's hands and headed for the kitchen. "Go on up, dear," she called over her shoulder. "Doc is checking on the men now. Maggie arrived a few minutes ago."

The Rawlings' two-story home housed Doc's offices on the first floor. Almost one week later, only the most severely wounded remained in his care. As she climbed the stairs to the surgery, she prayed. *Lord, heal the wounds of these men. Keep them free of infection and restore them to health.*

The days since the raid were a blur of activity. Ruth Ann had spent most of her time assisting Doc and Violet Rawlings treat the injured. She'd cleaned and dressed wounds, administered medicine, and spoon-fed those too weak to feed themselves. But none of it did anything to appease the heavy burden of responsibility she felt.

Despite Doc's best efforts, the bullet had severed Francis' femoral artery, and Doc couldn't save him.

The man at the center of all the hate and violence, Silas Hench, died in the blaze. She struggled with her lack of remorse at his loss. Surely some measure of compunction was due when a man lost his life.

Laughter floated through the hallway—Maggie and Edward. She would visit them first then begin Benjamin's ministrations. She passed Elias' empty room, a reminder of the fate that awaited each of the men arrested for participating in the raid. Deemed fit to travel, the sheriff had taken him to Leesburg yesterday to await trial.

She nudged the door open. "How are my favorite patients doing today?"

Maggie's warm smile greeted her. "Edward is doing well. He's had no laudanum since yesterday. If he keeps this up, Doc says he can go home tomorrow— as long as he promises to rest." She shot her patient a stony look. "And he will rest if he knows what's good for him."

Edward rolled his eyes. "We're not even married yet, and the woman is already bossing me around."

Ruth Ann grinned. "You don't fool me, Edward Simms. Your voice is complaining, but your eyes are twinkling."

He reached for Maggie's hand. "Nothing like surviving a harrowing ordeal to make you realize what's important in life."

She hugged Maggie tight. "I still can't believe you'll be a married woman before the summer is over." Winking at Edward over Maggie's shoulder she added, "That is if Edward follows Doc's orders so he can return to work in a few weeks. It would be a real shame to postpone the wedding for lack of funds."

Edward shifted his gaze out the window. "Why

don't you go check on Nate? You're a bad influence on my future bride." He glanced back at Ruth Ann, a slight grin tugging at his lips.

She shifted her attention to her sleeping friend. Shallow breaths punctuated his breathing. "How's Nate doing, Maggie?"

Maggie released Edward's hand and joined Ruth Ann beside Nate's bed. "About the same. Doc gave him some morphine this morning. He'll sleep for a while."

Ruth Ann patted Nate's hand. He lifted heavy-lidded eyes. A faint upturn to his mouth calmed her anxious heart before he gave way to sleep again.

"It's hard to believe his own father and brother could beat him senseless like this." She shuddered and fought against the lump forming in her throat. "Has Mrs. Hamilton come to see him yet?"

Maggie shook her head. "Nor is she likely to now that Elias has been transferred to the jail in Leesburg with his father."

"Have any arrangements been made for his care when he's discharged?"

"Nothing definite. I think Doc wants to speak with the Petersons. He'll need someone to help him for a while."

Moisture pooled in Ruth Ann's eyes. "If I hadn't—"

Maggie placed a hand to her shoulder. "He wanted to be his own man, remember?"

Edward winced as he pushed himself to sitting position. "You're not responsible for what those raiders did any more than you're responsible for Nate's choice to protect you. Or mine. Or Benjamin's."

She nodded, but inwardly, guilt gnawed at her for

the pain and suffering her friends were enduring. "I need to tend to Benjamin before he wakes."

Maggie handed Ruth Ann a copy of the *Mirror*. "Can you put this in Captain Reynolds' room? Edward is finished with it, and the captain will be looking for someone to read to him this afternoon."

"Sure." Ruth Ann took the paper from Maggie and gave Nate one last pat on the hand. Grinning, she paused by Edward's bed. "You'd better listen to Maggie. If she sees how ornery you are, she just might change her mind about marrying you."

Maggie's lips stretched into a wide grin. She swiped the hair from Edward's forehead. "We both know there is little chance of that."

She closed the door behind her and headed for the captain's room. Hearing Doc's voice behind Captain Reynolds' closed door, she tucked the newspaper under her arm and continued to Benjamin's room. She paused in the doorway—he looked so helpless. Nothing like the strong, self-assured man who had come calling at her door. She laid the newspaper on the bureau then scanned the doctor's instructions tacked to the wall above his bed. He was due for medication within the hour. From what she could decipher of Doc's scribblings, he was tapering Benjamin off the morphine. If she hurried, she should be able change his dressings before he roused from his medicated slumber.

Ruth Ann rolled up her sleeves and poured fresh water into the basin then washed her hands as Doc had instructed. Benjamin was flush. She laid a hand to his forehead—his fever persisted. A dark shadow outlined his chiseled jaw. Remembering the scruffy, bearded-man she first encountered at the creek, her lips tugged upward.

With a heavy breath, she pulled back his blankets. Using a small pair of shears, she snipped the dressings covering his injured shoulder then disposed of the soiled bandages. She dipped a clean cloth in the basin and wrung it out before gently cleansing his wound. The redness had diminished, but it still appeared swollen. A thin, clear liquid oozed from the site, but overall the stubborn abscess was gradually improving.

"I brought warm poultices." Violet stood in the doorway, tray in hand.

"You're a mind reader. I was just about to head to the kitchen for one of those. You'll need to teach me what herbs you use. They've made a huge difference for both Mr. Coulter and Captain Reynolds."

"All right, first thing tomorrow morning. If you like, you can grind them yourself with the mortar and pestle."

"Thank you." Ruth Ann retrieved a dish from the tray and scooped the warm paste from the bowl with her fingers. Leaning over Benjamin, she tenderly spread the mixture on his wound. Satisfied with her efforts, she cleaned her hands in the basin then applied fresh dressings.

Benjamin's eyes fluttered open. "Ru-Ruthie?"

"Yes, Mr. Coulter. It's me."

"I'll get my husband for you." Violet hurried from Benjamin's room.

"Would you like some water?"

Benjamin' strained to speak. "Yeeesss, pleeeese."

"Surely." After tying off his bandage, she poured a cup of water then slipped her arm behind his neck and lifted him forward enough to sip the cool liquid.

Benjamin winced.

"I'm sorry. Am I hurting you?"

He shook his head. "Mor-rre pleeeese."

"Easy now, your stomach has been empty for a few days. Drink too much and it will all come up." She carefully returned him to his pillow.

"Th-thank you."

"Well, look who's finally awake." Doc pressed his fingers against Benjamin's wrist. "You've given us all quite a scare." He placed his stethoscope on Benjamin's chest and instructed him to take several deep breaths. "Breathing is still a bit weak but, you have quite an impressive list of injuries young man, and it will take some time to get your strength back."

Doc examined his notes. "A buckshot wound to your left shoulder tops the list. It's a good thing you weren't shot at close range, or you may have lost your entire arm. As it is, the skin around the wound is seared and abraded, but Miss Sutton has been cleansing it twice daily and the infection is improving. You have two broken ribs. There doesn't appear to be any internal damage, but you'll need to keep your left arm wrapped snuggly to your side for at least a month. And if that's not enough, you've got several nasty lacerations on the back of your head—thirty stitches' worth. Sorry, had to shave the area at the base of your skull to do a proper job."

"Thhhanks, Doc." Benjamin scratched his arm then his cheek.

Doc examined his arm. "Itchy skin?"

He nodded.

"Don't see any irritation. Most likely a side effect from the morphine." He jotted something in Benjamin's medical notes then glanced at Ruth Ann. "If a rash develops let me know."

"Yes, Doc."

"Ya know, Benjamin, you're one lucky young man. Any one of those injuries could've taken you to glory, but thanks to Miss Sutton's dogged determination, I expect you to make a full recovery."

Not wanting her gaze to meet Benjamin's, she lowered her lashes.

"You'll need to stay here awhile longer and have those bandages changed several times a day." Doc patted his patient's hand. "Get some rest, son. That's the best thing for you right now."

Ruth Ann hastily gathered her supplies but paused at a feather light touch to her hand.

"Y-your face?" Benjamin strained to lift his arm a few inches above the bed. His eyes softened as he pointed to her busted lip and the discoloration on her cheek. "Y-you all right?"

"I'm fine."

His eyes pressed closed. "Those men...they didn't...?"

She reached for his hand and squeezed. "A few cuts and bruises, but that's all...thanks to you."

His eyes locked on hers, a contented smile forming on his lips. "You've...always been... a fighter, Ruthie."

Benjamin's eyes fluttered. It wouldn't be long until he slept again.

He patted the bed beside him. "Pleeease stay."

Despite his cruel rejection, the sight of Benjamin wounded and vulnerable drew her helplessly toward him, like a lamb to the slaughter. She tugged on her bottom lip. How could she still be attracted to him after what he'd said? Hadn't she learned anything?

"I can't. You get some rest." She closed the door behind her, quietly resolving to bury any flicker of attraction to Benjamin Coulter.

22

"Ouch!" Ruth Ann flinched.

Myra reworked the pins at her waist. "Sorry, child. I got to take it in some more." She tugged on the fabric. "I know that man upset you, but you best start eatin'."

She sighed. "You're right, Myra, but I have no appetite."

"Suppose a broken heart does that to a body."

Ruth Ann stared at her likeness in the full-length mirror while Myra altered the garment. A warm contentedness washed over her, something she had never known before. For the first time in her life she didn't despise her reflection. Fingering her curls with admiration, she thought about what the Psalmist wrote. *I will praise Thee; for I am fearfully and wonderfully made: marvelous are Thy works; and that my soul knoweth right well.* God had fashioned her in her mother's womb, just the way he wanted her. Her hands traced the outline of her buxom silhouette. If God was pleased with what He saw, then who was she, or Benjamin Coulter for that matter, to say otherwise.

"That man keep comin' 'round here. He still loves you." Myra slid a pin between her lips and nudged Ruth Ann sideways before removing it again. "It's been two months. You ever gonna let him say his piece or you gonna keep havin' Mrs. Sarah shoo him away?"

She didn't know why he came calling. He didn't want her. He wanted Rose and her hourglass figure. "It's better this way. With the railroad finally progressing to Round Hill, he'll be leaving town soon anyway." Eventually Benjamin would leave Virginia altogether and head west to Colorado or California. Only a few days more, then she'd never see him again.

Her gaze met Myra's in the mirror. She quirked a brow. "What?"

"Maybe you ain't as happy about not seein' that man as you lets on."

"Nonsense. I'm just nervous about the grand opening of the train station tomorrow."

"Mmmhmm. And seein' Mr. Benjamin while you on Mr. Thornton's arm."

Ruth Ann forced the air from her lungs. "Don't remind me."

A gentle rap preceded the creaking door hinge. Mama poked her head inside the room. "I thought I would see what progress you two are making."

"We just about finished, ma'am." Myra secured the final pin. "Turn 'round, child, and let us get a good look at you."

Ruth Ann moved slowly, careful not to step off the side of the cedar chest. She drew back the sides of the lavender floral polonaise and admired the gingham underskirt.

"Looks mighty fine. What you think, Mrs. Hannah?"

Mama clapped her hands together, her smile beaming with pride. "I never thought I would see you with any semblance of a trim figure, Ruth. While you are not as petite as your sister, you are every bit as beautiful. James will not be able to take his eyes off you tomorrow."

"I doubt that, Mama. As Master of Ceremonies, we both know James will be working the crowd and hobnobbing with railroad board members."

"Yes, dear, he will, with you right by his side." Mama stretched her hand out to Ruth Ann. "Your decision to entertain James again is very wise."

Ruth Ann lifted her skirts in her left hand and placed her right inside her mother's before stepping down from the cedar chest.

"Perhaps the attentions of a well-bred young man will shake these tiresome doldrums." Mama reached for the doorknob and paused. She glanced back over her shoulder. "You look lovely dear, but do try to work on your disposition."

Ruth Ann nodded. Her mother was right. Her nerves were a jumble. Between the ribbon cutting ceremony and her desire to avoid Benjamin, she was as sour as week-old milk. Even Jules Verne held little interest. Much of her spirit and opinionated nature had vanished. Her willful determination to teach the Negroes had cost her and many others she cared about, greatly.

"If we're done, Myra, I need to change and hurry over to the train station. I promised Maggie I'd help with the decorations."

Myra unfastened the buttons on the back of her dress and carefully slid the garment from her shoulders and hips. She hung the dress from the armoire then gently smoothed the linen fabric. "Lordy, child, when Mr. Benjamin sees you in this, his mouth gonna drop clean to the ground."

Ruth Ann worried her lip. What would her duplicitous heart do if it did?

~*~

Ruth Ann raised a hand to her brow, blocking the afternoon sun. "That end is too loose, Maggie. The first child who touches the bunting will pull it right down."

Maggie leaned over the rose bushes as far as she dared. "You're right, but even with this ladder, it's difficult for me to reach the far corner."

"Perhaps, I could help."

Ruth Ann stiffened at the deep timbre of Benjamin's voice. Oh well, she'd expected to see him at some point over the next two days. Might as well get it over with.

"Thank you, Benjamin." Maggie lowered the decoration. "That would be helpful. I'll fall into the roses if I lean any farther."

Ruth Ann glared at Maggie.

Benjamin took the bunting from Maggie's hand and stretched it taut against the railing. "How's that look?"

Maggie cocked her head. "Needs a bit of slack." She motioned for Ruth Ann to move toward Benjamin. "Perfect."

Benjamin pounded a small nail into the end of the railing. He wrapped the string around it several times before whacking it with the hammer again. He moved to where Ruth Ann stood and repeated the process. "Next."

Maggie retrieved another bunting from the crate. "The last one needs to be hung from the roof line."

He positioned the ladder then extended the hammer to Ruth Ann. "Hold this please until Maggie says we have it centered."

Ruth Ann tapped the hammer in her palm. She wanted to give him the hammer all right—right upside his hard head. She nodded slightly, acknowledging his request then glanced at Maggie. Her smug grin told Ruth Ann that Maggie was quite pleased with herself for engineering this move. She and Edward had been encouraging her to stop blustering about James and open her heart to Benjamin's contrition.

He stretched out his hand. "I need the hammer and a nail, please."

Her fingers grazed his, quickening her pulse. The hammer fell to the ground. "I-I'm so clumsy. I-I'll get that." She hurried down the steps and knelt between the rose bushes.

"Found it." Ruth Ann shook her hand as she stood. Her eyes darted around. "Where's Maggie? She was just here a—"

"Hmmm. Oh—uh, I'm not sure, but I can help you finish here."

She let out a breath. "If you hang that end of the bunting, it would be helpful." She brought her index finger to her lips then shook her hand again. "You can put the hammer in your pocket this time so I won't drop it again."

"You all right?"

"Yes, it's just a thorn. I'll be fine."

"Here, let me take a look at that." Benjamin scooped up her hand between his own, inspecting her finger. "It's the least I can do. I came by your house several times to thank you for caring for my wounds after the raid, but each time, Sarah told me you were unavailable."

"You needn't trouble yourself. It was nothing, really. I helped Doc care for all of the wounded."

He glanced over the tips of her fingers. "Oh. Maggie led me to believe you wouldn't allow anyone besides you or Doc to look after me."

Ruth Ann looked away, her heart beating wildly in her chest. How could he still affect her this way after what he'd done? "Maggie talks too much." She tried to wriggle free of his grasp. "I-I just wanted to make sure you were well taken care of. You risked your life for me, after all."

Benjamin's grip remained firm. "There it is. Hold on. This might hurt a bit."

She squirmed again. "Really, I'm fine."

"Hold still. Quit being such a baby."

"I'm not being a baby. I want to finish dec...ouch! That hurt!"

"Got it. Quite a nasty one, too." Benjamin brought her finger to his lips and kissed the spot pierced by the thorn. "All better."

"Let me go!"

~*~

Benjamin grinned as he released her hand. She was fun to tease, but there was nothing funny about the way that woman's touch stirred his blood. It had been months since he'd laid eyes on the curvaceous beauty, and all he wanted to do was take her in his arms and kiss her soundly. Since that would only earn him a well-deserved slap, he focused on the task at hand and climbed the ladder to secure the far end of the bunting to the roof. He tapped the nail two times then wrapped the string around it. "How's that look?"

"Good." Ruth Ann bit her bottom lip. "Why did you remain on the security patrols, Mr. Coulter? Captain Reynolds told Joseph you personally watched our home every night."

Benjamin secured the bunting with another nail.

"Captain Reynolds talks too much."

Ruth Ann pressed her lips together and furrowed her brow.

"You really want to know?"

She nodded.

He lowered himself from the ladder. "Because I still care about you, Ruthie. I can't get you out of my mind—or my heart." He reached for her hand. "Is that why you looked after my wounds, because you still care for me, too?"

She stepped away from him. "You need to refer to me as, Miss Sutton. I told you I simply wanted to repay your kindness for protecting me and my students."

Benjamin shook his head. Just when he thought he was making progress, she sidestepped him. It was probably best to go slow and not push her, but the fact that she took care of his wounds personally and wouldn't allow anyone but her or Doc to nurse him gave him hope that deep down she still loved him. "What else can I do to help?"

"Nothing, we're all done. That was the last of the buntings. I'm afraid I arrived late, and Maggie did most of it herself."

Benjamin put the hammer in the toolbox. "Where do the ladder and tools go?"

"Maggie borrowed them from the livery. I'll return them after I put these crates inside the train station." She stooped to lift one.

Benjamin took hold of the opposite side. "Let me help you with that."

"I'm fine, thank you."

He held firm. "A gentleman doesn't let a lady carry heavy crates while he stands idly by."

She tugged back. "Nor does he push his way upon

the lady."

"Fine. Have it your way." Benjamin released his hold. "You are the most stubborn woman..."

Ruth Ann stumbled backward. Unable to find her balance against the momentum of the crate, she plopped down hard against the wooden planks of the porch, sending her skirts and ruffled petticoats above her knees.

Benjamin dropped beside her. "Are you all right?"

"I'm fine."

He yanked her skirt across her shins, earning himself a swat in the process. "What did you do that for?"

"I can manage quite nicely."

Benjamin stood and dusted off his pants. "I guess I'll be going then since you don't need my assistance."

"Aren't you going to help me up?"

"No, I figure you have it under control."

Ruth Ann released a forced breath. "You insist on helping when I don't ask for it and then refuse me when I do." She set the crate to the side, struggled to her feet, and brushed off her skirts.

Benjamin peeked at her shapely backside. "Don't forget this side over here. I could help dust the back of your skirt if you want."

Her skirts twirled about her ankles as she spun away from him. "No, thank you. You have helped enough. Good day, Mr. Coulter."

"Then I'll be on my way." He touched the brim of his hat. "Good day, Miss Sutton."

She was the most mulish woman he'd ever known. He chuckled to himself, recalling the day they first met. Her stubborn refusal of assistance had landed her in the creek. Even angry, she was the most beautiful woman of his acquaintance. He might've been temporarily distracted by Rose, but Rose's appeal was only skin-deep. Ruth Ann's allurement lay in her heart, making her pretty face and shapeliness irresistible to him.

Why had that lesson been so painful to learn?

Benjamin paused and glanced toward the train depot. Only a week at most before he'd be camping in Snickers Gap until the tracks went over the Blue Ridge. He was more than willing to make the five-mile trip to call on her, but he had to have a reason. Leaving her in a lurch like he'd done would do nothing to help his cause. Showing himself a gentleman by returning the ladder and tool box to the livery would be a better choice.

A fancy carriage arrived as he neared the station.

Thornton? What was that dandy doing here? Benjamin pressed against the rear of the building and peered around the corner, his fists clenched at his sides.

He hadn't expected competition.

~*~

Ruth Ann placed the crates containing American flags and programs for tomorrow's ceremony inside the depot. She wiped the dust from her hands and stared out a nearby window. Benjamin's tall, muscular form disappeared behind an elm tree. Thoughts of what might've been flooded her mind. A heavy breath tore itself from her lungs. *Only a few more days until he's gone.* Then all of this can be forgotten.

"Hello, Ruth."

She startled. "James."

He leaned forward and kissed her cheek. "Myra told me I'd find you here. You look a bit...disheveled." He wiped dirt from her sleeve then straightened her hat.

"I'm all done here. I need to return the ladder and tool box to the livery. Then you can walk me home."

He removed a handkerchief from his pocket and dabbed the moisture beading on his brow. "Walk? When Zachariah is waiting in a luxurious carriage?"

"Please, James. It's such a beautiful day. The red buds and dogwoods are blooming, even some of the azaleas."

"All right. Just this once, but I do not intend to make a habit of it."

She smiled.

James brushed her cheek with the back of his fingers. "If pretty smiles are to be my reward, I may reconsider the practice. I'll tell Zachariah to return the ladder and tool box for you. He can take the carriage without us."

"Thank you."

He offered her his arm then steered her toward the Rockaway to give instructions to Zachariah before beginning their walk. "I was terribly concerned about you, Ruth. News of the raid made the papers in Richmond."

"I'm sorry I worried you. Your letters were very kind."

He tucked her hand inside the crook of his arm. "This is one reason why I strongly opposed you teaching the Negroes. It is not suitable for a young woman of your position—far too dangerous. I still can't fathom why on earth Joseph agreed to it."

James paused and cleared his throat. "My opinion

has not changed, Ruth. When we marry, you will not be allowed to volunteer with any organization that aids Negroes."

"I understand."

He patted her hand. "Excellent. I had every confidence you'd outgrow your youthful obstinance where the Negroes are concerned."

The laughter of children playing nearby drew her attention. Three boys knelt in the dirt, the scrawny carrot-top knuckled down, aligning his marble for the perfect shot. "You do want children, don't you, James?"

"Of course, I want heirs, Ruth. What a silly question."

"Heirs? James, they're children, our f-family." The word stuck in her throat. Could she really picture a future, a family with him?

"It's the same thing, darling." He patted her hand again. "Don't mince words with me."

His gaze drifted across the street to where the children played. A shoving match ensued when the redhead shouted "Keepsies," claiming all the marbles he'd won. "But ours will be well-mannered, not running loose unsupervised like those ruffians. Our children will have the advantage of the finest boarding schools in the country."

"Boarding schools?" She gulped, heart thrumming wildly. She'd assumed her children would be close by. What was the point of having children, or marrying James, if they were to be shipped away? What kind of father would he be? No doubt their children would never want for any material need, but would he love them? Would he hold them on his lap and tickle them as Benjamin had done with her nieces?

He studied her a moment. As if sensing her uneasiness, he squeezed her arm snug against him as they resumed their walk. "What is the matter, darling? Why are you so melancholy?" He lifted her hand to his lips then returned it to the pocket of his elbow. "I am home after all, and we have picked up where we left off last fall. Everything is fine. I hold no grudge against you for your dalliance with the railroad man."

Ruth Ann forced a smile. Should she be encouraging his attentions? What choice did she have? She needed to make the best she could of the only future that laid itself before her.

James led her up the stone walkway toward the front porch. "I wish you were joining us for dinner tonight. My parents would like to see you. I would enjoy showing you off to Mr. Heaton and the other Washington & Ohio board members who are joining us." James removed his watch from his vest pocket. "Where is Zachariah?" He craned his neck to look for the approaching carriage as he spoke. "I need to get home to Brook Lawn, change, and be ready for dinner in an hour. It would be wonderful to have you by my side, Ruth." His eyes settled on hers again. "Please come."

"I'm sorry, James. I'm just not up for a dinner party with strangers tonight."

Tiny red lines marred the whites of his watery eyes. He dabbed them with a handkerchief then sneezed. "Blasted pollen!"

Zachariah led the horses along the path toward the carriage house.

"There he is now. He is a good man—never disappoints me." James caressed the polished surface of the watch before nestling it inside his jacket.

She slipped her arm free of his hold. "Besides, you will be talking of nothing but business. You won't even miss me."

"Ah, but you are wrong, darling. I will miss you. However, I am determined to win your favor this time, so I will consent to your wishes." He grasped her hands and gently stroked them with his thumbs. "But once we marry, you will be expected to join me at functions like this as my wife."

As his wife? Her eyes drifted to their hands. His touch didn't make her tingle. The memory of his kiss didn't make her long for another. His eyes didn't smolder with passion for her. But what had that firestorm yielded? *Heartache, that's what.*

This was the right course. It had to be.

Without fire, she couldn't get burned.

~*~

Benjamin glanced at the cloudless sky—half past three, or thereabouts. He scanned the crowd gathered outside the depot. Where was she? The train was due shortly and from what he could tell, the Suttons nor the Palmers had arrived at the station.

Mr. Turner stepped to the podium. "Only ten minutes to the train, folks—ten minutes!"

The throng pressed closer to the platform. Businesses closed early, and farmers left their fields, all dressed in their Sunday best, to witness the arrival of the Washington & Ohio Railroad. A sense of pride filled Benjamin, knowing that his contribution to the rail line would bring continued prosperity to the community. Although he'd missed his certification exam while recuperating from his injuries during the raid, he was grateful to have been there to save Ruthie. He could reschedule as soon as he came up with the fee. The land mapping agency wasn't likely to pay for it a second time.

Neil tapped his shoulder and pointed toward the station. Ruth Ann stood at the edge of the platform, tying the bow on the back of Chloe's dress. His heart stuttered. Curls piled high in a fancy style, she'd left a few lose to drift in the breeze. Just enough to distract him. She waved her gloved hand at Maggie and Charlotte then took a seat next to Thornton.

Benjamin pushed forward through the crowd. Their eyes locked. She smiled then glanced away. His glare landed on his rival. A smug grin crossed Thorton's face as he lifted her hand to his lips. She couldn't be serious about that dandy—could she? Despite the mild temperatures, the heat scorched his neck. If he didn't know better, he'd think steam surged from his ears.

The approaching train whistle brought the cheering assembly to their feet. Excitement filled the air as fathers lifted their children to their shoulders to view the oncoming train. Red, white, and blue buntings decorated the depot and the town square. Everywhere American flags waved in the air. As the train pulled to a stop at the Catoctin Creek Station, John Dillon's coronet band played patriotic marches.

Mr. McKenzie, president of the railroad, emerged first from the train followed by Mr. Heaton and several other men he assumed were W&OR board members. Mr. Turner made his way to the podium and settled the crowd. Each dignitary stood and waved upon his introduction, inciting another round of cheering and flag waving.

"It is my great honor to introduce Ruth Ann Sutton. Her father, Charles Sutton, refused to allow the Washington & Ohio to bypass our little town on its way to Winchester. Along with William Thornton, they lobbied the state senate for the funds required…"

Benjamin stepped to the side to get a better glimpse of Ruth Ann. Her face paled and perspiration beaded on her lip. He noticed her trembling hands as she laid her notes on the lectern. Her eyes landed on him. *Come on, Ruthie. You can do this.*

Benjamin's heart swelled with pride, listening to Ruth Ann speak of the father she adored and how this day was the fulfillment of his dream.

Maggie nudged him with her elbow. "I see that look on your face, Benjamin. You need to let her know you still care."

"I've tried, Maggie. She either sends me away, or worse, we argue."

Edward put his hand on Benjamin's shoulder. "Don't give up. You'll need to be more stubborn than Ruth Ann if you're going to win her back."

He swiped a hand along the back of his neck. "That's a tall order." He tipped his head toward the platform where James Thornton was now speaking. "What about him?"

Maggie looked Benjamin directly in the eyes with an air of confidence he found unsettling. "She loves you, Benjamin, I know it. She's just too stubborn or too scared to admit it."

He shook his head. "Wooing women is hard work."

Edward laughed as he hooked his arm around Maggie's waist and pulled her to him. "It's a lot easier when you don't mess up so badly."

Benjamin chuckled. "I suppose there's truth enough in that." Taking a deep breath, he scanned the crowd. "Guess there's no time like the present."

Edward prodded him forward. "Go on, then."

Benjamin pushed his hat back on his head and surveyed the crowd. How would he find her in this mass of human activity? He'd wait on her porch—all day if he had to. She'd come home eventually, and the short walk between here and her home might help him think of something intelligent to say, some way to convince her of the sincerity of his contrition.

Anxious to get away from any additional sightings of Ruthie and that dandy, he'd practically ran the entire way to her home. He eased himself onto the top step and removed his hat. Idle fingers glided across its brim. *Lord, soften Ruthie's heart. Help her hear my regret.*

The soft plea of muffled cries reached his ears, interrupting his prayer. He followed the sorrowful weeping toward the garden. Crumpled in a puddle of fallen pink dogwood petals, Ruth Ann's shoulders shook, face buried in her knees. What was troubling her?

The latch creaked as he pushed the gate open. "Ruthie, you all right?"

She wiped her eyes on her sleeve and shrugged.

When she stood, Benjamin could make out the name *Buddy* carved into a wooden marker.

He tucked his hat beneath his arm. "Sorry you lost Buddy."

"Pretty silly to cry over a dog, huh?"

"Not at all." He wanted to take her in his arms and comfort her.

She sniffled. "By the end, he could barely walk. He died yesterday."

"I know how much he meant to you." Benjamin pulled a handkerchief from his pocket and offered it to her. "You must miss him terribly."

"I do. And Papa. The ceremony has me thinking on him, too." She dabbed her eyes. "What brings you by?"

His fingers skimmed the brim of his hat. "I wanted to let you know you did a fine job with your speech."

A smile flickered on her lips before she reined it in.

Benjamin held out his hand. "Will you sit on the steps with me?"

Ruth Ann stared at his offering. "Just for a minute."

Although she refused his hand, she had agreed to talk with him. It was a start.

"I couldn't take my eyes off you when you were on the platform. You were...stunning."

Her cheeks flushed.

"I had misgivings about leaving you at the train station yesterday with the heavy ladder and toolbox to put away. When I came back, I saw you with Thornton."

She remained silent. He searched her face, but she avoided his gaze, choosing instead to focus on her hands, resting in her lap.

"He still wants to marry you, doesn't he?"

A simple nod was her only response, yet it seized his heart in a vice-like grip. He forced the burning question from his lips, though he dreaded to hear the answer it may elicit. "And you're seriously considering his proposal?"

She shifted her gaze toward the mountains and shrugged. "He hasn't actually proposed, but we've been writing one another, and he's made his intentions clear."

There was still a chance. He pressed on, unsure her answers would bring relief to his aching heart. "Have your feelings changed toward him?"

Ruth Ann's chin hung low to her chest, her eyes pressed firmly shut. Was she fighting back tears? "I don't want to talk about this with you, Mr. Coulter." She stood on the bottom step. "Perhaps it's best if you leave now."

Benjamin tugged her hand. "Please don't go inside. Sit with me for a while. We'll talk about something else." His mind raced for a topic, anything that would keep her outside with him. "Uh...how is the search coming for a temporary school for the Negroes?"

She wriggled her hand lose from his hold and lowered herself beside him again. "The town has formed a committee, The Colored Man's Aid Society, to oversee the school since the Freedmen's Bureau has officially closed."

Benjamin leaned back on his hands, his long legs stretched out in front of him. "Will you be teaching there when it opens?"

"No. They'll only hire a Negro teacher for the position, but I will advise them on the curriculum and supplies for the school. Our goal is to offer not only the traditional subjects, but also the trades—carpentry, metal smithing, looming, and tailoring. Useful skills that will enable them to establish businesses and liberate them from the tenant farming that will be a deathblow to their freedom. We plan to partner with the Lincoln Society of Friends to offer apprenticeships for as many students as possible."

The passion in her voice rivaled the sparkle in her

eyes as she spoke, just as Benjamin remembered.

"I've been chosen to interview perspective teaching candidates. They even offered to name the school in my honor—*The Sutton School for the Advancement of Negroes*." She sighed. "But I declined."

The spark had diminished as quickly as it had arrived.

"Why, Ruthie?"

Her eyes pinched closed at the mention of his nickname for her. "I mean that's quite an honor, Miss Sutton. Why did you refuse?"

"James would never allow it."

Benjamin sneered. James Thornton grated on his last nerve.

"But that's not the only reason. I thought a more appropriate name would be *The Francis Jackson Negro School.*

Benjamin laid his hand on hers, still nestled in her lap. "Francis would be honored."

A lone tear escaped the corner of her eye. "He saved all our lives that night by ringing the bell faithfully for help. It's the least we can do." She squeezed his hand briefly then released it. "I owe you my undying gratitude as well." She peered up at him. "If you hadn't come when you did, Silas would have…"

Benjamin recalled the sight of the hooded man pressing himself against her. *Thank You, God for protecting her.*

Her breath hitched.

He hated to see her in distress. Instinctively his arm slid around her. A few minutes passed in comfortable silence and Benjamin felt himself drawn to her even more—to love her, protect her. He couldn't bear the thought of her not being part of his life.

Unexpectedly, she rested her head on his shoulder. "I'm testifying at the trial. Joseph thinks Elias and his father will hang with the others." Ruth Ann shuddered.

"He's probably right."

"I plan to speak on their behalf during the sentencing phase."

"You do?"

"Yes. Nate is one of my dearest friends. This has been so hard on him. I won't diminish what Elias and his father did during the raid, but I want to speak of the people I knew before—years ago. I am hoping their sentence will be reduced to hard labor."

"I know, Ru—uh, Miss Sutton, but after what they did—frankly, they deserve to hang."

She lifted her head abruptly, jarring his chin.

He rubbed his jaw. "Whatcha do that for?"

"There's been enough killing, Mr. Coulter. Enough prejudice. Enough hatred. It's time for healing. 'Forgive, as ye hath been forgiven.'" Ruth Ann stood and straightened her skirts. "I'm sorry, Mr. Coulter. I shouldn't have laid my troubles out for you to bear. You've made it perfectly clear that you don't want that responsibility any longer."

Was this the same woman who a few minutes ago was sharing her sorrows with him? Allowing him to comfort her? "I'm sorry if I overstepped my bounds, Miss Sutton. I only wanted to console you."

She hastily climbed the porch steps. "Thank you for stopping by."

"Ruthie, wait. I was hoping you'd allow me to call on you tomorrow evening."

She shook her head. "I don't think that is a good

idea. I didn't mean to give you the wrong impression."

Benjamin reached for her elbow, his jaw stiffening as he spoke. "How can you forgive Elias and his father after what they did to you and the others, but you can't forgive me?"

She jerked away from him. The softness in her eyes vanished. "It's not about forgiving you, Mr. Coulter. It's about trusting you. That, I don't know how to do."

23

Ruth Ann stepped inside the foyer and closed the heavy walnut door behind her. Resting her head against the frosted glass, she sighed. Every inch of her ached for that man, but she couldn't allow herself to trust him. She wasn't pretty or petite enough to grace his arm.

"Miss Ruth Ann, that you, child?"

"Yes."

Myra wiped her hands on her apron as she entered the foyer. "Your mama says you to go directly to your room and puts on the dress she laid out for you. The Thorntons comin' in less than an hour."

"All right." Ruth Ann breathed deeply. The smell of roast pork and potatoes filled the house. "Dinner smells wonderful."

"Thank you." Myra shook her head, a grin spreading across her face. "Your Mama talk me in to servin' it, too. She's as jumpy as a long-tailed cat in a room full of rockin' chairs. Mrs. Sarah is busy with the girls. Soon as I puts the bread in the oven, I gonna help you dress and re-pin your hair." Myra made a shooing motion with her hands. "Go on now."

Ruth Ann nodded and climbed the steps to the second story. Opening the door to her room, she spied her blue gown lying on the bed. She shook her head. Mama knew it was James' favorite. He claimed that particular shade accentuated the gold flecks in her eyes. But she wasn't fooled—it was the plunging

313

neckline he favored.

She sat on her bed and unlaced her shoes. Unlike Benjamin, James didn't seem to mind her fuller curves. Although robust may not be the highest flattery, it sure beat outright rejection. He could give her a home and children, as well as a very busy life as the wife of a prominent politician. She would learn to care for him, in time, as a wife should. Best of all—he was safe. If she'd listened to her mother, her heart wouldn't have been shattered into a million pieces she was still trying to put back together. No, if she'd learned anything, it was that romantic love was just another term for heartache and betrayal.

With nimble fingers, she unbuttoned her bodice. She stood and slid the sleeves from her shoulders, letting the fabric crumple at her feet. Her fingers glided along the silky blue fabric of the gown she would wear this evening. She needed to face facts. Benjamin was more persistent than she'd expected. Despite all that had passed between them, merely being in the man's presence still made her disloyal heart desire him. Her momentary lapse in judgment a few minutes ago didn't help. What was he supposed to think if she sat so intimately with him?

Getting a ring on her finger was the surest plan to send Benjamin Coulter away—forever. Normally unaccustomed to wearing the revealing gown, tonight it might be just what she needed to move James' talk of an impending engagement to an actual proposal.

Her gaze drifted to her image in the full-length mirror. With a jut of her chin, she studied her reflection.

She could do this.

She could marry James.

A light tap on the door stirred Ruth Ann from her thoughts. "Come in."

Myra smiled then reached for the blue gown.

"Not yet." Ruth Ann gripped the footboard. "Let's retie my corset first."

Myra arched a brow.

"As tight as you can make it, please."

~*~

Ruth Ann lifted the delicate rose-patterned cup to her lips, allowing the aromatic scent of orange bergamot to steel her nerves as she glanced around the parlor. Something was up. Maybe it was her imagination, but everyone appeared enraptured with secretive conversations in every corner of the room. James, Joseph, and Mr. Thornton huddled near the fireplace smoking cigars and pipes. Her mother, Sarah, and Mrs. Thornton clustered around the most recent copy of *Godey's Ladies Book* but rarely glanced at its pages.

Her gaze settled on James. The silver spoon on her saucer rattled against mother's good china. She slid a shaky hand across blue silk to steady her bouncing knee. The unspoken proposal hung in the air like the lemon oil Myra used to polish the woodwork. Although he'd been patient, James would be expecting matters between them to be resolved soon.

And so was she.

James patted Joseph's shoulder then crossed the parlor to join her on the settee. "I'd like to speak with you alone, darling. Would you join me on the porch?"

It was time. Her stomach twisted into knots like Bavarian pretzels. With two hands, she returned the teacup to the marble-top table and nodded. "Of course."

He led her outside to the swing but remained on his feet, puffing his Upmann. "My father and I have conceived a project that we think you would enjoy immensely, Ruth."

She lifted a brow. "Project?"

"Since it is inevitable that you will need to cease your association with organizations that assist the Freed Negroes, we have decided to establish a charitable foundation for you to manage." He tapped the ashes from the butt of his cigar. "You are very bright, Ruth, and this is exactly the type of work that will be meaningful to you and simultaneously advance my political ambitions."

"I'm afraid I don't quite understand. What would this charitable foundation do?"

"How would you like to organize a lending library? The first branch would be right here in Catoctin Creek with the ultimate goal being a countywide system of libraries. You and I, as Mr. & Mr. James Thornton, would provide a generous initial contribution. Then you would form a committee to raise additional funds, choose a location, oversee the construction of the library, select the titles, determine the lending rules, and establish a trust to fund the project in perpetuity."

"Really?"

James eased down beside her. "Well, Ruth, what do you say? I know how much you enjoy reading all those silly novels."

She squeezed his hand. "It's a wonderful idea. One that speaks to my heart."

He took one last puff from his cigar then raised his

chin and released a trail of smoke. "Excellent, but there is one more thing I should like to discuss with you."

He'd already mentioned her restriction from aiding the Freed Negroes. What else would he require form her?

"I have decided that when we marry, you may reside at Brook Lawn if you desire. That is, when you are not needed with me in Richmond. And you may instruct our offspring at home with the help of a tutor for the advanced subjects, like Latin and trigonometry, when the time comes. You would be much happier here, I think—closer to your mother and Sarah."

She managed a slight nod. "You'd do that—for me?"

He stroked her hand with his thumb. "Yes. As I have expressed before, I'm determined to win your favor, Ruth."

She leaned forward and kissed his cheek. "You've made me a very tempting offer."

Cigar protruding from his fingers, his hand slid over the spot where her lips had been moments before. A devilish grin skimmed his face as his gaze shifted to the neckline of her dress. "It's hard to take my eyes off you. You are breathtaking in this gown."

"Ah-hem."

He lifted his gaze.

"It's customary to look at a woman's face when you compliment her appearance."

He dropped the Upmann then ground it firmly with the toe of his shoe. "So noted. My apologies." He scooted close beside her. Thighs brushing, he leaned forward, his breath warm against her cheek. "I have made many concessions to earn your favor, Ruth. Now it is time for you to express your gratitude." His fingers caressed her bare arm, but his eyes lingered on her mouth. "I am a patient man, Ruth, but I have waited long enough."

She resisted the urge to turn from him. This was part of the arrangement. If she was going to marry James, she'd need to accept his kisses—and all that came with them.

Without warning, his mouth covered hers in a greedy surge of passion. Straining to breathe as he pressed himself tighter against her, she thrust away roaming hands. Wet kisses lumbered their way across her cheek and neck. The moist suction reminded her of Chloe slurping Myra's broth. She shuddered.

"James, that's enough." She wedged her palms against his chest in a vain attempt to push him away. Of all the nights for mother to abandon her post at the window.

He gasped for breath. Hair mussed over his temple, his gaze drifted to her heaving bosom. The porch swing creaked under his shifting weight as he inched closer. "But darling, we will be wed soon."

She struggled to keep him at arm's length. "We aren't…married…yet."

James stiffened. Whistling mingled with heavy footsteps on the stone walk terminated his amorous advances.

"Ruthie, is that you?"

~*~

Benjamin took the porch steps two at a time. His gut clenched as his eyes darted from James' disheveled appearance to the low neckline of Ruth Ann's dress. She was alone…in the dark, with him. His gaze dropped to their hands and thighs. He ran a finger along the inside of his collar. They were much too close for his liking.

James stood and swiped the hair from his forehead then straightened his suit coat. He extended his hand to Benjamin. "Nice to see you again, Mr. Coulter."

His southern drawl dripped with insincerity. James winced and leaned slightly to the right under the strength of Benjamin's grip. "Wish I could say the same for you, Thornton, but I'm an honest, God-fearing man. So exactly why are you here?"

Ruth Ann stood. "Benjamin, that is rude and none of your—"

"I came to pay a call on Miss Sutton this evening. We are discussing our future plans—whether she would like to live in Catoctin Creek or Richmond after we marry."

Hat in hand, Benjamin extended his arm in his rival's direction. "You can't seriously be considering marriage to this man, Ruthie?"

"Well,—"

"And why shouldn't Ruth consider marriage to me. I have far more to offer a woman than you'll ever have, Coulter."

Benjamin balled his fists, crumpling the brim of his hat in the process. He glanced past James until his eyes lighted on Ruth Ann. "Sometimes a woman needs more than material things, Thornton. She needs love."

James snickered. "You are as romantic and foolish as she used to be. But thanks to you, she is now taking a more practical approach to marriage." He kissed Ruth Ann on the cheek before taking one last gander at the neckline of her dress. "I will give you five minutes alone with the railroad man, darling, to say your last good-byes. Then I will expect you inside."

Ruth Ann nodded.

He shifted his steely gaze upward to meet Benjamin's eyes. "And I will expect you to keep your distance from my future wife." The screen door slapped behind him as he made his way inside.

Benjamin wanted to knock the condescending little weasel on his fancy-pants derriere, but that wouldn't win him any points with Ruth Ann. His determined steps pounded the floorboards between the lady and the railing on the opposite end of the porch "What were you thinking, sitting in the dark with him...and dressed like that?"

He paused, waiting for her response. When none came, he resumed his pacing. "His future wife? You've accepted his proposal?"

She remained quiet.

"You have nothing to say about the situation?"

With a jut of her chin, she folded her arms across her chest and drummed her fingers against her skin. "I haven't accepted him—yet. But I'm strongly considering it."

Benjamin swiped a hand over his cleanly shaven jaw. "You told me yourself he doesn't love you."

"Perhaps, but at least I know where I stand with James. He has always been honest about his feelings for me."

Desperation seized him. He grasped her arms. "How many times must I apologize, Ruthie? I'm sorry that I hurt you. You must believe me. I've changed. I'm not that man anymore."

"I don't see what concern any of this is to you. Why did you stop by this evening?"

Benjamin's voice grew louder. "Why did I stop

by?"

"Yes, I wasn't expecting you."

"That's obvious."

Ruth Ann slammed her hands against her hips. "Look, Benjamin, if you have something to say then say it, otherwise I'm going inside. We have guests."

Blood pounded in his temples. Maybe she no longer loved him, but that dandy? His tongue glided along the inside of his cheek. "I came over to mend fences between us."

Her foot tapped briskly against the wooden plank floor. "Well, in case you don't know, Benjamin Coulter, when someone wants to make amends, they usually express a more conciliatory manner."

Her icy tone could freeze water in August.

The latch clicked. Sarah poked her head around the screen door. "For heaven's sake, lower your voices."

"Sorry, Sarah. Mr. Coulter stopped by unexpectedly to mend fences. I dare say it's not going as he planned."

"Well, I suggest you keep your voices down before Mama makes her presence known. Good night."

He took a long breath and released it slowly. "I'm sorry for raising my voice earlier. I came by hoping to talk with you about what has happened between us and was very surprised to find you with that…that—"

"Gentleman."

He rolled his eyes." I'm not sure that word applies."

Ruth Ann walked toward the door. "James is waiting for me inside." Her tone softened as she glanced over her shoulder. "And I don't want—" She shook her head and reached for the latch. "It doesn't matter anymore."

"It matters to me. Tell me, Ruthie. What don't you want?"

She sighed. "I don't want to fight with you anymore."

"I don't want to fight with you either." He stepped closer. "I want to tell you how I've changed and—"

"I'm happy for you, Ben, but it has little to do with me."

He placed his hand on her arm. "You're wrong, Ruthie, it has everything to do with you…with us."

"There's no us, Benjamin." She eased the screen open. "Not anymore. Good night."

"Ruthie, wait." He pushed the door closed. His hand rested on the wooden frame, inches above her shoulder. "You still want to know why I came by tonight?"

She faced him again, her dark eyes searching his face.

"To do this."

In one sweeping motion Benjamin pressed her against the house showering her with impassioned kisses. Her stiffened response didn't discourage him as he twined his fingers through her hair. His lips forged a tender path to her ear and whispered, "I love you, Ruthie."

A weak gasp escaped her parted lips. His arms slid behind her and drew her close in a possessive hold. His lips lingered just above hers for the briefest of moments before he kissed her again, deeply this time. She melted into his embrace, responding with an intensity that rivaled his own before he tore himself away from her.

Gasping for air, she stood braced against the

house, chest heaving.

He folded his arms across his chest. "I know Thornton's kisses don't stir you like that, but I'm sure he tries."

In an instant, her hand connected with his face. "How dare you!"

Benjamin chuckled as his fingers grazed his smarting cheek. "Just remember, passion without love, is lust—plain and simple. Is that what you want for the rest of your life?"

He reached for the latch and nudged the door open before taking Ruth Ann by the elbow. "Go on inside, Ruthie. Your beau is waiting for you. But I suggest before you give Thornton his answer, you think long and hard about that kiss."

Dirt whirled around Benjamin's boots as he walked the dusty road back to the Petersons' boardinghouse. He replayed that stolen kiss in his mind. The mere thought stoked his insides hot enough to roast chestnuts. His confidence quickly waned as he touched his smarting cheek. He probably shouldn't have kissed her like that, but doggone it, this was war. Their passion for one another was a weapon he couldn't afford to leave holstered.

Oil lamps illuminated the first floor of the boardinghouse. He entered the parlor and tossed his hat on an empty chair.

"That woman is so..." He strode back and forth between the hearth and Mrs. Peterson's rocking chair. "Do you know what she was doing when I arrived?"

Neil removed his spectacles and stuffed them in his shirt pocket. He glanced at Charlotte who responded with a shrug of her shoulders.

"Entertaining James Thornton, that's what she was

doing. Alone. In the dark." Benjamin stopped mid-stride. "And that dress. It was more than a yard short of fabric in the bodice, I'd say." He renewed his agitated pacing. "She never wore anything like that when she was on my arm. And for good reason—I'd never stand for it!"

Neil pointed to the chair opposite him. "Why don't you sit down, Benjamin, and take a deep breath while you're at it. You keep that up and I'll be buying Trudy new rugs."

Benjamin flopped down onto the nearest chair. "That's great." He pulled his smooshed hat from underneath him. "Perfect ending to the evening."

Neil leaned forward on his elbows. "I take it Ruth Ann didn't accept your apology."

"I never had a chance to offer it. I got so riled up over James that I...I..."

"Lost your temper, son?"

"That's not all I did. I kissed her, too, with every ounce of desire I could muster."

Mrs. Peterson's fingers flew to her lips, stifling a gasp.

Neil cleared his throat. "And how'd that go over?"

"She resisted at first, but when I told her I still loved her, she kissed me back. Then she slapped me."

Charlotte grinned. "Serves you right, Benjamin. What were you thinking?"

He dropped his head into his hands, elbows resting on his knees. Images of Thornton kissing his Ruthie raced through his mind like a runaway locomotive. "I know it wasn't the most gentlemanly thing to do, but I'm leaving for Snickers Gap in just a few days. I don't have time to waste. I needed to remind her how we feel about each other."

Neil reached across the coffee table and put his hand on Benjamin's slouched shoulder. "Are you confident she's the woman God has chosen for you?"

"I wouldn't put myself through this otherwise. I love her, Neil, more than anyone or anything else...even more than myself, but she—"

"Then you mustn't give up."

Benjamin glanced at Mrs. Peterson. Her quiet determination had taken him off guard. He didn't want to quit on Ruth Ann, but it was hard to persevere, especially when she gave so little sign of encouragement. "I've told her repeatedly that I'm sorry and that I love her. What more can I say?"

Mrs. Peterson lowered her mending to her lap and gently pumped the rocker, eyeing him carefully. "A woman's heart is a tender thing. It will be your actions, not your words, that win her back. You need to do more than tell her you're sorry. You must ask for her forgiveness and her trust. Let her express her doubts and fears without raising your voice."

"Easier said than done. Obviously, I shouldn't have lost my temper tonight, but how should I have reacted when I saw her with that...that—"

"Gentleman caller."

He glared at Charlotte. "Humph. Ravenous wolf is more like it."

Mrs. Peterson squelched a grin as she thrust her needle through the plaid flannel of one of her husband's work shirts. "No one here doubts your love for Ruth Ann, or hers for you, for that matter. The question is whether she's willing to risk her heart again, and it can only be answered in your favor if your actions are consistent with your words."

Benjamin slumped back in his chair. Mrs.

Peterson's wisdom pricked his conscience. He hadn't spent much time looking at the situation from Ruth Ann's perspective. Loving her the way he did, he should spend more time considering her feelings rather than his own.

Oh Lord, please soften Ruthie's heart toward me.

Neil lifted Benjamin's crumpled hat from the coffee table, reshaping the crown as he spoke. "Nothing worthwhile in life is easy. And according to you, Ruth Ann is well worth the effort."

"That she is, Neil, but time is not on my side."

~*~

Benjamin stared at his shabby work boots. Why hadn't he worn his fine suit when he came begging for forgiveness? He'd rushed out the door without giving it a thought. Oh well. He lifted the brass knocker on the Suttons' door. An odd silence followed the heavy thud. No feisty Corgi announced his arrival.

He cleared his throat as the door swung open then extended his hand. "Hello, Joseph."

Joseph glanced at Benjamin's peace offering before looking him in the eyes. "Benjamin. I'm surprised to see you here after last night."

Benjamin forced himself to swallow. It wasn't like Joseph to ignore a hand offered in friendship. He wiped his sweaty palm against his pant leg. He had a long road ahead of him. "My apologies about the ruckus. It won't happen again."

"Glad to hear it." Joseph's expression soured. "Ruth Ann isn't here. James sent the carriage for her following breakfast. She's at Brook Lawn discussing..."

Benjamin cringed. *Oh Lord, please don't let him say*

wedding plans.

"...the library foundation."

His eyes closed briefly. *Thank You, Father.* "Might I have a word with you and Mrs. Sutton?"

Joseph stepped back, allowing him to enter.

Benjamin removed his hat. The familiar scent of lemon oil greeted him as he entered the parlor. "Good day, Mrs. Sutton. Sarah."

Chloe squirmed down from her mother's lap, knocking her *Mother Goose Rhymes* to the floor. She hurled herself at Benjamin, wrapping her tiny arms around his legs. "Uncle Benjamin. Why haven't you come to see me? I've missed you."

He lifted her up and placed a kiss on her cheek. "I've missed you, too, little one. How about if you sit on my lap while I talk with your parents and your grandmother."

Chloe leaned back against his chest, her small hand resting atop his. He took a deep breath then forged ahead. "I want you to know that I regret hurting Ruth Ann. I've been a fool." His gaze drifted to Mrs. Sutton. "I still love your daughter, and I intend to win her back."

Mrs. Sutton strummed her fingers on the plush arm of her wing back chair. "You are too late, young man. James has renewed his attentions to her. We are expecting to announce their engagement as early as today."

"I've heard." He dragged a hand over his face. "Pardon my frankness, ma'am, but why are you pushing her to marry so quickly?"

Her fingers clutched the broach fastened to the ribbon around her neck. "Ruth is more than halfway through her twentieth year. She needs to marry before she loses her bloom."

Before she loses her bloom? Benjamin shook his head at the absurdity of the idea. "I don't agree with Thornton on much, but I think it's fair to say neither one of us thinks she's in danger of her 'bloom' fading anytime soon."

Sarah stroked Lily's silky hair. "I think what Mama means to say is that she feels it's best for Ruth Ann to be settled soon, rather than not at all."

"Even if the man she is marrying doesn't love her?"

Mrs. Sutton pinched her lips together in a thin flat line. "Love? Love did not get her to the altar with you, did it?"

He troweled stiff fingers through his hair, frustration brimming. She was direct and to the point, much like her daughter. He hadn't expected this to be easy. He was tired and feeling more than a little hopeless. Mrs. Peterson had admonished him to keep an even keel if Ruth Ann refused his apology. He needed to try the same tactic now—remain calm and let Mrs. Sutton speak her mind. It would mean eating another helping of humble pie, something that left a bitter taste in his mouth. But if it won back even an ounce of their trust, it would be worth it. Having her family on his side, urging her to trust him again, would be a powerful weapon.

He shook his weary head. "No, ma'am."

"We all had such high hopes for you, Benjamin. Although her figure has always presented challenges where suitors are concerned, you made us believe that you loved her. But in the end, you rejected her for another woman—a more petite woman." Eyes narrowing, her voice strained. "It was against my better judgment to let you court her. I encouraged your attentions, hoping she would find whatever it was her heart longed for. I worried from the beginning all this romantic nonsense would end badly, and I was correct. Perhaps James doesn't love her, but he does care for her, and I am confident they will have a successful union."

Benjamin skimmed the brim of his hat between his thumb and forefinger. Head down, his eyes fixated on a knot in the wood flooring, anywhere but her penetrating gaze.

Mrs. Sutton shifted in her chair, exposing the thick sole of her right shoe. Is that why she discouraged 'romantic nonsense'? Had her heart been broken by a suitor who couldn't see past her deformed leg? The same way he'd rejected Ruth Ann because of her figure? It all made sense now. She wasn't trying to persuade her daughter to marry for money. Instead, she was trying to protect her heart—from a man like him. Or at least the type of man he used to be.

He hadn't considered that the heartache he'd inflicted on Ruth Ann extended to her family. His gaze traveled from Joseph, to Sarah, then Mrs. Sutton. It was clear to him now—the pain in Mrs. Sutton's voice and Chloe's tight embrace, even the disappointment in Joseph's eyes when he'd first arrived. He had become part of this family, and when he broke Ruth Ann's heart, he'd wounded them all.

"You're right, ma'am. I chose to end our courtship for shallow reasons. Please forgive me. You welcomed me into your home as part of your family, and I misused your trust."

Sarah rested her cheek on Lily's head, eyes glistening.

"I've regretted that decision every day since. But I want you to know that I don't feel that way about her appearance any longer. Your daughter is a beautiful woman—in every way imaginable." He paused then forced himself to continue. "There is no excuse for my behavior. I lost my way. I've seen a glimpse of what my life would be like without Ruth Ann, and it's nothing I relish. I intend to do everything in my power to win her back. I won't rest until she agrees to marry me."

Mrs. Sutton remained expressionless.

Joseph offered his hand. "Thank you, Benjamin. We all needed to hear you give voice to both your regrets and affections where Ruth Ann is concerned. You still have my blessing to marry Ruth Ann if you can persuade her to accept."

Benjamin slid Chloe onto the settee and walked beside Mrs. Sutton's chair. "And you, Mrs. Sutton? Do I have your blessing as well?"

She tilted her head and held Benjamin's gaze. Her intense look reminded him of Ruth Ann. She could look deep inside a person and take their measure. A trait she must have taught her daughter. "I will not urge her to consider you, Benjamin."

A heaviness settled on him. Even opening his mouth to speak took concerted effort. "I see."

"Nor will I oppose you."

Jaw unhinged, he rested a hand on the back of her chair. "Pardon?"

"I said I will not oppose you. I will allow Ruth Ann to make her own decision."

"Thank you, ma'am."

"Don't thank me yet. I'm not convinced you are the right choice for her. James has been very attentive, and he has offered her the library foundation—a stroke of genius, if you ask me. You have your work cut out for you, young man."

He glanced at Joseph. "Library foundation?"

"I'll explain as I walk you out." Joseph stood. "Sarah, would you join us, please?"

She nodded and set Lily on her Mimi's lap.

"Bye, Uncle Benjamin."

Uncle Benjamin. If the child only knew how he wished that were true. He tousled her hair. "Good-bye, Chloe."

Joseph leaned against the porch railing. "Don't let grass grow under your feet, Benjamin. I can't believe I'm saying this, but James is close to winning her hand. He's offered her two enticing carrots. She may split her time between Richmond and Catoctin Creek, living at Brook Lawn, of course, and the library foundation."

Benjamin frowned. "You've mentioned that several times. What is the library foundation?"

"Once married, she will no longer be teaching, but James won't allow her to continue volunteering with the Colored Man's Aid Society either. However, it seems the Thorntons have found something to rival her affections for teaching Negroes—establishing libraries in towns throughout the county."

Sarah shook her head. "Mother is right. This library foundation is a stroke of genius. She's so excited about the project that I don't think she slept a wink."

Benjamin rubbed his jaw. This was war, and Thornton knew it, too. The dandy couldn't awaken her passion toward him, so he was doing the next best thing—stirring her love for reading and literature.

"That guy doesn't play fair," he mumbled.

"Pardon?"

Benjamin plopped his hat on his head. "Nothing. I have an idea to win her back, but I could use some help."

Joseph slid his arm around Sarah's waist and pulled her close. "Anything, Benjamin. We're rooting for you. What do you need?"

A wide grin stretched across his face. Thornton wouldn't even know what hit him. "Well, I was thinking…"

24

"Come in."

Mama peeked around the door. "I would like to speak with you privately before James arrives."

Ruth Ann laid her dog-eared copy of *Pride and Prejudice* on the window seat. She'd managed to avoid her mother's probing questions regarding James' proposal thus far. Although heavily inclined to accept him, she wanted one more night to sleep on it—without interference.

"I see you are dressed for dinner."

"Punctuality is essential to James."

"What an elegant coiffure. Did Sarah arrange those pearls in your hair?"

Ruth Ann nodded as she fingered the elaborate braids. "You know I don't have the patience for a hairstyle this intricate."

"With the extra attention given to your appearance, I assume you have decided to accept his offer?"

She nodded. "I will not tell him until tomorrow, just before he returns to Richmond."

"I see." Mama pointed to the pink flowers on the bureau. "James has excellent taste."

Ruth Ann reached for the vase and pulled the roses close, inhaling their fragrance. "They're from the hot houses at Brook Lawn." She idly fondled a rose petal between her thumb and forefinger. "Fresh ones will be delivered to my room daily after we marry."

"You seem indifferent, Ruth. I would think such a gesture would please you."

"I suppose it should." She forced a smile as she returned the vase to her dresser.

Mama studied her. "Benjamin came by to visit today."

Ruth Ann pressed a hand against her middle. Why did the mere mention of that man's name cause fluttering in her stomach? "I trust you sent him away."

Mama shook her head. "He was hoping to see you, of course. When he learned you had gone to Brook Lawn, he spoke with the family."

She snapped her attention toward her mother. "The family? W-what did he say?"

"He apologized to us for his treatment of you and asked our forgiveness then professed to a major change of heart where you are concerned."

Ruth Ann's gaze drifted to her lap. Her fingers traced the thin yellow stripe of her evening dress. "You don't believe him, do you?"

"I do. Benjamin seemed very sincere. He had many complimentary things to say about you and—" Mama's voice cracked. "He reminded me of what a special young woman you are."

Lips parted, she peered up at her mother's face.

"I've never been very comfortable expressing my feelings, Ruth." Mama hesitated and reached for her daughter's hand. "But I want you to know that there are many qualities I admire about you. You have an inner beauty and quiet strength that draws people to you. You are kind, smart, and of strong character. Every one of our acquaintance tells me how affable you are."

Ruth Ann's breath hitched. She yearned to believe

her mother's words, but they didn't fit the narrative of her life.

Moisture pooled at the rim of Mama's eyes. "You have reason to doubt what I say?"

She tugged her bottom lip between her teeth. "Sometimes, Mama, when you look at me, I think all you see are my—" Lowering her gaze she whispered, "My imperfections. For a very long time, that is all I saw as well."

"I am sorry, Ruth Ann."

Ruth Ann? She lifted her head. Her mother hadn't addressed her that way since childhood.

A single tear traveled Mama's cheek. "I have been too harsh on you in the past. I placed entirely too much emphasis on your outward appearance and not enough on your character. We all have our weaknesses, Ruth Ann. I am profoundly sorry for exaggerating yours."

She rested her head on her mother's shoulder.

"I've made quite a mess of things. Can you find it in your heart to forgive me?"

Ruth Ann clutched her mother close. "Of course, Mama. I love you."

Mama pulled her close again, caressing her back. She rested her cheek atop Ruth Ann's head. "Now, about this marriage offer..."

~*~

A light breeze fluttered the yellow toile curtains at the Sutton's kitchen window. Mumbling to herself as she wrote, the steel nib of Ruth Ann's pen glided effortlessly across the paper tablet barely able to keep pace with the flourish of ideas churning in her head.

"Three-week lending period. No fees unless more than five days late. No more than two books lent to any one patron during a single lending period."

"Have you seen my pipe and tobacco box, Ruth Ann?"

Pen in hand, Ruth Ann pointed to the counter nearest the icebox. She dipped the nib in the inkbottle and returned to her list-making with nary a glance in Joseph's direction.

"Thank you." Joseph peered over her shoulder. "If I'd put things away where they belong, as I tell Chloe on a daily basis, perhaps I could find them when I need them."

Lost in her own thoughts, Ruth Ann continued penning and mumbling. "Negroes must be allowed access to the library."

She paused, pen to cheek. James would never allow it. Sighing, she scratched a line through her last entry. Tapping the wooden shaft of her pen against her jaw, she continued pondering how to make the lending library accessible to all of Catoctin Creek's residents.

The pen descended on the paper, etching her idea in ink. "Discuss lending library for Francis Jackson Negro School before resigning from Colored Man's Aid Society."

Joseph struck a match across the strike plate on the stove and lowered it to the bowl of his pipe. Soon the kitchen smelled of cherry and vanilla as his rich Virginia Cavendish floated in the air. "What has you so engrossed, Ruth Ann?"

"I'm making a list of all my ideas for the library foundation." She hastily scribbled another idea on her list.

"Mmm. Then you've decided to accept James'

proposal?"

Ruth Ann froze, nib to paper. "Yes. I have." She swallowed the lump in her throat, eyes fixed to her list. "I will tell him tomorrow."

Joseph pointed to the empty seat beside her at the table. "May I?"

"Of course. You needn't ask."

Joseph straddled the chair beside her. "And what of your feelings for Benjamin?"

Squaring her shoulders, she met Joseph's gaze. "That's irrelevant. After what he's done, how can I ever trust him again?"

He clenched the stem of his pipe between his teeth. "Your sister and I found our way back to each other after our courtship ended. We learned to trust again. You and Benjamin can as well."

She closed her eyes and shook her head. "I love you, Joseph. You know that, but I'm not as gentle spirited as Sarah. I don't know how she learned to trust you again."

He lowered the pipe from his mouth. "It wasn't Sarah that needed to learn to trust again—it was me."

Ruth Ann stared, mouth agape. "I—I just assumed it was you who had ended the relationship. I was barely fourteen. Sarah didn't confide in me then." She shook her head as she struggled to reconcile Joseph's words with her memories. "But I remember her tears and malaise. She barely ate for months."

Joseph removed the pen from her hand and rested it in the ink bottle. "Yes, all of that is true, but only many months later. Perhaps you should ask Sarah about this."

"I'd rather hear about it from you."

Joseph hesitated, brow wrinkled. "All right, but

only because I think it may help where Benjamin is concerned."

Ruth Ann rolled her eyes. "What does Benjamin have to do with anything? I know Sarah didn't cast you aside because your appearance was lacking." She grinned. "You are one of the handsomest men I've ever seen—even with the whiskers. And you know I'm not inclined toward a man with a beard."

Joseph's neck sported a nice shade of crimson as his discomfiture spread upward from his neck. "Thank you. I suppose I should be accustomed to your frankness by now, but sometimes, you still surprise me."

She smiled. "Good. Stop stalling and tell me what you did to my sister to make her end the courtship."

The gleam in Joseph's eyes disappeared, replaced by a thoughtful stare. "I wasn't born first."

"Sarah broke the courtship because you won't inherit Oak Hill?"

Joseph nodded.

She slouched against the back of her chair. "I can't believe it. That doesn't sound like Sarah."

"Not only that, she began receiving calls from my older brother, Richard."

"Why would she do such a thing?"

Joseph raised a brow. "Why has your mother encouraged a match between you and James?"

Ruth Ann swiftly raised her hand in a failed effort to prevent a gasp from escaping her lips. "To secure a wealthy, well-connected husband."

Joseph sighed. "I could've stayed at the farm and lavished Sarah with my family's money, but I had a dream to own my own business. I had requested and received a chunk of my inheritance to open my liveries.

However, your mother felt I was untested—too much of a risk."

A stiff breeze swooshed through the open window, swaying the curtains. The pages of Ruth Ann's tablet flipped well past the point of her meticulous list. She moved to the window and lowered the sash.

"That doesn't make any sense. Mama depends on you, and Sarah—she adores you."

A smile crossed Joseph's whiskered face. "And I her, but the sweet peacemaker we both know and love is void of your tenacity and determination, Ruth Ann. Sarah is compliant. Sometimes to her own detriment. She bowed to your mother's wishes where I was concerned."

"What did you think when she told you she wanted to step out with Richard?"

"Ah, that part she didn't tell me at first. Initially, she tried to convince me that we weren't well suited for one another. A few weeks later, Richard told me he intended to court Sarah and that she was amenable to the idea." Joseph raised the pipe to his lips and took another puff, his mind seeming to drift away before releasing the smoke from his mouth. "When I confronted her, she didn't deny it. She said simply that despite her love for me, she could not stand to disappoint your mother."

Ruth Ann leaned against the dry sink, eyes trained on Joseph, struggling to accept this version of events so foreign to her.

"I begged her several times to reconsider, but after discovering that she had chosen Richard, not for love but for his inheritance, I was devastated." Joseph's voice cracked as he fought to contain his emotions.

"The thought of my brother, whom I idolized, with Sarah, nearly drove me insane. I had not only lost my best friend in my brother, but the love of my life as well." Joseph shuddered. "I bought my first livery, in Middleburg. I bunked there and refused to speak to either Richard or Sarah for months."

"What changed?"

Joseph's eyes softened as he reached for Ruth Ann's hand.

Placing her hand inside his, she returned to her seat.

"Your father passed, and I came to pay my respects. It had been six months since we'd spoken, and Sarah was surprised to see me. Richard, on the other hand, had sent a telegram with his condolences. He told her it was foaling season, but if she sent word of the arrangements, he would do his best to come to the funeral."

Her voice strained. "He was courting Sarah, and he would 'do his best to come'?"

Joseph nodded. "If you recall, Richard and my parents did attend the funeral, but his first love has always been the horses—a lesson Sarah learned quite painfully. They departed the next day, leaving Sarah with all your father's affairs to manage. She pleaded with Richard to stay and assist her, but he refused, saying he had a business to run and suggested your mother hire an attorney to handle your father's estate."

Removing the pipe from his lips, Joseph leaned it against the tobacco box. "I saw her distress, and I couldn't abandon her as Richard had, though it pained me to stay and not be able to console her grief as I would have liked." Joseph rubbed his whiskers as he continued. "I sent word to my foreman that I wouldn't be returning for at least two weeks and took a room at the Peterson's. Fortunately, your father was an organized man. In just a few hours alone in his study I found his will, bank documents, and investment papers. A few days later, your mother and I traveled to Leesburg to settle all of his accounts and file his will with the court."

She'd always known Joseph to be an honorable man, but this—taking care of their father's affairs when Sarah had rejected him. Her esteem for her brother-in-law grew tenfold. Her voice wavered. "H-How did you reconcile?"

"We didn't for several more months, but Sarah ended her courtship with Richard immediately after I returned to Middleburg. This is when the malaise you mentioned earlier initiated. Although I loved her deeply, my heart was not yet ready to trust her. Sarah took to her bed and wouldn't eat or receive company."

"I remember. We were so worried about her, and on the heels of Papa's death, it was more than Mama could bear."

"Your mother came to see me in Middleburg. She informed me of Sarah's condition and begged me to visit her. My willingness to place my fledgling business on hold to assist your family in their time of need convinced your mother of my honorable character and love for your sister. She apologized for judging me solely by my bank account and asked me to forgive Sarah for complying with her wishes."

"But how did you trust her, Joseph? What made you believe that Sarah loved you?"

Joseph placed his free hand on top of Ruth Ann's. "I just knew in my heart that she had always loved me in spite of her misguided actions." He paused. "Your father and I are not the only honorable men in your life, Ruth Ann. I can think of at least one other. One who risked his life for you, with no expectation of ever receiving your love or trust again."

Moisture pooled in the corner of her eyes.

"The same one who missed his certification exam recuperating from his injuries."

She sucked in a breath. Images of Benjamin weak and bed-ridden invaded her thoughts. "I-I had no idea. He never told me."

"Why would he? He has no regrets sacrificing on your behalf. He loves you."

"But how can I be sure he will never tire of my appearance again?"

"You can't. There are no guarantees. Love is a leap of faith."

The kitchen door swung open. "I see you found your pipe." Sarah's mouth tilted upward in a playful smile. "I thought you had gone to awaken Malachi to purchase a new one."

Joseph looped his arm around his wife's waist and pulled her close. "Ruth Ann and I have been talking." He tapped the tip of Sarah's nose with his finger. "You never told her that you broke my heart all those years ago. She assumed I had done the dirty deed."

Sarah brushed the back of her hand along Joseph's whiskered jaw. "I thank God every day you had the courage to trust me again. I would be lost without you."

Joseph pulled Sarah's hand forward and lovingly kissed her fingers.

Ruth Ann doubted she would ever know the type of love Joseph displayed so tenderly for Sarah. Her thoughts roamed to the conversation with James in the gazebo last autumn. *Perhaps, in time, we will have a deep abiding affection and concern for one another.* She sighed. It may not be all that her heart desired, but at least he couldn't shatter it to pieces as Benjamin had.

Sarah leaned forward and kissed the top of her husband's head before addressing her sister. "Benjamin came to visit today while you were at Brook Lawn."

She pressed a hand to her stomach hoping to quell the unwelcome churning of emotions. "I heard. Mama told me."

"He apologized for the way he treated you." Sarah placed a hand on her sister's shoulder. "Joseph and I believe he is contrite and that he has changed."

Deep down, Ruth Ann knew it, too. She had sensed it when they talked about the Colored Man's Aid Society, and she saw it in his jealousy over James. Having given him no reason to think she would consider him again, he'd come back repeatedly seeking to make amends. She shook her head. *Stay strong so he doesn't break your heart again.*

Sarah tucked a stray curl behind her sister's ear. "He still loves you, and he's determined to win you back."

"Too little, too late. Tomorrow, I will accept James' proposal." She gathered her writing supplies and whisked past Sarah and Joseph. "Good night."

"Ruth Ann," Joseph called just as her hand pushed open the swinging door.

She paused but refused to face him.

"Accepting James doesn't guarantee your life will be free from heartache. The only assurance you have is that James doesn't love you. I'm sure he will be a kind husband to you, or I wouldn't allow the union." His strong hand gripped her shoulder, coaxing her to face him. "A loveless marriage will bring its own type of heartache to be sure. If that is all you desire from your marriage, then you should be well pleased."

He pulled her into a brotherly embrace. "If you desire to be loved deeply, then Sarah and I urge you to open your heart to Benjamin and trust him again." His gaze wandered to Sarah. "I have no regrets that I chose to take a leap of faith."

Taking a leap of faith sounded simple enough.

Then again, one misstep on the side of a steep cliff could send her hurling to her death.

~*~

Moonlight streamed through Ruth Ann's bedroom window, casting shadows on the wall. The chant of a distant whip-poor-will coupled with the sweet scent of peonies floated on the breeze. She flopped onto her back and stared at the ceiling, her arm draped across her forehead. James expected an answer tomorrow. He'd been so attentive at supper and interested in all her ideas for the library foundation. She glanced at the roses on the bureau. A faint smile passed her lips. He was trying hard to win her hand. Life as Mrs. James Robert Thornton wouldn't be so bad.

She rolled onto her side and allowed her eyelids to drift shut. Disturbing thoughts of their kiss on the swing derailed her slumber. Unwittingly, her hand swiped her lips. She shuddered. Surely, that would improve with time. Her eyes sprung open.

What if it didn't?

She sat up and pulled her knees close. Could she lie in his bed? Conceive his children? There'd be no denying him if they married—and she did want children. How bad could it be? Women had endured their marital obligations for centuries. Besides, if he resided in Richmond six to nine months out of the year, the frequency of her wifely duties would be severely diminished. It would be fine. She nestled into her pillow and forced herself to concentrate on more pleasant thoughts—like the library foundation.

Titles by Dickens, Austen, Emerson, and Verne tallied in her thoughts. Without warning or invitation, Benjamin's amber eyes infiltrated her list making. She flung herself over, once again staring at the ceiling. He'd been genuinely concerned when he learned of Buddy's passing. Unlike James, Ben had cared for her dog and had supported her involvement with the Freedmen's School. Alone in the dark she chuckled at how flustered he was when he found her on the porch with James. Served him right.

But that kiss! She shoved one leg from underneath the blanket and fanned herself with *Pride and Prejudice*. There was no denying that man could spark heat in every inch of her body. His contrition did appear genuine. Even Mama thought so. She sighed. Should she put James off a bit longer and try opening her heart to Benjamin again as Sarah and Joseph encouraged?

Images of the petite Rose Martin on Benjamin's arm taunted her. The leather straps supporting her bedding groaned as she flipped onto her stomach. She punched her pillow. Insufferable man.

Ping.

Ruth Ann glanced toward the window.

Ping.

She pushed herself onto her elbows.

Ping. "Ru-thie!"

Huh?

"It's me, Ben."

For heaven's sake, didn't he know what time it was?

"There's a yellow rose of Texas that I am going to see-"

The familiar chorus drifted through her open window. Was he playing a guitar?

"She cried so when I left her, it like to break my heart. And if I ever find her, we never more will part."

Ruth Ann cast off the blanket and hurried toward the source of the disturbance. With one knee bent on the window seat, she lifted the sash above her head and leaned out. "Benjamin? What are you doing?"

He stepped into the moonlight. "I have some things to say to you, and I want you to come down to the porch and hear me out."

"It's late."

"I'm not leaving until I've said my piece."

"I'm not—"

"—her eyes are bright as di'monds, they sparkle like the dew—"

"Stop that at once! You'll wake the entire house."

"Then you'd better come down here, Ruthie."

"I will not. Besides, I'm in my nightclothes."

"Have it your way. *Oh, now I'm going to find her, for my heart is full of woe. And we'll sing the songs together that we sung so long ago. We'll play the bango gaily, and we'll sing the songs of yore, And the Yellow Rose of Texas shall be mine forevermore—*"

"All right. All right. I'll come." She dressed quickly and crept down the stairs then peeked through the open crack in the front door.

"I'm here. Now what is it you wanted to say to me?"

"Nope. You need to come out here on the porch and talk with me."

She shook her head. "It must be after ten o'clock."

His fingers plucked the strings. *"There's a yellow rose of Texas that I am going to see—"*

Ruth Ann scurried through the door, closing it tight behind her. "Okay, you win."

~*~

Benjamin lifted the strap from his shoulder and leaned the guitar against the porch railing. His eyes fixated on the dark mass of curls unfurled across her shoulders. His throat felt thicker than a stack of pancakes smothered in molasses. He wiped his sweaty palms against his pant leg and removed his hat. "Evenin', Ruthie."

Ruth Ann folded her arms across her chest and pursed her lips. Her slippered foot tapped the wooden porch boards. She didn't look too pleased with his starlight serenade. He swiped his tongue around the inside of his mouth, hoping to remove the mass of cotton that had somehow collected there. His heart thundered in his chest. This was it—now or never.

His last chance.

Pulse hammering in his head, words tumbled from his lips. "I've come here tonight to persuade you to trust me again. I love you, Ruthie. My heart beats for none but you."

"I'm sorry, Ben, it's too late—"

A faint hissing escaped his constricting lungs.

"I'm accepting James' proposal tomorrow."

He doubled-over, hands sliding to his knees.

She rushed to his side. "Are you ill?"

"Woman...you...scared me." He took several deep breaths and straightened. "It's not too late, and you need to listen to what I have to say, before you make a huge mistake like the one I made calling on Rose."

She stepped away from him, shaking her head.

"Please, Ruthie. Listen to what I have to say, and if I don't convince you, then I'll leave you alone and you can marry Thornton with no more interference from me."

"Promise?"

Benjamin raised his right hand. "On my honor."

A faint smile passed her lips. "I agree to your terms."

"Allow me, Miss Sutton." He offered his arm.

She raised a brow. "Why can't we talk right here?"

"I have a surprise."

Her gaze wandered to the guitar. "I hope it's quieter than your last one."

"That depends on you. If you give me any trouble, I'll have to start singing again."

She slipped her hand into the fold of his arm. "I'll be on my best behavior."

Benjamin escorted her down the stairs and across the well-worn path to her mother's cutting garden. As they rounded the corner of the house, a small fire came in view. Two chairs sat nearby with a wooden crate between them serving as a makeshift table. A pair of coffee mugs sat on the crate, one on either side of a pitcher filled with pale pink Peonies.

Ruth Ann cradled her cheeks between her palms. "You did this for me?"

"Let's say it's been a group effort."

"But why?"

He pointed to the canopy of stars. "Because God

made nights like this for wooing women."

She smiled, revealing one of her dimples, then took a seat by the fire.

Benjamin handed her a mug and took the empty chair beside her. A few minutes passed before he broke the silence. "Ruthie, there are no words to tell you how sorry I am for hurting you."

"I don't want to—"

He weaved his fingers between hers and squeezed. "No doubt some of what I say will be hard to hear, but you agreed to hear me out, and I intend to hold you to it."

Ruth Ann nodded and sipped her coffee.

"You told me I was brave for rescuing you at the Freedmen's school. But truth is, when it really mattered, I was a coward."

"That's not—"

He held up his hand, quieting her objections. "Yes, it is. I was a coward and a fool to walk away from you. I was afraid of what others would think of me if the woman on my arm was less than perfect. And the truth is, there was never anything wrong with you, Ruthie, but there was definitely something wrong with me."

He glanced in her direction. Their eyes met briefly before she focused on the crackling fire.

"I've spent most of my life ashamed of my upbringing. I've already told you that my parents were illiterate and how we scraped to get by, but I never told you much about my family—especially my mother. She has always been…a portly woman. Doing the simplest tasks would tucker her out, so many things were put off or left undone altogether. People stared whenever we went to town, or worse yet, whispered and pointed in our direction. It got so bad, I'd offer to do errands for Ma in town because I was embarrassed to be seen with her. I ran ahead of my mother to church and chose a pew with friends so I wouldn't have to sit with her."

Ruth Ann wriggled her fingers lose from his grip and moved closer to the fire. Keeping her back to him, she stretched her palms out against the warmth of the flames.

Would that be the last time he ever touched her? *Please, Lord, soften her heart toward me.* He swallowed the lump in his throat and trudged on.

"The sad part is, I love my mother, but I wasn't courageous enough to confront those who judged her solely on her outward appearance." Benjamin hung his head, fearful and ashamed of what he would say next. "Somewhere along the line, I resolved that my life would be different. No matter what it took, I would be respected, not ridiculed and I...I promised myself that I wouldn't marry a plump woman."

Ruth Ann gasped and covered her mouth, refusing to look his direction. "You alluded to something like this when I forced you to tell me why we couldn't be together, but to hear you put voice to it—" A soft whimper accompanied the shaking of her head. "There's something I don't understand. If you made such a promise to yourself, why did you pursue me in the first place?"

He moved behind her. "Because you're so pretty, Ruthie. I've been smitten with you since the first day I came across you barefoot at the creek. You're smart, kind, and patient. You're refined but satisfied with simple things."

She faced him now, wrinkles creasing her brow. "So, what changed?"

"What changed?"

"My figure hasn't altered from the day we met to the day you stepped out with Rose Martin. Why did it suddenly become an issue for you?"

"Oh." Benjamin took a deep breath. He knew if there was any hope of righting things with Ruth Ann, he needed to be brutally honest with her, but he didn't want to cause her any more pain. "Comments from the men in camp about your figure."

"Like what?"

He hadn't planned on traveling this road. What good could come from it? "It's not important now."

"It's important to me. Tell me, Ben."

A sweaty palm stroked the back of his neck. "Remember the day you came to see me at the railroad camp with Maggie and Charlotte?"

She nodded.

"When you left, several of the men teased me saying you had eyes for me and that I'd better be careful. They made jokes about your ample curves and how hips like yours were made for pushing out babies and…"

Her eyes bore into him like a hammer pummeling a nail. "And you didn't stand up to the truth of your feelings for me."

Her icy tone nicked his heart, but he deserved it. He squatted and stoked the fire with a stick. "No. I'm ashamed to say I didn't."

"So you tossed me aside in the hopes of a relationship with Rose. Well, that makes sense. Rose is slim and petite—quite the opposite of me, isn't she?"

"Yes, she is. In every way imaginable."

~*~

Unbelievable.

Ruth Ann folded her arms tightly against her chest, doubting her decision to come outside and listen to more of this nonsense.

The fire hissed and popped as Benjamin shoved his makeshift poker under a log. "Rose may have been the petite woman I thought I wanted, but she has none of your qualities. She spoke only of fashion and gossip. When she asked about my work, she nearly fell asleep before my answer was through."

Ruth Ann's lips curved into a satisfied grin.

Benjamin paused, keeping his gaze fixed on the flames. "Rose represents everything I thought I needed to garner the attention and respect of other men. However, I've learned that a man can't respect himself if he doesn't pursue the woman he loves because of what others think about him. God taught me that respect comes from my character—not my job, my possessions, or the woman who graces my arm." He tossed the stick into the fire and stepped toward her. "And you taught me how to look deeper within myself to find the courage to stand up for what I want."

"Me?"

He grasped her folded elbows. "You risked everything to teach at the Freedmen's school because you didn't see Negroes. You saw people made in the image and likeness of God. And you didn't back down."

"I was foolhardy and reckless. I nearly got myself and everyone I care about killed."

"No. You stood up for what you believed, no matter what others thought. That's what I intend to do from this day forward. With or without you by my side."

"Aren't you forgetting something?"

"What?"

"Nothing has changed in that regard. I have the same broad shoulders and fuller curves I've always had." She looked away from him, biting her lip to keep her emotions in check.

"Ruthie, everything I could ever want or need is in my two hands right now."

Her lips quivered and moisture pooled in her eyes.

"I've always thought you were pretty, but now…"

Benjamin's eyes widened and the smile that graced his lips expanded. Why was he staring at her as if he didn't know her? "How do you see me now, Ben?"

"I think you're the most beautiful woman I've ever seen."

Her jaw slackened. "Y-you think I'm beautiful? But I'm still…"

"Shhh," he whispered, gently cupping her face in his hands. "All I see…is you."

Tears streamed unchecked now. No one had ever thought she was beautiful. No one, except her Heavenly Father. The tender sincerity of his words bore witness in her heart. This was exactly what she wanted him to say—what she needed him to say.

He removed the handkerchief from his pocket and dabbed her eyes. "You are all my heart desires. Without you, Ruthie, I'm nothing. I need you by my side, helping me to become the man God wants me to be."

Her chest tightened as her resolve dwindled like candle wax near a burning a flame.

"Ruthie, look at me."

"Uh-uh." She clamped her eyelids closed, summoning strength from somewhere deep inside she didn't know she still possessed.

He lifted her chin with his finger, but she still refused to open her eyes and look at him. He leaned forward, his soft breath tickling her ear. "You're a stubborn woman, Ruth Ann Sutton."

She chuckled and complied with his request as her gaze rested on his honey-colored eyes.

"Ruthie, I know I don't deserve it, but can you find it in your heart to forgive me? To trust me? I will never hurt you like that again."

Ruth Ann pressed her lips together, heart pounding. It was no use. She could not deny her love for him any more than she could deny air to her lungs. "I already have."

Benjamin drew her gently toward him. His fingers traced her hairline then across her jaw before dropping to her shoulders and down the length of her arm.

She trembled at his touch and pulled back slightly. Disappointment clouded his eyes. Any doubt soon vanished as she stroked his cheek with the back of her hand. "No matter how hard I tried, I couldn't make myself stop loving you, Ben."

He pulled her into a snug embrace. "What will you tell Thornton?"

A contented sigh escaped her lips. "That I can't marry him because I'm in love with you."

He raised her hand to his mouth. A sultry grin claimed his lips as he kissed her open palm.

Her breath stilled as a trail of tiny kisses showered her forehead, her temple, her cheek. One strong hand in the small of her back held her tight against him while the other tenderly caressed her face. She rested her cheek in his palm, savoring his touch.

He angled closer. "Ruthie."

His warm breath fluttered against her skin dispatching fiery vibrations to every quarter. Pulse skittering, her eyes flickered closed, anticipating the reunion of their lips.

"I can't imagine my life without you. Marry me. Let me cherish you for the rest of my life."

25

Ruth Ann's eyes whisked open. She'd expected a kiss, not a marriage proposal. They'd reconciled only moments ago and now Ben sent her hurling off a precipice into the great unknown. She massaged her temple. What was she to say? Joy, fear, and desperation tangled her heart and head together like a ball of Myra's knitting yarn. Heart throbbing in her chest, she desperately weighed Benjamin's declarations. Were they enough to bind herself to him for the remainder of their lives?

"Ben I'm not—"

Calloused fingers pressed against her lips, silencing her protests. "I'm sure this seems very sudden, but I've wanted you to be my bride for a long time."

She shook her head. "But, I—"

"Shhh. Don't answer me now. Take a few days to think and pray about your decision."

She forced a short breath from her lips and nodded.

"Good. I'll come by for you on Tuesday. We can have a picnic at the stream and you can tell me your answer then."

~*~

Ruth Ann leaned back on her hands and twirled her feet in the cool water of the creek. Three days had passed since Benjamin proposed, and she still didn't know how to answer him. She didn't doubt their love for one another, but was his change of heart real or would the first woman with a trim figure and a pretty smile lure him away? Would he regret his choice? That would be too much to bear. She needed to find a way to renew their courtship but postpone any engagement until he'd proven himself. After all he'd put her through, he'd understand she needed more time.

Or would he?

Maybe even a postponement would sting of enough rejection to chase him away. Injuring a man's pride was dangerous territory. Sighing, she picked up a pebble and tossed it into the creek. The ripples spread across the stream. Her thoughts pondered the verse in Joel that Charlotte had shared during those dark days when she'd first learned why Benjamin had really ended their courtship. *And I will restore to you the years that the locust hath eaten.*

She glanced heavenward. "Is that what You're doing between Ben and me, Lord? Are You restoring all that the locust have eaten? I love him, and I believe he loves me, but I'm afraid. Give me the words, Lord, so he'll understand I need to wait—just a bit longer."

Her gaze rested on the stream where mating dragonflies skimmed the water's surface. How would she tell him? What words would he—

This is your husband.

A cool prickle raced from her shoulders to her ankles.

This is your husband.

She glanced behind her. No one was there. The gentle, loving voice had been so clear, so vivid—like the dreadful evening she'd clutched the laudanum.

Benjamin is your husband.

What? No. She'd asked for God's guidance, but this wasn't the answer she'd prayed for. Her stomach roiled. Short, desperate breaths blew through her parted lips. She wanted to wait until Benjamin had proven himself. Tilting her head back, her fingers clutched the fabric of her bodice.

"I can't. I'm not ready, Lord. I need to see proof that he's changed before I—"

Benjamin is My best for you.

Crying, she cradled her face in her hands. "Please! I beg you, Father. Don't ask this of me."

I will not leave you or forsake you when you follow after Me. I love you, child, as I love, Benjamin. He is the one I have chosen for you.

God had chosen Ben? For her? Her breathing relaxed to a steady rhythmic pace. A divine serenity washed over her just as the cool current of the stream flapped against her bare feet, easing the tightness gripping her chest.

"I'm afraid, Lord. Please give me the courage to go where You lead."

Horse hooves clomped in the meadow behind her. She retrieved the handkerchief from her sleeve and dried her tears. What a sight she must be. Puffy, swollen eyes and a red nose would most likely greet Benjamin. She straightened her shoulders. God would give her the words—and the courage to speak them.

~*~

Benjamin guided the team into the clearing. He spied Ruth Ann perched on that same rock overhanging the creek. Why had she gone ahead without him? This didn't bode well for the answer he wanted to his proposal. *May Your will be done, Lord.*

She waved.

"Hello, sweetheart." He fastened the brake and tethered the team to a low branch then grabbed the blanket and picnic basket from the back of the wagon. "I was surprised to hear you'd gone ahead."

She smiled. "I wanted to save us a good spot."

"Your eyes are red." His stomach tightened. "Have you been crying?"

"Only a smidge. I was lonely without you." She stretched up on tiptoes and kissed his cheek. "Let me take the basket while you spread the blanket."

He doubted her excuse, but he also wasn't sure he wanted to know why she'd been crying either. Not when he was hoping to hear she would become his bride.

He pointed to her grassy feet. "I see you've been enjoying the creek without me again."

Ruth Ann wiggled her toes. "I can't deny it. Want to join me?"

"Don't mind if I do." He plopped down and removed his boots and socks then took her hand and headed in the direction of the water.

After only a few steps, she resisted. "Wait a minute. If I didn't know you better I'd think you were a city slicker, Ben Coulter."

He wrinkled his brow and looked at the clothes he wore. Not his usual work pants, but not his Sunday best either. "What's wrong with my clothes?"

"Nothing." She stooped and rolled up Benjamin's pant legs. "But any country boy worth his salt knows to roll up his britches before wading in the creek."

Grinning, she straightened to her full height. "You

have hairy feet."

He glanced at her toes, peeking out beneath the hem of her blue skirt. "I'm glad you don't."

He slipped an arm around her waist and pulled her close. His lips grazed her cheek, not once, but several times as they inched forward on their quest to secure her lips with his own.

She shoved her hands between them. "Please don't."

He nodded and released her, his heart pinching in his chest. Just when he thought perhaps he'd misunderstood her earlier tears. But now, the hope of her acceptance seemed more dismal than ever.

She tugged on his hand. "Did you hear that?"

"What?"

"It sounded like a whimper coming from over there near your wagon."

"I didn't hear anything. Come on. Let's go wading." He led her toward the creek bank.

She stopped just a few feet shy of the water. "Listen. There it is again. Don't you hear it?"

He shook his head.

Twisting her hand free, she picked up her skirts and headed for the wagon. He followed, fast on her heels.

"Oh, Ben, a Corgi puppy!" She lifted the small dog from the wagon and rubbed its soft fur against her cheek. "It's the cutest thing I've ever seen."

He stroked the soft tuft of hair on the pup's head. "Yeah, she's pretty darn cute. I hope you don't mind that she's slightly deformed."

Ruth Ann raised the pup above her head, inspecting her. "She looks perfect to me. What's the matter with her?"

"Look at her ears. One's up and the other is only half up. And the tip is bent, but she has the most beautiful eyes."

She lowered the pup to her face, touching its cold, wet nose to her own. "That's normal. Their ears are floppy when they're born. They'll stand up on their own before long. Where did you get her?"

"Joseph and I visited Oak Hill yesterday and picked her out. Mr. Palmer said you were welcome to come back and choose another if she's not to your liking."

Ruth Ann's grin broadened until her smile lighted her entire face. Her dark eyes sparkling. "She's for me?"

Both dimples. He hadn't seen that stunning pair in far too long. His throat constricted, making it difficult to form an intelligent sound. "W...uh...She's..." He kicked a clod of grass with his bare toes then bit back a foul word. "That smarts. I forgot I'd taken my boots off."

She snickered.

"What I'm trying to say is that I'm hoping she's for us. But, yes, she's yours whether you accept my proposal or not."

"Thank you. This was so thoughtful and speaks to my heart."

"Better than a library foundation?"

Her eyes softened as she snuggled the pup under her chin. "No comparison."

Warmth radiated through his chest. Maybe all wasn't lost. "Let's take her over to the blanket."

Yipping and pouncing, the rambunctious canine nipped and tugged at Ruth Ann's skirts. "No you don't, little one."

Ben grabbed a twig from the grass. "Here you go, squirt. Chew on this."

The pup wedged the stick between her paws and gnawed intently. Before long she yawned and stretched then curled up in Ruth Ann's lap and fell asleep.

Ruth Ann stroked the pup's red and white fur. "Did you know the word *Corgi* means dwarf dog?"

"No, but I can see that with those short stubby legs of hers."

She chuckled.

He tore a tall blade of grass from its roots, split it, and stuck half between his teeth. No need to entice her. He knew her well enough to know she'd continue without any prodding on his part.

She pointed to the ring of white fur circling the back of the dog's neck. "Legend has it that a Corgi wandering in the Welsh countryside came upon a maiden who had fallen off her horse. She asked the dog if he would help her get home. He obliged her, and when they reached her castle, the maiden revealed that she was a fairy princess, and for his gallant deed, he would ever be marked with a white fairy saddle so all would know of the Corgi's noble heart."

Benjamin grinned. Life with her would never be dull. He reclined on his elbow and removed the stalk from his mouth. "You're the most fascinating woman I've ever met."

A touch of pink graced her cheeks before she glanced away. The breeze blew a loose curl across her jaw, taunting him to wrap it around his finger. Anxiety plagued him. She'd given no hint as to whether or not she'd accept his proposal. In fact, she seemed oblivious to the fact that she owed him an answer about their future. If she said yes, they could begin planning their life together—right now. But what if her answer was no? Indecision might not be so bad after all.

Buck up, Coulter and just ask.

He retrieved a coin from his pocket and offered it to her. "Penny for your thoughts?"

She smiled and took the penny. "What would you like to know?"

Benjamin held her gaze, hoping he'd have this privilege for the rest of his life. He suppressed the uncertainty constricting his voice. "Will you be my bride?"

Moisture pooled in her dark eyes.

Piercing pain gripped him, puncturing his heart. How would he ever recover? Air creaked from his lungs, bottling in his chest.

Tears streaked her cheeks.

He took her hand in his, probably for the last time. His thumb caressed her soft skin. "I suppose some things can't be fixed with an 'I'm sorry.' I know it doesn't make any sense, but I still need to hear you say it, Ruthie."

Her crying escalated into shoulder-shaking sobs, garbling her words. "God s-said...you...I...to...m-m...you."

Benjamin stared lovingly at the hand he had hoped would adorn his grandmother's ring. Why had he let a momentary fascination with Rose Martin ruin everything? He'd never forgive himself. "I want you to know that I'll always love you, Ruthie, but as I promised, I won't bother you anymore. You are free to marry Thornton with no further interference from me."

Her breath hitched as she struggled to find her voice. "B-But...I w-want you...to bother me."

His brows furrowed as he cocked his head to the side.

"G-God told me...you're His...best for me."

He leaned closer. "What are you saying, Ruthie?"

"I'm saying...I love you...and...I...I want to be your wife."

Benjamin sprung to his knees and grasped Ruth Ann by the shoulders. "Then goodness gracious, woman, why are you crying?"

"They're h-happy tears...because I l-love you...and I-I can't fight it anymore."

"Happy tears?" He pulled her into a tight embrace. "Ruthie, you scared me near to death."

She dabbed her nose with the handkerchief she'd tucked inside her sleeve. "S-sorry."

"Dry those eyes of yours. We've got celebrating to do." He kissed her forehead then swiped the pup from her lap. "If you'll set out the food, I'll take her to the privy."

She chuckled. "Privy?"

Benjamin crouched behind some bushes and removed a tiny green velvet bag from his pocket. He untied the gold string and dumped the contents into the palm of his hand. *Thank You, God for giving me the desires of my heart! Help me to be the man she deserves.* He tied his grandmother's pearl ring to the red ribbon around the dog's neck then kissed her head. "You're too cute for your own good."

He placed the pup next to Ruth Ann on the blanket. "She feels much better now that she's made water."

Ruth Ann grinned and handed him a plate.

"Thanks. I'm famished." Benjamin stuffed a deviled egg into his mouth.

She stretched her arm and pointed to the edge of his lips. "You have a smidge of egg on the corner of your mouth."

He waggled his brows. "Why don't you get that for me?"

She lifted a cloth to his mouth.

"Nope, no napkins allowed."

"Well, how am I supposed to...oh."

A devilish grin spread across her pretty face. She leaned forward, her mouth hovering inches from his. "It would be my pleasure."

Anticipating her kiss, Benjamin closed his eyes and moistened his lips. She was coming to him. Warm, stale breath preceded the slobbery tongue bathing his face. His eyelids flew open as he swiped the back of his hand across his mouth. "Bleck. Dog kisses?"

"Well, you said no napkins, so I was left to my own devices."

"Why you little..." Benjamin grabbed Ruth Ann, tickling her waist.

She giggled and attempted to return the torture. "It's not a fair fight. You're not ticklish."

"You're right, but I'll stop if you kiss me."

"Okay, you rogue. You win. I'll kiss you." She leaned across Benjamin's chest and pressed her lips tenderly against his. Pulling back, she lowered her gaze, her mouth curving into a shy smile.

Their kiss was way too brief for Benjamin's liking. Sighing, he tucked a stray curl behind her ear. How could he ever have thought she was anything less than beautiful?

~*~

Ruth Ann lifted her eyes, quivering as Benjamin's fingers grazed her jaw. "How soon will you be leaving for Snickers Gap?"

"I'm not."

Her eyes widened. "You're not?"

"Seems the W&OR is finally out of funds. The line will end at Round Hill."

She squeezed his hand. "But you'll never get your chance to take it over the mountain."

He shrugged. "That's all right. I'll be closer to you, and I can study for my certification exam in September."

"We won't be heading west until then?"

He shook his head. "I hope you're not disappointed, but I told Mr. Farrell that I'd finish the line to Round Hill."

"Well that won't take long. It can't be more than three miles from here."

He shook his head. "The Virginia Creeper is living up to her name. With financing dwindling, they've already let go more than half the crew. They're not expecting to open the station until December."

"December?"

"Is that a problem?"

She tugged her bottom lip with her teeth. "No. It's just...where will we live?"

He scraped the back of his neck. "I hadn't given that any thought." His gaze shifted to meet hers, eyes twinkling. "Didn't really have any reason to—until now."

Heat rushed to her cheeks. "I suppose we could leave things the way they are until then."

Benjamin glanced at the pup still sleeping in Ruth Ann's lap before setting his plate on the blanket.

His eyes swept over her, and she gulped. She hadn't seen that cat-that-had-eaten-the-cream look in his eyes since their first kiss at the old homestead.

He removed the plate from her jittery hands and leaned closer. "Why on earth would I want to continue with our current arrangements when you've finally agreed to be my wife?"

Ruth Ann shrugged. If her cheeks were warm before, then they must be flaming now.

Benjamin cradled her face in his hands and gently tugged her close as his thumb brushed her lips. "It won't be a terribly long engagement, will it?"

"No," she whispered, her mouth hovering near his. "I don't think that would be a good idea."

"Me, either."

His arms slid around her, pulling her close. Tender lips consumed hers, savoring her as if she were a rare and precious gift. Soft words tickled her ear. "I love you, Ruthie."

She blinked back tears threatening to creep from the corners of her eyes as she laced his fingers with her own.

He cocked his head, brows furrowed. "What are you thinking?"

Staring into his golden-brown eyes, Ruth Ann barely believed she sat poised to entrust her heart to him again. Never would she have imagined that possible a few months ago—even a few days ago for that matter. "That we'll get to do this for the rest of our lives."

His free hand slipped behind her neck, drawing her forward.

A cold, wet nose wiggled itself between them.

She stifled a grin as disappointment etched

Benjamin's handsome face. "I guess someone is jealous and looking for attention. We need a name for her."

"How about Zeus?"

She cradled the dog in her arms, stroking her white belly. "Oh, be serious, Ben. She's a girl, and she's not a German shepherd."

"Athena?"

Ruth Ann gave him a gentle nudge.

"Okay, how about a character from one of your favorite novels?"

She tilted her head. He might just be on something. "Like what?"

Benjamin rubbed his jaw. "Josephine, from *Little Women*. You can call her Jo."

Ruth Ann stared at the pup for a moment then wrinkled her nose.

"What about Darcy, from *Pride and Prejudice*?"

"Darcy was a man, but it might work." She tapped her finger against her jaw. "Do you like it, Ben?

He shrugged. "I'd prefer Athena."

Ruth Ann rolled her eyes in playful exasperation.

He lifted the pup's chin, examining her. "I've got it. Jules. For one of our favorite authors, Jules Verne."

"Jules is perfect."

Sunlight sparkled near Jules' neck. Ruth Ann laid the animal in her lap and examined her coat. Eyes glistening, she gasped. "A ring?"

He kissed her temple. "No more tears today, Ruthie, happy or otherwise. I forbid it."

"Can you help me untie it please? My hands are shaking."

Benjamin loosened the knot then slid the ring onto Ruth Ann's trembling finger.

She bussed his cheek, her mouth loitering longer

than necessary against his skin. "It's lovely," she whispered. "Thank you." Lifting her hand, she admired the beautiful pearl.

"It belonged to my grandmother. I hope you don't mind it being secondhand."

"I don't mind. Besides, it's not secondhand. It's a family heirloom. And I'm proud to wear it. But after all you've shared about your family, I'm surprised to see such a treasure."

"My grandfather won it in a poker game in the Mexican War. But you should know that ring comes with a string attached."

She quirked a brow.

"You have to agree to travel with me to Pennsylvania to meet my family."

She held out her hand. "Deal."

He slipped his arm around her shoulders and tugged her close.

Ruth Ann held his gaze a moment longer, enjoying the intoxicating mix of love and mirth that twinkled in his eyes. She glanced at their hands, fingers threaded and resting in her lap. Only a few months ago destructive phrases from their pasts had collided, tearing them apart. Through prayer, God had changed the way they thought about themselves and each other. He had healed all the old wounds, freeing them to experience the fullness of God's unconditional love.

A love they would now share with one another as husband and wife.

Weightlessness swept over her as the burdens of the last few months vanished, taking with them any lingering doubts she may have harbored in her heart. She shook her head in awe of the miracle God had done. He had replaced a lifetime of hurt and rejection with His unfailing promise of love and acceptance, and He sealed His promise with Benjamin.

God had not only chosen to heal—He had chosen to restore.

Thank you

We appreciate you reading this Prism title. For other Christian fiction and clean-and-wholesome stories, please visit our on-line bookstore at www.prismbookgroup.com.

For questions or more information, contact us at customer@pelicanbookgroup.com.

Prism is an imprint of
Pelican Book Group
www.PelicanBookGroup.com

Connect with Us
www.facebook.com/Pelicanbookgroup
www.twitter.com/pelicanbookgrp

To receive news and specials, subscribe to our bulletin
http://pelink.us/bulletin

May God's glory shine through
this inspirational work of fiction.

AMDG

You Can Help!

At Pelican Book Group it is our mission to entertain readers with fiction that uplifts the Gospel. It is our privilege to spend time with you awhile as you read our stories.

We believe you can help us to bring Christ into the lives of people across the globe. And you don't have to open your wallet or even leave your house!

Here are 3 simple things you can do to help us bring illuminating fiction™ to people everywhere.

1) If you enjoyed this book, write a positive review. Post it at online retailers and websites where readers gather. And share your review with us at reviews@pelicanbookgroup.com (this does give us permission to reprint your review in whole or in part.)

2) If you enjoyed this book, recommend it to a friend in person, at a book club or on social media.

3) If you have suggestions on how we can improve or expand our selection, let us know. We value your opinion. Use the contact form on our web site or e-mail us at customer@pelicanbookgroup.com

God Can Help!

Are you in need? The Almighty can do great things for you. Holy is His Name! He has mercy in every generation. He can lift up the lowly and accomplish all things. Reach out today.

Do not fear: I am with you; do not be anxious: I am your God. I will strengthen you, I will help you, I will uphold you with my victorious right hand.

~Isaiah 41:10 (NAB)

We pray daily, and we especially pray for everyone connected to Pelican Book Group—that includes you! If you have a specific need, we welcome the opportunity to pray for you. Share your needs or praise reports at http://pelink.us/pray4us

Free Book Offer

We're looking for booklovers like you to partner with us! Join our team of influencers today and periodically receive free eBooks and exclusive offers.

For more information
Visit http://pelicanbookgroup.com/booklovers